Dramatic, emo...
world of a casu...
and forging bo...

Just What She Always Wanted

Three heart-warming romances from three
favourite Mills & Boon authors

Just What She Always Wanted

AMY ANDREWS

ALISON ROBERTS

LUCY CLARK

MILLS & BOON

First published in Great Britain 2012
by Mills & Boon, an imprint of Harlequin (UK) Limited,
Eton House, 18-24 Paradise Road, Richmond, Surrey TW9 1SR

JUST WHAT SHE ALWAYS WANTED
© by Harlequin Enterprises II B.V./S.à.r.l 2012

The Nurse's Secret Son, The Surgeon's Engagement Wish and *The Emergency Doctor's Daughter* were first published in Great Britain by Harlequin (UK) Limited in separate, single volumes.

The Nurse's Secret Son © Amy Andrews 2006
The Surgeon's Engagement Wish © Alison Roberts 2005
The Emergency Doctor's Daughter © Lucy Clark 2007

ISBN: 978 0 263 89676 3

05-0112

Printed and bound in Spain
by Blackprint CPI, Barcelona

THE NURSE'S SECRET SON

BY
AMY ANDREWS

This book is dedicated to all my colleagues in the
Samford First Responder Group, and to Mick
at Grovely for his mentoring

PROLOGUE

DANIEL MONDAY frowned as the ringing of the bedside phone interrupted his familiar dream. The woman beside him protested sleepily as he rose on one elbow and plucked it off the cradle. The red digital figures of the clock told him it was three a.m.

'Yes?' He heard the tension that had crawled across his shoulders reflected in his voice. His blue eyes mirrored his concern. No one rang at three in the morning with good news.

There was silence on the other end and Daniel felt his ire rise at being woken in the middle of the night by a prank call. 'Is anyone there?' he asked curtly.

'Daniel…it's me…Sophie.'

Daniel felt the tension in his shoulder muscles intensify as the woman from his dream spoke into his ear. He rose slowly from the bed, careful not to disturb the leggy redhead, and wandered into the lounge room. What did Sophie want?

'It's three in the morning, Sophie—what do you want?' He knew he sounded gruff but it was late and…he didn't need this. He didn't need a late-night trans-Pacific phone call undoing all the emotional distance he'd achieved. Hell!

He'd moved to New York. Started a new life. He didn't need her to unsettle his equilibrium again.

'It's John…'

Daniel heard the catch in her voice and felt his heart start to pound. Something really bad must have occurred for her to be ringing at this time. 'Grandfather? What's happened to G.?'

'He's had a CVA.'

'A stroke?' The pounding was almost deafening now as he tried to recall everything he knew about cerebral-vascular accidents. 'But he's so fit and healthy.'

'He's eighty-four, Daniel.'

'Which side is it? Is it bad?' His medical training had taken over now, the questions he needed to ask to assess his grandfather's condition forming clearly in his mind.

'It was a right CVA. He's totally paralysed down his left side. He's stable but the next 48 hours will be critical. His neurologist won't know the full residual effect until the swelling dissipates. He's asking for you, Daniel. He's very distressed.'

Daniel clutched the phone, forcing himself to concentrate on the information and not to dwell on the emotion in Sophie's voice. 'So his speech is OK?' asked Daniel, still in clinical mode. That was positive.

'It's not great. He's very difficult to understand.'

Daniel closed his eyes and imagined his strong, intelligent grandfather lying helpless in a hospital bed. How he would hate it.

'Will you come home, Daniel?'

'As soon as I can arrange it. I'll get on to the airline now. It'll still probably be the day after tomorrow with the time difference.'

A silence fell over the line. Was she thinking the same as him? Did John have that long? Would he get there in time?

'Thank you, Daniel. If anyone can get him through this, you can.'

He nodded, knowing she was right. He had always known he was the apple of his grandfather's eye. Not seeing John was probably one of the hardest parts of his self-imposed exile.

'Are you OK?' Daniel said the words before he could stop himself. Before he could remind himself that he was still angry with her. But her voice sounded shaky and he knew how close she also was to John.

'Sure,' she said, and he could hear her sniff. 'It's been a shock and it's awful to see him so…still. Max is very upset. He found John on the floor and he's too young to understand. He keeps asking for his G.G.'

Daniel felt his heart go out to his nephew. The poor little guy. He'd already lost his father. It must have been awful for a three-year-old to discover his normally active great-grandfather sprawled helplessly on the floor. Even from the other side of the world Daniel knew that Max and John had a very close relationship.

'Where is the little tyke?'

'He's at Arabella with Sally.'

Thank goodness for Sally. Daniel wondered with all the things that had happened in the last four years how the Monday family would have coped without their unflappable housekeeper.

'Have you rung the rest of the family?'

'Your parents are flying back from Europe as we speak.'

'Good. OK,' said Daniel. It was time for him to ring off

but now her voice was in his ear again he found it an almost impossible task. Her voice stirred memories. 'I should go—get things organised.'

Sophie walked silently into Max's bedroom and watched him sleep. She'd been by John's side all day and she had missed her little man. She hoped to take him to see his G.G. as soon as possible to allay Max's fears and she was certain it would also be a real boost for John.

Not as much as Daniel's arrival would be, however. The prodigal grandson would be greeted with much joy even if John Monday would be physically incapable of expressing it. She could feel her own anticipation building and had to remind herself how much Daniel had hurt her. How the hurt and anger had erected a wall of bitterness between them.

Sophie stroked her finger down Max's cute button nose and watched his chest rise and fall.

'Daddy's coming home, my baby,' she whispered. 'Daddy's coming home.'

CHAPTER ONE

SOPHIE buckled a sleeping Max into his car seat and shut the door. She looked up at the leaden sky and thought, How appropriate! Still, at least the inclement weather had held off until now.

Getting away had been just what she had needed. The stress of the last few days had taken its toll. Watching John slip in and out of consciousness had been very worrying.

Worse was witnessing his frustration at being unable to communicate properly during his waking moments. For such an articulate man, being robbed of his speech had been the worst insult.

She had gratefully accepted her mother-in-law's invitation to get away to the holiday house for a couple of days. John's condition had stabilised and now they were back from Europe she had been relieved from her bedside vigil.

Max had needed this time away, too. He had been clingy and upset since his great-grandfather had been taken ill, and dividing herself between her son and John had been exhausting. He had needed reassurance and she had been able to give him that these last two days when it had been just the two of them.

And then there was Daniel. His plane had touched down yesterday and Sophie had felt too wrung out and emotionally shot to deal with all their personal baggage as well. She was going to have to face him soon but the lingering memory of the last time they'd seen each other and the shame and loathing it always aroused didn't make her in any hurry.

She threw her small bag into the boot of her car and let her hand linger on the bright yellow paintwork as she shut it. She loved her Beetle. Michael had bought it for her for their first anniversary.

Michael. Sophie felt the familiar rush of mixed feelings rise like a tidal wave inside. The acute sense of loss and grief had started to dissipate but it occasionally still threatened to overwhelm her. She made a conscious effort to concentrate on the pink flower on her dashboard as she buckled up. She felt the wave ebb and sighed gratefully.

Not for the first time, she wondered how different her life would be now if Michael hadn't become a paraplegic and she had been emotionally free to marry the man she had truly loved, instead of settling for his brother. Guilt and pity and platonic love and long-standing friendship had been a strong catalyst and she'd been…happy.

But with Daniel back on the scene, he would be a constant reminder of a tumultuous part of her life. There was bound to be a resurfacing of all the hurt and guilt and anger that had made their previously carefree relationship a minefield of recriminations.

She reversed out of the garage into the steadily falling rain and thanked the gods for the divine weather of the last two days. Max loved visiting the holiday home. But, then, so did she. Set high on a hill overlooking the beckoning Pacific, a short drive from Noosa, who wouldn't?

They'd had a ball, building sandcastles on the beach and swimming in the luxurious pool. She had seen the worry in her son's eyes ease and the incessant questions about John slow to a trickle as he'd realised that his world hadn't changed too much.

Of course, visiting his great-grandfather briefly at St Jude's on their way to the coast had been very beneficial in this process. Max had been able to see for himself that John wasn't dead, that they hadn't been lying to him.

Sophie's eyes had welled with tears as Max had planted a kiss on John's cheek and said, 'I wuv you, G.G.' She'd noticed tears shining in the old man's eyes, too and she had swallowed hard and looked away, battling to regain her composure. John didn't need his support structures falling apart. That's why this break had been so important. To re-group. But now it was time to go home.

She looked down at the sleeveless white vest she had thrown on after whipping off her bikini top down on the secluded beach. Her denim cut-off shorts were damp from having climbed into them while she'd still been wet from the ocean. There wouldn't be much call for her to wear this outfit for a while.

It was amazing that in just two days the sun had coaxed her slender arms and long legs to turn a lovely shade of caramel brown. It emphasised her dark blue eyes and the natural caramel streaks in her blonde hair.

The car crawled down the winding dirt driveway as the rain and the encroaching dusk reduced visibility. The surface was a little slippery too and Sophie was grateful when the road flattened out. She rounded the last bend before the gate and slammed her brakes on hard, sliding to a halt.

A ute blocked the road at a crazy angle, the driver's door wide open. Sophie recognised the vehicle immediately as belonging to Charlie, Sally's husband. The couple had kept house for the Mondays for two decades and Charlie had been responsible for the magnificence of the gardens, both here and at Arabella, the Monday family mansion in Brisbane.

Sophie was momentarily puzzled. The car didn't appear to be damaged so an accident seemed unlikely despite the atrocious driving conditions. A breakdown maybe? But…where was Charlie?

And then she saw him through the gloom. A figure lying on the ground, face up, near a rear wheel.

'Oh, my God,' she whispered as her nursing instincts urged her body to action. She glanced at Max, who was still sleeping soundly. She grabbed her mobile, praying for decent coverage, and flung her door open. She went directly to her boot, pulled out the first-aid kit and bolted to Charlie's side.

The rain drenched her in seconds. It didn't matter. Only Charlie mattered.

'Charlie! Charlie!' she called, as she knelt in the mud and shook him. She ignored the tiny hard rocks that dug into her knees like needles. She grabbed the torch from the first-aid kit and shone it in his face.

'Damn,' she swore, as the gravity of the situation became apparent.

It was obvious Charlie had had a massive allergic reaction to something. He'd seemed perfectly fine ten minutes ago when she had waved him good bye, so it had to be anaphylactic shock. Bees. She remembered he was allergic to bees.

His face had swollen dramatically, his eyes puffed to the point of being shut. His face looked grotesque. Ogre-like. The skin was shiny, stretched beyond its normal elasticity. He was flushed and had huge red welts covering his body.

'Charlie!' she called again as she ground her fist into his sternum, hoping to gain some response. He was unconscious. She felt his carotid pulse and was relieved to find he had one but unsurprised by its weak, erratic beat. He was fading. Fast.

Sophie heard the distinctive raspy noise of obstructed breathing. She prised his mouth open and inspected his large swollen tongue. Soon it would totally occlude his airway.

She dialled triple zero. 'Yes, I need an ambulance,' she said, raising her voice to be heard above the rain which was bucketing down, plastering her caramel blonde hair to her head and her clothes to her body.

Sophie gave the details to the ambulance call-taker while monitoring Charlie's pulse and breathing. As she talked she was thinking. Adrenaline. Didn't Charlie usually carry the lifesaving drug?

She looked around and noticed for the first time the contents of a small toiletry bag strewn on the ground around Charlie. Had he been trying to get to his vital injection when he'd lost consciousness?

She nearly cheered out loud as she shone the torch on the Adrenipen, which had rolled out of Charlie's reach just under the car. It was aptly named. Looking like an ordinary pen, inside the barrel a cartridge of adrenaline replaced ink. The nib was a fine needle. It was a simple single-use unit that anyone could be taught to use, even a child.

She reached over him, extracting it and checking it was ready to go. Still talking to the ambulance call-taker, Sophie plunged the pen into his upper arm muscle and depressed the button on the end to deliver the entire contents into his system.

Sophie was relieved to feel Charlie's pulse strengthen but dismayed to hear that the inclement weather had stretched the ambulance service to its limit. Paramedics were being despatched but due to their relative isolation the ETA was twenty minutes. Charlie didn't have twenty minutes.

Just then a car engine and a set of headlights intruded into her frantic thoughts. Sophie could have cried she was that grateful. She watched the man get out of his car, the heavy rain obscuring his face, and waved him over.

'What happened?' he asked, kneeling beside her.

Sophie turned to explain and stopped, the words dying on her lips. 'Daniel?' she shouted above the rain, drips of water hanging off her sodden fringe.

'Sophie?'

They stared at each other. Years of love, hate, anger, friendship, guilt, bitterness and…yearning filled the space between them.

'What are you doing here?' she asked. 'I thought you were with John? He's OK, isn't he?' Alarm raised her voice even further. He should be with John.

'He's fine. I came to talk to you. But,' he said, looking down at Charlie, 'it can wait.' They clearly had an emergency on their hands. He had to concentrate on that. 'What's happened to Charlie?'

Sophie made room for Daniel to assess their patient. Relief to have an intensive care paramedic by her side flooded through her. She could put all the other issues aside if he could. Charlie would die unless they did something.

'Allergic reaction?'

'I'm assuming it was a bee,' she confirmed.

'How long ago?'

'Not sure. He was ten minutes ahead of me and I've been here close to ten minutes. Depends when he was bitten. Twenty minutes tops.'

'He's lucky you came along.'

'He's had a hit of adrenaline but he needs more.'

'And some hydrocortisone and an antihistamine,' he agreed, switching to clinical mode.

'Oxygen would be handy, too.'

'He's barely breathing and cyanosed,' Daniel observed as Sophie noticed the blue tinge starting to stain Charlie's lips.

'Ambulance is still fifteen minutes away,' she said, using the torchlight to consult her watch.

Daniel had never wanted his trauma kit more. Here, on the roadside in the pouring rain with no equipment, no drugs and no shelter, there didn't seem much hope. But he did have a fully qualified emergency nurse by his side, which was an asset he knew you couldn't put a value on.

He had to think of her like that. As a nurse. An asset. A card he held to help save Charlie's life. Because if he thought of her as Sophie, his Sophie—the girl he'd taught to climb trees, to ride a bike and where to kick a guy who wouldn't take no for an answer—he would be of no use to Charlie.

He shook his head, flinging water droplets into the air that joined the others belting down from the sky. Damn the rain! Damn the bad visibility. And damn Sophie. Damn her for still being as beautiful as she was in his dreams.

Daniel put his head right down to Charlie's mouth, concerned that the laboured breathing they were both so attuned to, despite the noise of the rain, had stopped. It had!

'He's stopped breathing.'

'Damn it, Charlie! Don't do this to us.' Sophie gave their patient a shake. She pulled a resus mask out of her first-aid kit and fitted it over Charlie's nose and mouth.

'I don't think you're going to be able to oxygenate him that way,' said Daniel, adjusting Charlie's neck for her so she could hold the mask in place properly. 'His airway is totally obstructed.'

'I know,' she admitted, 'but maybe we can get some through. You watch his chest.'

Sophie blew into the port at the top of the rubber mask that formed a mouthpiece. She repeated the exercise a few times.

'No chest movement,' said Daniel. 'It's no good, we'll have to trachy him.'

'What?' Sophie stared at him like he'd just suggested they put a gun to Charlie's head and shoot him. 'Are you crazy? How? What with? We can hardly see each other, let alone perform an operation on his neck!'

'It's the only way, Sophie, trust me,' he said, running to his car.

Twice. Since he'd left for New York she'd seen him twice. And now he was asking her to trust him. Sophie frantically attempted to push some more air into Charlie's lungs but his chest remained deathly still. The strange thing was, she did trust him. Before this rocky patch she had trusted him implicitly and, despite everything, here in the pouring rain, trying to save Charlie's life, she still did.

Daniel hurried back with a pocket-knife and a black

ballpoint pen with the ink cartridge removed. It was now just a hollow plastic tube.

She stared at him through the lashing rain and swallowed hard. He was really going to do this. Sophie had seen many tracheostomies being performed, both in the controlled environment of an operating theatre and in critical situations in the accident and emergency department. But in the field?

She didn't want to think about it. Only she had to because every second Charlie went without oxygen took him a step closer to irreversible brain damage, cardiac arrest and death.

'Please, tell me you've done this before.' She placed a stilling hand on his as he quickly prepared his equipment.

'I've done this before.'

She smiled at him then. Water rivulets ran over her lips, moistening them, and a sudden rush of desire kicked him hard in the solar plexus.

'Come on, then, Daniel.' She smiled, his confidence infectious. 'Time is brain cells.'

He instructed Sophie to extend Charlie's neck. She did so with one hand and held the torch with the other. Daniel noted her professional hold, knowing that she was monitoring Charlie's carotid pulse, as well as giving Charlie good jaw support to optimise his airway. Once again he found himself grateful to have such a skilled assistant.

Daniel ran an index finger down the hard ridges of cartilage that formed Charlie's trachea until he identified the Adam's apple, or thyroid cartilage. He kept his finger there and slid his middle finger lower until he found the cricoid cartilage. The indentation between the two was where he would make his incision.

He drew a steadying breath and sensed Sophie tense as he positioned the knife. Daniel made a small horizontal incision in the cricothyroid membrane and felt the give as the knife entered the trachea. There was surprisingly little blood.

He placed his finger inside the slit to open it slightly to allow passage of the hollow pen. He pushed the plastic tube into the stoma he had created—it was a snug fit. He blew some deep breaths into the artificial airway and only acknowledged his thundering heart when he saw Charlie's chest rise and fall again.

'You did it, Daniel! You did it!' It had seemed like an age to Sophie yet in reality the procedure had taken about twenty seconds.

Daniel smiled around the pen keeping his eyes down so he couldn't see her brilliant smile, her triumphant face or the way the rivulets of rain ran down her neck and chest into her soaked and clinging shirt. Seeing that was not good for his concentration.

Sophie's celebrations were short-lived, however, as she felt Charlie's pulse slow, become irregular and then stop.

'Lost his pulse.' Sophie tried to keep the alarm out of her voice. She was a professional. She knew what to do. But this wasn't some anonymous patient. This was Charlie.

'You do chest compressions,' Daniel said between breaths.

Sophie shifted position and started compressing Charlie's sternum with her interlocked hands. They couldn't lose him after all this.

They fell into a routine, he delivered one breath for every five of her compressions. Daniel couldn't help himself. He looked out the corner of his eye as her rhythmic shoulder movements caused her breasts to bounce. The rain ran down her bare arms and plastered the fabric of her shirt to her breasts, moulding them, the nipples on show to the world. He tried not to think of the hours he had spent touching them and how she used to beg him to never stop.

Sophie glanced at him and caught him staring. There was an intensity in his incredibly blue eyes that was compelling. Was he…he appeared to be…staring at her breasts? She looked down at them as she kept up the rhythm on Charlie's chest.

She almost gasped. Her top was clinging to her braless form, leaving nothing to the imagination. She was mortified. She may as well have PLEASE OGLE MY BOOBS tattooed on her forehead! She felt her cheeks grow warm and looked away.

A rush of memories assailed her. It was hard to believe from their current strained relationship that there had been a time when they hadn't been able to get enough of each other. When making love had been a desperate, urgent need that they had slaked as often as they could.

A siren blaring in the distance pulled her out of the past and an ambulance pulled up a minute later. Three paramedics dressed in rain gear hurried to them.

'Hi, Jane Carter, I'm a paramedic. What's happened here?' Her friendly voice was a welcome distraction and Sophie noted the stripes on her shoulder indicating Jane's intensive care status.

'Sophie, swap with me,' said Daniel, shuffling along so they could change positions. Daniel took over chest compressions, allowing him to talk.

'Daniel Monday, off-duty paramedic. Anaphylactic

shock following an assumed beesting. Adrenaline administered via Adrenipen. I performed a tracheostomy due to
complete upper airway obstruction from the tongue—'

'You did?'

Sophie smiled at the incredulous note in Jane's voice.
'Don't worry, Jane, he's an IC para, like you,' she said, lifting her mouth briefly from the plastic tube and then returning to her task.

'He needs a trachy tube, IV access, fluids, more adrenaline, as well as some hydrocortisone and Phenergan.'

'You trachied him,' Jane repeated, her stunned expression still firmly in place. 'Good call.'

The paramedics sprang into action, relieving Sophie of
her job. She rose slowly, the skin on her knees abraded by
the constant needling of tiny sharp rocks. They were
muddy and bloodied.

'Get in the back of the ambulance,' one of the paramedics offered. 'There's blankets to dry off and keep warm.'

Sophie checked on a still sleeping Max first and then
gratefully sought the shelter offered. The flashing red
emergency lights still active on its roof gave the ambulance
a welcoming glow. It beckoned her, all dry and warm.

She wrapped a white cellular blanket around herself
and watched as Daniel and the three paramedics continued
to work on Charlie.

Daniel placed a proper tube into the hole he had created
in Charlie's trachea and they attached a bag to the end to
administer lungfuls of one hundred per cent oxygen.

'How long has he been down?' Jane asked.

'He went into cardiac arrest only a couple minutes before you got here. He stopped breathing about ten minutes

ago but his ventilation has probably been severely compromised for about twenty minutes.' Daniel's reply was methodical. Concise.

Sophie was relieved to see a cardiac rhythm come back quickly after adrenaline was administered down the trachy tube and directly into the lungs. She started to feel a spark of hope.

Twenty minutes later Charlie was as stabilised as they could get him in the rain on a roadside. They loaded him into the ambulance and Daniel and Sophie watched its flashing red lights until it disappeared from sight.

They stood in silence for a moment as the rain finally eased to a light shower.

'Well, this'll be something I won't forget in a hurry,' said Daniel.

'You can say that again,' she said, and gave a half-laugh. She turned to face him. Now the emergency was over she didn't know what to say. It had been two years since she'd last seen him and the terrible things they had both said still seemed so fresh they could have spoken them yesterday.

'Why don't we go back to the house? I think we need to talk.'

'No.' She shook her head. 'I need to get back. Sally needs to know about Charlie. I don't want her to hear it over the phone and I have Max in the car.'

He shot her a measured look. 'How is my little nephew? Mum said you took him to see G.'

'Yes, he's much happier now.'

The rain continued to sprinkle down around them as another silence fell between them.

'We need to talk, Sophie. We're going to be seeing a lot of each other. G. needs support and harmony, not—'

'I assume you're staying at Arabella?' she asked, interrupting him as she thought quickly ahead. She didn't want to have this conversation with him now. In the growing darkness, in the rain, in soaked clothes, with Max asleep in the car and with Charlie's emergency and John's stroke weighing heavily on her mind. She was a little too overwhelmed to think straight. If this conversation turned out like their last then she'd need to have her wits about her.

'In my old room,' he said, a small smile on his lips.

'OK,' she said, shrugging the heavy, sodden blanket from her shoulders and opening her car door. She needed action. Anything to take her mind off the things they had done in that room. 'We can talk tomorrow.'

Sophie seated her drenched body in her beautiful car pleased to see that Max had slept his way through the whole incident. She started the car and realised she hadn't even thanked Daniel. They may have had their problems but she knew one thing for sure—Charlie would be dead right now if he hadn't come along when he had. She pressed the button for the electric window and it slid down with a soft whirr.

'Thanks,' she said, hating the husky note that had crept into her voice.

He nodded at her wordlessly and she drove away carefully. Sophie watched the unmoving form of Daniel in her rear-view mirror until the rain and night totally obscured him. Her arms and legs started to shake as reaction from the events of the night sank in. She shivered and turned the heater on high.

So, Daniel had come back. She had asked and he had come. And he was living at Arabella. Well, it was his home after all. Much more his than hers. She shifted uncomfortably in her seat, the wet denim of her shorts chafing her thighs. Could they live under the same roof?

She pushed her disturbing thoughts aside and switched on the radio. The DJ announced a mushy love song in a chirpy voice and she quickly changed channels. A hard rock song blared out and she turned up the volume. Anything to stop herself thinking about Daniel.

Daniel stayed rooted to the spot for who knew how long. Long after her car lights disappeared. Long after the rain finally stopped.

She was still exactly the same.

Still the same girl who had shadowed him constantly when she'd been five and he eleven.

Still the beautiful teenager who had begged him for her first kiss when she'd been sixteen.

Still the desirable woman who had given him the gift of her virginity and had told him she loved him.

Still the woman who had married his brother instead.

Still the woman who had slept with him mere hours after they had laid his brother, cold and dead, in his grave.

How could she have done that? How could he?

CHAPTER TWO

DANIEL tracked Sophie down the next afternoon on his return from the beach house. They had to have that talk. The way things had been left between them could make living under the same roof very difficult. There were things that needed to be said.

After enquiring about Charlie and finding out he'd already been transferred from ICU to a ward, Daniel came straight to the point. 'About what happened after Michael's funeral, the things we said.'

Sophie felt nauseous, thinking about it. It hadn't been the highlight of their tangled relationship.

'It was something that shouldn't have happened,' Daniel said.

'Yes, thank you, I got that.'

'Look. I'm sorry. I shouldn't have said the things that I did. I was just a little…shocked at our—my—behaviour and I handled it very badly.'

Sophie almost laughed out loud at the extent of his understatement.

'I'd just buried my brother, Sophie. I wasn't thinking straight.'

OK. That was it. He wasn't going to pull the grieving brother card. 'Well, gee, Daniel, I'd just buried my husband but I didn't accuse you of being some kind of Jezebel or whatever the hell the male equivalent is.'

'I know. I know. I'm sorry. I really am.'

'It takes two to tango, Daniel. I didn't notice you trying to put the brakes on.' Sophie was surprised at how raw her hurt still was.

He shut his eyes and tried to erase the images that sprang into his head. He didn't want to go over that night blow by blow—he just wanted to clear the air over it. Obviously she was still hurting from their angry exchange of words.

'Look. All I wanted to say was I'm sorry that it happened and sorry for what I said. We both have to live under this roof and I'd like to be able to get past what happened.'

And if they did? Weren't there still a thousand other things between them that were also hard to get past? 'And what about all the other stuff, Daniel?'

'Well, I don't know about you but I'm over all the other stuff. I thought you would be by now, too.' It was important that she knew that up front. He was over her.

Sophie saw red. What exactly was he trying to imply? 'I am one hundred per cent over you, Daniel Monday. As far as I'm concerned, you and I never existed.'

Good, he thought, they understood each other. He didn't need any rekindling of old flames. Michael might be dead but his obligations to his brother hadn't died with him. He owed his brother and Sophie belonged to Michael. Period.

And that was the last conversation they had for a while. The entire family devoted their time to keeping John company at St Jude's and Daniel and Sophie fell into a pattern.

For the three weeks John was hospitalised they rarely saw each other. Sophie took some leave, spending the days with Max and then heading off to St Jude's at night, while Max was sleeping, to read to John.

Daniel spent the mornings with John and spent the afternoons making the necessary arrangements to pack up his New York life and find a job. He wanted to be around for John. Seeing his strong, able-bodied grandfather so dependent had been a wake-up call. John wasn't a young man and Daniel wanted to be there for his grandfather's twilight years, just as his grandfather had always been there for him.

Once John's cerebral oedema had settled he improved quite quickly, regaining a good portion of the function he had lost. His gag and swallow reflex had returned to almost normal by the end of the first week and his speech improved dramatically with just occasional slurring of some words. That had been a great relief to everyone as John's frustration was making him very cranky.

The left-sided paralysis had lessened but there was still a significant residual deficit on that side and he was going to need intense physiotherapy to regain the power and use of his limbs. Mobilisation was limited, with John relying heavily on a wheelchair.

But nothing on earth was going to keep John in St Jude's a moment longer than he needed to be. Not the private room, not the attentions of the top neurologist or the very best of everything St Jude's could lay on. He had spent too many years walking its corridors as an eminent professor of microbiology to suddenly be in a position where he felt vulnerable and powerless.

And the stroke certainly hadn't affected his obstinate

streak. He was eighty-four and had suffered a huge cerebral insult, but he remained sharp as a tack and determined
to make a full recovery. At home. At Arabella. Surrounded
by his family and everything dear and familiar to him.

Luckily Arabella was already equipped for a wheelchair. It had been fully converted for Michael—ramps,
rails and even a lift to the upper storey had been installed.
Hallways and doorways had been widened where necessary. All the conversions money could buy had been put in
place. Little had they known that not one but two Mondays
would benefit from the changes.

The family had arranged the best care in Brisbane. A private physiotherapist and nurse had been arranged to come
in on a daily basis. They'd also consulted other allied health
fields and a private occupational and speech therapist
would also be involved in John's care.

When the big homecoming day finally arrived, Sophie
was relieved as splitting herself in two was quite exhausting. She and Max had shifted from their wing to make way
for John as these rooms were the most wheelchair friendly.
Michael, Sophie and Max had lived in them as a family so
they were decked out with every device imaginable to
make living in a wheelchair as easy as possible.

They moved into the guest wing with much excitement
on Max's side. Sophie not as much. She knew that it was
the most sensible thing for John but she had a sense that
things were changing in her life that were beyond her control. Daniel's presence only intensified this feeling.

Her living space hadn't changed in four years and she'd
never realised what a security blanket it was. The love and
the laughter the three of them had shared in these rooms was

difficult to let go of. It was so silly. She was just moving down the corridor and yet it seemed like a whole new world.

In fact, as she had shifted their belongings she had even contemplated moving out altogether. Maybe it was time to make a clean break? Living with Daniel was going to be awkward and even though Sophie looked upon Arabella as her home she had no real claim on it and even less now that Michael was dead.

Wendy and Edward, Michael and Daniel's parents, were horrified when she had broached the subject at dinner one night.

'Goodness, Sophie! What do you mean, move out? That's the most ridiculous thing I've ever heard!' Edward had said, dropping his fork on his plate with a clatter.

'It's getting a little crowded here now. I don't want you to feel you have to keep providing a place for me to live. You've been very generous, opening up your home to me.'

'Yours as well, Sophie,' Wendy interrupted, tears shining in her eyes. 'It's high time you started thinking of Arabella as your home, too. For goodness' sake, you've been coming here every school holiday since you were five and lived here permanently since your uni years. Max hasn't known another home. No.' She shook her head. 'We won't hear of it. Arabella is as much your home as ours.'

Sophie had felt warmed by her mother-in-law's affirmation but as she and Max sat waiting for John to arrive she also remembered Daniel's silence during that conversation.

This house held plenty of their history, too. So many happy times. She smiled as she thought about them now. Times when Michael and Sophie had followed the older Daniel around like puppies.

Times the three of them had spent up the mulberry tree, eating handfuls of the sweet berries until their clothes and fingers and lips had been stained dark purple. Times when they'd splashed in the pool. Times when they'd skipped stones across the surface of the Brisbane river that lapped at the edges of Arabella's extensive grounds.

And the time when, long after he'd moved out, she and Daniel had realised they loved each other and had spent weeks sneaking around, meeting secretly to kiss and touch and whisper sweet nothings.

They had kept their new relationship quiet, wanting to savour it by themselves for a while. Carry on without the fuss and attention that they'd known would be made of it. Kissing in the gardens, in the pool, in the bathrooms and in his bedroom. Finally making love on his old bed and knowing they wanted to be together for ever.

And as Max jumped off the bed at the sound of the car in the driveway and she saw Daniel in the driver's seat, she remembered the bad times as well.

Learning about the accident and that Michael, her best friend, was going to be a paraplegic for the rest of his life, discovering she was pregnant and then Daniel's rejection.

'I don't love you. I never loved you. I just said that so you'd have sex with me.'

She remembered how harsh his voice had been and his sneer and her total devastation as her world, already crumbling from Michael's tragedy, had crashed in a heap around her. How the news about their baby had died on her lips and she'd realised she couldn't tell him. Not after he had said such an awful thing.

'Come on, Mummy,' said Max, jumping up and down on the bed excitedly. 'G.G.'s home!'

He grabbed her hand and heaved with all his three-year-old might to pull her off the bed. She smiled at her snowy-haired son and felt tears sting her eyes. Oh, to be so carefree!

'Mummy's coming,' she sniffed, and swallowed the hurt along with her tears.

A week later Sophie walked into the entrance to St Jude's Hospital and made her way through the sliding doors of the ground-floor accident and emergency department. She greeted the three other RNs who were waiting for handover from Georgina, the department's nurse manager.

She sighed contentedly—it was great to be back at work. It would give her a break from the constant state of wariness she now lived in. Running into Daniel was becoming a more frequent occurrence now that John was home, and she was finding the situation increasingly difficult.

Her anger with him warred with rekindled memories and she found herself increasingly just wanting to shout at him. For his rejection, for his distance and for seducing her at an emotionally crippling time of her life and then treating her like…Eve who had tempted him with the forbidden apple. Oh, yeah. She was definitely mad at him.

'In cubicle one,' Georgina interrupted Sophie's turbulent thoughts, 'we have a twenty-three-year-old female with abdominal pain. We're waiting on blood and urine results. She's had fifty of pethidine and her pain has settled.'

'Any bleeding?' asked Sophie, snapping into her clinical role.

'No. Not gynae. Preg. test is negative.'

'Cube two is a sixty-year-old female with a chest infection. X-ray shows left lobe consolidation.'

'Antibiotics?' asked Richard.

'Stat dose of penicillin. Sputum samples have been sent.'

'Let me guess. We're waiting on a ward bed,' said Richard, his voice heavy with derision. Bed shortages were always a problem.

Georgina nodded and continued. 'Cubes three and four are empty. Cube five is a forty-two-year-old male who sliced open his left lower arm on some kind of industrial saw thing at work a couple of hours ago.'

'Ugh! Did he lose much blood?' asked Leah.

'Estimated loss of approximately two hundred mils. He's lucky there's been no damage to any major vessels, tendons or nerves. He's scheduled for suturing as soon as Todd's ready.'

Oh, goody! Todd was on—they were definitely going to have a great night. Dr Todd Hutchinson was one of the department's registrars. He was nearly at the end of his six-month rotation. He had blond curly hair and looked about nineteen instead of thirty. His youthful looks gave him an air of innocence despite his dreadful habit of practical joking. He was a laugh a minute. And a dreadful flirt. Sophie really enjoyed working with him.

'Cubes six, seven and eight are also vacant. The six beds in Short Stay, however, are packed to the roof. There's been a vomiting and diarrhoea bug going around since the Ekka started. Everyone's on IV fluids and anti-emetics.'

They all had a chuckle. Every year the same thing happened. The yearly agricultural exhibition came to town

with its sideshow alley and carnival atmosphere, and everyone in Brisbane came down with whatever the prevalent
illness happened to be at the time. Last year it had been flu,
the year before conjunctivitis. When hundreds of thou-
sands of people mingled, there was bound to be some germ
swapping!

'No one's in Resus and there's nothing around the ridges
that I know of. You should have a quiet shift.'

Leah looked at Sophie then at her boss and said,
'Thanks, George! Give us the kiss of death, why don't
you? When the bus-crash victims start rolling though the
door you'll be the first one we call.' They all laughed.

As Sophie had seniority it was her job to allocate the
late-shift staff to the areas they would work in until they
knocked off at eleven p.m.

'Richard, can I give you Short Stay?' She batted her
eyelids dramatically and smiled her sweetest pleading
smile. Eight hours with vomit bowls and bedpans was a very
long time!

'But, of course, Sophie, my dear. I love vomit. I live for
vomit. Vomit is my best friend.' He rolled his eyes.

'You're a darling.' She giggled. They watched as he
stuffed his pockets full of disposable gloves until they were
bulging then donned special splash goggles and a plastic
apron. He looked ready to do battle.

'Karen, you can do Triage.'

'Are you sure?' Karen's smile was hesitant. She was a
new graduate who had only been in the department for a
few months and this would be her first time solo at the
triage desk.

'Positive. You'll be great. You're a natural.' Sophie shot

her a reassuring smile and watched as Karen blushed. 'Just come and ask if you're not sure about anything.'

They watched as Karen headed to the desk, a spring in her step. 'OK, babe,' she said to Leah. 'You and me got the cubes. Reckon we can handle it?'

'With our eyes shut.'

Sophie grinned at her friend. She felt the stress of the last month lift a little. She loved her work here at St Jude's. Being an emergency nurse had always been her goal and she had come straight to the department from her training five years before.

They had been tremendous during her times of need. Like Michael's accident and the numerous times she had needed leave at a moment's notice in the beginning to grapple with some new crisis due to his paralysis. And then maternity leave and the whole awful time surrounding Michael's sudden death two years later. She couldn't have asked for a more supportive workplace.

She only worked part time these days, mainly night duty with the occasional late shift. She didn't want to be disruptive to Max and his routine and found these shifts suited best.

Michael had been house-husband when he'd been alive and she had worked full time. His male pride had occasionally been pricked but he had thrived in his role and Sophie had loved how close he and Max had been. Especially when Michael had always known Max was not his son but had loved him like his own regardless.

'Sophie, don't forget you're rostered on at the city station for your yearly ambulance ride-along on Saturday night,' Georgina reminded her as she walked past on her way out.

Damn it! She had forgotten, with everything that had happened recently.

'Sophie!'

A low whistle from behind had her turning around. 'Hey, Todd.' She grinned.

'Look at you.' He laughed. 'You look great. Fantastic tan,' he said, stroking his hand lightly down her sun-kissed arm. 'How's the professor?'

'In much better humour now he's at home,' she said.

Their conversation was interrupted by a commotion coming from the triage desk. Leah, Richard, Todd and herself went to investigate.

An elderly woman—Sophie thought she might be in her eighties—was babbling away in a foreign language and gesticulating wildly at Karen. The young nurse looked bewildered, getting a word in when she could. Another woman—about her own age, Sophie thought—was adding her voice to the hubbub, trying to calm the older woman.

Sophie dug Richard in the ribs. His smooth charm had calmed many an agitated patient. He moved forward into the fray, ever-present vomit bowl in hand.

He stood beside the elderly lady and she turned to glare at him. Then she said something that sounded suspiciously like an insult and promptly threw up into Richard's bowl.

A few seconds of stunned silence followed.

'Well done, good catch, Richard,' said Todd, and everyone smothered laughter.

'My grandmother has been vomiting all day,' the younger woman said into the silence. 'She doesn't seem to be able to stop.'

With great difficulty they ushered the pair into an empty

cubicle. Sophie left Leah with them as she went to gather the paperwork.

'Hello, Sophie.'

She looked up to find Daniel standing on the other side of the desk in his navy blue paramedic overalls. They fitted him superbly, the stripes on his shoulders completing the image of a professional intensive care paramedic. He had started work a few days ago.

Daniel swallowed hard and forced his facial features into neutrality as his body reacted to seeing Sophie in her uniform. It had been years since he had seen her dressed as a nurse. He remembered how it had turned him on, the virginal, don't-touch-me aura that the pristine white uniform had given her. It had made him want to get her dirty and the front zipper had always been too much of a temptation for him.

His eyes were drawn to the way the white cotton pulled across her bust and how her fob watch swung lazily across the fabric at her breast with each movement. It was hypnotising, the swish and sway mesmerising.

'Daniel,' she said, surprised. She knew that their paths were bound to cross at work from time to time but she hadn't been prepared to see him tonight.

The patient on the trolley coughed and Sophie remembered that there was actually a purpose to Daniel being here.

'Beryl!' Sophie recognised Daniel's patient instantly. She was a regular to the department and one of Sophie's favourites. Beryl had been Sophie's first-ever patient as a student nurse and she had nursed her on and off ever since.

'Hello…my…lovely.'

Beryl's speech was forced out between snatched breaths.

She sat bolt upright on the trolley, leaning forward slightly, her outstretched neck reminding Sophie of a turtle. An oxygen mask was pressed desperately by one shaky hand to her face.

She looked pale and pasty with a film of sweat on her creased forehead. Her eyes were large and round—fear of dying bulging them to their full extent. She clutched Sophie's hand across the desk. 'In…a…bad…way,' she said.

'Cube three,' she said to Daniel, and followed them into the cubicle.

Sophie busied herself getting Beryl settled while Daniel relayed the incident details and his treatment. Sophie tuned into the low rumble of his voice and her mind drifted to how she had loved to listen to him talk after they had made love and her head had been snuggled on his chest, her ear pressed to his skin.

'Sophie?'

She looked at Daniel blankly. Had he said something? He held the end of the oxygen tubing towards her and she stared at him for a few seconds before she realised he wanted her to plug it into their wall supply. She took it, feeling foolish, lecturing herself on appropriate workplace thoughts. She connected it and placed a finger probe on Beryl to assess her oxygen saturations.

She noticed the yellow staining on her patient's clubbed fingertips and the cigarette packet hanging out of Beryl's open handbag. It didn't take a genius to figure out what had been the cause of this acute exacerbation of her chronic airway disease.

'Beryl,' she chided gently, 'I thought you were giving up after your last scare.'

'Too old…too…set in my…ways,' Beryl wheezed. 'I'm old… I need some…pleasure.'

Pleasure. The word settled between them. Sophie looked at Daniel. Daniel looked at Sophie. Then they both looked away, busying themselves. Todd entered the cubicle and stood close to Sophie. She'd never been more grateful to see another human being. She beamed at Todd and relayed the information to him, tuning Daniel out altogether. When Daniel took his leave she almost sagged to the floor in relief.

Daniel pushed the trolley to the waiting ambulance, refusing to dwell on what had just happened inside. He helped the crew of the transport vehicle to restock and talked with them briefly about Beryl's case. He waved to them as they departed then climbed into his own single-officer vehicle.

The white Jeep was a compact mini emergency department equipped with almost everything he could ever require in any situation. Two people could be seated in the front but it was strictly a non-transport vehicle. IC paras were there to provide a higher skill set. Their cars were not equipped for patient transport.

As he drove out of the ambulance bay he remembered how Sophie had smiled at Todd and had seemed to only have eyes for him. Were they in a relationship? His mother hadn't mentioned anything in her regular phone calls and she'd always given him the rundown on Sophie and Max's goings on.

They were obviously very friendly, but was there something else going on? He felt sick. It had been bad enough thinking about Michael touching her, but this Todd guy? He was just too damn cute!

Back at St Jude's, Sophie didn't have time to reflect as Beryl kept them busy for a while. She was requiring regular Ventolin nebuliser treatments to improve the wheeze. A chest X-ray didn't show any new changes but it did reveal a slightly enlarged heart.

'Keep the nebs up every fifteen minutes to start with,' Todd ordered, scribbling on Beryl's bed chart. 'If she starts to become less short of breath, we'll knock it back.' He smiled at Sophie with his thousand-watt smile.

'I'll just reduce her oxygen now her saturations are in the mid-nineties,' Sophie said as she switched the neb mask for the oxygen one.

'Good idea. We don't want to knock off her respiratory drive.'

People with chronic airway disease operated on a hypoxic drive. The general population depended on rising carbon-dioxide levels in the bloodstream to stimulate a breath. Chronic airway sufferers had persistently elevated levels as their norm. Their bodies compensated for this by reverting to falling oxygen levels to stimulate a breath. Too much high-concentration oxygen could knock off this vital drive and the patient could just stop breathing.

'Nurse…Nurse.' Beryl clutched Sophie's arm and then the lapel of her uniform in a bid to bring Sophie closer.

'It's OK, Beryl, I'm here,' Sophie reassured her patient.

'I'm scared,' the old lady gasped out.

'Beryl, we've got you now.' Sophie softened her voice and spoke gently, trying to ease her favourite patient's distress. 'I know your breathing is difficult at the moment, but you are improving. Try not to panic, it'll just make your breathing worse.'

Beryl gulped in air like a fish floundering on the shore after it had been hooked. She fixed Sophie with frightened eyes. 'I don't…want to…die.'

Sophie squeezed Beryl's hand as Todd left the cubicle.

'That's just what I mean, Beryl. You need to think positively here. Come on, breathe with me. In…' Sophie sucked in a deep breath and held it. 'Now out…' she said, exhaling slowly. She repeated the exercise with Beryl, who quickly calmed down.

Half an hour later Sophie left the cubicle, satisfied that Beryl had settled. She gathered paperwork at the nurses' station.

'How's Beryl doing?' asked Todd.

'Better now.'

This time anyway. Both of them knew that Beryl was smoking herself to death. Today had been a close call and unfortunately they were becoming more and more frequent. One day soon she wouldn't be so lucky. Sophie hoped it wouldn't happen on her shift.

Two hours later Beryl's condition had stabilised and she was happy to go home. Her breathing had settled back to its normal level and her husband had arrived with her home oxygen cylinder for the trip back. As Sophie waved them off she wondered how long it would be until she saw Beryl again.

Sophie's thoughts were distracted by raised voices behind the curtain in cubicle four. It was the old lady in full swing again, pointing and swearing in Polish. Mrs Schmidt had vomited down her shirt and Leah was trying to remove the putrid clothing and put her into a fresh gown.

The old lady clutched at her top, ignoring the desperate pleas of Anna, her granddaughter, to let them help.

'I'm so sorry,' Anna apologized. 'My grandmother was in a refugee camp after the war. She has dementia now and thinks she's still back in the camp.'

Leah and Sophie looked at each other. Sophie didn't need to ask to know that Leah would be thinking the same thing. How awful to lose your mind and be stuck in an era that would have been dreadful enough the first time around. It would be like constantly reliving your worst nightmare.

They let the old woman be for a moment and her rantings stopped—temporarily. She continued to eye them suspiciously. Sophie's heart went out to Anna. She looked embarrassed and...exhausted.

'Does she live with you?' she asked.

'Yes. My grandfather died two years ago just as she was getting a bit forgetful. My husband and I have been looking after her ever since. The last few months have been very difficult with a new baby and all.'

'Does she have any periods of lucidity?' Leah asked.

'Not any more.'

Tears welled in Anna's eyes and she brushed them away quickly. Sophie put her arm around the young woman's shoulders and gave them a squeeze—she looked at her wits' end.

'Come on,' she said. 'Leah and I will change your grandmother and then we'll discuss getting her admitted and having her assessed by the geriatric assessment team.'

'But they'll put her in a home,' Anna sobbed. 'I promised Papa I'd look after her. I don't want her to be with strangers.'

'It doesn't have to come to that,' Sophie reassured her. 'They can help with all sorts of things—medication and respite and helping you with adapting your home for her needs.'

'Papa would never forgive me if I put her in a home.'

Sophie was moved by Anna's loyalty. 'Does she recognise you at all these days?'

'No,' the girl sniffed. 'She thinks she's in the camp. It wasn't a particularly pleasant place and she thinks I'm one of the guards.' Anna started to sob and Sophie comforted her a bit more.

'Hey, come on, now, we're going to need you to help us. Does your grandmother speak any English?'

'She used to be able to but she hasn't recognised it for about the last six months.'

'Well, we'll need you to translate. Talk to her and tell her what we're doing. It might help.'

'OK, Mrs Schmidt,' said Leah, 'time to get you cleaned up.'

They operated as a team, trying to remove Mrs Schmidt's blouse and dodge her fists as well. She fought and yelled and flailed her arms and hurled insults at the top of her lungs.

It was difficult work but Sophie had dealt with worse. She could only imagine the old woman's fright as she battled with her would-be attackers. She had to wonder, as Mrs Schmidt fought them tooth and nail, what kind of memory she was stuck in now.

It would have been comical had it not been so sad. One wizened old lady fighting off two nurses with a strength that belied her bird-like size and a mouth a wharfie would have been proud of. She may have been speaking Polish but everyone in the cube got the gist!

What happened next took Sophie completely by surprise. Afterwards she couldn't even recall how it had unfolded. Sophie turned to say something to Anna and as she turned back Mrs Schmidt's open hand connected with Sophie's face and knocked her backwards into the wall.

'Mama!' gasped Anna, yelling at her in Polish.

Sophie felt the wall behind her as she slid down it, cradling her stinging face and tasting the metallic taste of blood in her mouth.

'Sophie!' Leah rushed to her side. 'Are you OK?'

'Not really, no,' Sophie muttered, as stars floated in front of her eyes.

Leah poked her head out of the curtain. She couldn't see Todd but she did spy Daniel with a patient in tow, who was talking to Karen at the triage desk. 'Good. You'll do.' And she dragged him behind the curtain.

The noise in the cubicle was the first thing Daniel noticed. The elderly woman on the trolley was yelling in a strange language and the younger woman was yelling back at her between bouts of hysterical sobbing.

Then he noticed Sophie crouched on the floor and his heart almost stopped. She looked pale and shocked and he noticed the livid red mark on her face not adequately covered by her hand. He forgot all his angst and responded to her as he had always done when she had hurt herself, helping her up from the floor.

'Daniel?' Sophie looked at him, surprise adding to her dazed look.

He led her gently out of the cubicle.

'I'm OK, really,' said Sophie, the stars and buzzing noise starting to clear from her head. 'It was my fault. I wasn't quick enough. I didn't duck quick enough.'

Daniel sat Sophie on a chair in the staffroom, gently pried her fingers from her injured face and inspected the damage. 'You were assaulted, Sophie,' said Daniel testily. 'It wasn't your fault.' He probed her jaw and cheekbone and she grimaced slightly. 'Do you have ice packs?'

'Fridge,' she said, pointing to it.

Relieved to be moving away from her, he opened the door and retrieved an ice pack from the freezer. Sophie winced slightly as he knelt before her again and applied the chilled pack to the angry red mark.

'Put your teeth together and smile at me,' he said.

'I'm all right, Daniel,' she protested.

'Smile,' he reiterated, his blue eyes brooking no argument.

She did as she was told. 'Doesn't appear to be any major malformation. You should get an X-ray just in case, though.'

As he spoke he traced the outline of the ugly red weal with his fingertips. Back and forth. Back and forth. Sophie realised how close he was to her and found the caress hypnotising. Staring into his blue eyes as his fingers lightly stroked her aching face was compelling. She almost sighed as the faint touch took her back four years.

Todd rushed into the room and broke up the intimate scene. He all put pushed Daniel aside, repeating the quick checks he had just completed.

Daniel's earlier misgivings about Todd intensified. He felt the unnatural urge to pick the doctor up and throw him across the room as he watched Todd's fingers touching Sophie's face.

'We'll get an X-ray,' Todd said.

'No,' said Sophie rising from the chair. She was feeling

better now, her cheek just a dull ache. 'I'm fine. Nothing's broken. I'm just going to sport a shiner for a few days.'

'He's right,' Daniel butted in, the admission rankling. 'An X-ray would be sensible.'

'If I had an X-ray for every time a patient has whacked me, I'd be glowing green by now,' Sophie said dismissively.

'This happens a lot?' Daniel couldn't believe what he was hearing.

'More often than you think,' she admitted.

'That's appalling!'

'What are you going to do, Daniel? The majority of incidences occur with demented patients. Mrs Schmidt thinks she's in a refugee camp. I'm more cranky with myself than anything. I'm pretty good at ducking and weaving. I was silly for not being more on guard.'

Todd's pager went off. 'I have to go,' he said.

'Todd, make sure you document in Mrs Schmidt's chart that she needs her dementia assessed by the geriatric team.'

'Are you sure you'll be all right? I feel a little guilty about leaving,' he said, and pouted dramatically.

Sophie smiled and rolled her eyes as she sat back down. 'I'm fine. Go!' she ordered.

Daniel could have cheered when Todd left. He knelt before Sophie and placed his hand over hers as she cradled the ice pack to her cheek. He gently drew her hand away to inspect the injury. It was looking better. 'You'll live,' he said gruffly.

'Thank you, Daniel,' she said, because she had to say something to hide the confusion she was feeling.

They stared at each other for a few moments. His blue eyes compelling. His short, salt and pepper hair tempting.

His clean-shaven jawline strong and somehow comforting. Now thirty-one, Sophie had to admit he'd aged well. In fact, if anything, he looked better now, like he'd grown into his face.

Daniel became aware of his body's response to her closeness and quelled the reaction from years of practice. Her stare meant nothing. It was probably the way she stared at everyone. Probably the way she stared at Todd. No. Don't think about Todd.

'How's Beryl?' he asked huskily.

'We discharged her a little while ago. She'll be fine until next time. She's such a darling.'

Daniel heard the obvious affection in her voice and worried about her professional perspective where this particular patient was concerned. 'You do know, Sophie, that one day soon, especially if she continues irritating her airways with cigarette smoke, she's going to come in here and she'll die?'

'Of course, Daniel,' she said, annoyed at his statement of the obvious. 'So does she. That's why she's so scared.'

'Well, are you going to be OK with that?' he queried. 'I thought health-care workers were supposed to maintain a professional distance?'

'What are you saying, Daniel? Are you trying to tell me I don't know how to do my job?' She pushed him aside as she got up from the chair. She found herself angry again as four years of resentment bubbled to the surface.

'I think you may be too close to her, yes. As a nurse, I think you should know the dangers of that better than anyone.'

'I'm well aware of my professional boundaries, thank you very much. But sometimes the odd patient slips under the radar and, yes, I do have a soft spot for Beryl. You can think that's terrible if you like, but personally I believe it separates the good nurses from the great nurses. And I'm a bloody great nurse, Daniel. Not that you would know.'

'What's that supposed to mean?' he asked quietly.

'It means don't lecture me on my professionalism when you don't know the first thing about me. Don't jet off to the other side of the world and waltz back in from time to time and think you deserve to pass judgement on how I do my job.'

He heard the barely suppressed anger in her voice as her chest rose and fell. Rose and fell. 'Well, pardon me for caring,' he said sarcastically. 'There was a time when you used to care about what I thought, valued my opinion.'

'Oh, so now you care? Is that right, Daniel?'

'I've always cared, Sophie,' he sighed.

'Well, that's not what you said four years ago.'

Four years ago he'd said what he'd said to make sure she would fall into Michael's arms. And she had. Had been in them all along apparently. Max was proof of that. 'You recovered quickly enough,' he reminded her, a hard edge to his voice.

She gasped, stunned at the accusation. He had told her to marry Michael, to be with Michael. 'At least Michael knew how to love. Was capable of it,' she said bitterly.

'Sophie.' Leah called her name as she bustled into the room, stopping dead when she realised she'd obviously interrupted something. 'Everything OK in here?'

'Fine,' said Sophie smiling an overbright smile at her friend and then wincing as a sharp pain tore through the swelling on her cheekbone. 'I was just leaving.'

Sophie left the room with Leah with as much dignity as she could muster. Her body was quaking by the time she reached the desk. The gall. The absolute gall of the man to land back in her life and tell her how to do her job!

And for him to accuse her of rushing straight from his arms to Michael's. How dared he? He had practically offered her on a platter to his brother and now he was angry with her that she had done as he'd wanted?

Or was he just angry that she had thrown herself into it with one hundred per cent commitment? She had loved Michael. Had always loved him. She may not have fallen in love with him but he had been her best friend and confidant. Becoming his wife had seemed the most natural thing in the world when he had needed her so much and she had needed a father for Max.

And she was damned if she would be hanged for it!

CHAPTER THREE

SOPHIE woke with a start on Saturday morning to discover Max, who had got into bed with her at five a.m., was gone. It was now seven. Where was he? It was unusual for him to stir and for her not be aware of it. She must have been more tired than she'd thought. She hadn't got away from her shift last night until close to midnight and her feet had throbbed and her calves had ached as she had fallen into bed.

'Max,' she called out, presuming he would just be playing in their suite of rooms somewhere. No answer. He was probably watching the morning cartoons, she decided as she dragged herself out of bed and headed for the sitting room. TV off, no sign of Max.

John. He would be with John. Sophie quickly threw on her red gown with the large Chinese dragon embroidered on the back. She tightened the belt around her waist, ensuring her skimpy thong and tight T-shirt were fully covered.

It was too hot at this time of the year to wear anything but the bare minimum of clothes to bed. It was only because of Max that she wore anything at all—it wasn't that she hid her nudity from her son but a three-year-old's curiosity could be exhausting!

She walked briskly down the hallways. John wasn't quite up to his regular morning visit from Max. It was a routine that they had fallen into and John had loved his early morning wake-up calls. Max would take a book and climb in next to his G.G., snuggling into the crook of his arm, and John would make his great-grandson giggle with his silly voices.

She stopped at John's door and peered through the small gap created by the door having been left slightly ajar. She could see John's sleeping form and hear him snoring. No Max. Relief that he hadn't disturbed John didn't last long. If Max wasn't there, where was he?

She heard Max's high-pitched giggle coming from further down the hallway and followed the joyous sound to…Daniel's door. Great! She heard the low rumble of Daniel's voice and gave up all hope of being able to extract her son from the room without Daniel noticing.

She waited outside for a few moments, gathering the courage to enter. Something was obviously very funny. It sounded as if Max was being tickled if his squeals of delight were anything to go by. She didn't want to see what waited for her behind the door. Coward, she admonished herself. It can't be that bad.

She knocked quietly and opened the door slowly. It was. It *was* that bad, and more! A shirtless Daniel was throwing Max up in to the air and catching him again in smooth easy movements. Max was laughing so hard they hadn't even heard her enter. It was such an endearing picture Sophie felt her heart contract with love. To see her son with his father was way beyond anything she had words for.

'Mummy!' said Max, finally spying Sophie by the door. 'Dan's throwing me in the air!'

'Uncle Dan,' she corrected automatically, and then felt guilty at her deceit. The secret she had kept for four years suddenly weighing heavily on her.

Daniel stopped his activity and plonked a protesting Max on the bed beside him. She was wearing his gown. The one he had bought her for her twenty-first birthday. Back when they had made love at every opportunity and she had worn it with nothing underneath.

He drew his legs up beneath the sheet, tenting it to hide his quick reaction to the mental image that had flashed on his inward eye. His chest heaved a little still from the energy it had taken to repeatedly throw Max and then catch him. His arm muscles were already protesting the exercise.

She looked beautiful this morning. Her blonde hair all messed up and her sleepy eyes regarding him warily. The belt of the gown emphasised her small waist and even the T-shirt that peeked out from the V of the gown wasn't enough to disguise her braless state.

'Again, Unca Dan, again,' said Max, climbing onto Daniel's chest and straddling it. 'Giddy-up, Unca Dan.' He laughed, riding Daniel like a horse.

Daniel's gaze unlocked from hers as he turned his attention back to Max and made a clippity-clop noise with his tongue and bounced Max up and down.

'I'm sorry,' Sophie said, dragging her gaze away from his half-naked chest and finding her voice. 'I hope he didn't wake you.'

'I was dozing,' he said dismissively, not looking at her.

'Come on, Max. Let's leave Uncle Daniel to get some more sleep.'

'Oh, Mum. Dan's fun,' Max said, and continued his ride.

'He's OK,' Daniel assured her, concentrating on giving Max the bumpiest ride he could.

She stood there awkwardly. They hadn't seen each other since their heated discussion two nights ago and she was conscious of the strain between them.

'I…I thought you'd be at work by now,' she said, casting around for conversation.

'I start nights tonight.'

'Oh.' Nights! He was working nights? And she had a ride-along scheduled for tonight. Was there some conspiracy going on somewhere to deliberately throw them together? John's stroke. Charlie's emergency. How were they supposed to spend twelve hours together in the close confines of an ambulance?

'Problem?' he asked, finally looking at her.

'I'm rostered to do a ride-along tonight.'

Silence enveloped them. Daniel had stopped being a horse and Max seemed content to just sit on his uncle's chest. Damn it! He had known an RN was rostered on with him tonight; he'd just never thought it would be Sophie.

'Oh,' he replied.

'I'm hungry, Mummy.'

Grateful for the interruption, Sophie focussed on Max. 'Why don't you go down to the kitchen and see what Sally can fix you? Mummy will be there in a minute.' There were things to say if they were going to get through their shift together.

'Okey-dokey,' chirped Max, giving Daniel's abs one last giddy-up before scrambling off the bed and tearing out of the room.

'Are we going to be OK tonight or should I try and reschedule?' Sophie didn't see any point in beating about the bush. If he didn't think they could work together, she'd rather know now. Ride-alongs were notoriously difficult to switch due to advanced ambulance rostering. She wouldn't be popular with the ambulance brass if she interfered with their tightly run ship.

'I'm sure we're both mature enough to put our differences aside for a night. Right?'

Did he think she wouldn't be able to? 'I can if you can,' she said testily.

'Good. Well, I'll see you tonight. Shall we go together or take two cars?'

Sophie paused. It made perfect sense to take just one car. They were both going to the same place and had to be there at the same time. But something held her back. At least if she had her own car she could escape if she needed to. Why she would need to escape she wasn't quite sure, but carpooling seemed a little intimate. They *had* to share the ambulance—there was no choice in that matter. But she did have a choice over this and the idea of having space from him appealed to her.

'Let's each get there under our own steam.'

He looked at her wordlessly and nodded his head. If that was what she wanted, so be it. He didn't want to think about it any more than he had to.

She turned to go.

'You're still wearing my gown.'

Sophie's heart slammed hard in her chest as her hand stilled on the doorframe. His gown. She blushed as she remembered the times she had spent with him in and out of the red floor-length gown. 'This old thing?' she said, keeping her voice deliberately light. 'I've had it for ages.'

'I know,' he said, his blue eyes boring into hers. 'I bought it for you. Don't you remember?'

She laughed, forcing the shaky note from her voice. 'Really? Goodness, I'd forgotten all about that.'

'Your twenty-first birthday present.'

She shook her head and smiled at him blankly.

'You put it on for me after the party and we made love with you still wearing it.' He couldn't believe she could have forgotten it. The gown, or what had happened later.

Sophie swallowed as she remembered the magical night. The night they had made love for the first time. It was one of her most treasured memories. She could only hope that if she ever got dementia, like poor Mrs Schmidt, it would be a memory that she could hold onto for ever. But for now it was better to play dumb. To pretend that the events of that night were so distant she could barely recall them.

'I think dredging up the past is kind of pointless. A lot of water has flowed under the bridge since then. I'll see you at seven o'clock.'

She turned on her heel and walked out of the room on very shaky legs. He had recognised the gown. She hadn't even realised its significance when she'd thrown it on but, then, she hadn't expected to be talking to Daniel in it either. He had been really pushing her to recall the memories. Why? What was the point? Nothing would change the past and, as they had both categorically stated, they were over each other.

Daniel brooded over the past as he checked his watch and absently stirred his coffee. She'd be here any minute.

He tried to be calm about it and sucked in a breath to dispel the disappointment he felt over her vagueness that morning.

Surely she hadn't really forgotten that he had given her the gown and the times he had pulled the belt to reveal her naked body beneath it? She had to be lying. Or had their time together come to mean so little? Had he hurt her that badly by rejecting her love four years ago that she had erased the memories from her mind for ever?

Such thoughts were going to get him nowhere but crazy! He must at all costs think of her and treat her as just another nurse riding along for the shift. Just another nurse.

Not as Sophie, his Sophie, Sophie of the dragon gown, Sophie his first and only love. But Sophie his sister-in-law. Sophie whose pinched and distraught face at Michael's funeral had haunted him. Sophie who had broken down as he had presented the eulogy, her sobs chilling him to the core. Because that Sophie was out of bounds!

Sophie drove to the inner-city ambulance station with some apprehension. How was she going to spend the next twelve hours in Daniel's company? The thought of awkward silences and loaded conversations was too awful to contemplate. She had the feeling that something was about to give and it was going to be ugly.

Maybe a pre-emptive strike was called for? Sure, they had talked about the incident after Michael's funeral but had steadfastly ignored all their other history. And they had history to burn! Lots of highs and some pretty awful lows.

She had spent a lot of the last four years being angry with him. And where had it got her? On a ride-along, that's where. So maybe it was time to let bygones be bygones. Be the bigger person, acknowledge the past and move on.

They didn't have to spend hours pulling everything to pieces, psychoanalysing every word, every action. They could just admit that the past was part of their lives so they could get on with their futures.

She came to a decision as she parked the car and shut her door firmly. She would talk to him about it. First thing. Clear the air. Agree to start anew, whether they liked it or not!

Once inside the building she pushed open the door that said INTENSIVE CARE PARAMEDIC SERVICES. It opened quietly and she spied Daniel immediately. He was standing in the small kitchen area, seemingly engrossed in the contents of the mug he was stirring. He didn't hear her enter.

She took a moment to study him. His navy blue overalls fitted him snugly from the back. He was tall and lean. Taller than Michael even, who had been six feet. His uniform only hinted at the attributes she had witnessed that morning as he had played with Max. Broad shoulders, firm back sloping to a narrower waist.

His short back and sides hairstyle suited him. It looked spiky but she knew from experience it was actually soft and quite fine. The longer hair on top fell in soft layers and was peppered with grey highlights, brushing his forehead in a shortish fringe. He was as sexy as—there was no denying it.

'Are you trying to read your tealeaves?'

And then he turned around and smiled at her, holding her gaze easily. His eyes crinkled at the corners and Sophie was drawn to the grey at his temples. The smile tipped her off balance. She hadn't expected it after that morning's conversation. It seemed as unfettered as his smiles of old.

'Come in,' he said, breaking eye contact. 'I'll show you around.'

She walked towards him and he braced himself for the impact of her nearness. Her perfume floated his way, reaching him before she did, and he felt as if an invisible tentacle had shimmered forward and wrapped itself around his waist.

'This is it, I'm afraid. It's not very big.' He gestured around him.

Sophie had to agree. The room was tiny. Most paramedics worked out of large city or suburban stations but because there were so few IC paras they only got a small-ish room situated at Ambulance Service Headquarters.

There was a kitchenette, a toilet and shower and a lounge area that housed two recliner chairs, a large-screen television and video.

He showed her where to stash her bag and handed her a fluorescent pop-over vest with OBSERVER emblazoned on the back and front in reflective lettering.

'What happens now?' she asked.

'Make yourself a cuppa and have a seat. It's all a waiting game from now on. Saturday nights are pretty busy but it doesn't usually hot up until after ten.'

She followed his advice and sat in the recliner next to him. She feigned interest in the TV sports show he seemed to be engrossed in. She sipped at her tea and formulated the words she would say to end this awkwardness. She despaired at the kind of night she was going to have if he continued to ignore her like this.

Daniel gripped the arms of the chair and kept his face turned forward. If he looked at her he might not want to stop. He could feel her presence to the left of him like an encroaching force field. Every movement she made rippled the energy closer and closer. Soon he would be totally swallowed up by it and every cell in his body screamed, *danger!*

Sophie could bear it no longer. She had to clear the air. 'Daniel.'

'Mmm?' he said, his eyes not leaving the screen.

And then she chickened out. Her carefully planned speech dried in her throat. This wasn't going to be as easy as she'd thought! 'Do you think I could have a look in the ambulance? I know the IC para cars are different to the standard ones and I'd like to familiarise myself with the layout if I'm going to be of any use to you tonight.'

He leapt up, pleased for the opportunity to put some distance between them. 'Good idea.' He nodded. 'This way.'

Daniel opened the door that led to the outside world and the white two-seater Jeep sitting idle in the driveway. Red reflective lettering that read INTENSIVE CARE PARAMEDIC decorated the side panels and the bonnet. The ambulance service crest was on both doors. The red beacons on the roof completed the look.

'The supplies are in the back here,' Daniel announced as he opened up the doors and stepped back to allow for their outward swing.

Sophie inspected the equipment, all stowed on special shelves and securely fastened. A Lifepak that doubled as a heart monitor and defibrillator was in easy reach. There was also portable oxygen and suction apparatus, a large orange box full of drug ampoules and IV therapy supplies.

Several pre-packed bundles, sterilised and single use, were also available. A chest tube pack, a maternity pack, a tracheostomy pack and a trauma kit. There was also a soft-sided, multi-pocketed bag full of dressing and bandage supplies.

Cervical collars and splints were in special net holders attached to the interior roof. A spinal board ran down the center, reaching right down between the front bucket seats.

'It's well equipped,' Sophie commented, turning to face him.

He nodded. 'What we don't carry the standard ambulances do. IC paras usually get despatched as code-two back-ups. Rarely are we first on scene. More often than not they stand us down once the first crew on scene assesses the situation and calls in their sitrep.'

'The cases you do attend, what do they usually involve?'

'We're mainly used for IV access or pain relief. IC paras are the only paramedic level that carries narcotics so we do a lot of those kinds of jobs. Occasionally we get a big multi-trauma or intubation, something that really tests our skills.'

'It must be very different from your last job. I'd imagine even on its worst Saturday night ever, the streets of Brisbane are chicken feed compared to New York.'

'Oh, yeah.'

He laughed and his eyes crinkled, and it took Sophie back to her childhood. When he would beat her at chess and her crankiness would amuse him.

'But, still, I don't mind the slower pace. You so often don't get time to even think properly over there. You just react. It's all go, go, go. And it's nice, living in a city where violence isn't a way of life.'

Sophie was surprised to gain this small insight into his

life over the last few years. They'd not spoken about anything personal since his return. Maybe this was a good opening to discuss their issues.

But his pager had other ideas as it interrupted with its insistent beep, beep, beep. She watched as he pulled it off his belt clip and scrolled through the message.

'House fire out at Sunvalley. You ready?' he asked.

She nodded and watched as he shut the back doors and briskly got into the Jeep. She donned her pop-over vest and climbed in next to him.

'Coms, this is unit 001.' Daniel spoke into the handheld radio hanging off the centre console.

Sophie noticed how his full lips were pressed to the black plastic of the microphone as he spoke.

'Unit 001, have you proceeding to a house fire at number six Riverbed Drive at Sunvalley. Map reference 102 Lima twelve. You'll be backing up unit 990. The fire service reports unknown casualties at this stage. Proceed code two, pending sitrep. The Sunvalley first responder group will also be attending.'

'Roger that, Coms.'

They drove in silence for a while, each preparing mentally for what they might find when they arrived on scene.

'What is the first responder group Coms was talking about?' asked Sophie.

'It was an initiative by the ambulance service to provide for the more remote parts of Brisbane where response times can be delayed. They're volunteers who have been trained and respond to accident and medical emergencies in their area.'

'Sounds like a good idea.'

'It's fantastic,' he agreed, enthusiasm evident in his voice. 'I've been out to a couple of jobs there already and they're a great bunch of people. Dedicated to their community.'

Sophie was about to respond when the radio crackled to life.

'Coms, this is unit 990. Two patients. One with minor injuries. The other with extensive burns. Can we have the IC upgraded to code one?'

'Roger, 990. Do you copy, 001?'

'Copy,' replied Daniel, flicking a switch on the dashboard that activated the beacons and siren as he accelerated quickly.

Sophie held on as the sirens wailed. Daniel thrust the Brisbane directory at her and ordered her to navigate. Ten minutes later they pulled up at the scene.

'Sophie, grab the dressing and IV kit,' he said as they alighted from the vehicle. 'I'll get the drugs and the Lifepak.'

Sophie had put on her clinical mask, as had Daniel. The seriousness of the situation had banished her feelings of unease. At least in this arena they were on a level playing field.

They rushed to the badly burnt man and received a brief handover from the paramedics already on scene. One of the first response team had placed a sterile burns sheet over the victim and was dousing it with water, while another held an oxygen mask close to the man's badly burnt face. The man was groaning and shaking quite visibly beneath the sheet.

'Let's pull the sheet back so we can assess the damage,' suggested Daniel, and nodded to Larry, one of the responders, who gently peeled it back.

Sophie swallowed the gasp that rose in her throat. The

burns were extensive. The patient's clothes had been burnt away, leaving the charred flesh exposed. It looked like it had been peeled back in places and was all red and fleshy. Mostly, however, it was quite black—charred.

The man's entire front had borne the full fury of the fire. His chest, abdomen, groin and legs had all been burned. His face didn't look as bad—maybe only superficial burns—but the rest looked partial to deep thickness to Sophie.

'Anything on his back?' Daniel asked Larry.

'Nothing,' he confirmed.

Poor guy, Daniel thought as he did a quick calculation in his head, using the rule of nines, an internationally recognised system for estimating the extent of a patient's burns. Fifty to sixty per cent, Daniel calculated quickly.

He nodded to Larry to replace the sheet and to continue the water treatment.

'What's your name, mate?' Daniel asked the patient.

'Simon,' he croaked.

'I'm Daniel. I'm a paramedic. This is Sophie. How's your pain, Simon?'

'It hurts real bad.'

'Right. What I'll do is put a couple of intravenous lines in and give you some morphine. We'll also start some fluids and get you to hospital as quick as we can. OK?'

'Whatever. Just hurry!'

'Sophie, get a line in that side,' he ordered. 'I'll get one this side.'

Thankfully Simon's arms were relatively unscathed so finding a vein wasn't going to be too difficult. Still, she felt a pressure to get it right the first time. One thing Simon needed more than anything at this moment, even getting to hospital, was fluid.

She'd seen a lot of major burns patients in her time and it was usually awful. But this? This was different again. Here, tending to the patient on the ground, in the dark, with the intense heat emanating from the smouldering house behind them, was a startling reality check.

There was a rawness about this scene that didn't exist in the hospital situation. When patients arrived at St Jude's they seemed…cleaner somehow. The freshness and the newness of the situation had ebbed and the real sense of urgency had dissipated. Back in the department things were clean and white and ordered. Here it was dark and dirty and messy.

This was real touch-and-go stuff, even more so than in the emergency department. What they did here could determine Simon's outcome. She shivered at the huge responsibility and wondered how Daniel did it day after day.

The needle slipped in easily and she ran a bag of fluid through a giving set and attached it, commandeering Larry to act as a human IV pole. She checked the ampoule of morphine with Daniel and he pushed it straight into the IV line.

'OK, Simon. The pain should start to ease off now,' Daniel assured him.

The thing Daniel had to worry about now was any respiratory involvement. He shone his penlight up Simon's nose and noted the singed nasal hairs. He'd obviously sustained some inhalation burn injury to his respiratory tract.

The extent was difficult to assess, looking from the outside. Simon's airway could be swelling right now. There was no audible respiratory stridor at the moment, which was a plus. But his voice had sounded croaky. They should load him and go. If he should need intubating, that was something better done at the hospital.

'Do you want the fluids running to the standard formula?' Sophie asked.

'Sure,' he said. 'I'll get the stretcher.'

One of the major problems with burns victims was the dramatic fluid shifts that went on inside their bodies. Fluid that usually circulated through their vessels was pushed out, into the interstitial spaces. It was imperative that this fluid be replaced and for further losses to be accommodated.

An international protocol governed the type and the amount of intravenous fluids to be given, depending on body weight, surface area, burns percentage and time elapsed since the initial injury.

As Sophie did the calculations, Daniel, with the help of the first responders and the other two paramedics, loaded Simon into the back of the ambulance. The second patient, who had sustained a minor burn to one hand, was also going with them.

Daniel handed the Jeep keys to Sophie. 'Follow us,' he said. 'We're going to St Jude's.'

Sophie's hand closed around the keys. Obviously Daniel was going to ride in the back of the ambulance with Simon and he wanted her to drive the Jeep.

The ambulance pulled away, light and sirens blazing. Sophie stopped to thank the first responders and then got in the Jeep and followed at a more sedate pace, listening to the radio chatter. She parked near the emergency doors on her arrival at St Jude's and found Daniel completing his paperwork in the back of the ambulance.

'How is he?' she asked.

'He's just developed a mild stridor. They're going to electively intubate him and send him to ICU.'

Fifteen minutes later Daniel had filled out his report form, restocked the Jeep, called himself clear at Coms and they were on their way back to Headquarters.

He watched Sophie surreptitiously and noticed how quiet she was, just sitting and staring out the window.

'You OK, Sophie?' he asked gently.

'Uh-huh.' She nodded and turned to face him. 'It's just…you know. Different.'

'What is?'

'Your job and mine. It's so…raw. You see people at the worst possible moments in their lives. At least when they get to us the initial shock has worn off and they're…I don't know, cleaner or something. Your job's pretty confronting.'

'It can be—sure,' he admitted, holding her gaze as he pulled up at a traffic light. She'd obviously been affected by Simon's case. Seeing him writhing on the ground, extreme pain racking his charred body, was about as raw as it got.

Sophie gazed into Daniel's blue eyes. Even in the semi-darkness of the car they glowed. He saw stuff like this all the time. How did he cope with it?

The pager beeped into the silence and she looked away, quickly reining in her emotions.

'Here we go again,' he murmured.

The next few hours flew by with no real chance to talk. They spoke about clinical things and directions and possible scenarios they might encounter. They communicated well on that level, comfortable with each other at last. They were despatched to seven cases and stood down from five.

Sophie felt dizzy from all the going back and forth and the turning around and the noise of the siren and the irritating strobing of the vehicle beacons. She was relieved when they finally got back to Headquarters.

'We should try and get some sleep,' Daniel said, passing her a blanket. 'There's no telling when we'll be needed next. It's nearly one a.m.'

Now they were alone again Daniel had slipped back into his awkwardness. She watched as he pushed his recliner back and dimmed the overhead lights, not looking at her once. He turned his back to her so he was lying on his side, facing the wall.

She'd enjoyed the last few hours. She'd never worked with him before and was surprised by their synchronicity. There had been an ease that had echoed past times. Their angst had been forgotten as they had worked like a team that had been together for years.

It seemed they could talk for hours about medical matters with no evidence of strain. Work side by side to save a patient's life, no problems. But now they were back at HQ, with no lives hanging in the balance, four years of baggage loomed large.

Sophie adjusted the blanket around her and got comfortable in the chair but she lay awake, unable to sleep.

'Daniel.' It was now or never.

'Yes, Sophie.' He didn't turn to face her.

'Truce?'

'I wasn't aware we were fighting,' he hedged, talking to the wall.

'We can't go on like this. We've got the rest of the shift to get through and I think for John's sake and your parents and even Max, we should be able to get along.'

Daniel squeezed his eyes tight and stifled a sigh. That was easier said than done when he only had to look at her and his emotions became tangled in such a bitter-sweet jumble he didn't know whether he wanted to spank her or kiss her.

'Daniel?'

He moved around in his chair until he was sitting properly and turned his head to look at her. 'Can we do that, Sophie? Can we put everything behind us? You were sleeping with my brother at the same time you were sleeping with me. Did you tell Michael you loved him as well or did you only save that particular honour for me?'

Sophie shut her eyes at the accusation in his voice. How could he think that of her? The denial came to her lips but she quashed the impulse to clear her character. There had been four years of lies trapping her in a web that just got stickier. She had let him think the worst because it was the only plausible explanation for Max.

'What do you care? You never loved me anyway.'

'See,' he whispered into the gloom. 'Difficult, isn't it?'

Sophie swallowed hard as his point hit home. 'Difficult, sure...but not impossible. If we just agree to leave the past where it belongs—'

'Ignore it, you mean?'

'No. Acknowledge that we have one but let the emotions go. I don't think we're ever going to get anywhere if we go ten rounds of I-said-you-said.'

He was silent for a few minutes, digesting her suggestion. Maybe she was right. It would make life a lot easier around the house. Of course he couldn't control where his mind wandered but he could control what came out of his mouth and the way he acted towards her. 'OK. Truce,' he agreed.

Sophie let out the breath she'd been holding. For the foreseeable future they would be living under the same roof—hopefully their agreement would ease the way.

The beeper went off an hour later as Daniel lay staring at the ceiling, still wide awake.

'What is it?' Sophie murmured sleepily.

'"Seventy-year-old female. Difficulty breathing. History of COAD,"' he read off the pager. 'Come on, sleepyhead.' He deliberately used a light teasing tone, rising quickly and grabbing her hand to pull her to her feet. 'Let's hustle.'

They got in the car and Daniel contacted Coms on the radio.

'Thank you, 001. You are proceeding to one hundred and fifty Peermont Road, Newfarm. Code one, please. You should be first unit on scene.'

'Roger,' said Daniel, and put the mike down. 'That's Beryl,' he said, urgency in his voice and actions as he switched the sirens on and planted his foot on the accelerator.

Sophie almost groaned. Just when they had found some common ground they were going to have to confront a situation that would once again put them at odds. Well, if he thought she was going to be anything other than herself with Beryl, he could think again! She wasn't going to be cool or distant because he disapproved of her relationship with a patient.

They arrived at Beryl's in just under five minutes. Sophie lugged the oxygen and Lifepak as Daniel came up behind with the drug box.

Beryl's husband ushered them through the door and Sophie was instantly aware of the ingrained odour of cigarette smoke. It permeated everything—the curtains, the carpets, the linen on her bed. No wonder her airways were constantly irritated.

Beryl was sitting bolt upright in bed, one leg over the side, her foot planted on the floor, pushing herself as far forward as possible. A Ventolin nebuliser misted out around the mask she was clutching to her face. She looked frightened. Not even the sight of Sophie erased the fear.

'Beryl,' Sophie said, going straight to her and swapping the oxygen tubing over to their cylinder and cranking it up. 'It's OK. We're here now,' she soothed.

Sophie quickly attached three electrodes to her patient's chest and switched on the Lifepak. The heart rhythm looked normal, albeit a little fast.

'Can't…breathe,' Beryl forced out, holding Sophie's hand desperately.

Sophie sat beside her on the bed and worked through the elderly woman's breathing with her. Beryl's hand was sweaty but Sophie didn't mind. She watched Daniel out of the corner of her eye and wondered what he was thinking. If this one small comfort helped ease her patient's fears, he could go to hell. Beryl's anxiety was only making her breathing worse. And besides, Sophie was a nurse, she comforted—that was her job!

Daniel busied himself with setting up an IV line just in case they needed it. Beryl seemed worse to him than she had the other day, snatching every breath she could. She was pale and clammy and as Sophie applied the BP cuff he also noticed she was hypertensive. They needed to get her to hospital pronto. If she were to go into respiratory arrest out here, he didn't fancy her chances.

The smell of cigarette smoke polluted the air inside the house and Daniel found his ire rising. Why did people do this to themselves? It was all well and good to say nicotine was addictive but surely not being able to breathe was a good incentive to kick the habit? Daniel despised smoking with a passion. He'd seen too many people like Beryl throw their lives away.

Sophie removed the nebuliser mask now that the dose was finished, put on a normal mask and delivered the oxygen at six litres per minute as Beryl's oxygen saturations weren't too bad. The urge to really crank it up was tempting but Sophie didn't want to confuse Beryl's hypoxic drive.

They heard the other ambulance arrive and Sophie went to meet them, instructing them to bring the stretcher, as they would be transporting as soon as possible.

Once again Sophie drove the Jeep to St Jude's behind the ambulance, pulling in simultaneously this time. Beryl had settled quite a bit on the brief ride to St Jude's, as was often the case. Patients' conditions could be exacerbated by their anxiety. The knowledge that they had a trained professional tending them and they were in good hands often had a beneficial effect.

'Good luck, Beryl.' Sophie squeezed her favourite patient's hand as Richard, who was on Triage, took her through to the cubicles.

Sophie waved to her until she disappeared behind the

curtains. She would be very sad when Beryl finally passed from this world. Daniel was right about that. But as much as it angered her that her favourite patient was smoking herself to death, Sophie knew that Beryl was a mature adult who understood what she was doing.

Todd came out from a nearby cubicle. 'Hey. Sophie. Wow! Sexy vest.'

She laughed and did a little pirouette. 'Oh, yes. Very glam!'

'It is on you, sugar doll. But, then, you'd look good in a sack.'

A sack? Or *the* sack. Daniel had heard their banter as he'd rounded the corner. It was obvious Todd had a major crush on Sophie. His tongue was hanging out a mile. The guy was just too smooth for Daniel's liking.

'Let's go,' he said, trying to keep the terse note out of his voice.

Daniel drove back to HQ, mulling over the Todd thing. Of course other men would find Sophie attractive. She wasn't exclusively available to Monday men after all. One day he supposed she would find someone else. It was easy to forget she was only twenty-five, she'd been around in his life for so long.

Snippets of memories flitted through his mind as he navigated the Jeep. The day he and Michael had first met her, a gawky, gangly five-year-old, sent to spend the school holidays at Arabella while her mother had recovered from depression. And the many other school holidays that had been the highlight of his younger years.

G., teaching them all to play chess, and the many games she'd insisted they play together so she could get good enough to beat him. The cake she had harangued Sally to let her cook for his sixteenth birthday, complete with a very wobbly DANIEL that her eleven-year-old fingers had personally iced. And…the red gown.

Daniel pulled up in the driveway of Headquarters and switched off the engine. OK, so he'd agreed to let the past go but…surely she hadn't really forgotten? The hours he had spent searching for just the right gown returned to him. The embarrassment of hanging out in lingerie departments. The shop assistant who had winked and taken pity on him, helping him to find exactly what he had been looking for.

'Daniel?'

Her quiet interruption brought him back to the present. He turned to face her and he knew he couldn't let it be.

'Are we going in?' she asked, looking at him oddly.

He looked at her some more, his intense blue gaze holding hers. Was that her breathing he could hear roughening? Was she licking her lips because they were dry or was she nervous or something else?

'Were you serious this morning about the gown?'

Sophie's breath stuttered out into the close confines of the Jeep. Must they talk about this again? She looked down into her lap. 'Daniel, I thought we agreed—'

He placed two fingers beneath her chin and turned her head towards him. She looked tired and wary and fragile and…beautiful.

'The gown, Sophie. Don't tell me you don't remember.'

'I…'

'I've pulled that belt so many times.'

'Stop it, Daniel,' she begged in a hoarse whisper. 'This just gets us nowhere.'

'Tell me you remember,' he insisted softly.

'No,' she said, shaking her head and dislodging his fingers, hardening the wobbly edge to her voice. 'I don't. I won't.' She had to deny it. If she admitted it now, if she put it out there, she feared that all their suppressed intimacy would be unleashed and overwhelm the tiny space that separated them.

He lifted her face again and he could see the determination glitter in her eyes.

'Tell me.'

She shook her head mutinously. Staring him down. Every cell rebelled at his request, screamed at her to get out, but there was something compelling about his eyes, his stare, that she couldn't resist.

Daniel felt his breathing roughen and fall into sync with hers. He knew if he didn't kiss her right now he was going to die.

But instead of being soft and gentle and giving, it was insistent, punishing. His fingers held her jaw steady as he plundered her mouth for a few brief seconds and then pulled away. 'Tell me,' he gasped.

'Go to hell,' she said through clenched teeth.

He lowered his head again and repossessed her soft lips, revelling in her resistance as she shook her head from side to side. They pulled apart again and the air seemed to crackle like a brooding sky before a thunderstorm. Their harsh breathing louder than a cyclonic wind. 'Say it and I'll stop.'

Her eyes grew large. He was seriously going to blackmail her over this? 'I remember,' she whispered, because she had to stop this craziness and she didn't think she could cope if he kissed her again.

But he kissed her again anyway. Softer this time. Slower. His fingers stroking her jaw, her cheek. 'What do you remember?'

She heard the pleading note in his voice and responded to it just as she always had. 'I remember that the gown was a gift from you,' she said quietly, leaning her forehead against his, 'and that I used to tease you by wearing nothing underneath it so you would pull the cord and take it off and make love to me.'

She felt the gentle kiss he pressed to her forehead and tears pricked at her eyes. Was he satisfied now?

'Thank you,' he whispered, kissing her forehead again.

They pulled apart and sat quietly, each staring out of the windscreen straight ahead, collecting their thoughts and letting their breathing settle.

What had possessed him? He didn't know. It had suddenly been so important to him for her to acknowledge their past. Their earlier decision to ignore it had made it seem all the more crucial. 'I'm sorry,' he said. 'I shouldn't have done that.'

'Damn right,' she said, reaching for the doorhandle and letting herself out.

She walked into the staffroom, collected her bag and was out of the door again as he was just alighting from the vehicle.

'Where are you going? Shift's not over yet.'

'It is as far as I'm concerned,' she threw over her shoulder, walking briskly to her car.

Daniel watched her leave, mentally berating himself for his stupidity. He hadn't meant for things to get so out of hand. They were supposed to be moving on. He'd acted impulsively and had really ticked her off.

Worse, their kiss had stirred something inside that he'd managed to put into deep freeze for four years. Maybe he wasn't as over her as he thought?

CHAPTER FOUR

MAX jumped on Sophie at four o'clock the next day. She didn't usually sleep this late after a night shift but she'd tossed and turned for hours, reliving the incident with Daniel before finally getting to sleep midmorning.

'Come on, Mummy. Wake up. You've been asleep for ages. It's Family Sunday.'

Sophie stretched and woke to find eyes as blue as Daniel's staring back at her.

'Helwo, Mummy,' said Max smiling at her.

'Hello, my Maxster,' said Sophie.

'I wuv you, Mummy,' he said.

'I love you, too.' She grinned and closed her eyes as Max stuck his thumb in his mouth and reached for a strand of her hair, rubbing it against his cheek. Max gave her another five minutes' sleep, indulging in a rare moment of tranquillity, the comfort of his old routine still having a calming effect. But the joys of Family Sunday beckoned.

'Mummy,' he whispered, opening one eye for her with a chubby finger.

'I'm coming,' she said, opening both eyes before Max did damage to her eyeball.

She got out of bed and threw on a pair of shorts and a T-shirt. Max left her to it, satisfied that she was up. She gave herself a once-over in her mirror. Her hair looked a little worse for wear so she scraped it up into a ponytail. Still average, but it would have to do.

She tried not to think about last night as she slowly made her way to the formal lounge room. Walking out on Daniel like that had been highly unprofessional but, then, so was what he had done. Kissing her like that—she could have him for sexual harassment, no contest!

'Afternoon everyone,' she said, suppressing a yawn as she joined the clan.

They were all there—John, Edward and Wendy, Sally and a fully recovered Charlie, Max and…Daniel. Someone had put a CD on and the light music was a perfect backdrop to the lively conversation.

Family Sunday was a Monday tradition that had been around for longer than Sophie had been on the scene. It involved the family coming together on Sunday afternoons and spending time with each other, afternoon cocktails and conversation leading to a wonderfully cooked dinner courtesy of Sally.

Wendy had introduced it when Michael and Daniel had been little to ensure there was one day in the week they all came together. A family of doctors didn't make for the most regular routine and as the boys had got older they, too, had had many activities that had taken them away from regular family time.

Sophie and Michael had continued it with Max. John had usually joined them, with Edward and Wendy there as well between jaunts on the European lecture circuit. And since John's stroke, Family Sunday was going stronger than ever.

Sophie accepted a glass of champagne from Edward and laughed at a joke Charlie was telling. She was reminded of happier times before Michael's accident when the family, no matter where they had been or what they had been doing had all tried to make it to Arabella for Family Sunday.

'Mummy,' Max said, running to her and hugging her around her legs, his little face beaming with excitement. Her son loved Family Sunday more than any of them. The fact that he was usually the centre of attention the obvious reason.

Sophie was excruciatingly aware of Daniel. She glanced at him over her champagne glass as he popped a roasted cashew into his mouth and looked directly at her. Was he angry about her storming off last night? He didn't seem to be.

Max headed for the bowl of nuts and Sophie picked them up out of his reach, placing them on the high table next to John.

'Oh, I want a nut, Mummy.' Max pouted.

'You're too little for nuts, Maxy. Have one of Sally's chocolate crackles instead,' she said, offering him the plate of assorted nibbles Sally had put out for everyone.

The next half-hour was full of laughter. Sophie had doubted she could laugh today with the events of last night still fresh in her mind, but the Monday family intimacy worked its magic. There was just something about being with people who knew you. Really knew you and loved you unconditionally.

Having John in his wheelchair brought a touch of *déjà*

vu to the proceedings. Michael had loved Family Sunday almost as much as Max. Looking around the room, it seemed strange that they were all together without him. It was hard to believe that it had been over two years since his death.

A squeal of pure delight interrupted her thoughts as Daniel lifted Max up onto his shoulders and jigged him up and down. Max giggled and held onto Daniel's head. She watched them together, noting the similarities between father and son. They had the same eyes and the same lazy smile. When Max cracked up at something funny it reminded her so much of Daniel's childhood chuckle that it almost took her breath away.

But that was pretty much where the similarities ended. In fact, in many ways he had looked much more like his uncle, which had made it easier for Michael to pass him off as his own. Looking at the four generations of Monday men present in the lounge, Sophie could see the strong family resemblance shared by all the men in the family. Yes. Max was definitely a Monday.

Sophie had promised Michael the day he'd proposed to her that she would never reveal the truth to Daniel. She had been hurt and angry at the time and Michael had been right when he'd said it would be too complicated. He had wanted to raise her baby as his and he had loved her and needed her and they had been best friends. It had been the perfect solution.

'Look at me, Mummy. Look at me,' said Max from his lofty perch. He stood on his father's shoulders now, stretched out to his full height, his chubby hands held firmly in Daniel's. The pure joy of being a child glowed in his eyes and she felt absurdly like crying. He definitely had his father's eyes.

'Yes, darling, look at you,' Sophie agreed, blinking back the tears that momentarily blurred her vision.

Daniel saw the shimmer of moisture in Sophie's eyes and frowned slightly. Was this about last night or just one of those things that made women such a mystery?

He remembered how sentimental she had always been.

How she cried at Anzac Day marches and got all misty-eyed whenever she saw a bride. In his teens he had enjoyed teasing her about it and had taken great delight in how huffy she would become and even more so when she would storm out in disgust. Just like she had last night.

He saw her blink rapidly and look away, and was grateful to Max who started to tap dance on his shoulder-blades, demanding to be put down. He aeroplaned his squealing nephew onto John's lap and watched with satisfaction as Max's little arms twined around the old man's neck. It reminded him of the many hours he had spent sitting in the same spot and how close he had always been to his grandfather.

Max whispered something in John's ear that made him laugh, and Daniel was pleased that John had this little boy's adoration to help him through the tough times. And for the first time in his life he felt a streak of envy.

Sophie was talking to Sally and Charlie when she heard Max coughing. She turned instinctively, a sixth sense shooting a tremor of unease through her gut. Max appeared to be choking, coughing and gasping, panic widening his eyes.

'Max!' Sophie leapt up and was at his side in seconds, plucking him off John's lap and slapping him on the back.

'What have you eaten, Maxy?' she demanded, slapping him some more as he continued to choke.

Sophie was shaking. Adrenaline surged through her system. Logically she knew that the obstruction should clear but this was her child and he couldn't breathe and he was looking at her in sheer terror.

'It must have been the nuts!' John's alarm said it all.

'He'll be right,' said Daniel, coming to Sophie's side, trying to be calm, hoping this would ease the gut-wrenching fright stamped on her face.

'He can't breathe, Daniel.' She turned to him, her dark blue eyes beseeching him as she watched the pink of Max's lips lose their colour.

'Call an ambulance, Mum,' he said pulling Max away from Sophie, who was crazily slapping her son's back. He felt confident that Max would clear his own airway soon enough but back-up wouldn't hurt. 'Dad, in my car boot is my kit. Grab it for me.'

Sophie watched Max's lips become dusky and his body go limp. Tears fell unchecked from her eyes. 'Please, help him, Daniel. Do something,' she yelled. She couldn't lose Max. She'd already lost her mother and Michael. The very thought made her frantic.

Daniel flipped his nephew over until his head was lying face down in Daniel's hand. He supported the little body with his forearm and then laid him along his extended leg. He administered several sharp blows to Max's back between his little shoulder blades. No luck.

'Ambulance is on its way,' Wendy said, running back into the room. She put her arm around Sophie, pulling her daughter-in-law close. 'He'll be OK,' she soothed. If any one knew the mind-numbing panic of losing a child, it was Wendy.

'It's been too long,' Sophie wailed. 'He should have coughed it out by now.'

Edward arrived with Daniel's bag. Daniel's heart thumped in his chest. He quashed the rising tide of despair and worry. If he let his emotions get in the way he'd be as useless as Sophie. Someone needed to take charge.

What he was doing wasn't working. He knew he had to take a look and see if he could remove the obstruction himself. Luckily he had the equipment to do so.

He laid Max's limp body on the floor.

'Here, Daniel,' said Edward, passing his son a laryngoscope and Magill's forceps he'd found in Daniel's kit.

Daniel was grateful that his father also seemed to be keeping his head. As a renowned paediatric cardiologist, he certainly knew his way around the equipment.

'Hurry, Daniel,' Sophie begged, her voice holding an urgency that bordered on hysteria.

Daniel blocked it out. He blocked everything out and talked silently to Max. Don't do this to us, buddy. Mummy needs you. We all need you.

He opened Max's mouth and inserted the blade of the laryngoscope down the side of his tongue, extending Max's neck slightly as he manoeuvred the instrument to view his nephew's airway. The light source illuminated the small space well and he almost cheered when he located the offending nut occluding the trachea just past the epiglottis.

His father held the forceps by their angled neck for ease of transfer, and Daniel took them from him without even looking up. Everyone in the room held their breath.

He inserted the metal forceps down the line of the laryngoscope, their angled head and long arms allowing deep access. He grasped the nut with the round flat tips and pulled it out in one easy movement. Sophie burst into tears, running to her son's side.

'Why isn't he breathing yet, Daniel?' said Sophie, her relief short lived as Max lay deathly still.

'He will,' said Daniel confidently. 'How about I give him a little incentive?'

He quickly pinched his nephew's nose, took a deep breath and blew gently twice into the little mouth. Max took a breath and started to cough and then vomited and began to cry. Daniel felt a surge of relief almost overwhelm him.

Max's little lips and mottled skin pinked up almost instantly and Sophie picked him up and crushed her to him. She sobbed as she hugged her little boy for dear life. He cried in her arms, his fright and her hysteria upsetting him even more.

When the paramedics arrived a short time later they were pleased to see the crisis was over but put Max on some oxygen for a while anyway. It was purely for prophylaxis, given Max's brief spell of hypoxia.

Sophie couldn't believe the whole incident had lasted less than two minutes! It had seemed like an eternity when her son's life had hung in the balance and Daniel had brought him back from the brink.

The paramedics advised Sophie to transport Max to St Jude's so he could be monitored for a few hours but looking at him now, dancing to the music and giggling like the Max she knew and loved, Sophie declined. There was enough medical expertise in the house and should they be concerned about him they would get him there pronto.

Luckily the rest of the family backed her and the paramedics left, happy that they had discharged their duties. Everyone was still so relieved that Max was OK that they didn't want to let him out of their sight. They all just sat for a while and stared, watching him, drinking in his life and energy.

Sophie trembled whenever she thought about how close she had come to losing him. She sniffled and sucked in a deep breath. It hadn't happened. Max was OK. But the what ifs were never far away. She glanced at Daniel. What if he hadn't been there?

Max was nonplussed by all the fuss.

As Sophie tucked him into bed later she lectured him about nuts. He didn't look like he needed much convincing. Max had scared himself more than anyone and Sophie doubted he'd eat nuts ever again.

She watched him as he drifted to sleep, reluctant to leave his side. She lay beside him, snuggling his little body close to hers. Subconsciously Max reached for her hair and sucked his thumb. Sophie just lay there, inhaling his smell and counting her blessings. It had been a very scary day.

She woke an hour later with a kink in her neck and quietly crept out of his room. Sophie heard conversation drifting up from the lounge but didn't feel like company. She slipped out the back door and found herself heading for the wooden jetty where she had always gone to mull things over.

It was old and rickety but Sophie found the sound of the waves slapping the wood comforting and felt a strong connection with her childhood. She had fished and swum from this jetty. Skipped stones from it. Star-gazed from it on hot summer nights, lying on the rough boards, peering into the inky night sky. She'd even kissed Daniel on it.

The view from the end was as magnificent as always. A fairyland of lights on the opposite side of the river illuminated the CBD. She inhaled and the salty aroma filled her senses.

'You OK, Sophie?'

She didn't turn. She hadn't heard Daniel's approach but, then, she wasn't surprised by it either. If anyone had known where to find her after the events of the day, it would be Daniel.

She sensed rather than heard him come closer. The weathered boards always creaked underfoot but Daniel knew from years of sneaking up on her where to tread for maximum surprise. They had all known.

He sat beside her. He didn't say anything more and she was grateful for that. They just sat in companionable silence for a while. The magnitude of what could have happened was too horrific to speak about.

'Thank you, Daniel,' Sophie said, realising that she hadn't expressed her gratitude. 'I was so useless today. If you hadn't had been there… I don't know what came over me.'

'You're his mother, Sophie.'

'I'm a nurse—an emergency nurse—and I just went to pieces.'

'You're a mother first. I doubt I would have been any good either if it had been my child.'

Sophie closed her eyes as the tempo of her heartbeat increased. For the first time in a long time she didn't feel guilty about keeping the secret. She had needed Daniel today. To be the strong one, the one in control. Would he have been so calm if he had known that Max was really his son? Or would he have been as useless as her? Sophie suppressed a shudder.

They were quiet again for a while, only the lapping of the gentle tide and the sound of a passing boat interrupting their thoughts.

Daniel turned so he was facing her and not the view. 'What were you thinking about earlier today when Max was on my shoulders, before he decided to scare the hell out of us? You looked a little misty-eyed there for a moment.'

Sophie searched back through the jumbled haze that was her memory of the day. What had she been thinking about?

'I was thinking how Max had his father's eyes.' She turned to face him as well, their thighs almost touching. A very small space separated them.

'It's weird, isn't it? Not having Michael around? It just doesn't seem right somehow,' he said pensively.

'Nothing's been right since he died,' she said quietly.

She looked away as her mind drifted to that awful night two years ago. Michael had taken a tumble out of his wheelchair during the day, playing basketball, and had fractured his femur. She remembered how funny, how ironic he had thought it that a fracture, usually enormously painful, had been completely painless.

'Cheer up, babe.' He had laughed at her worried face. 'Just another advantage of being crippled.' And he had smiled to soften the words.

Later that night she'd had a phone call from St Jude's.

Michael had been rushed to ICU. The family had charged to the hospital but it had already been too late. They hadn't been able to revive him.

An autopsy later revealed what the doctors had suspected. A massive fat embolism, liberated from his bone marrow at the time of the fracture, had lodged in his pulmonary artery and sent him into cardiac arrest.

Daniel shifted beside her and called her back from the past. She turned to him again and they stared at each other for a short while.

'I'm sorry about last night. It was unforgivable.'

Sophie nodded. Yes. It had been. But that had been last night and tonight her son was sleeping in his bed soundly because Daniel had saved his life, and nothing else mattered next to that.

'I don't know what came over me, Soph,' he said huskily as she continued her silence.

Her arms prickled as goose-bumps broke out. He had called her Soph. Just like in the old days. She inhaled deeply to quell the mad stirrings in her body and the salty, earthy atmosphere took her further into her past.

'Sophie, please,' he begged.

She blinked at the ragged tone of his voice and snapped back to the present. 'Don't worry about it, Daniel,' she sighed. 'We both behaved unprofessionally. Let's leave it at that.'

'But—'

'Shh.' Sophie cut him off, placing her fingers against his lips. It was an impulsive move but in the circumstances seemed right.

She took her hand away. 'I just want to sit here and listen to the waves and be grateful that Max is alive. Can we do that?' she asked softly.

'Sure.'

They both turned back to face the view. After a while, Daniel lay back against the boards, his legs dangling over the edge. The waves and the insects were soothing, the breeze was balmy and the stars glistened like teardrops.

They sat for ages just as they had as children, absorbing the night. The years melted away. Max was alive. Their problems were insignificant.

CHAPTER FIVE

THE next morning at breakfast Sophie and Max were already eating when Daniel pushed John to the breakfast table.

'Morning, Maxy,' said John.

'Hello, G.G.,' said Max through a mouthful of corn-flakes.

'He doesn't seem to be suffering any adverse effects from yesterday,' John commented to Sophie as he held his cup out with his good arm for Sally to fill with coffee.

'No.' She shuddered. It made her feel sick whenever she thought about it. 'Thanks to Daniel.'

Daniel looked at her and she smiled at him and he smiled back. Something had happened last night out on the jetty. They hadn't discussed it—in fact, they'd barely spoken at all—but their relationship felt easier this morning. Free of some excess baggage.

'Yes,' John agreed, looking at his grandson. 'She's right, Danny, boy. You were brilliant. There may just be something to this paramedic nonsense after all.'

Sophie laughed. John had taken it hard when his favourite grandson had decided not to follow Monday family tradition. Under Arabella's roof alone there was a mi-

crobiology professor and a paediatric cardiologist, and
Wendy was a geneticist. In fact, all the Mondays for generations had been involved in the medical profession. Even
Michael had been studying to become a doctor when the
car accident had crippled him.

Daniel had been the one exception. Nothing John had said
had been able to dissuade him. There had been many heated
exchanges. Diatribes about wasting his grades and his tal-
ents and how poor the pay was had had no effect. Daniel had
stuck to his guns. More than that, he had excelled. Intensive
Care Paramedic was a difficult status to achieve.

'Thanks, G.,' said Daniel, 'I'll take that as a compliment.'

'No, I mean it, Danny. I'm proud of you. I really am.'

Daniel stopped eating and put his knife and fork down.
This was high praise indeed from John. He thought he saw
a shimmer of tears in the old man's eyes and felt humbled.
Disappointing his grandfather had always been one of his
biggest regrets. 'I appreciate that, G. I really do.'

Sophie watched the exchange, feeling a little teary herself. Having been privy to a lot of the commotion that
Daniel's decision had caused, she understood the magnitude of John's statement.

She knew Daniel had struggled about letting his grandfather down. In fact, at one stage he had felt so pressured
that he had confided in her he was going to give in, give
up his dreams and follow the Monday path.

'No!' She had been horrified. 'This is hard for you. You
love John and don't want to disappoint him, but this is *your*
life, Daniel. You have to do what's right for you.'

He had been eighteen then. And frankly, after yesterday,
she had never been gladder that he had listened to a squirt
of a kid, a twelve-year-old, and fulfilled his dream.

* * *

Life after Max's choking episode settled back to normal. Or as near normal as it could with John's rehabilitation dictating their days. His physical therapy became a family project.

Tina, the physio, was a tough taskmaster and just what a cantankerous old man needed. John was impatient with his weakness, wanting to move as quickly through his therapy as possible to a full recovery.

Tina knew he had to learn to crawl before he could walk and kept him on task with her persistence and iron will. John was stubborn but Tina was more so. She was also canny, involving everyone to keep her client on the straight and narrow.

Max loved 'helping' John and the little boy seemed to be the only one who could soothe John when his frustration got the better of him. Tina used Max to full advantage to bully John into just one more set of exercises.

The phone rang one morning after breakfast and Daniel picked it up. It was Tina.

'Something's come up and I can't make it today. I'd scheduled some hydrotherapy for John this morning. Are any of you free to do that with him? He was really looking forward to it. He knows the exercises.'

'I don't go on shift till tonight—I'll do it.'

'You may need a hand, getting him in and out,' she said, and rang off.

Daniel got changed into his swimmers and went looking for John. Martin, John's nurse, who came every morning for an hour, had helped his patient get ready for the pool. He handed the wheelchair over to Daniel and left as he was already running late for his next client.

Sophie and Max were in the water when they arrived.

The pool had been fully modified for Michael, who had swum every day, even in winter. It was fortuitous for John as it meant he could have regular hydrotherapy at home.

Daniel discarded his shirt and adjusted the waist drawstring on his boardies. A wet and smiling Sophie propelled herself out of the pool in one fluid movement, the water sluicing off her body like a waterfall. She sat on the edge and wrung the excess water out of her hair.

'Want a hand?' she called, keeping one eye on Max who was splashing around in the deep end, the yellow floaties attached to his upper arms keeping him above water.

She was wearing a bikini. A very tiny bikini. And it was the first time Daniel had seen her with so little on in a long time. Would it actually stay attached to her body if she helped?

Sophie walked towards him and he was struck by how her body had changed over the years. Her breasts seemed fuller, her hips slightly rounder. Her waist more obvious. She looked fantastic. The leanness of four years ago had been replaced by subtle curves—very womanly.

Maybe that was the difference. She was no longer a girl. She'd grown into a woman. She'd nurtured a baby in her womb, suckled him at her breast. She was a mother and had flowered accordingly. And he liked it! He liked it a lot.

She came close and between the three of them they got John into the pool. If there was one thing they both knew well, it was the manual handling of patients. Their jobs involved a lot of lifting and safe techniques were essential to prevent back injuries.

Sophie left them to it, joining Max at the other end of the pool. Daniel tried hard to concentrate on John's exercises. He knew water was an excellent medium to work on arm and leg strength—the exercise aided by the natural buoyancy. Still, the splashing and the giggling from the deep end was distracting.

'Why don't you go and join them?' said John.

'Hmm? What?' said Daniel.

'I'm perfectly capable of doing this myself, Danny, boy. The stroke didn't affect my intelligence.'

'Tina wouldn't approve of me shirking my responsibilities.'

'I won't tell her if you don't.'

'Unca Dan, Unca Dan.'

Daniel hesitated midway through manipulating John's arm through the water. He really didn't want to turn round.

'Go,' John insisted.

'Unca Da-a-an,' Max called again.

Daniel sighed as his grandfather winked at him. 'Stay close to the edge in case you lose your balance,' said Daniel.

'Aye, aye, Danny, boy.' John saluted him with his good arm.

Daniel rolled his eyes at his grandfather and pushed himself off the wall with his toes, swimming leisurely towards his insistent nephew. He ducked under the water as he approached and came up underneath Max, lifting him out of the water and tossing him. The floaties ensured he bobbed harmlessly in the water and the little boy squealed for more.

'He'll never tire of it,' warned Sophie, laughing at their antics.

She swam down to John, feeling a tad superfluous. Max

had taken to his Uncle Dan like a duck to water. He'd always been a boy who had identified with men. Max had grown up with several strong male role models and, apart from her and Sally and his grandmother, he much preferred male company.

He had adored Michael. His little face had lit up every time Michael had come into the room and, with him being a stay-at-home dad, they had formed a deep bond. If Sophie could find one positive aspect of Michael's death it was that, at two years of age, Max had been too young to fully understand. Just over two years later Max had no recall of the man who had been his father in every way that mattered.

Sophie watched John go through his exercises, helping him occasionally as he required. It was amazing how much he had improved in the last month. John's doctors and even Tina were certain he would always have a residual weakness due to the extent of the stroke, but John was determined to reduce the deficit to something only he was aware of.

John watched Sophie pretending to keep him company but not fooling him in the slightest. The squealing and laughter and splashing hadn't abated and he could read the wistful look in her eyes as easily as he had always been able to read her expressions.

'He'll make a great father,' John commented.

'Hmm,' said Sophie noncommittally, her eyes not leaving the other end. If only John knew the half of it!

'When are you going to tell Daniel he's Max's father?'

That got her attention! Her head snapped back to face him instantly.

'Wh-what?' said Sophie. John knew? But how?

'I'm not stupid, Sophie,' said John gently, to soften the blow.

'Stupid, no. Wrong, definitely.' Sophie gathered her wits. She hadn't kept Max's paternity a secret for four years to baulk the first time someone called her on it.

'You don't think I knew what was going on between you and Daniel just before the accident?'

'I don't know what you're talking about,' she spluttered turning her face away. She felt slightly dizzy from the rush of blood to her head.

'I know you thought you were being discreet but it was written all over both of your faces.'

'You're wrong, John,' she denied again. Her heart pounded. Had they been that obvious?

'I may be old but I know what young love looks like, my dear. You two had it bad.'

Sophie looked back at him again. She thought they'd hidden it so well. She didn't know what to say. It seemed pointless to continue to deny it when he so obviously knew what had happened. John's face told her the game was up. She should have been horrified, but perversely she wasn't. She was, what? Relieved?

John watched the play of emotions on her face and recognised the moment she surrendered. 'And then the accident happened and you and Michael announced your engagement and your pregnancy, and I put two and two together.'

'Why did you never say anything?' she asked quietly. The raucous noises from the deep end of the pool faded as she conceded. It was just her and John and this conversation. And the surprising lightening of a burden.

'Because for the first time in a month Michael was

happy. We'd been very worried about him. You know how terribly depressed he'd been and suddenly he was his old self again. You gave him a reason to live. You and Max. I didn't have the heart to mess with that, and I knew that Daniel and you had quarrelled and that you would love Michael just as you always had. I knew Michael needed you much more than Daniel. It makes me ashamed to admit it to you now but it seemed better to stay silent at the time.'

Sophie swallowed the lump rising in her throat. She could hear her heart pounding and was amazed to see that the water surrounding her wasn't vibrating in unison.

'Who else knows?' she asked quietly.

'Just me,' said John, 'although I suspect that Sally has an inkling. But we've never really spoken about it. Edward and Wendy were on the lecture circuit in Europe at the time of your affair and the accident, so they were unaware of what was happening.'

Sophie nodded, remembering that awful time. She'd come back to Arabella late at night after being out with some friends to find two policemen at the door talking to John. She'd never forget the dreadful feeling of foreboding that had settled in her gut.

'What?' she had said to John. One look at his stricken face had confirmed her worst fears. She had felt her legs buckle and one of the policemen had grabbed her around the waist as she had sagged against him.

They had charged up to St Jude's. The information had been sketchy. Just that both Daniel and Michael had been involved in a serious car accident and had been admitted to hospital, badly injured.

Sophie's overwhelming relief to find Daniel relatively unscathed had been tempered by Michael's critical status. It had been so hard to believe her dearest friend was lying so still and so close to death in St Jude's specialised spinal unit.

As the days had gone by and the three of them had maintained a bedside vigil, her relationship with Daniel had been put on hold. Edward and Wendy had rushed back from Europe just as Michael had improved enough to be out of Intensive Care. But with his paraplegia confirmed, Michael entered a dark depression.

He was alive, yes, but losing the use of his legs had been a major blow and his mood was difficult. But she went to see him every day, hoping by sheer force of will alone that she could make a difference to his life. She couldn't desert her best friend in his hour of need.

It was at the same time she discovered she was pregnant. It was the worst timing possible. The Monday family were dealing with enough, without putting this on their plate as well. What would Daniel think?

They'd seen each other rarely in the month since the accident and their time together was tempered with guilt. Guilt that they were both walking around, able to enjoy themselves, while the one other person who meant the world to both of them couldn't.

Daniel felt it most acutely. He had been driving the car and Sophie watched as guilt tore at his soul. It didn't matter that they had been struck by a car that had veered into their path from the other side of the road. It didn't matter that no one else blamed him for the accident, least of all Michael. His brother was crippled and that was all that mattered to Daniel. Injured in a car that he had been driving!

Daniel's self-reproach made him difficult to face about

her news. Sophie still hadn't told him when she burst into tears one morning in front of Michael, who had been particularly cantankerous and impatient. It had probably been the jolt Michael needed to jar him out of his self-pity. He certainly looked startled as he tried to comfort her and she blurted out her awful secret.

He was just like the old Michael, her dear, dear friend. He told her it would be OK and not to worry, and if Daniel didn't realise what a lucky man he was then he'd marry her and they'd bring up the baby together.

She laughed through her tears at his suggestion. But then Daniel rejected her love so callously later that night she found herself crying all over Michael again and he restated his proposal.

She dismissed the idea but when he explained how happy it would make him and she looked into his eager face, smiling for the first time in a month, she felt the strings of their longstanding friendship pull tight. It was the perfect solution.

'Michael made me promise I wouldn't tell,' she said quietly to John, coming back from the past.

'I can understand that,' said John, swishing his arms back and forth, using the natural resistance of the water. 'But he's dead now, Sophie. Do you think he meant you to take the secret to your grave?'

Had he? She didn't know any more. And just how did you have that kind of conversation anyway? 'It doesn't get any easier to tell him, you know?'

'Of course, my dear, of course. And whether you do or not makes no difference to me, but I think maybe he deserves to know. Look at him,' he said, nodding towards

Daniel frolicking merrily with his son. 'Look at Max. Maybe he also deserves a father?'

'He doesn't love me, John. We don't love each other.'

'And you and Michael did I suppose?'

He'd caught her out there. Michael had loved her. As a man. As a husband. Even though their marriage had been totally non-sexual, due to the level of Michael's paraplegia, he had never made any secret of the depth of his feelings for her. And he had understood her position. That she had loved him as a friend. A best friend. But that was all it would ever be for her.

'This is different, John.'

'Why? Because you still love him?'

'No,' she said. Because she didn't. Any love she may have felt for him once upon a time had died a painful death. 'Because it is. It just is.'

'Mummy!'

Max's excited yell interrupted the conversation.

Sophie and John turned to look at Max. He was standing on his uncle's shoulders, Daniel's big hands were holding Max by his thighs, steadying him. 'Watch me dive, Mummy.'

With that, he pushed off Daniel's shoulders like a little spring, holding both of his hands out in front of him with a diver's poise. He disappeared under the water briefly before the flotation devices on his arms bobbed him to the surface again.

Max beamed as his audience broke into spontaneous applause. 'That's definitely a ten, Maxy,' said John proudly.

Sophie caught Daniel's eye and they stared wordlessly at each other for a few moments.

'He's a chip off the old block,' said Daniel, as he held a squirming Max tightly in his arms.

Michael had been a champion diver at school. 'Yes,' said Sophie, burying herself even deeper in the lie. 'I guess he is.'

Sophie checked her watch. It was nine p.m. Only two hours to go until the late shift was over. Her feet ached from being on them for seven hours solid and she yawned as the familiar pool-induced tiredness she'd been fending off all day crept into her bones.

After splashing around for another hour, she and Max had got out of the pool. Max had fallen asleep as soon she had put him down for his midday nap. She'd known how he'd felt. The sun and the exercise had been conducive to sleep but Sophie had had to go to work and had resisted the temptation to lie down with her son.

The shift had been frantic and had helped to keep Sophie's mind off John's startling revelation. Two car accidents had kept them on their toes and despite their best efforts they had been unable to save two teenagers from dying.

It had been heavy going with the families and Sophie could still feel the chill down her spine as a mother's grief had reverberated around the walls of the department. It was like that sometimes. Some shifts just sucked.

It was always difficult to remain aloof from the tragedies that could occur here, and something they all struggled with but tonight held a particular element of reality for Sophie. It was hard not draw comparisons with Michael and Daniel's accident.

Michael had been left a paraplegic. Daniel had spent

every day since haunted by his guilt. But they had lived. And it took a night like tonight to really make her see how lucky they had been. Yes, Michael had suffered. But…what if they had both died?

How much more awful and tragic would it have been to lose her best friend and her lover in one dreadful blow? To have never seen Daniel's face again or talked to him or been near him. To have never had his son.

She closed her eyes, sickened by the notion, the cries of anguished mothers filtering through her disturbed thoughts. Just because she was over him, it didn't mean she wanted to live in a world where there was no Daniel.

It was with a heavy heart that she finally got the chance to take a teabreak. She didn't feel much like sitting alone in the tearoom so she sat down at the triage desk and started to load backlogged data onto the computer.

Looking at the stats, Sophie wasn't surprised to see that seventy-six patients had been triaged over the course of the shift. She took a sip of hot tea and glanced over to the empty waiting area—a most satisfying sight!

'Here she is,' said Todd, motioning to Leah. The two of them stood before her with silly grins.

'Hey, guys. What are you up to?' she asked, feeling the dullness leave her chest at the mischievousness in their eyes.

'Sophie Monday, may we present the Todd and Leah tap show,' said Todd in his very best radio DJ voice.

'What?' she asked, looking at them like they'd both escaped from the psych ward.

They laughed and began their routine, their work shoes clicking away on the hard linoleum of the department floor just like real tap shoes. Sophie laughed. How had they done that?

Todd hummed a tune and they tapped and leapt and pirouetted their way through an entire song. Sophie was laughing so hard as they built up to their grand finale she could hardly see. But thankfully she didn't miss the beautifully executed dip and the playful kiss Todd placed on his partner's lips.

'What exactly is going on here?' A shrill voice interrupted Sophie's clapping and Todd quickly pulled Leah to her feet.

'Ross,' said Sophie, sobering quickly and groaning inwardly. Not Ross, please. The after-hours nurse manager didn't have a humorous bone in his body.

'Doctor, I do not appreciate you leading my nursing staff astray. Sister Monday,' he went on, pointing his pencil at her, 'I expected more of you.'

'Ross, it's not as bad as it looks,' sighed Sophie. 'I was a bit down after what happened earlier and they were just trying to cheer me up.' Heaven forbid they should actually enjoy their work!

'I shouldn't have to lecture either of you on appropriate workplace behaviour.' His pencil jabbed the air again. Sophie looked behind Ross's head to see Leah pulling a funny face. She had to chew down on the inside of her cheek to stop herself from smiling.

'If you have nothing to do, I'm sure I could send you to another ward to help out.' With that he stuck his pencil behind his ear and turned on his heel, leaving them feeling like naughty schoolchildren.

They waited five seconds until they heard the squeaking of Ross's rubber soles fade away. And promptly burst out laughing. They laughed so hard they had to take it to the tearoom. Todd and Leah tippy-tapped in behind her.

'OK, what did you two do to your shoes?'

Leah bent her knee and flipped her foot up behind her, exposing the sole of her shoe. Two ECG dots, normally used when monitoring a patient's heart rhythm, were stuck to her shoes. They were round with a raised central metal nipple. And made a perfect tapping noise against the floor.

Sophie shook her head at the pair of them and laughed again. They each got a cup of tea and sat at the table.

'Is that guy for real or what?' asked Todd.

'Unfortunately, yes. Ross is a bureaucrat. He acts like every glove, syringe and bandage is paid for out of his own pocket. It's not important to like your job, just to do it well.'

'What's with that pencil? Where did it come from? He acts like he walks around with it shoved up his you know what!'

Sophie laughed at the image Todd had evoked.

'I would have thought something larger than the pencil.' Leah grinned and they laughed again. Oh, it was good to forget about their awful night.

'Speaking of which, I saw someone with a pineapple in his rectum a few years ago,' said Todd.

Leah and Sophie turned and looked at him with horrified expressions.

'True story,' he said, crossing his heart.

'Ouch,' said Leah.

'How did he do that?' asked Sophie.

'Slipped in the shower,' said Todd.

Sophie thought Leah was going to choke to death, she

was trying so hard to breathe and laugh at the same time. She slapped her on the back and they all had a quiet chuckle.

They were still there fifteen minutes later when Daniel strode into the room. Daniel had heard Sophie's familiar laugh from out in the hallway and noticed the slight kick of anticipation quicken his step. He had some paperwork to complete and needed a cup of coffee. Sophie's presence would be a bonus.

The first thing he saw was Todd touching Sophie on the shoulder. Something else kicked him this time. And it wasn't pleasant! He felt his stomach clench as the mere thought of Todd with Sophie did alarming things to his pulse rate. They didn't belong together. It was all wrong.

The second thing was that something was obviously highly amusing. All three of them looked like they'd been caught with their hands in the cookie jar. He noted the relief on their faces as they realised it was only him.

'Hello, Daniel,' Sophie said.

'Something funny?' he asked.

'Todd was just telling us about a patient with a foreign body in an awkward spot,' she said.

'That's one way of putting it, Soph. Seen any of those in your time, Daniel?' Todd asked.

Daniel watched as Todd kept his arm loosely around the back of Sophie's chair. Todd had called her Soph. Only he ever called her that. He felt his hackles rise. He didn't know why but...he just didn't like this guy. 'I've seen a few,' said Daniel quietly.

'Funny, isn't it?'

Sophie could tell from Daniel's face that he didn't find

it particularly amusing. His face looked closed, tense. He looked kind of angry and she really wasn't sure why.

'I've never found them to be particularly funny.'

Daniel's comment clanged like a loud bell around the room. Sophie shut her eyes and shook her head. Would it have killed him to have agreed? Was he going to make a scene now?

'O-O-K, then,' said Todd dropping his arms to his side and standing to go. 'Well…I have charts to tend to so I think I'll get going.'

Leah followed him quickly.

'What?' said Daniel, as Sophie glared at him.

'What the hell was that all about?' she demanded.

'I think laughing at a patient's expense is extremely poor form, don't you?'

'What?' she asked incredulously.

'Very unprofessional.'

She stared at him like he'd grown another head. Why was *he* acting like he had something shoved up his rectum? 'What?' she repeated.

Oh, damn! He sounded so pompous. Even to his own ears he sounded like a disapproving school teacher. He couldn't help himself—Todd irritated him big time! 'I mean, did the man not take the Hippocratic oath? And I don't think he needs any further encouragement from his groupies. Do you?' What was wrong with him? Why couldn't he just shut up?

'Groupies?' Was he implying that she was some simpering brainless fan?

'Yes, groupies. Is there something going on between you two? Because you're looking pretty damn cosy.'

Sophie's head was spinning. She was finding it hard to keep up. Her and Todd? Was he insane? Todd no more wanted to settle into a relationship than fly to the moon. And, besides, he was too…too…cute!

'And what if there is? What the hell's it got to do with you?' She was too angry to give him the satisfaction of a denial.

'You're right, it's got nothing to do with me. You just do whatever the hell you want. I keep forgetting that. I keep forgetting that you jump from man to man without a backward glance!'

Sophie felt sure her gasp could be heard all over the department. The unfairness of his comment stung. She heaved in some ragged breaths, two angry spots of colour staining her cheeks.

'How dare you?' she spat, dragging air into her lungs. 'How dare you come in here and accuse me of things and completely absolve yourself from any responsibility? Everything I've done you've driven me to, you sanctimonious bastard!'

Daniel immediately regretted his words. Too late. They were out now. He watched her as her dark blue eyes blazed in outrage. 'I'm sorry. OK? Hell, Sophie, I'm so sorry! That was unforgivable.'

She didn't look very mollified as she continued to glare daggers at him. 'I just think he has designs on you that you're maybe not aware of. Are you ready for that, Sophie? I mean, really ready?'

He had to be joking, right? He was so wrong about this it was almost laughable. 'Two things, Daniel. It's been two years since Michael died. I hardly think that constitutes jumping from man to man, do you? Secondly,' she went on, not wanting or caring for him to answer, 'you have no idea what we've been through tonight. I've watched a seventeen- and an eighteen-year-old die. I've comforted their fathers and I've held their mothers. I'm sorry that we seemed a little callous to you, but we *really* needed to laugh about something.'

Daniel shut his eyes. He'd stuffed up—big time. He knew that sometimes you had to laugh or you'd cry. Was sorry going to cut it? It seemed inadequate. 'Soph, I'm so sorry. I don't know what came over me.'

'Frankly, Daniel, I don't really care. I didn't think you could possibly hurt me any more than you already have over the years. Guess I was wrong about that.'

And with as much dignity as she could muster, she brushed past him without a backward glance.

CHAPTER SIX

SOPHIE'S legs shook all the way to her car. Daniel's accusations had hurt. She heaved in a breath and closed her eyes hard to stop the tears that were threatening. She'd cried too many tears over Daniel Monday.

But the tears were easier to stop than the memories, and as she drove to Arabella they crashed all around her and flooded her with their smells and voices. Michael's funeral replayed in her head, the grief and sorrow still there two years on.

The heady smell of roses that Charlie had cultivated over the years and picked from Arabella's rose garden to place on the coffin. The poignant notes of the flute that had played as Michael had been committed to the ground. The smell of the rain hitting the earth as the drizzly weather had mirrored the sombre mood.

The utter misery of Wendy's sobs as she'd thrown soil into the hole in the ground and Max's confusion as he had grizzled and clung to her, too young to understand but canny enough to know something really awful had happened.

People had been so kind. Marquees had been erected in Arabella's gardens and everyone had made a special effort to seek her out and express their deepest sympathies. Even Daniel's presence hadn't managed to pierce the bubble of grief that had encapsulated her. Her husband, her best friend was dead. Michael…

Later that night Max had taken for ever to go to sleep. He had cried for his daddy and she had lain with him, hugging his little body close, their tears mingling. She had rocked him gently and crooned 'Beautiful boy' to him, just as Michael had done every night of Max's life. Finally they had both fallen into an exhausted sleep.

Sophie woke a few hours later taking a few seconds before she orientated herself and the unrelenting grief settled around her again. She got up carefully and didn't know what to do with herself. She couldn't face going to bed. Lying alone in the king-sized bed was too painful to think about.

She wandered around the house for a bit, finally coming to the formal lounge. She moved to the bay window and absently fingered one of the two comfy, over-stuffed chairs that faced each other. A low coffee-table that held the chessboard separated the two.

This room held so many memories. This was where John had taught the three of them to play chess. Michael hadn't been overly interested but Daniel had and so, therefore, had she. The hours they had spent, the games they had played, sitting on these chairs.

A noise from behind disturbed her and she turned to discover Daniel standing in the doorway.

'Sophie,' he said in a voice that echoed her misery and grief.

She didn't answer him. Just turned back to cast her unseeing gaze to the river view. She heard him approach and could feel her body tremble with a build-up of emotion.

'I'm so sorry, Soph,' he whispered, and placed his hands on her shoulders.

And it was her total undoing. She crumpled. Days of putting on a brave face and being strong for Max disintegrated in an instant. She turned in his arms and he pulled her tight into his chest and she let it all flow out.

If there was one person in this world who understood how she felt, it was Daniel. For so many years they had been like the Three Musketeers. Inseparable. Her memories of Michael were so joined with those of Daniel that it was hard to separate them. She knew he was grieving every bit as much as her.

He held her and whispered his sorrow and kissed her forehead and her cheeks, as he had always done when she had hurt herself as a child. It was comforting and seemed so right, so natural. And then she stopped crying and just stood in the circle of his arms, listening to his heartbeat.

She wasn't sure when it changed, if there had been a moment or a nuance when she had become aware of his body on a physical level. But suddenly it felt different. Like he was holding her differently or his breathing had changed.

And then she became aware of his hardness. The events unfolded as if in slow motion. His obvious arousal, the thudding of his heart against her ear, the sudden stiff-armed, robot-like way he held her. Kind of awkward, like he was trying to create some space between them.

She looked into his eyes and even in the gloom she could see the flash of desire that dilated his pupils and took her back to the days when they had been lovers.

'Sophie,' he said again, and his voice was full of aching and need and want, and he was so close and smelt so good and felt so wonderful.

And then they were kissing. Flashpoint had been reached and they exploded. Sophie couldn't get enough of him. He tasted just like she remembered. Kissed just like she remembered. And she hadn't been kissed in the longest time.

Sure, Michael had kissed her but their marriage had never been consummated. After many frustrating attempts they had let the idea go. Michael had said if he couldn't have it all then he didn't want anything, and she had been more than happy to agree.

They'd shared a bed and been as close physically as was possible for two people who weren't having sex. She'd never had sexual feelings for him anyway and apart from the odd frustrated episode she'd put all those emotions on ice.

But Daniel had melted them away with one kiss and she was so hungry for more she was frightened she'd die of starvation before she could be sated.

The inevitable happened. They gave no thought to the consequences or the guilt that would follow. All they could think and feel was the moment and the wonderful sensation of coming home.

It took about a minute after they'd made love for the realisation to kick in.

'Oh, God. What have we done?' Daniel sat up, pushing himself away from her, disgust at his actions in every line of his semi-naked body.

She didn't answer and he turned back to look at her. She remembered flinching as his eyes, full of disgust, had flicked over her. Her blouse had been yanked open, her bra pushed aside, her skirt had ridden up around her waist.

He had stood, straightening his clothes as she'd lain there, still trying to work out what had happened. 'For heaven's sake, Sophie, fix yourself up,' he had snapped.

She had got up from the floor feeling sullied and used. He'd refused to look at her and she hadn't understood why he'd seemed to think it had been her fault. 'Daniel?' she said, her voice small.

He ignored her. 'What were we thinking?' he asked, turning to her, his eyes beseeching her, looking for an answer she didn't have.

They hadn't been thinking. It had just happened. A reaction to their grief and loss at a time when they were both seeking comfort. It hadn't made it right. It hadn't made it any easier to swallow. But it was what it was.

'Why did you let me do that?' he demanded.

'Daniel—'

'We just put your husband in the ground a few hours ago. How could you do this to him?'

Sophie knew that Daniel was struggling with what had happened, struggling with his own guilt, but his words stung and she remembered the deafeningly sound of her slap as it connected with his cheek. 'My husband. Your brother. How could *you*, Daniel? How could you?'

She walked out on him then and Daniel went back to New York a couple of days later. They hadn't talked about it then and had only skirted around it the other night. As Sophie parked her car she acknowledged it was still there between them. Still a thorn in their sides.

* * *

'Unit 001, thirty-year-old male. GSW to left femur. Is conscious and breathing but leg is apparently haemorrhaging significantly. Injury followed a bungled bank robbery. Assailants have left the scene and police are present. Being backed up by unit 912.'

'Roger, Coms.'

Daniel hung up the radio and sped, lights and sirens blazing, to the address in Fortitude Valley given to him by the communications centre. Years of living in New York had fostered a certain nonchalance concerning gunshot wounds. He'd seen hundreds of them! Rarely would a day go by on the job when he hadn't dealt with at least one.

So, consequently, his mind wasn't full of possible scenarios and clinical issues. It was full of Sophie. He hadn't slept a wink the last couple of nights, thinking about what had transpired between them. He pushed those thoughts aside and tapped into the hum of adrenaline running through his system and channelled it to sharpen his mind and prepare his body.

He reached the scene fairly quickly. The experience of years of being a paramedic came to the fore as he climbed out of his vehicle. Someone had been shot and needed him. Everything else took a back seat.

There was chaos at the scene as Daniel approached. Four police cars blocked the road. The victim had been shot on the footpath outside the bank and a crowd of curious onlookers, being held at bay by the police, was adding to the noise.

The man was clutching his bloodied leg and groaning in agony. A large pool of blood was congealing on the cement. Another bank employee was trying to apply pressure but quite ineffectually as the victim kept rolling around.

Daniel's mind was in purely clinical mode as he drew nearer. D for danger. Police were present and the bad guys had fled. Check.

R for response. Patient was groaning and swearing about the pain. Normal response. Check.

A for airway. The man appeared to have a perfectly patent airway if the swear words were any indication. Check.

B for breathing. Well, it was a bit hard to swear if you couldn't breathe. Check.

C for circulation. Again, swearing was exceedingly difficult to achieve if you were pulseless. Check.

H for haemorrhage. Bingo! 'Hey, mate,' said Daniel, snapping on some gloves and pulling a sterile dressing pad out of his kit. The assistant gratefully gave up his spot so Daniel had room to work. 'I'm Daniel. I'm a paramedic. What's your name?'

Daniel eased the makeshift dressing away from the wound gently so he could assess the damage, not wanting to disturb any clot that may have formed. The injury was in mid-thigh. Not pumping and the blood seemed darker and therefore venous. That was good but it was still oozing considerably. Taking a rough guess at his patient's blood loss, Daniel thought he'd probably lost close to a litre.

'Gordon,' he groaned. 'He shot me. I can't believe he bloody shot me!'

'Are you hurt anywhere else?' asked Daniel as he replaced the pad with a sterile one and bandaged it firmly in place, exerting more pressure over the top with his hand. He did a quick visual head-to-toe check.

The man shook his head vigorously. 'It's just me bloody leg!'

'Right, you,' said Daniel, pointing to the person who had been helping when Daniel had arrived. He'd introduced himself as Reg. 'You were doing a great job, Reg. You reckon you can hold this for me again? Firm pressure, OK?'

His helper did as he was asked but their patient continued to roll around a bit.

'Gordon, you need to keep still so we can apply effective pressure.'

'Hurts too bloody much to stay still,' he yelled, and groaned again.

Daniel heard his back-up arrive. 'I'm going to put you on oxygen and then put in a drip. We'll be able to give you some pain relief then. OK?'

'Whatever, mate! Just do it,' he snapped.

The back-up paramedics joined the scene and Daniel quickly allocated them jobs. Being an IC para, Daniel had seniority and controlled the scene. As he inserted the IV, Gordon was being hooked up to a monitor and having his vital signs recorded.

'BP ninety systolic.'

Daniel assessed the information. It wasn't too low but for a man in extreme pain you'd have expected it to be higher, unless he'd lost a large amount of circulating blood volume. Hypovolaemic shock was to be avoided at all costs.

Daniel hooked up a plasma supplement and ran it in as fast as it would go to replace the blood loss. He also administered a dose of morphine and Gordon became easier to manage.

Daniel's next concern was whether Gordon's femur was

fractured. That could be causing a large part of Gordon's pain. Daniel suspected it had been, and guessed it had probably splintered into many shards if it had taken the full force of the bullet.

If he could splint the leg, using a figure-of-eight technique applied to Gordon's feet, he would be able to apply traction to his injured leg and hopefully reduce his pain further. Daniel didn't want to move him until they'd stabilised his femur.

Working as a team, the three paramedics quickly and efficiently applied the figure-of-eight bandage and then splinted both legs together. Daniel was satisfied they could load Gordon now his haemorrhage was being efficiently controlled, his fracture reduced and his lost fluids were being replaced.

Daniel drove to the hospital behind the ambulance. His patient was as stabilised as he could be in a pre-hospital setting, so he found his thoughts returning to Sophie. He knew she was working today. What were the chances they would meet?

Very good actually. Sophie's face was the first he saw as he entered St Jude's. He stared at her and saw her momentary surprise.

'Sophie.'

'Daniel.' Her tone was brisk. Her actions methodical. 'What have we got here?' she asked, refusing to look him in the eye.

Daniel sighed and handed his patient over to her with the most professional façade he could muster. If she could pretend nothing had happened, so could he. He fought the urge to stick around, guessing it would make her job a lot easier without him hovering in the background. Gordon was in good hands and he had definitely been dismissed!

The silent treatment continued at Arabella. Thank goodness for Max. At least he didn't treat him like a pariah. Not that he didn't deserve it. Daniel knew he had been way out of line the other night. He had tried to talk to Sophie about it a couple of times but she was obviously still pretty angry with him.

'What did you do to my mummy?' Max asked him one morning after Sophie had left the breakfast table the minute Daniel had arrived—again.

'What makes you think I did something?' asked Daniel, amused by the observation skills of his three-year-old nephew. It must be fairly obvious if Max had noticed!

'She does that dippy thing with her eyebrows when she looks at you,' he said, stuffing some toast into his mouth. 'Like she does at me when I've been naughty.' Max did a fairly good impression of his mother's frown.

'Oh,' said Daniel, chuckling. Out of the mouths of babes… 'I said something to upset Mummy. Something I shouldn't have said.'

'Don't worry, Unca Dan,' said Max, patting Daniel on the hand. 'Mummy never stays angry for long.'

Oh? The way he figured it she'd been angry at him for longer than Max had been on the planet. He looked down at his nephew's hand on his and felt a little pang in his gut. Oh, to be so innocent, so trusting! Sophie had done a great job. Michael, too. The pang intensified. How lucky his brother had been.

In many ways he hadn't, of course. He'd been a paraplegic and had died too young, but he'd also had Sophie and sired a son. Surely, in the grand scheme of things, those were the things that mattered?

Looking down at the little hand, he found himself absurdly jealous of his brother. And something else. Determination crystallised in his mind. Determination to be a part of this little boy's life, maybe pick up where his brother had been so cruelly torn away.

He suddenly regretted the last two years he had wasted on the other side of the world. Max needed him. As a role model, a father figure, even as a link to Michael. What was that old saying? It took a whole village to raise a good child. He knew with sudden clarity as the little hand warmed his that he wanted to be a big part of his nephew's life.

Daniel hung onto the side of his seat as the ambulance flew through the streets of Brisbane. The first rays of daylight streaked the sky. He was in the back with Beryl and she was in serious trouble. He could hear the screaming sirens from the inside and hoped they'd make it in time. If she stopped breathing and they had to pull over so he could intubate her, the outlook would be extremely grim.

'What's our ETA?' Daniel called to Adam, the student paramedic, who, despite his inexperience, was driving like a rally car professional. Beryl's husband, Fred, was in front beside Adam.

'Two minutes.'

'Radio Coms to update St Jude's on our ETA. Let them know she's developing ST elevation.' Daniel put on his best clinical voice so as not to alarm Fred, but the changes to Beryl's heart rhythm were worrying.

Beryl was sitting upright on the trolley, hanging onto the rails for stability as the ambulance swayed from side to side. She reminded him of a frog—large frightened eyes practically bulging out of her head, leaning as far forward as she could get, her neck outstretched and gulping in the oxygen through the mask like a frog catching flies. The effort to breathe was so severe she couldn't even manage the occasional word.

'Beryl, have you got any chest pain?' he asked, touching her sweaty arm.

She nodded, unable to talk. He looked at her blood-pressure reading on the monitor and decided it could handle a shot of glyceryl trinitrate. If, as he suspected, she was developing cardiac ischaemia due to hypoxia then a quick spray of the drug under her tongue should dilate the coronary arteries and improve the blood flow to the heart muscle itself.

An infarction of her cardiac tissue would indeed be a very bad complication and anything he could do to avert such an event was essential. He administered one spray underneath her tongue with barely a disruption to her oxygenation.

The vehicle swung into St Jude's ambulance bay shortly after that and Daniel didn't wait to be let out. He opened the doors from the inside and had the trolley half out by the time Adam joined him.

'Let's hustle,' he said, his jaw set in a grim line as they rushed the trolley inside.

The team met them on their way in and rushed the trolley through to the resus bay. Sophie was there and Daniel nodded silently as he helped the team move Beryl quickly and efficiently from his stretcher to their trolley.

'Acute exacerbation of COAD. Administered bron-chodilators and IV steroids on scene with no noticeable improvement. Poor bilateral air entry. Developed ST elevation in the last two minutes. One dose of GTN given.'

Sophie listened to Daniel's concise handover as she hooked her patient up to the monitor. She looked at him and saw his blue eyes convey the things that he hadn't said. He was worried. Really worried.

A quick assessment of Beryl had her agreeing. It was the worst she had ever seen the elderly woman. She was cold, pale and clammy and gulping in air as fast as she could. Her body was desperately trying to get as much oxygen as possible. If that meant snatching the next breath before the last one had finished then so be it. She can't go on like this, Sophie thought.

'She's going to arrest,' said Daniel softly, standing behind her.

Sophie nodded. Beryl certainly couldn't keep this up for much longer. She moved closer to Beryl and covered her hand with her own.

'Please, Beryl. Try and slow your breathing down.' Sophie smiled and spoke in a confident manner. The last thing she wanted to do was panic Beryl by allowing her alarm to colour her voice.

The old woman clutched Beryl's hand and she noted the iciness. 'I know you're scared but you're here now. Let us take care of you.'

'H…h…' Beryl stuttered in a fragile whisper.

Sophie brought her head closer to try and catch what her patient was saying.

'Help.'

Then suddenly, just as Daniel had predicted, Beryl stopped breathing. Her eyes rolled back and she lost consciousness. Daniel was paged away to another call as the team sprang into action. He left reluctantly, sure that Beryl would not make it through this episode, and he worried how Sophie would cope.

Sophie didn't even notice his departure as dread settled in the pit of her stomach. Beryl! No. Don't do this to us, please. Sophie's thoughts were frantic as she quickly laid the back of the bed flat. For a few minutes as they bagged oxygen into her lungs via a resus mask, her heart trace on the monitor continued. But Sophie watched in dismay as it slowed and the ST elevation returned, indicating major cardiac involvement.

Sophie remembered the heart enlargement on the last chest X-ray Beryl had had. It was a common side effect of chronic airway disease. Years of lung dysfunction eventually put a strain on the heart. The heart grew larger, trying to compensate, and eventually it became too stretched and baggy to work effectively.

Thanks to the two IV lines Daniel had placed on scene, they were able to give drugs to speed up her heart rate and support her blood pressure.

'I'm in,' said Todd.

Sophie attached the black bag to the end of the endotracheal tube Todd had placed in Beryl's throat to allow them to ventilate Beryl's lungs. She met immediate resistance to her attempts to push air into the lungs.

'Her lungs are incredibly stiff,' she stated, her brow puckering in concentration. 'I can hardly ventilate them at all.'

'She's in VF,' said Richard as the monitor blared a warning at them. He started chest compressions.

'Charging the defib,' said Karen as she slapped two self-adhesive pads on Beryl's bare chest. The machine pinged its readiness. 'All clear,' Karen said in a firm, loud voice.

Sophie dropped the bag and stepped back. Everyone stopped what they were doing and did the same. Karen pushed the shock button and delivered the current.

'Still VF,' said Todd as they all resumed their places. 'Charge to 360,' he said, listening to Beryl's chest with a stethoscope. 'She's not shifting any air at all,' he confirmed with Sophie. 'Her lungs have had it.'

Years of chronic airway disease had made Beryl's lungs difficult to oxygenate adequately. During an acute episode such as this, the airways constricted right down, making it almost impossible to push air into them. Beryl's lungs had come to the end of the road.

The team worked on her for another fifteen minutes but when they couldn't ventilate her or restart her heart it became obvious it was futile. They stopped the resuscitation, Todd declaring Beryl's life extinct.

'I'd say she had significant cardiac infarction by the look of those ST segments,' Todd said.

Sophie agreed. Beryl's lungs were bad enough. Her heart failing also had made it a lethal combination. And it had only ever been a matter of time while she had continued to smoke. Sophie knew that. But that didn't make it any less sad.

In fact, it probably made it harder. Knowing Beryl could have avoided dying in such a way just highlighted the absolute waste. It was always sad when a favourite patient passed away and more so when their death could have been prevented.

Half an hour later Sophie was startled by the harsh clatter of the curtain being pulled back.

'Hi,' said Leah.

Sophie was surprised that the time had got away from her and the morning shift had arrived. She had gathered everything she needed and prepared to make Beryl presentable for Fred.

'Off home for you,' Leah said, feigning a stern voice. 'You've had an awful night. No one expects you to do this.'

'No,' said Sophie, smiling gently at her friend. 'I can't leave her like this. I promised her hubby I'd see to her and anyway…I think I need to do it for me as well.'

'I'll help.'

'No,' Sophie said firmly. 'It won't take long. I'll yell when I need a hand.'

Sophie was grateful that Leah had been around long enough to understand that there were some things you had to do by yourself. Laying someone out was never a great job but if you were particularly fond of a patient it was the final respectful thing you could do for them. It was an honour and a privilege and Sophie didn't know one nurse who didn't treat the often sad job with the utmost reverence.

Sophie talked quietly to Beryl as she gently washed the old lady's wrinkled, papery skin. She removed the endotracheal tube and the IV cannulas. She chatted about the time they had first met when Sophie had been a student nurse.

Leah gave her a hand to change the sheets and put a clean hospital gown on Beryl. Sophie combed Beryl's thin grey hair as Leah went to find Fred. She pulled a chair up close to the trolley so Fred could sit with her as long as he liked.

He entered a few moments later, looking older than his

eighty-odd years, and sat in the chair. Sophie felt her eyes well with tears as Fred took his wife's hand and a sob choked in his throat.

'What am I going to do without you, my girl?' he asked her. He laid his head on the bed beside her and placed her hand against his cheek.

Sophie left quietly, not wanting to intrude on such an intimate moment. It was humbling to witness and Sophie had to remind herself that some people stayed together for a lifetime. That their love for each other at the end of their lives had grown and magnified into something beautiful and ageless.

Sophie left work an hour late that morning but didn't mind. Tending to Beryl and chatting with Fred for a while had been very rewarding. He had thanked her for making Beryl look as beautiful as the day he had met her and Sophie had blinked rapidly to dispel the tears that had pricked at her eyes.

He obviously hadn't seen the external ravages of age or chronic disease that Sophie had seen when she'd looked at Beryl. His love and devotion had blinded him to such details. He had seen only the girl he had once known.

Sophie wondered if she'd ever have anyone in her life who would love her that much.

CHAPTER SEVEN

JOHN was an astute old goat, thought Sophie as she headed for the beach house. His suggestion that she get away overnight by herself had been a good one. Beryl's death had affected her more than she had realized, and with all the recent upheaval it was just one more thing she hadn't needed.

Sally had urged her as well, insisting that Max would be treated like a king and spoilt rotten until her return. When she had pointed out that that wasn't exactly what Max needed, Sally had shooed her away and gathered her surrogate grandchild to her ample bosom.

Max had squealed in delight and Sophie had felt a niggle of jealousy. It had looked pretty comforting there in Sally's arms and for the first time in a long time she found herself missing her mother.

Not that her mother had had the capacity to nurture and love that screamed from every cell of Sally's body. No, she had always been much too fragile for that. But there was the odd memory of being held tight and feeling totally loved. And it was that that Sophie chose to hold dear.

Sophie heard the crash of waves as she opened the door

of her Beetle and the sea breeze lifted her caramel hair off her neck. She looked at the big old bungalow with its wide wrap-around verandah facing the ocean and felt the cloud lift a little.

The water beckoned. She parked her car in the garage and stripped off her clothes to reveal the bikini beneath. She left her overnight bag by the front door and set off for the ten-minute walk down to the sand. She would open up after she'd had her fix of sand and sea.

The water was cool on her hot skin and Sophie dived eagerly into the waves. The ocean was just the right medicine for a hot day and a preoccupied mind. It was hard to think of anything other than one's place in the cosmos as the rhythm of the waves, as old as time, surged around your body.

Half an hour later Sophie walked out of the ocean and towelled off. The temptation to lie in the sun for a while almost won out, but her common sense overrode it.

She would, no doubt, fall asleep lulled by the rhythmic slapping of the waves against the shoreline and the drugging caress of the UV rays. She'd wake up two hours later burnt to a crisp even though it was getting past the hottest part of the day.

She walked a little further up the beach where the treeline met the sand and sat in the shade. She donned her sunglasses and absorbed the natural beauty, feeling her tensions ease as each wave hit the beach.

Sally and John were chatting in the kitchen when Daniel entered, looking for something to eat. Sally fixed him a sandwich.

'I was thinking I might go to the beach house tonight.

I've got a couple of days off now and I can hear the ocean calling my name.'

Sally and John looked at each other. 'That's a good idea,' said Sally. 'There's nothing like a bit of salt air to clear the head.'

John looked at her, a small smile on his face. Just as he had always suspected—Sally knew more than she let on! 'I agree,' said John, still looking at their mischievous housekeeper. 'That's a good idea, Danny, boy.'

Sally turned away and busied herself at the sink but not before John caught her widening smile and the speculative glint in her eyes.

'I'd better go and pack, then,' Daniel said, putting his plate in the dishwasher. 'Where's Max? I'll just say goodbye to him.'

'He's asleep,' said Sally, turning back quickly to face Daniel. It was the truth, but the last thing she needed was for Daniel to hang around waiting for Max to wake up. She loved that child like her own but, as dear as he was, she knew he was a blabbermouth. 'I'll tell him.'

John and Sally's collective sigh when Daniel finally left was audible all over Arabella.

'So,' said John, amusement lighting his eyes, 'playing Cupid, Sally Jones?'

'You know as well as I, John Monday, that those two belong together and always have, and if Michael hadn't been paralysed they'd be married by now with maybe another Max or two.' She said it sternly but spoilt it totally by grinning a moment after her little speech had ended.

'Sally Jones, you old fox.' He'd always had an inkling that the ever-present housekeeper knew more than she let on.

'I'd be careful who I was calling old, John Monday,' she sniffed, and gave him a wink as she turned back to the sink.

The walk back up the hill was much more taxing, and Sophie was glad to have reached the top. She stopped and washed off the sand at the outdoor shower, before making her way to the front door and inserting the key.

She was really tired now, the exercise and the sun and the salt air combining with her paltry sleep that morning to eradicate thoughts of anything other than bed.

She headed straight for the bedroom she usually occupied, switched on the air-conditioner and fell onto the bed, still in her bikini. Not Beryl's death, not Max, not John, not even Daniel, who had occupied too much of her head space lately, intruded on her deep, dreamless sleep.

When Daniel pulled up a little while later he, too, felt the pull of the ocean and went for a swim before he did anything else. When he finally entered the house the shadows were lengthening, although there was still probably a couple of hours of daylight left.

He could smell the stuffiness caused by the house having been locked up for so long and methodically went through the entire place, opening all the windows so air could circulate. One of the guest bedrooms' doors was closed and he thought how odd that was when all the others weren't. He pushed it open and stopped dead.

Sophie was startled from her sleep, sitting bolt upright as the noise of the door being opened knifed through her.

'Daniel? You scared the daylights out of me,' she said as her heart pounded frantically in her chest.

'Sorry…I didn't know you were here.' And that you would be wearing next to nothing.

'Hmm.' She yawned, lying back down and shutting her eyes, the pull of slumber beckoning her back to its enticing embrace. His presence didn't really register she was so tired!

Daniel tried not to stare at her barely covered body. It was hardly an itsy-bitsy bikini by any stretch of the imagination. Boy-leg chocolate brown bottom and a crop-top style matching bra. His eyes were drawn to a delicate silver chain adorning her neck. A butterfly with mother-of-pearl wings hung from the chain fluttering at her cleavage.

He shut the door and shook his head to clear it, trying not to think about her bare skin and curves. She was here, too. Maybe he should leave? By the look of her not-quite-awake eyes he doubted she'd even remember he had been here. But it seemed so ridiculous to drive two hours just for a swim. Surely they were both adult enough to get along for one night?

Actually, the more he thought about it the more confident he became. He owed her an apology and she hadn't really given him the chance to do so. Alone with him tonight, she wouldn't really have a choice. He would cook for her, his very best cuisine. A special, please-forgive-me, apology dinner. He grabbed his car keys and went out for supplies.

The room was dark when Sophie finally woke up. She jumped in the *en suite* shower and dressed in a denim miniskirt and a purple V-necked T-shirt. She opened the bedroom door and the most delicious aroma tickled her senses. The image of Daniel bursting into her room came abruptly back to her. Maybe it hadn't been a dream. Maybe he really was here, too.

But why? Surely he had told John or someone at the house his plans? And surely they had told him she was already here? Had he followed her here for a reason? Did he want to thrash things out with her again? Revisit their awful argument and try and explain himself?

Sophie shook her head. Things had been awkward since their row, sure, but Beryl's death had made their angry words insignificant. They were both alive. That was something to be grateful for. It was just another argument, one of many they'd had and probably, knowing them, just one of many still to come.

She made her way through the house and leaned against the archway that led into the kitchen and beyond to the open-plan dining and lounge room and eventually to the massive deck overlooking the ocean.

Daniel was humming to himself as he cooked. He was chopping something on the chopping board, his back to her, and she took a moment to just stare. He was dressed in denim shorts and a white T-shirt, looking very casual and comfortable in such a domestic scene. A man who was comfortable with cooking—what woman could resist that?

He turned to get something from the fridge and spotted her.

'Hi,' he said hesitantly. 'I'm making us some tea. I hope you don't mind?'

'What are you doing here, Daniel?' she sighed. 'I'm really not in the mood to go round and round the houses with you tonight.'

'I know, I'm sorry, I didn't know you were here. John

didn't mention it when I told him I was coming. I wouldn't have come if I'd had known, Sophie.'

Sophie accepted Daniel's words at face value. She had a sneaking suspicion the old man was trying to pull their strings. Did John expect her to blurt out the truth simply because they were alone? Didn't he realise how difficult it was for her?

'Look, you've had a tough day and, whether we like it or not, we're both here. Let's just make the best of it. I made you a tropical cocktail.' He plonked it in her hand. 'Go outside and drink it. Tea is half an hour away.'

She didn't argue with him. The sight of him cooking dinner seemed too cosy, too appealing, so getting as far away as possible seemed like a most sensible suggestion. She wandered out to the deck and noticed that he'd turned the fairy lights on so she walked down the steps to the garden and made her way to the love seat.

She sipped at her drink, its fruity taste and the crushed ice very pleasant on this balmy night. The house looked magnificent and Sophie knew that from its elevated position the lights could be seen from miles around. Max would love them when the whole family came up next week for the annual pilgrimage to celebrate his birthday.

She watched as Daniel walked towards her, a drink in his hand.

'Do you mind if I join you?' he asked.

She shuffled over and they swung together silently for a few minutes as his weight caused the love seat to rock.

'So…Beryl…' he said gently.

'Died.'

'Yes. I rang St Jude's. I'm so sorry, Sophie. I know she was a favourite of yours.'

'*Que sera sera*,' she said, and smiled sadly.

'I—'

'Please, Daniel,' she interrupted, 'don't spoil the moment with I told-you-sos.'

'I wasn't going to, Soph, I'm not totally without tact! I was just going to say that it seemed like such a waste of a life.'

'Yes,' she said quietly, 'it was.'

They sat, not speaking, absorbing the night atmosphere. They could hear the waves crashing on the beach below, the insects humming raucously, and the vision of the fairy lights completed the magic.

Daniel finished his drink. 'Come on, dinner is served,' he said, and walked into the house with Sophie trailing behind.

She sat at the beautifully set table and whistled. 'Did you invite the Queen?' She smiled. 'What's this all about, then?'

'It's my way of apologising,' he said as he served up their food. 'I was totally out of line the other night. I don't know what came over me. It was unforgivable.'

'You're right, it was, but lucky for you I'm a very forgiving person.'

'That's sounds promising,' he said as he placed a glass of wine in front of her.

'It's amazing how very little it seems to matter now. John's stroke, Max's choking episode, Beryl…things like that put petty differences into perspective.'

'Amen,' he said, and clinked his glass with hers.

Their meal got under way and Daniel was grateful he could occupy himself with something other than looking at Sophie. The damn butterfly necklace was most distracting, his eyes drawn to it over and over again.

Cooking was one of his passions and with Sally's tutoring, as well as living alone for years, his culinary skills had been well and truly honed. He had skipped the idea of keeping it simple and had cooked to impress. It was only what Sophie deserved after what he had accused her of.

And when Sophie bit into the superbly cooked beef Wellington and shut her eyes and sighed blissfully, well…it was the greatest compliment. Some tiny pieces of flaky pastry stuck to her lips before she licked them away and Daniel stared, helpless to stop.

They talked. Actually talked, just like the old days. He'd forgotten how much they'd once laughed together. They stuck to safe subjects—work, Max, John and Max's upcoming birthday. And Daniel relaxed and actually enjoyed himself.

Daniel served the dessert—a melt-in-the-mouth chocolate mousse—and then they moved to the lounge for coffee.

'Port?' Daniel asked as he placed her mug on the coffee-table along with a plate of colourfully wrapped chocolate mints.

'Mmm, sure,' she said, feeling very relaxed from a full stomach and the excellent wine.

They sipped at the fiery liquid in silence, only the steady thrum of the waves intruding into the quietness. She realised how much she had missed this aspect of their friendship. The intimate conversations. Even the comfortable silences.

She stared at him over the rim of her glass, aware suddenly of his intense blue stare. The queerest sensation started burning between her hipbones and she felt a pressure flare to life. A very familiar pressure.

Her eyes fell on the chessboard that sat on a low table in front of the bank of floor-to-ceiling windows that separated the deck from the house. She'd never felt so much like kissing an inanimate object. They needed to keep occupied. Something was happening that shouldn't be.

'How about a game?' She indicated the board with a nod of her head.

Game? Sure. He could think of plenty. Strip chess sounded good, he thought as the butterfly swung tantalisingly against the swell of her breasts. When had the night gone from companionable to combustible? 'Sure,' he said, clearing his throat.

They moved to the other table and sat opposite each other.

'White or black?' she asked, admiring the familiar, intricate wooden pieces.

'Your choice,' he said.

'We'll draw for it,' she said picking up a white and a black piece and shifting them between her hands behind her back.

The action thrust her chest slightly forward and emphasised the glorious outline of her breasts. The butterfly got caught in her cleavage temporarily and Daniel suppressed the urge to lean forward and release it from its fleshy prison.

She thrust her downturned fists towards him. 'You pick,' she invited.

He tapped her right hand and she turned it over to reveal a white rook. 'You go first.' She smiled.

He was grateful to get the game under way, desperately needing a distraction. Not that it seemed to work. The damn butterfly messed up his concentration and it was no wonder she checkmated him quite early in the game.

'Rematch?' he asked.

What the hell? thought Sophie. Why not? It was great to play chess with someone who wasn't such a stickler for strategy. She and John still played quite a bit but he was very rigid and didn't like a lot of chat while playing, preferring to concentrate. At least with Daniel they could play and talk at the same time.

The second game was over quickly. Daniel shut down all thoughts other than victory and had her beaten in ten minutes.

'Checkmate,' he said triumphantly.

She eyed the board sceptically from every angle. She hadn't even seen that one coming. How had he done that? Her concentration was broken by Daniel's laughter.

'You haven't changed one bit.' He chuckled. 'Still as competitive as ever. Still disbelieving that anyone could beat you. Just like when we were kids.'

'Watch it or I'll tip the board up,' she threatened lightly. 'John's not here to pick on me for being a bad sport.'

They laughed together and Sophie couldn't help but be flooded by memories. They'd had such great times once. She sobered a little at how different things were now. How simple everything had been when they'd been younger.

She felt absurdly like crying and felt tears well in her eyes. She blinked them away but to her dismay one fell down her cheek unchecked. She turned away from Daniel, getting out of the chair and moving the short space to the bank of windows that led to the deck. The moonlit ocean shimmered through her tears.

Daniel rose, cursing himself as he went to comfort her. Her tears were surprising but, then, she'd had an emo-

tional day. And he'd gone and brought up their childhood—
memories that must still cause her heartache.

'Sophie,' he said quietly, coming up behind her and
touching her shoulder.

She turned to face him. 'I'm sorry, Daniel. Don't worry
about me, I'm fine. I don't know what's the matter with me
lately.'

She looked so confused and they were so close. Close
enough for him to wipe away the next tear that spilled
from her lashes. Even though he knew he shouldn't.

Sophie felt strangely energised as his thumb moved
across her cheek, gently capturing the tear. Something was
happening. She held her breath as his fingers reached out
and gently lifted the silver butterfly off her suddenly burning skin. He fingered it gently for a few moments and then
placed it back onto the swell of her breast.

She sucked in a breath as his fingers lingered there,
stroking the feverish skin lightly. Hot desire lanced her like
a thrust from a dagger. She felt a tingling deep inside her
and knew with sudden clarity that she needed him inside
her like she needed her next breath.

Daniel's eyes widened at the pure sexual need reflected
in her eyes. He *really* shouldn't be doing this. He needed
to stop. Now! Somewhere inside him there was still a sker-
rick of sense telling him to step back.

But her skin felt so soft beneath his fingers and her perfume was mixing with another powerful essence—that of
a woman ready for pleasure. His nostrils flared as they
filled with the intoxicating scent. Even so, he knew he still
possessed enough control to walk away.

'Danny,' she half groaned, half whispered, her voice

husky, her lips moist and swollen as her teeth bit into her bottom lip.

Now he was lost. No one but his grandfather called him Danny. But the way she said it, full of need and aching and promise, totally undid him.

He swooped his head down and claimed her mouth, closing the distance between them in an instant. Crushing her sweet skin against his. Desire exploded inside him as she opened her mouth to the urgent demand of his tongue. Fireworks sizzled and sparkled behind his eyes as his need to feel every inch of her against him had him pushing her hard against the glass. Closer. He had to get closer.

Sophie understood his need to get closer as she yanked his shirt out of his trousers and tore at the buttons until she could feel the glide of his smooth naked flesh under her hands.

'Oh, Danny. Danny!' she groaned, as the feel of his chest stirred her primal lust. She wanted him, needed him, and only the feel of him hard and hot and thrusting was going to obliterate it. 'I need you, Danny. Now!' she gasped, and fumbled with his belt buckle.

His kisses were driving her mad. His hand up her shirt, yanking her bra aside and rubbing her impossibly erect nipple, had her screaming for more. 'Help me,' she cried in frustration as desire rendered her fingers useless.

'Slow down,' he gasped, and laughed huskily as he helped her with his belt and zipper.

'No, Danny. If you don't come in me right now, I'm going to die.' And she kissed him again. Hot and long and deep, thrusting her hands into his underpants and grabbing his erection triumphantly. 'Danny,' she whimpered softly.

For heaven's sake, they were both standing half-naked

up against a glass wall like sex-crazed teenagers. 'Sophie…slow down,' he panted into her neck covering her hands where they were stroking him.

She shoved him half away from her. 'I'm serious, Danny. I need you like I need oxygen.'

'I want you, too,' he gasped, his chest heaving.

'Please, Danny, now,' she breathed, and pushed aside his clothing until he was blissfully free of any restrictions and completely hers to touch.

Sophie couldn't explain it. She didn't understand it. All she knew was that if she didn't feel the hardness she held in her hand inside her in the next second she would scream. She didn't care whether she orgasmed or not. This was beyond the need for gratification. This was something primal. And it was such a turn-on she could hardly see straight.

'Danny!' she demanded again.

He didn't usually operate this way. He always gave pleasure before he took it. Always. But the caveman in him was emerging with Sophie's desperate urgings and he felt his desire surge to new heights. There was something passionate about a woman wanting you inside her this badly.

He pushed her pants aside impatiently and groaned into her mouth as he plunged his fingers into her heat.

She practically screamed into his mouth and he felt her legs buckle. He quickly shoved her further up the wall.

'No. Please, Danny. This. I want this,' she breathed, pushing him to her entrance, squirming and grinding her hips against his swollen erection.

He entered her in one swift movement, no longer able to deny his body or hers the thing they both wanted. He heard her cry out and almost roared in triumph as her tightness captured him and stroked him. He kissed her harshly, brutally almost, as her wild urgings and moans hurtled him close to his release.

There was something incredibly primitive and ardent about their act. Her head bumped against the glass as each thrust drove her against it. The silver butterfly moved in unison as he yanked her shirt aside and feasted on an engorged nipple.

Sophie was a whimpering mass of nerve endings. Her eyes rolled back as the pressure inside her was caressed by each masterstroke from Daniel. His wet mouth taunting her nipple was almost too much to bear and Sophie knew she was going to faint from the sheer sating of her need.

She cried out as the unbearable pressure ruptured and released inside her. The pleasure wave surged through her with all the power and force of a tornado. She heard and felt him as he joined her and together they rode the almighty heights as it took them to the stars and back.

It took an age to float back down to earth. Their ragged breathing was the only noise in the room. Daniel had slumped against Sophie, his chest heaving, his head burrowed into her shoulder as her sated body relaxed against him and he supported her weight.

They were still joined. He could still feel her internal muscles as they sporadically pulsed around him. It felt incredibly erotic and made it impossible for his erection to settle. Never in his wildest dreams had he imagined it could be this good.

Their breathing took for ever to settle. Sophie could feel Daniel still hard inside her, the length of him teasing her already sensitive nerve endings. She could feel her arousal build again, her release of a few moments ago already not enough. It had been two long years and she didn't want to let go of this moment. Not yet.

She moved against him and felt his instantaneous response.

'Sophie,' he moaned into her shoulder.

She kissed his head, her face caressed by the soft, fine hair, and moved again.

'Sophie.' His voice held a desperate strangled note and he raised his head to look at her.

'More,' she said huskily.

'More?'

'More,' she said, and moved again as she lowered her head and gave him a deep lingering kiss.

'Not like this,' he said, releasing her and lowering her to the floor.

'Please, Danny,' she whispered. She needed him again.

'My way this time,' he whispered back, kissing her swollen mouth and swinging her up into his arms.

He placed her gently on his bed, kissing her deeply before pulling away and stripping off his clothes. He helped her off with hers and it was the most amazing feeling to be totally naked with her again. Just like old times. She was looking at him like she always had—with pure desire. And he felt the thrumming of his blood pound in anticipation.

He took his time, rediscovering every inch of her body. All the places that made her shiver, the ones that made her skin goosy and the ones that made her cry out loud. Her neck, her knees, her breasts and finally her moist centre.

When her orgasm arched her back and tore through her body it was his mouth that swallowed her cries and his mouth that kissed her eyes as tears fell on her cheeks and his mouth that covered hers with tiny butterfly kisses until the last whimper had left her lips.

And then, just as she was getting her head around the mind-blowing pleasure he had unleashed upon her, she felt his erection nudging her as he pushed himself into her. She took him to the hilt, kissing him, and a surge of moisture inside her caused him to groan into her mouth.

'Sophie,' he muttered, breaking away from her kiss.

'Oh, yes, Danny,' she whispered, opening her eyes to find him staring at her, his blue eyes glazed with passion.

'Sophie,' he muttered again, incredibly turned on by her flushed cheeks and the swollen moistness of her bottom lip and the look of complete abandonment.

'Don't stop,' she begged, hypnotised by the passion in his stare.

His breathing became rough and unsteady again with each stroke into her tightness.

'Oh, Danny. Yes. I'm—I'm...'

'Me, too,' he breathed, feeling his body start to tremble uncontrollably as he claimed her mouth and with one final thrust brought the sky shattering down around them.

Sophie felt like she'd left her body as the pleasure undulated through her. Sharp and intense at first and then deep and slow as the first manic surge ebbed. She could hear their mingled cries somewhere below her but her thundering heartbeat obliterated all other noises.

And somewhere between flying up into the stratosphere and floating back to the ground, Sophie realised the horrible truth. She still loved him. Nothing had changed. It was just like old times.

Making love to him was one thing but *falling* in love? That was going to be a lot harder to rationalise.

CHAPTER EIGHT

THEIR breathing settled more quickly this time and Sophie felt a malaise invade her bones. Daniel took a couple of deep breaths and slowly pushed himself away from her. They stared at each other wordlessly, their breathing almost normal.

'What happens now?' Daniel asked.

Sophie shrugged and licked her lips and noticed the flare in Daniel's eyes as he followed the motion. What had they done? How were they ever going to be brother and sister-in-law again?

'I don't know, Daniel,' she said, sitting up and dragging the sheet around her. 'I don't have a guide book about what to do after you've just had sex with your dead husband's brother.'

She hadn't meant it to sound so callous but she couldn't remember ever feeling this confused. Not even after he had so suddenly rejected her all those years ago. How could they have done this again and how could she have been in love with him all these years and not realised it? But she knew without a doubt that she'd never stopped loving him.

He flinched at the harshness of her words. Wasn't he more than that? He watched as she avoided looking at him—she regretted it already. He nodded slowly. 'We shouldn't have done it,' he said matter-of-factly, massaging his temples.

She closed her eyes as his words wounded—he regretted it already. Oh, God! She couldn't bear a repeat of the recriminations that had happened when they had succumbed to temptation hours after Michael's funeral.

Sophie felt herself becoming angry. She wanted to yell, Of course we shouldn't have done it, but I love you, you idiot, and it's not how I loved your brother. It's all-consuming, it's in every cell of my body and every fibre of my being. It even hurts to breathe when I think about it.

'Of course we shouldn't have,' she said into the silence because she'd be damned if he'd hurt her with his words again. She was getting in first this time. 'Maybe if you hadn't taken advantage of my vulnerability, it wouldn't have happened at all.'

'I'm sorry?' Daniel's fingers stilled. What exactly did she mean by that?

'I was upset about Beryl…you knew that.'

'No. Wait. I didn't do anything that you didn't want me to do. Begged me to do.' His blue eyes glittered dangerously.

She had made him angry. Good! Maybe he could taste some of how she was feeling.

'I was grieving, Daniel. No one thinks straight in that frame of mind.'

'Grieving? That's a bit strong, isn't it? Upset, maybe. She was just a patient, Sophie. It wasn't—'

'Who? Michael? Hmm, yes, I'm seeing a pattern here.

You pop up in my life at significant sad moments, have sex with me and then tell me you shouldn't have done it.'

'Sophïe, it's not like that.'

'Really? Oh, no, that's right. It's usually my fault. How could I do it to you—et cetera, et cetera? That's right. I'm remembering now.'

'I think you're being a little unfair. I've told you I was sorry for what I said to you after Michael's funeral. And I don't feel that what just happened now is the same thing. But, Sophie, we can't keep doing this. It's not right.'

'Doing what, Daniel? What are we doing?'

'Playing with fire. That's what. You are my brother's wife—'

'No. I am your brother's widow.'

'It doesn't matter. There can never be anything between us, Sophie. There's too much history and too much angst. And it's just too…complicated!'

They stared at each other for a few more moments. Sophie felt her body stirring again. She almost screamed out loud at the unfairness of it all. Here she was in bed with the person she loved and a dead man stood between them.

'And what if I still love you, Daniel? What happens then?' It was impossible. She couldn't love him. She shouldn't. Tears tracked down her face. And, funnily enough, she didn't care. This situation was crazy and if they didn't get some resolution, they'd need to send for the men in white coats.

'Don't be ridiculous, Sophie. You don't love me. You love Michael.' He needed to hang onto that. That was how it was supposed to be. It was the only thing that had kept him away for four years. 'We both love him and we can't do this to him. He deserves our loyalty not our disrespect. What we just did, twice, is disrespectful to his memory.'

Daniel held onto his belief. He'd stuffed up his brother's life and the guilt had never gone away. He owed him and he'd struggled with that obligation ever since. He'd even given up Sophie for Michael. And now he was dead, a death that wouldn't have happened had he not been confined to that damned wheelchair. The wheelchair that *he* had put him in.

Had his death changed things? No. If anything, Daniel felt it demanded a greater commitment from him. Just because his brother was gone, it didn't negate *his* obligation, and he was damned if he was going to let Michael down again.

Sophie was talking crazily. It was easy to confuse feelings from the past when the intimacies they had shared were still so fresh. But his feelings were exactly that—in the past.

'Don't tell me what I feel.'

'You'll feel differently tomorrow. You just need a bit of perspective.'

Was he mad? Did he really believe that? Sophie looked at him with fresh eyes. He did. She could see the almost zealous belief stamped on his face and she knew that nothing she could say to him tonight would make a blind bit of difference.

Well, that was fine, but she loved him and she didn't want to sit around and have him talk her out of it. She had to get out of here. Daniel had broken her heart one too many times and she wasn't about to start hitting her head against the wall, waiting for him to throw her some crumbs.

He had told her four years ago that he didn't love her,

and despite her utter devastation she had survived. And she would do it again.

She slid out of bed and walked out of the room. He let her go, quelling the urge to call her back. He wasn't sure what had just happened but it was obvious she was upset. If he could start the night over he would, but what was done was done.

He loaded the dishes into the dishwasher and tidied the kitchen. His first instinct was to flee back to New York. But he'd promised John he would stay for as long as his recovery took and then there was the pledge he had made himself about being around for Max. Going back wasn't an option.

'I'm going.'

Sophie's voice pulled him out of his thoughts and he focussed on her, noting her packed bag at her feet. 'No, Soph. Please, don't leave.'

'I can't stay,' she said huskily, picking up the bag and walking away before she changed her mind and threw herself at his feet and begged him to love her.

Daniel stayed still, listening to the door shut and then, a few moments later, her car drive away. Damn! He'd handled that really badly. They'd been close tonight, before they'd ruined it by becoming physical. And while the intimacy had been fantastic, the feeling that they had been on the road to rebuilding their friendship had been better.

He didn't want it to end like this. He threw down the teatowel he was holding, quickly switched out the lights and locked the door behind him. He didn't have time to shut up properly and would have to remember to talk to Charlie about it in the morning. Right now all he cared about was catching up with Sophie and making her see sense.

He estimated he was maybe fifteen minutes behind her as he got into his car. It was nine p.m. so traffic wasn't going to be a problem. He was glad when he reached the gate to the property and turned out onto the main road. He'd have a chance to really accelerate now.

He caught up with her yellow VW on the highway back to Brisbane and reduced his speed to sit behind her until the highway exit. There was really no where for them to pull over on the dual carriageway so he'd have to cool his heels for the next hour or so.

He didn't want them to go back to their corners and prepare for the next round. He was tired of the continual undercurrent of blame and anger. Whether it had been wise or not, they had crossed a line tonight that neither of them could ignore. They had to find a way to accept their mistake and go on with their lives.

Because they were involved with each other, whether they liked it or not. They were family, and while it had been much easier when a whole world had separated them, that was no longer the case. He was going to be around a lot, for John and for Max, and they had to finally deal with it. Tonight.

Sophie didn't realise it was Daniel's car behind her and even if she had been aware of it her tears wouldn't have allowed her a clear view. How many types of fool were there in the world? How many times was she bound to make the same mistake? When would she learn that falling in love with Daniel Monday was always doomed to fail?

Apart from a few brief happy months when they had been lovers and a son he didn't realise he had, Daniel had caused her no end of heartache these last four years. She had thought her defences against him were rock solid and had been prepared for any new onslaught he could possibly unleash. But solid defences didn't help you if the enemy lurked within!

Fresh tears fell as she berated herself for her foolishness. When she had told Daniel she was one hundred per cent over him she had genuinely meant it. How could she have lied to herself all these years? He had never truly left her heart, she'd just managed to move into a state of extreme denial. Damn it, she swore silently, and slammed one palm into the steering-wheel for good measure.

An ambulance flashed past her with its lights and sirens blazing, and it brought her out of her thoughts as she immediately eased her foot off the accelerator. She wondered where they were going and to what, and sent a little prayer heavenwards that no one was seriously ill or injured.

It became apparent a few minutes later as she rounded a bend that her prayer had been too late. She braked gently as a scene of total road carnage greeted her. Three cars, one turned over, the others smashed and twisted, lay scattered on the highway. Broken glass, car parts and walking wounded added to the scene of devastation. A lone policeman was controlling traffic and the ambulance that had passed her was the only one on the scene.

Sophie pulled to the side of the road, thinking she could help a little before reinforcements arrived. She got out of her car and was making her way towards the scene when a familiar voice called her name.

'Sophie.'

She turned and saw Daniel walking towards her. 'Daniel?' Despite the situation, she felt her stomach flip-flop. How had he got here? But now wasn't the time for questions or to pick up where they had left off, and they both knew it. People needed them and that took priority.

The policeman tried to stop them as they walked quickly into the fray. 'Step back, please,' he ordered. 'Go back to your vehicles.'

'I'm a paramedic and Sophie's an emergency nurse. We just thought the crew over there could do with a hand,' said Daniel.

The young policeman hesitated for a second.

'Come on, mate, they're snowed under. At least let us help until some back-up arrives.'

The policeman waved them through and they raced over to one of the paramedics. It was Jane Carter, the ICP who had helped that night in the rain with Charlie.

'Am I glad to see you guys,' she said, recognising them instantly and giving them each a pop-over vest with AMBULANCE emblazoned in reflective lettering front and back. 'There's twelve victims from three cars as far as we've been able to assess. We're trying to triage at the moment. There's two entrapments, one in a bad way, the other negative. The rest appear to be relatively unscathed. If you guys could do some quick head to toes on them, that will free me and my partner up to deal with the girl who's trapped in her vehicle.'

'How far away is your back-up?' asked Sophie.

'Another fifteen minutes,' Jane replied, before heading off to the flattened car where a human being's life hung in the balance.

Daniel and Sophie worked as a team, organising those who could walk to sit by the ambulance where the light was best and they could assess them more easily. They put cervical collars on as many people as they could, checked neurological states and looked for broken bones and haemorrhages.

Several fire engines arrived, adding to the colourful strobing of lights. Sophie heard the guttural growl of a motor starting up in the background, followed by the crunching of metal as the jaws of life sliced through the frame of a vehicle as if it were a tin can. It wouldn't be long now until the girl was released from her squashed car.

Three ambulances pulled up, shining their headlights across the carnage and into the night, the glass on the road sparkling like diamonds in the glare. Several paramedics descended upon them and Daniel gratefully handed their patients over.

As the ambulances began to leave with the injured Sophie noticed a girl she hadn't seen before wandering around aimlessly. She had some dried blood on her forehead and was muttering to herself. She had panda-like eyes where tears had mingled with her mascara, causing it to run.

'Hi, I'm Sophie. Were you involved in the accident? How about you come over to the ambulance and we can check you out?'

The girl, who looked about nineteen, stared at her blankly. She seemed dazed and Sophie was concerned that she might be concussed.

'James. I can't find James,' she said, looking straight through Sophie.

Sophie felt a prickle of alarm. 'Was James in the car with you?' she asked gently.

'He was driving,' she said absently.

Sophie searched her memory. The name didn't ring a bell from any of the people she had treated tonight, but she hadn't seen them all. Maybe Daniel had treated him?

She led the confused young woman over to Daniel, reaching into the back of the ambulance to grab a blanket and put it around her patient's slim shoulders. The girl was shaking and was obviously shocked.

'Daniel, did you treat anyone called James tonight?'

'No,' said Daniel, automatically checking out the girl, concern creasing his brow. 'What's your name?' he asked as he shone a penlight into her eyes, relieved to find her pupils equal and reactive.

'Donna,' she said. 'I'm fine, really, I had my seat belt on but James didn't. I told him he should put it on…I told him.'

Daniel flicked a glance at Sophie and she knew, without asking him, what he wanted. She located the scene controller and informed him they'd have to search the area for another potential patient.

Sophie and Daniel joined in the search along with available fire crews and police. Torches in hand, they searched the overgrown nature strips either side of the highway, the beams of light probing the darkness.

'Found him,' a voice called, and Sophie and Daniel rushed to the ditch, where James had been thrown clear of his car.

Daniel took one look at the young man and knew he was dead. His body was twisted at an awkward angle and his head skewed in the opposite direction. A sudden vision of Michael's body lying on the road flashed into his mind, and Daniel blinked hard to erase it.

Donna had managed to break through the crowd surrounding James's body. She threw herself on the ground and knelt over the inert form. He appeared to be about the same age as her.

'James, James!' she yelled frantically, shaking his body. 'Help him. Help him,' she begged, looking at Daniel with wild, frightened eyes. 'Why won't he wake up? He won't wake up.' She intermittently shook his body and wrung her hands.

A few of the searchers tried to pull her back but Daniel signalled to them to leave her. The girl grabbed Daniel's hand and yanked him down beside her.

'Fix him,' she begged, pushing his hands onto the young man's chest.

Sophie sank to her knees beside Donna and put her arm around the girl's shoulders.

Daniel looked at Sophie wordlessly and she shrugged, knowing that the situation was futile but also knowing that Donna needed to see something being done.

Daniel placed his fingers over the young man's carotid pulse. Absent. He put his stethoscope in his ears and placed it on the dead man's chest. Breathing—absent. Heartbeat—absent. He'd broken his neck and had probably died instantly.

Starting any resuscitation measures now would be futile and probably not welcomed by this fit-looking young man who would, if by some miracle they were successful, spend the rest of his life in a wheelchair hooked up to a ventilator with major brain damage.

He thought about how angry Michael had been that Daniel had resuscitated him at the scene of their accident, only to be left a paraplegic.

'James,' Donna sniffed, wiping her eyes, smearing her

mascara further. 'You can help him, can't you?' she pleaded, choking on her sobs as Daniel removed the stethoscope from his ears.

'James is dead. I'm very sorry. He's broken his neck.' Daniel's voice was gentle as he covered her hand that gripped his arm. It was a horrible thing to have to tell her in less than ideal surroundings.

'No, no.' She shook her head violently from side to side, looking from Daniel to Sophie and back to Daniel again. 'No. You have to fix him. You have to make him wake up. I didn't get to tell him I loved him. You have to make him wake up!' She was sobbing hysterically now, and shaking Daniel's arm.

'I'm sorry, there's nothing I can do,' he said quietly.

Her face crumpled and she let out a cry of such agony that it raised goose-bumps on Daniel's arms. She threw herself at her boyfriend's body, her head against his chest, her hands clutching his shoulders.

'No, James. No,' she sobbed. 'I love you. I love you. Can you hear me? Don't leave me. I love you.'

Daniel and Sophie sat with the girl as she wept, and the small crowd of people surrounding them peeled away, knowing there was nothing further they could do. The scene controller, in his fluorescent yellow vest, approached.

'Your patient?' he asked Daniel.

'Negative,' Daniel said softly, and the man nodded and backed away.

An over-zealous official brought a sheet to place over the body, but Daniel waved him away. Donna was still holding onto James. The girl needed time to grieve, she would let him go when she was ready.

The girl's cries were chilling. She kept touching her boyfriend's face as if the sheer depth of her love alone could bring him back. She kept asking, 'Why? Why didn't I tell you?'

Sophie blinked back tears as the young woman's grief chilled her to the core. She looked away, the intensity of Donna's grief almost too painful to witness.

She surveyed the carnage of the three-car pile-up strewn all over the highway. Twisted car bodies, stray pieces of luggage, personal items and broken glass littered the road surface. A multitude of flashing lights strobed into the night like glitter balls at a gruesome discotheque.

Two young people lay dead from a lethal mix of alcohol and no seat belts. Ten others had been very lucky to escape major injury. What a waste of life.

They stayed with the girl until she had cried herself out, neither of them wanting to leave her in such an overwrought state. She eventually let go of James's body and allowed Sophie to take her to a waiting ambulance.

Sophie caught a glimpse of the utterly defeated young woman before the back doors slammed and they took her to St Jude's for observation. She looked small and forlorn, her panda eyes all but gone now—a million tears having washed the mascara away altogether.

Sophie knew what Donna was going through. Knew how the suddenness of death sucked your breath away, how your mind reeled and you couldn't take in the awful truth. How, just when you thought you'd finished crying and there could not possibly be any more tears left, they came again. And again.

Sophie leant against her car now there was nothing for

her to do, and waited for Daniel to finish talking to the accident investigation squad. She had already given her statement. The road was obviously going to be blocked for hours as nothing could be moved until the investigation was complete.

After what had happened at the beach house she should just get in her car and go. Take the detour the police had set up and drive home to Arabella. But she couldn't. As mad as she was at Daniel, at the moment part of her knew that James's death had to have been hard for him.

Sure, he'd been the consummate professional tonight but something like that was just too close to home. There must have been some memories stirred for him.

'You OK?' he asked half an hour later as he approached her. He remembered her quietness after the Sunvalley house fire and how she had been affected by the rawness of his job. Well, this had been pretty raw, too.

'Sure,' she said. 'What about you?'

'What about me?' He smiled.

'I thought the whole James thing might be a little confronting for you.'

'Ah,' he said. She was astute. She was leaning against her car for support and he copied her pose, standing beside her, their arms brushing lightly.

They didn't speak for a while. The incident at the beach house had taken a back seat. Their minds were full of the carnage they had witnessed and the people they had treated and the two young people who weren't going home tonight, or any night.

And another car accident four years ago that had dramatically altered the course of their lives for ever.

'I could have tried to resuscitate him,' said Daniel into the now eerily quiet night air.

'It was too late, Daniel. He'd broken his neck. Too much time had elapsed. You know you wouldn't have got him back.'

'I resuscitated Michael.'

'It's different, and you know it. You were right there, you were able to administer immediate first aid to Michael. James had been in that ditch for who knows how long. Besides, Michael's spinal cord injury was much lower. We didn't need a CAT scan or an MRI to tell us that. People's heads don't twist that far unless something's snapped.'

Daniel nodded. 'I just kept seeing Michael's face,' he whispered. 'Remembering that night.'

'It wasn't your fault, Daniel.'

'Of course it was. I was driving.'

'A man had a heart attack at the wheel on the opposite side of the road, veered across into your lane and smashed into you. It was a freak accident.'

'Well, why do I still feel so guilty?'

'I don't know, Daniel. Why do you?'

He was silent for a moment. 'Because I was thinking about you, that's why, when the other car veered. And I know it all happened very suddenly but maybe if I hadn't been so preoccupied with you and how great you looked naked and how wonderful you smelt and how lucky I was to have you, then maybe I would have seen it coming sooner. Maybe I could have swerved or braked or done anything other than let it happen.'

Sophie swallowed the lump in her throat. She heard the anguish and accusation in his voice. So it had been her fault? No. She wasn't going to take that on. She couldn't control who was thinking about her and when, and if Daniel really thought a split second would have made a difference to the outcome of their accident, he was crazy.

'I was looking into James's face tonight and Donna was begging me to do something, and all I could hear was Michael yelling at me how I should have let him die, and I just couldn't put James through that.'

Sophie remembered the anger and the bitterness that Michael had felt in that first month and how in the deepest part of his depression he had said those things to Daniel and had even begged her to help him end his life.

She looked at the man she loved and felt his pain. 'You did what anyone would have done, especially a paramedic. Especially a brother. Michael went on to have a full and happy and productive life. James would be a ventilator-dependent quadriplegic.'

'I know…I know,' he sighed, and turned on his side so he was facing her. 'It just kind of sucks, though, doesn't it?'

'Absolutely,' she agreed, turning to face him also. 'It does. But it doesn't make it your fault. What happened with Michael was just coincidence. Two sets of strangers in the wrong place at the wrong time. There's no rhyme or reason to it. It was bad luck. That's all. And, yes, that sucks, too.'

She rose on tiptoe to kiss him on the cheek. It was a platonic gesture because she couldn't bear it that he still blamed himself for something that had been a tragic accident, and wanted to comfort him somehow.

But she knew even before she reached his face that it would be his mouth she would kiss. Something compelled her and with the memory of their love-making so fresh it was an urge she couldn't quell. She pressed her lips against his and then pulled back slightly. She felt reaction to the kiss slam into her and saw his nostrils flare and his eyes glaze.

She kissed him again and felt her lips open to the demanding pressure of his. His arm came around her waist, drawing her against him, and Sophie felt her head bend further back as the heat from his mouth drugged her into submission. Her heartbeat pounded in her ears and she could feel her internal muscles stir to life again. Man! Could he kiss!

With a supreme effort she broke away and they shared an unfathomable look, chests heaving.

'I'm going home now,' she said huskily. She opened the door and got in, and Daniel crouched beside her window. She pressed the button and the glass whirred down.

'Drive carefully, Soph,' he said quietly, his blue-eyed stare mesmerising. It wasn't something he needed to say with the horror of the night still close. 'And kiss Max for me.'

She drove off, his last words reminding her of yet another reason why she loved him. Their son. Their beautiful Max.

She sure didn't make things easy for herself. She was in love with someone she shouldn't be in love with. Someone whose emotional commitment to his brother was steeped in guilt so thick that it prevented him from feeling and loving freely.

Sophie despaired at what she could do to change it. She had a feeling that only Michael himself could release Daniel from his self-imposed feelings of obligation. And Michael was dead. It didn't bode well.

CHAPTER NINE

SOPHIE went to work gratefully a few days later no closer to finding a resolution to the stalemate that existed between her and Daniel. Being at home, catching glimpses of him, sharing meals and finding Max in bed with him every morning made life difficult. Worse were the memories of happier times that screamed from every nook and cranny of Arabella.

It was becoming apparent that she couldn't go on like this. She couldn't live under the same roof as him and love him and not go mad. He seemed hell-bent on sticking to his guns and pretending nothing had happened between them. Sophie knew staying would only make her unhappy in the long run.

Her suggestion a couple of months ago that she move out was sounding better by the day. The Monday clan wouldn't like it. Hell, neither would she. Max would hate it and probably her to boot. But she couldn't continue to pretend like this. If Daniel wouldn't let her love him, she had to get out.

But first things first. There was this late shift to get through at St Jude's and then tomorrow they were off to the beach house with the rest of the family and then the next day was Max's birthday. She wasn't going to spoil this happy occasion with her unwelcome news. There'd be time enough for that later.

It was good to slip into her Sophie the nurse persona. The familiar aspects of her job had a soothing effect on her raging thoughts. Taking blood pressures and temperatures. Doing urine tests and hooking people up to monitors. Dressing wounds and cleaning up vomit. Drawing blood and inserting IVs. Things she had done a thousand times were strangely therapeutic tonight.

It was a busy shift and Sophie was grateful that there was no time for personal introspection. Two broken arms, three abdo pains, a chest pain, a major nosebleed, a sore eye, a case of suspected meningitis and a gangrenous toe. Way too busy to think.

'Sophie, can you come and take some blood on the lady in cube five, please? I've had two tries. Her veins are awful.'

Sophie followed Karen into the cubicle. Mrs Schmidt lay on the trolley. Her granddaughter was sitting on a chair nearby.

'Oh, Sister,' Anna said, recognising Sophie immediately. 'How's your face? Nothing broken, I hope.'

'No. It was fine,' Sophie assured the younger woman. 'I'm going to see if I can get some blood from your grandmother. She has difficult veins.'

'Yes,' agreed Anna. 'We always have trouble.'

'Well, Sophie's the best,' Karen's chirped. 'If she can't get it then there's none there to get.'

Sophie smiled at the younger nurse. It was a nice compliment. It was also true. Taking blood and putting in IVs were skills she had mastered.

Mrs Schmidt lay docilely on the trolley, staring into space.

'How was she when you tried?' she asked Karen.

'Quiet as a lamb.'

Still, Sophie gloved up with some trepidation. The woman lying on the trolley was a far cry from the agitated patient who had come into the department a couple of months ago, but she didn't really want a repeat performance.

'She seems a lot calmer,' commented Sophie to Anna.

'Oh, yes. She's much easier to handle now. The geriatric team said there wasn't a whole lot they could do for her as her dementia was quite advanced, but they put her on some medication and it's really helped. Coming here that night was a godsend, Sister. I was at the end of my tether.'

'That's excellent.' Sophie smiled. 'What brings you here today?'

'Well, I was a bit worried that she's over-medicated. She's been very sleepy the last few days and is often hard to rouse. I rang the geriatric doctor and he advised me to come here and have some drug levels done.'

Sophie nodded and snapped on the tourniquet. Karen held Mrs Schmidt's arm and Anna stood on the other side, ready if the old lady let fly again.

Sophie prodded the crook of her patient's arm with her gloved fingers. Taking blood, particularly from difficult veins, with gloves on made the job even harder. The latex barrier really reduced the ability to 'feel' a vein.

Concentration creased Sophie's brow as she thought she felt one quite deep. There were several closer to the skin surface but Sophie could feel the knotting and guessed they were probably too sclerosed to be of any use.

She took a breath and slid the needle in. Mrs Schmidt didn't even flinch and Sophie closed her eyes as she advanced the needle deeper, sensing the vein position as much as feeling it. She got a flashback and almost whooped as dark red blood filled the syringe.

Mrs Schmidt remained docile throughout the procedure and Sophie felt admiration for Anna. After the months of abuse she'd had from her grandmother she could be forgiven for wanting docility. But she obviously loved the old lady a lot and preferred to see a happy balance rather than an extreme either way.

Sophie shut the curtains behind her and placed the blood tubes and path form in the box that was regularly collected by a pathology courier. She spied Daniel coming in through the ambulance bay and her stomach flopped at the sight of his long-legged stride, reminding her of her one and only ride on a roller-coaster.

Memories from the other night came flooding back, making it impossible to get off the ride. How he had felt inside her, how good his lips had felt on her breast, how erotic it felt to be pinned high against the glass by the force of his surging desire.

He chose that moment to look up and fix her with a blue stare. She knew his thoughts were on that night, too. The look of pure sexual hunger transmitted in his stare had her stomach looping the loop. She felt her cheeks grow warm as his lustful gaze continued.

'Sophie.' He nodded, still staring as he drew the trolley to a halt beside her.

'Daniel.' She tried to steady her voice but even to her own ears she sounded like a swooning heroine from an old black-and-white movie.

They stared at each other for a few more moments until Ben, the other paramedic, cleared his throat loudly. Daniel gave himself a mental shake. 'Unknown female. Probably early twenties. Found OD'd in the valley. Probably heroin. Not a known junkie. No track marks. Given Narcan after some bag-masking failed to produce a response. She is rousable. Haven't been able to identify her or elicit any info from her. I inserted an IV at the scene.'

Sophie watched his lips move as he formed his words. She tried not to stare at them or think about the magic they had weaved.

'Sophie?' he prompted quietly.

'Hmm? Oh, yes…right,' she said, dragging her eyes away to look at the patient on the trolley. The woman was lying on her side and had on an oxygen mask. An oropharyngeal airway protruded from between her lips. A white cellular blanket covered her slight form.

'Oh, my God. It's Jenny.' Sophie recognised her instantly as they pushed the trolley into a cubicle. 'She was a patient here a few months ago. She'd been raped by two men. Jenny? Jenny, can you hear me?' Sophie spoke loudly as she shook the girl's shoulder firmly. 'Jenny. Open your eyes and talk to me.'

The patient roused at the insistent note in Sophie's voice and coughed on the airway, which she promptly spat out as she pulled the mask away. She tried to sit up, obviously disorientated from the side effects of the drug.

She was as tiny as Sophie remembered. Maybe more so,

her arms looking almost skeletal. But she was a far cry from the woman who had presented to the department a few months ago. That Jenny's face had been swollen and bloodied, her upper lip cut and a nasty bruise had blackened her right eye. Her blouse had been torn and there had been grazing to her hands and arms.

'Where am I?' she asked.

'You're at St Jude's. It's Sophie. I looked after you when you came in before. Do you remember?'

'Oh, no, no, no,' Jenny groaned, and threw herself back as tears rolled down her cheeks. 'I don't want to be here. I just want to die. Just leave me to die.' Sobs choked from her throat as she curled herself into a ball.

Daniel lingered and watched Sophie for a few minutes as she worked. She leaned forward and spoke softly to her distraught patient. She held Jenny's hand and stroked it and was quick with the vomit bowl as Jenny started to retch.

She was professional and efficient and in control. Very different from the woman he had held the other night. Her blind need had brought her to a state of begging and he hardened, just thinking about how she had pleaded with him. Time to go!

A couple of hours later, after Jenny had had a chance to sleep and recoup, Sophie was able to talk to her. She brought her some juice to drink and some sandwiches.

'What happened today, Jenny?'

'I just couldn't stand it any longer.' A tear trickled down her cheek. 'I've just felt so dirty, so violated. The police haven't caught them yet and I see their faces in every man who passes. I'm so scared all the time.'

'What did you take?'

'I went to the valley because I'd heard you could get heroin there. I didn't want to just take a whole bunch of pills. I wanted to do it properly. I bought some off a dealer and he showed me how to inject it. I went back to the alley where…where…' She stopped and struggled to pull herself together.

'It just seemed fitting, you know? To die there. In that alley where they raped me. It seemed like the perfect place to end it all. I can't believe someone found me.'

Sophie put her arm around Jenny as she sobbed anew, and stayed until she had calmed down.

'Have you been going to your counselling sessions?'

Jenny shook her head. 'I can't talk about it with a complete stranger. How could they possibly know how I feel?'

'Remember how I told you the rape crisis counsellors are all women who have been raped? They have professional counselling qualifications and they specialise in rape recovery.'

'Really? I don't remember that,' said Jenny. Her voice wobbled as she dried her tears.

That was hardly surprising. It was hard to take everything in after such a vile act had been perpetrated against you. 'Really. And you know what? Sometimes it's easier to talk to someone you don't know than those close to you. Particularly if they've been through the same thing as you.'

Sophie rang the crisis centre at Jenny's request. A counsellor arrived promptly and Sophie left them to it. She hoped desperately that Jenny had taken a big step towards recovery tonight.

Sometimes people had to hit rock bottom before they

could climb back up again. Lying in an alley with a needle sticking out of your arm had hopefully been Jenny's.

With Jenny's issues as resolved as she could make them this shift, Sophie's thoughts returned to Daniel. The heat that had flared between them had taken her by surprise. She had understood her reaction but interestingly it definitely hadn't been one-sided. Maybe he wasn't as indifferent to her as he tried to make out.

A little while later, Sophie stood at the triage desk, chatting with Richard and Ross, the after-hours nurse manager. He had his pencil out and was tapping it against his teeth. Todd was at the other end of the desk, inputting data on the computer. The waiting room had all but emptied and in thirty minutes their shift would be over.

What happened next occurred so quickly that Sophie didn't have time to register it or even scream. Suddenly she felt the sharp edge of something cold and metallic pressed to her throat. A filthy arm grabbed her around the chest and dragged her backwards. Her nostrils filled with the fetid stench of unwashed skin.

'Don't move!' A chilling snarl cut through the confusion in her mind. It had happened too swiftly to assimilate all the messages coming from her brain.

'Nobody move,' the man roared, swinging wildly from side to side, yanking Sophie with him. 'Everyone stay calm. I'll let her go as soon as I get morphine. But I swear I'll cut her up right here in front of you all if you screw with me. Morphine! Now!'

Sophie swallowed hard and tried not to panic. He was a junkie. She could feel his violent trembling and smell the cold sweat covering his bony body. He needed a fix.

Obviously badly to pull this stunt. Her heart rate soared and she felt the knife point press a little closer to her jugular vein.

'Listen, mate,' said Richard, standing slowly and putting his hands out. 'Don't do anything crazy.'

'That's right,' said Todd, clearing his throat. 'Just take it easy.'

'Morphine,' the man roared again.

'It's not as easy as all that. There are procedures for dangerous drugs. Counts,' Ross hedged.

Sophie couldn't believe what she was hearing. She and Ross had never seen eye to eye. He typified a management stereotype that she'd never had much time for, but even so she would have expected his support in this instance.

Surely he was joking! OK, it was Ross's job to manage and this incident would swamp him in paperwork, but surely he could see through the bureaucratic haze long enough to know that the man with the knife was serious.

'Just get the drugs, Ross,' she hissed.

'You'd better listen to her, mister,' the junkie advised. 'All of it, everything in the cupboard.'

Sophie watched as Richard handed the drug-cupboard keys to Ross. Richard's eyes communicated his worry to her. He looked down quickly and pointedly and then looked back at her.

Sophie was confused at first and then remembered the panic button that had been installed beneath the triage desk last year. She shook her head imperceptibly at Richard. She was fairly certain that the arrival of several security guards would only worsen the situation.

She shut her eyes and thought, Please, don't let me die tonight. Max needed her. She thought about never seeing him again and couldn't breathe. He'd be well looked after, she knew that, and she guessed that John would tell Daniel the truth and Max would finally be with his father. But it wouldn't be fair to deprive a little boy of his mother, too.

Her life flashed before her and she thought about all the other people she would miss. John and Michael's parents and Sally and Charlie. And Daniel. What if she never saw Daniel again? What if she never got the chance to tell him she loved him?

'Sophie!'

Daniel's voice. Had her fear and panic managed to conjure him up? Was he real? She opened her eyes and there he was.

'Stop right there, mate.' The guy sounded panicky at Daniel's arrival. 'I'll kill her. I swear it. Where's my drugs?' he roared in Sophie's ear, and she shut her eyes again.

Daniel stood beside the trolley he'd been bringing in, immobilised with fear. Sophie. His Sophie being pawed by a man with a dirty, rusty kitchen knife held to her throat. She looked frightened and pale and Daniel felt fear and then rage build inside him.

'What's taking him so long?' Sophie's attacker yelled.

Daniel spied an insipid-looking man standing at the end of the corridor, drugs in hand, talking to four security guards. For heaven's sake! Who had rung them?

Four years in New York had given Daniel lots of experience with drug addicts and how desperate they could be. Any signs of force could panic them and that made them unpredictable.

The man was obviously close to the edge. His eyes were darting around the room and there was sweat running down his pale, sickly face. Daniel felt ill. The fear on the beautiful face of the woman he loved twisted in his gut.

And there it was. A true light-bulb moment. The woman he loved. It was as if there had been an invisible curtain between them all this time and it had taken one drug-crazed lunatic to tear it down and reveal the truth. He loved her. It was so simple and so powerful all at the same time.

'Stay back,' Daniel commanded the security guards in a loud voice. 'He's got a knife and he'll use it.'

The junkie swung around nervously, sensing he was about to lose control of the situation. 'Listen to him,' he shouted. 'I'll cut her. I swear it!'

'You. Bring the drugs—now!' Daniel's demand brooked no argument.

Sophie held her breath and felt tears threaten. She would not cry. Tears weren't going to help now. She needed to think clearly. Thank God Daniel had arrived. He was taking charge of the situation and she began to feel like it might just turn out OK. If only Ross complied.

Daniel had had enough. If this guy walked any slower down the corridor he'd arrive some time tomorrow. He strode off and seized the drugs from him, shooting Ross a look of pure contempt. As far as human beings went, Daniel thought, he was a waste of good oxygen.

He turned around and in five large strides was back at the triage desk, holding the boxes of morphine out to Sophie's captor.

'Let her go,' he demanded, his heart banging loudly.

'Give me the drugs first. Put them in the bag,' he said, dropping a filthy backpack off his shoulder to the floor and kicking it towards Daniel.

Daniel stuffed the boxes inside.

'Kick it back.'

Daniel did as he was told and the junkie slowly reached down and gathered it up.

'Let her go,' Daniel demanded again.

The man smiled triumphantly and licked his lips, showing a bunch of yellowed rotting teeth. He pushed Sophie away with a force that belied his state of ill health and ran towards the door, but before he could even make good his escape the security guards had tackled him to the ground.

Sophie crashed into Daniel's body and he pulled her to him, crushing her against him as overwhelming relief swept through her body and she sobbed from the shock of her close brush with death.

'Are you OK?' he asked, pulling her head off his chest, his hands on either side of her face, his fingers buried in her hair.

'I thought I was never going to see Max again,' she cried, her face crumpling, and he pulled her head into his shoulder.

'I know,' he soothed, stroking her hair. 'I know.'

Sophie felt her fears recede as she wept and Daniel held her. Once again he had saved the day. Just as he had with Charlie and with Max. The horrifying events faded from her mind as she absorbed his calm strength and the sheer enormity of her love blossomed.

He held her while she cried and he kissed her hair, his own heart hammering. She was safe. She was safe. And he loved her. Not that it helped anything. In fact, it complicated everything, but it could not be ignored.

She moved in his arms and he felt her snuggle closer. How had he let this happen? And what was he going to do?

It was an impossible situation. As far as his head was concerned, she was still his brother's wife.

And, heaven help him, he loved her.

CHAPTER TEN

MAX launched himself at his mother's sleeping form. 'Mummy, Mummy, Mummy,' he said, bouncing up and down beside her. 'Wake up. It's my birthday.'

Sophie opened her eyes slowly, the bright sunlight causing her to squint. 'Morning, baby,' she said, and accepted his sloppy kiss that missed her cheek and landed on her eye.

'You should see all my presents. It's so exciting, Mummy, come and see,' he said, dragging her up by her hand.

'All right, all right.' She laughed. 'Let me put my gown on. Anyone else up yet?'

'No. Just us,' he said.

'Lucky us.' She smiled. Max's blue eyes twinkled his excitement and she could feel herself respond to his childish wonder.

She flung on the red gown and tied the belt at her waist. She almost hadn't brought it but had changed her mind at the last minute. If Daniel wanted to be stoic then so be it, but she was damned if she'd make it easy for him.

'Better go and wake everyone up, sweetie,' she said and laughed as Max charged out of the room, yelling for everyone to get up because he wanted to open his presents.

Sophie shook her head. It was hard to believe it had only been two days ago that a maniac had held a knife to her throat. Life had quickly gone on as if nothing had happened, and she'd actually recovered quite quickly.

On this special day Sophie spared a thought for the poor soul who had held her for ransom. She had seen enough drug addicts come through St Jude's doors to know they had an illness. Once the immediate danger to her life had dissipated she had been able to look at the incident quite objectively.

The man had been caught within a few minutes. He hadn't stood a chance with four burly, fit security guards chasing him. Sophie marvelled at how he'd ever imagined he was going to pull it off.

But, she supposed, that was the tragedy of drugs. People did things they would never have done before they had got hooked, and how they scored their next hit didn't matter. As long as they scored.

Sophie actually felt sorry for the man in a lot of ways. What had happened in his life that had pushed him to addiction? Had he been an intelligent kid with promise or had he not stood much of a chance in life to begin with? What catalyst had driven him to the state of desperation he'd been in that night?

She shook her head—she would never know. She needed to stick to problems she could solve. Which brought her to Daniel. He was a different kind of addict. Addicted to his sense of obligation towards his brother born from his overriding guilt. She didn't know what to do about it either.

Sophie wandered into the lounge room where everyone was gathering around the central coffee-table laden with multicoloured gifts. Max was bouncing up and down on his haunches, impatient for the adults to join him. Sophie sat cross-legged on the floor and Max quickly jumped into her lap.

She could feel his little body trembling in anticipation and felt a pang of jealousy. Oh, to be a child and not have the worries of the world on your shoulders. As her mind buzzed with all her adult problems Max's simple life seemed very appealing.

Daniel sat on the lounge chair behind her. She didn't have to turn to confirm it, she could sense it. She didn't have to look either to know he would be wearing his boxer shorts and black snug-fitting T-shirt. And she didn't need eyes in the back of her head to feel his gaze boring straight through her.

Edward dished out the presents one at a time, as he did every year. The family watched as Max ripped the paper off each one, tearing through the pile of presents like a mini-tornado. He was disgustingly spoilt, as he was every year, but Sophie had given up protesting. He was a much-loved only grandchild, the littlest Monday, and though the family was generous they also expected him to be well mannered, polite and good.

'Here you are, Maxy,' said Daniel from behind, plonking a small wicker basket with a lid in front of them. It had a huge red bow tied around it and Sophie knew instantly what it was.

'Oh, wow, Unca Dan,' said Max, lifting the lid. 'A kitten, a kitten. Mummy, Unca Dan got me a kitten.' He lifted the tiny sleeping ball of fur gently out of the basket and brought it to his face, rubbing his cheek against the soft fur. 'How did you know, Unca Dan? How did you know?'

Everyone laughed. Max had wanted a kitten all year and hadn't exactly been keeping it a secret!

'Daniel!' she exclaimed, turning to look at him.

'He wanted a kitten.' He shrugged and grinned at his Max's totally enchanted expression.

'He's too young,' she protested.

'He'll be fine, I'll teach him how to care for her.'

Sophie shot him a dubious look. 'I think Daniel needs a big kiss for that, don't you?' she said to her son, and Daniel grinned, knowing he had won.

Max rose from her lap, taking his precious bundle with him, crawling up onto Daniel's lap and pressing a kiss on Daniel's cheek.

'This is the best present ever, Unca Dan. I love you.' Max snuggled into Daniel's embrace a little further, the sleeping kitten cradled between Max's little chest and Daniel's flat stomach. Father and son stared at the tiny animal, totally engrossed.

'I love you too, Maxy.'

Sophie turned away, blinking hard. A lump rose in her throat. She caught John's eye and felt a surge of guilt. She knew she should tell Daniel about his son, and in a lot of ways it would probably get her what she wanted. But she didn't want Daniel out of obligation. He was very good at obligation and he would want to do the right thing by her, but she was only interested if he loved her, wanted her.

If they were to ever get past everything, it would need to be because he loved her, not because he wanted to be a father to Max. She'd waited too long to settle for less.

The more she thought about it, the more it crystallised in her mind. She needed to get away. She couldn't live with

Daniel and this thing between them and stay sane. Finding somewhere new to live would become a priority when they returned to Brisbane.

The morning idled by. Sophie and Max walked down to the beach for a swim around nine before the sun got too hot. When they came back Sophie joined everyone in the kitchen and helped prepare the birthday lunch.

Daniel took Max out onto the deck and they played with the now awake and playful kitten. He talked to his young charge about cats and Max listened with rapt attention. Daniel's deep rumbling voice would occasionally be heard, followed by Max's higher giggle.

Sophie tried not to watch them as she helped with the meal preparations, but the bank of windows running the full length of the massive deck gave them spectacular ocean views and so the two figures on the deck were a little hard to ignore.

Plus, every time she looked out through the windows she was reminded of exactly what she and Daniel had done against that glass, and she spent an inordinate amount of time blushing. Her body was swamped with images from that night and how she managed to not cut herself on the vegetable peeler was a miracle, given the trembling of her hands.

They ate at about one and Daniel brought Max in on his shoulders, the kitten held firmly in place on Daniel's head by a chubby little hand.

'Ah. Hands, both of you, and put the cat back in her basket, sweetie. No kittens at the table.'

'Come on, matey,' said Daniel, rolling his eyes at Max dramatically and being rewarded by a naughty giggle. 'Better do as Mummy says.'

They ate until they were all groaning, only just managing to fit in a slice of Max's birthday cake. Shortly after that Sophie put a sleepy Max to bed for his nap and sat and watched her blond-haired, blue-eyed boy for a while. The kitten, who had been named Clementine, lay curled up beside him and he looked so happy Sophie almost changed her mind about moving out.

Max would hate it. The family would hate it. She'd hate it. But it wasn't like she was going to drop out of the Mondays' lives altogether. She just needed a breather from the constant ache inside that seemed to magnify every time she ran into Daniel. It would still be there, she knew that, but hopefully it would plateau instead of constantly peaking to new highs.

Sophie heard the front doorbell chime as she shut Max's door, and heard Daniel answer it. Edward, Wendy, John, Sally and Charlie were out on the deck and Sophie thought about joining them, but the comfy double lounge beckoned and she lay on it, thinking that a small nap was in order.

'Anthony!' said Daniel, surprised to see the family lawyer standing on their doorstep. 'What brings you here? Come in.'

'Ah, no, thanks, Daniel. I'm on my way to my wife's family for dinner I just had to drop this in.'

The elderly lawyer, not that much younger than John, handed Daniel a yellow envelope with something that felt like a videotape inside. It was addressed to him and to Sophie—or rather Mrs Michael Monday.

Daniel ran his fingers over her name. It sure put things into perspective. She was Mrs Michael Monday and he would do well to keep reminding himself of that. 'What is it?' he asked.

'It's a videotape that Michael made for both of you just before he and Sophie got married. He asked me to keep it safe and in the event of his death deliver it to you on Max's birthday two years after the date of his demise.'

Daniel felt his heart start to thud a little harder in his chest. What was on the tape?

'OK? If that's it, I'll be going,' said Anthony, interrupting Daniel's swirling thoughts. He mopped the sweat off his brow, the hot sun beaming down on his bald head.

'Of course,' said Daniel. 'Thank you for coming all this way, Anthony.' He shook the lawyer's hand before closing the door.

Michael, what have you done? He was tempted to go and watch it himself first but as it was addressed to both of them he knew that wasn't his right. Still, his hand trembled in anticipation.

'Sophie.'

'Hmm?' She didn't open her eyes. She didn't need the sight of Daniel in his boardies unsettling her equilibrium.

'This just arrived for us.'

She sighed sleepily and opened her eyes. 'What is it?'

'A videotape that Michael made. For you. And me.'

Sophie sat up and looked at the yellow envelope. She looked at Daniel and he seemed to be just as puzzled.

'What do we do with it?' she asked, afraid and nervous and apprehensive.

'Watch it, I guess,' he said quietly.

They went into the den and shut the door. Sophie watched as Daniel loaded the tape into the machine and pressed the play button. Neither of them sat down, but stood and waited for the tape to begin.

There was a minute of 'snow' and then Michael appeared on the screen, looking fit and alive. Sophie could feel herself choking up. She sat down on the chair behind her. It was too cruel for life to have taken Michael from them.

'Well, I guess if you're watching this I'm dead and have been for a couple of years. Poor me.' Michael laughed but it didn't really reach his eyes and she could tell that this video hadn't been easy for him to make.

'I guess you're wondering why I'm making this video. Well, tomorrow I'm marrying the girl I love. The girl I've loved since we were five and we played catch and kiss in the backyard.'

Sophie felt a tear spill down her cheek and she pulled a tissue out of the box that sat on the coffee-table in front of her.

'Sophie, I know you're going to make me the happiest man in the world. I'd like to thank you now for the time you gave me and for the son you bore me. He's not here yet but I want you to know that you've given me the greatest gift. One that, thanks to this wheelchair, I won't ever get a chance at again.'

Daniel could hear Sophie sniffling behind him and couldn't bear to look.

'But I'm doing this because I owe you an apology—owe you both an apology, actually. I know that you love me, Soph, as a best friend, a brother even, but not as a lover or a husband…and that's fine. I know you're in love with Daniel, have always been in love with Daniel, and I'm sorry that I've used our friendship and my…condition to get you to marry me. I should have encouraged you to patch things up with Daniel instead of seeing it as a way of having you for myself. I can only hope and pray that our marriage will be as happy for you as I know it's going to be for me. I'm going to make it my mission, Soph, to make you the happiest woman on earth.'

The tears were flowing freely down her face now. It had been. No, it hadn't been a marriage in the truest sense of the word, but she'd been very happy married to Michael.

'I guess I owe the biggest apology to you, Daniel. It doesn't matter how many times I tell you that it wasn't your fault and I don't blame you, I can still feel your guilt. You said to me not long ago that there must be some part of me that blames you, and you know what? I think you're right. I think there is a small part of me that's pissed at you about the accident. Not because I think it was your fault but because you walked away without a scratch and I'm crippled.'

Daniel felt his breath being torn out of his lungs and he reached back and sat in the chair next to Sophie. To hear Michael talk about this was cathartic. He'd always known that his brother had to have held some grudge, and to hear it finally was a relief.

'And I think it's that part that's been able to rationalise the terrible thing I've done to both of you. You see, Daniel, I knew Sophie was pregnant that day I intimated to you that she and I had also been fooling around.'

Sophie gasped at Michael's admission. He had told Daniel that he and her…that they'd… What on earth for? Why would he do such a thing?

'She visited me that morning and broke down about being pregnant and how worried she was about what you would say because you'd hardly been speaking since the accident and what bad timing it was. And I told her that you'd be a fool not to sweep her up in your arms and that if you didn't, I'd marry her. And that got me thinking that day about the possibility, and how marrying Sophie would make life in a wheelchair bearable. Because I loved her and always had, but I knew that, while she loved me, she was *in* love with you and I would never stand a chance. So that's when I decided to meddle.'

Daniel couldn't believe what he was hearing. All the things he had believed over the last couple of years were being shattered. He looked at Sophie and she looked back at him equally bewildered.

'That part of me that was pissed at you decided that you owed me. Now, that's not rational or fair, I know that, but I was a little desperate a couple of months ago. I knew that day that I'd be seeing you before she would and so I told you that the only thing that would make me want to go on with my life would be to marry Sophie. I led you to believe we were having a sexual relationship when we weren't, and I told you that if you really wanted me to be happy you'd let Sophie go and suggest she marry me instead. I knew your guilt ran deep and I played on it. And you did the rest. Much better than I could have planned. You dumped her that night before she had a chance to tell you about the baby, and she came straight to me.'

Sophie sat shell-shocked, listening to Michael's admissions. Daniel had given her to Michael because his brother had emotionally blackmailed him into it. Not because he hadn't loved her but because his brother had orchestrated it. Michael had played with their lives. Sophie felt anger mix with her disbelief.

'Am I proud of what I've done? No. I can only say in

my defence that two months ago I wasn't sure if I even wanted to live, and the only thing that dragged me out of the terrible, terrible darkness was the thought of forming a family with you and the baby, Sophie.'

She felt her anger soften. He was right. What a totally screwed-up time it had been for all of them emotionally. There had been anger and sadness, blame, guilt and desperation. Michael's depression had worried the entire family and they had all been grateful, not least her, when their engagement had given him a new lease of life.

It would be easy to judge Michael harshly now, his four-year-old actions removed from the dreadful roller-coaster of feelings they had all suffered. What a terrible time it had been. None of them had been thinking very rationally.

'So, I guess you're wondering why I've decided to make this tape? Easy. Guilt. I guess that's something we all know a lot about. I'd like to think that, as I'm obviously not around any more, you two will have found a way to come together. But if I know Daniel as well as I think I do then he's probably still in New York, nursing his guilt, trying to keep away from you, Sophie. I figured you two might need a little nudge.

'So why now? Why did I instruct Anthony to deliver it to you now? I thought two years seemed like a reasonable amount of time to have elapsed. I figured any sooner and society might not have thought it proper for you two to get together. I just hope I'm not too late. If you're both sitting here, watching this, and have already worked it out or are married to different people then I guess I'm going to look like a right idiot.

'I'm just really sorry to have meddled in your lives and

interrupted a great love match. I expect you'll both be pretty mad at me by now. I only hope you can forgive me in time and realise that we were all victims of circumstance to a degree.

'Daniel, let it go, man. This isn't your fault and you've paid the price too long. If you really feel like you need to make atonement, I think you have more than done that, don't you? Love her, man. Love her like she deserves to be loved.

'Sophie, remember me to our son. I love you and I'm sorry. I love you both and I hope you both live happily ever after.'

The screen went blank and they both sat staring at it. Neither of them moved for a while and then Daniel got up and walked over to the window, watching the gulls ride the air currents.

'So…I'm Max's father.'

'Yes,' said Sophie quietly.

There was silence again. Where did they even begin? There was so much to say, to talk about.

'Did you really believe that I was having sex with Michael at the same time we were lovers? How could you have thought that of me?'

'Honestly? Deep down I didn't. It seems like this is the day for honesty so I think I can finally admit it to myself. I think a part of me knew that Michael was lying and I just suppressed it, ignored it. He was asking me for you and it was easier to do it when I could pretend that you were unfaithful.'

'Your guilt really ran that deep? That you would give me up like I was some kind of prize?' Outrage at the disregard of both Michael and Daniel for her as a person, a human being, took over. They had traded her like some bartering chip. Your lover for your guilt!

'My brother couldn't walk because of me, Soph. That was a terrible burden. I know I had no right to use you to assuage my guilt but I just wanted to make it right for him.'

'Damn right. You had no right.'

'Hey, it wasn't my idea and anyway…it didn't help.'

Sophie sighed and walked over to where he stood. He was right. Michael had definitely been pulling their strings. 'And what about now? Does the tape help?'

'Yes, it does, actually. It was freaky to see him again, so alive. A bit like a ghost. But I do feel absolved. Michael being pissed at me I can handle. We were brothers. But I took that as blame and I didn't need his when I had so much of my own.'

'So if part of you knew I hadn't been unfaithful then you must have known Max was yours.'

'I guess…yes,' he said. 'But I didn't know you were pregnant until I was in New York and I knew what being a father meant to Michael. He'd told me the accident had left him impotent, and it was just another thing to feel guilty about, so when he had this chance I couldn't deny it. I blocked out the little voice that kept whispering the truth. Again, it was easier to ignore the truth and believe what he wanted me to believe.'

Sophie nodded again. Michael had sure done a number on their heads. 'So when you told me that you didn't love me, that you had lied to get me into bed…that was a lie?'

'Of course it was,' he sighed. 'I would never have told you I loved you if I hadn't. But I needed to make sure that you sought solace in Michael's arms. I'm so sorry, it was harsh, but I needed to destroy the love you had for me to push you to Michael. I needed there to be no doubt whatsoever in your mind that you and I were over.'

'Well, it worked.'

'I'm so sorry,' he said, stroking his hand down her cheek. 'I've never stopped loving you. I fooled myself for a while. Moving away helped, but the other night, when that guy held a knife to your throat, it hit me. I still loved you.'

She nodded. His admission started her heart beating erratically. Still, caution was required. 'Seems like there's a *but* there.'

'No buts, Sophie. For the first time in four years I feel free. I feel free to tell you how I feel and to think we could have a life together. But I've behaved so badly since I've been back that I can't possibly expect you to feel the same way. I know I've hurt you a lot over the years. I can't blame you if you hate me and want nothing to do with me. I do want to be involved with Max but I'll be guided by you. I won't push.'

'Daniel, you idiot.' She laughed, hardly believing what she was hearing. 'I love you. Yes, between you and your brother I've been hurt and I thought, like you, that I was over this, but when we made love the other night I knew I'd never stopped loving you. I want us to be together and for Max to know you as his father. We've spent too many years apart, lets not waste any more time.'

Daniel stood still. There was only a small gap separating them but he was too stunned to close it. He blinked hard and opened his eyes again and she was still there with that silly grin on her face and that look of expectancy. Had she really said those words? Did she really mean them? Surely this was too good to be true.

'Really? You want us to be a family?'

'Really, you silly man. I love you, Danny. I've always loved you. From the moment you called me brat when I was five and you were eleven, I was a goner.'

Sophie couldn't believe that he still hadn't moved to close the gap between them. She wanted to feel his lips against hers so badly she could practically taste him.

'Danny! If you don't kiss me in the next second I'm going to think this is all a cruel joke.'

Sophie wasn't sure if he kissed her or she kissed him in the end. All she knew was that she was in the arms of the man she loved and that finally everything was right with the world.

'How are we going to tell the family?' she asked some time later as she sat cuddled in his arms in the lounge chair.

'I guess we'll just show them the tape,' Daniel said.

Max chose that moment to barge into the room and spied his mother and uncle curled up together on the couch.

'There you are, Mummy,' he said, and plonked himself and Clementine between them. He squirmed a bit, making himself a nice comfy spot, and relaxed against Daniel's chest.

'Why are you hugging my mummy, Unca Dan?' asked Max.

'Um…ah..' Daniel shrugged at Sophie, lost for words.

'Do you love Mummy?'

'Ah…yes, I do, actually, Max. Is that OK?'

'Sure. Are you gonna marry her?'

'As long as it's OK by you,' said Daniel, shooting a withering look at Sophie who was trying hard not to laugh.

'Does that mean you'll be my daddy?'

'I guess it does.'

'Will I have to call you Daddy or can I keep calling you Unca Dan?'

'Whatever you want, Maxy,' said Daniel, holding his breath for his son's next decree.

'I think I'll call you Daddy.'

'Okey-dokey,' said Daniel, wanting to shout his joy from the rooftops. He ruffled Max's hair instead, not wanting to frighten his son with the strength of his feelings.

'That OK, Mummy?' asked Max.

'Sure,' said Sophie, all choked up. She was thankful that Max was too engrossed in Clementine to pay any heed to the tears that were falling down her face.

Daniel kissed her forehead and she was surprised to see moisture shimmering in his blue eyes.

'I love you,' she mouthed over the top of Max's head, and he mouthed it back.

The trio sat cuddling contentedly on the lounge, being the family they should have been before life had got in the way. Sophie stroked Max's hair and reflected on the irony of the situation. The person who had kept them apart was the same person who had brought them back together. And now, thanks to Michael, they were finally free to love each other for ever.

THE SURGEON'S ENGAGEMENT WISH

BY
ALISON ROBERTS

For Sandra, my friend
in the NZ Department of Conservation
who helped me find out how to save whales. With love.

CHAPTER ONE

THE car should *not* have been there.

In the small car park adjacent to the emergency department of Ocean View hospital, yes. In the space reserved for the ambulance, even, if the emergency was dire enough.

But three quarters of the way through the wide electronic doors that led into the reception and triage area?

No *way*!

Nurse Elizabeth Dawson's astonishment rapidly gave way to alarm. The car would have been suspicious enough tucked neatly into an acceptable car-parking slot. An ancient, rusting hulk of a V8. A status symbol amongst the elements of society who preferred to simply ignore any restrictions the law might impose on their lifestyle.

The man climbing out of the driver's seat was even more intimidating. Clad in battered leathers with the 'patch' of his gang emblazoned on the back of the jacket, the heavily tattooed and menacing figure would have alarmed even the most confident of any emergency department staff.

And Beth Dawson was far from the most confident

right now. She had started a new job in a new town only a couple of hours ago, for heaven's sake, and everything was still completely unfamiliar.

No. Not quite everything. The aggression emanating from the gang member she was watching was all *too* familiar.

An unexpected flash of anger cut through her fear. This type of scenario was precisely why she'd left her job in a huge south Auckland hospital so recently. She'd had a gutsful of dealing with violent and uncooperative patients who took any pleasure or even satisfaction out of demonstrating the level of skill she had attained in her chosen profession.

The anger couldn't last long enough to fuel courage, however, given the fact that she was alone in this part of the department. At 1 a.m. in a semi-rural area you wouldn't expect a full waiting room, and the only patient who had come in since midnight was now having his chest pain investigated in one of the two resuscitation rooms.

Beth's finger was pressed firmly against the button summoning assistance and any trace of saliva vanished from her mouth as she watched another two figures emerge from the vehicle. The bizarre sight of the car under the bright lights and filthy tyres on the spotless linoleum had already become just a background to an unpleasant drama unfolding. So had the rhythmic and futile attempts the electronic doors were making to close the small gap left around the obstacle. They touched the rear of the car and then bounced open again. And again.

The movement of the doors did not impede two of the men dragging the final occupant from the rear seat of the car. Little care was afforded the potential injuries of an apparently unconscious victim and a large smear of blood appeared on the pale floor as his feet dragged.

Two more nurses rushed into the space behind Beth, closely followed by the only doctor on duty, Mike Harris. Beth could feel all three of them virtually skidding to a halt as they caught sight of the car inside the building, but she didn't turn her head. Her gaze was fixed on the slumped figure being held up by the armpits. She drew back instinctively as the gang member who had been driving the car started walking towards them.

'Jackal's been shot.'

Beth was aware of broken teeth and the smell of alcohol as the man spoke. She was also quite well aware that the incongruously casual tone of voice was no insurance against the level of implied threat in his next succinct words.

'You'd better *do* something.'

They would be armed, Beth had no doubts about that. There would be knives tucked inside those commando-style boots. At least one of the men was wearing knuckle-dusters and she was quite certain there would be more than one sawn-off shotgun easily accessible in that vehicle.

Her breath escaped in something like a strangled laugh. She had left a big city hospital that had proto-cols for dealing with precisely this type of incident. Any number of security personnel would be available within seconds and a well-rehearsed police squad only minutes away. And even that kind of back-up hadn't been enough to prevent her best friend, Neroli, giving up her nursing career, having been held at knife point in Beth's old emergency department.

Beth had come to a small-town hospital near the tip of the south island of New Zealand to find a peaceful place to settle and refocus her life. She had barely begun her first night duty in this tiny emergency department and here she was, facing one of her worst nightmares. A recurrent one, thanks to the trauma she had unsuccessfully tried to help Neroli overcome.

Did Ocean View hospital even have security?

How far away were any police? The closest large town was Nelson and that would be at least ninety minutes away by road.

The tension escalated several more notches as the spokesmen for the gang members moved. His shoulders hunched and the fingers of one hand flexed and then clenched. The fist was thrust towards the only male member staff member present.

'*Now!*'

Just do what he says, Mike, Beth urged silently. *Please!* But Dr Harris hadn't even flinched.

'Sure.' Mike's face was impassive and Beth found herself suddenly feeling slightly more confident. Well into his fifties now, Ocean View hospital's emergency department consultant probably had more than enough experience to cope with situations such as this. 'But I'm not going to tolerate my staff—or anyone else—being intimidated.'

There was a tiny silence as each side weighed up the implications of non-cooperation. It was broken by a groan from the injured gang member and the attention of everybody present was instantly diverted.

'What's happened exactly?'

'He's been shot, man. I told you.'

'Yes, but where? And how long ago? How much

blood has he lost?' Mike was moving calmly towards the victim. Beth looked at her nursing colleagues. Should they all follow him? Chelsea was looking as nervous as she felt herself, and Maureen looked grim. The older nurse tilted her head.

'Chelsea, why don't you and Beth go and get a stretcher? I'll stay and help Mike.' She turned as she spoke so that her back was towards the gang members. 'Call the police,' she whispered faintly, her lips barely moving. 'Fast.'

Chelsea's nervousness seemed to wear off the moment she was assigned a task. She even grinned at Beth as they hurried from the triage area.

'Here we go,' she said almost cheerfully. 'Again!'

Beth's heart sank to a new low. 'You mean you get this type of incident on a regular basis?'

'We do get bit of trouble from gangs now and then.' Chelsea paused as they entered the main section of the emergency department and she reached for the wall phone. 'You'd be used to it, though, wouldn't you? Didn't you say you've been working in south Auckland?'

'Yes, but I didn't expect…' Beth's words trailed off as Chelsea started speaking to whoever was on the other end of the phone.

'We seem to have a code yellow in ED,' she said briskly. She listened for only a few seconds. 'Cool… thanks.'

Beth grabbed the tail end of the stretcher and she and Chelsea headed back the moment the phone was replaced.

'What's a code yellow?'

'Trouble with gangs.'

Good grief! So it happened often enough to have its own code?

'What happens on a code yellow?'

'Sid will get here first. He's our night orderly cum security guard. Then one of the local cops who lives just down the road will come in.' Chelsea was looking almost excited now as she glanced back at Beth. 'If he thinks it's necessary, he'll call Nelson and they'll chopper in the armed offender squad to help out.'

'But there's only one patient!'

'So far.' Chelsea gave Beth a questioning glance now. 'This really bothers you, doesn't it?'

'I'm OK.' Beth wasn't about to demonstrate any inadequacy on her first shift. 'Like you said, I'm used to it. A bit too used to it, maybe. A friend of mine had a knife held to her throat by a gang member not so long ago.'

Chelsea looked horrified. 'Was she hurt?'

'Not physically. She's given up nursing, though, and gone to work in her sister's coffee-shop in Melbourne.'

'Was that why you decided to move as well?'

'Partly.' Beth smiled wryly as they turned the corner. 'I *was* rather hoping I'd be getting away from this kind of thing by moving down here.'

Chelsea's quick smile was sympathetic. 'I hope it wasn't the main incentive for the shift, then.'

'It wasn't.'

Beth's words were lost as they entered the front of the department to find the stretcher was now superfluous. The injured man's colleagues had dragged or lifted him as far as the bed in the empty resuscitation area.

'I said *don't* cut his leathers, man!'

'We've got to get his jacket off so I can assess his

breathing.' Mike was still managing to sound calm but Beth could see that his frown lines had deepened perceptibly.

Maureen was plugging the tubing attached to an oxygen mask onto the overhead outlet. 'I'm just going to put this on your face,' she warned their patient.

The stream of obscene language made Maureen look even grimmer than she had on first spotting this patient.

'Airway appears clear,' she told Mike dryly. Stepping back as two silent gang members unceremoniously stripped the leather jacket off the now groaning man, she noticed the return of the younger nurses.

'Perhaps you two could clear Resus 2.' She and Mike seemed practised in trying to keep the atmosphere as casual as possible, but the undercurrent of urgency was easy enough for Beth to detect.

And no wonder. The man in the adjacent resuscitation area was looking alarmed and his wife was terrified. It was just as well that the chest pain he was having investigated had been deemed to be angina rather than a heart attack because otherwise the anxiety caused by the arrival of the new patient might have made his condition a lot worse. He probably didn't need admission but he certainly needed to be moved.

It took a minute or two to disentangle the patient from the ECG electrodes and other monitoring equipment anchoring him to the area. Beth looked over her shoulder as she pushed the foot end of the bed clear of Resus 2. The injured man in Resus 1 was alone with his medical attendants now. The other gang members had vanished. A second later they all heard the roar of an unmuffled engine as the car blocking the doors was restarted.

'Our first job is to clear the department of any other

patients if it's possible,' Chelsea told Beth as they manoeuvred the bed along the corridor separating the emergency department from the rest of the hospital. 'We close the department to any arrivals that could be seen by a GP as well.' She shook her head. 'There was a major riot in the department a few years back apparently, and a bystander in the waiting room got stabbed. That was when code yellow came into force.'

Their patient's wife was clutching her handbag in both hands as she trotted beside the swiftly moving bed. 'Did you hear them say they were going to deal with whoever did the shooting? Where's it going to end?'

'At least most of them are out of the department for a while,' Chelsea responded. 'It'll give the police time to deal with them before there's any *real* trouble here.'

There was a curious calm in the emergency department when Beth and Chelsea returned. Mike was doing an ultrasound on the exposed, tattooed belly of their patient. Maureen was setting up a new bag of IV fluids.

A burly man wearing an orderly's uniform was standing with his arms folded by the head of the bed, and an equally solid man in police uniform stood in an identical pose at the foot. They both gave Beth a curious stare.

'Gidday,' the orderly said. 'You're new here, aren't you?'

'This is Beth,' Chelsea told them. 'It's her first shift tonight. Beth, this is Sid and that's Dennis.'

The nods and smiles from the two men were both welcoming and sympathetic. Not a great way to start a new job, they conveyed, but they were pleased to meet her and would make sure she was safe. And Beth smiled back. Suddenly things didn't seem nearly so disheartening.

She would never have been introduced to members of security back-up in her old department and they certainly wouldn't have made any non-verbal promises about making sure she was looked after. Working in a small community *was* going to be different.

Better.

'Who's on call for surgery tonight?' Mike's query broke an almost companionable silence.

'Luke,' Maureen told him.

'Good. He won't mind being woken up.'

'Can you call him in, please, Chelsea?'

'Sure.'

Beth watched as Chelsea headed for the wall phone. She knew there were five surgeons associated with Ocean View hospital. Three general and two orthopaedic. What were the odds that one of them would end up being called Luke?

And how many other reminders would there be for her tonight to let her know that you could never really escape the past and make a brand-new start? Beth shook herself mentally, bending over to pick up packaging from dressings and IV gear that littered the floor.

For heaven's sake. It had been six years ago. It was pathetic that hearing that particular name could still have any effect on her. And it was weird that it was so much stronger tonight than it had been for a very long time. Maybe that was just because she was displaced. Feeling a little lost in a new environment and seeking links with her past to anchor herself.

'He's on his way,' Chelsea reported. 'Do you need theatre staff called in?'

Mike angled the ultrasound probe in a new direction, still peering at the screen. Then he nodded. 'Yes, thanks,

Chels. I reckon Jackal here is going to need more of an inside look than I'm getting.'

The gang member's nickname suddenly seemed quite appropriate. The flash of fear as the comprehension of what was being organised on his behalf filtered through was swiftly followed by an aggressive snarl.

'No way! You're not cutting me, man! I'm outta here.'

'*Oi!*' The barked response from both Sid and Dennis was not enough to stop Jackal making an unexpectedly vigorous move to sit up, ripping the IV line from his arm in the process and actually managing to swing both legs over the side of the bed.

Restrained by the larger men, who latched onto both arms, he subsided instantly. In fact, he looked decidedly green within seconds and then, much to Sid's obvious disgust, he vomited. Sid gamely kept hold of the arm but the restraint was no longer needed. Sitting up had been enough to cut an already diminished blood supply to Jackal's brain and his level of consciousness was dropping fast.

'Lay him down.' Mike sounded almost weary. 'And watch out for that blood, Sid.' The orderly was wearing gloves but Jackal's IV site was bleeding quite heavily. He leaned closer to their patient. 'Listen, mate. You're sick. You've had a bullet go through your belly. You're lucky it hasn't killed you but it's still done a lot of damage to Jackal's spleen. You're losing blood. Jump up now and you might make things a whole lot worse in a hurry.'

The response was not incoherent enough to disguise the obscenities but Mike simply straightened and reached for a fresh pair of gloves.

'I'll get that IV line back in. I don't think he's going to put up much of a fight with his blood pressure in his boots.'

Beth looked at the monitor. The pressure reading was 85 over 40. Jackal had to be losing a significant amount of blood. The glance that passed between Sid and Dennis was significant. If this became a homicide, they could all be in for a lot more drama.

Maybe they would be anyway.

Beth handed Mike a new wide-bore cannula and was ready with the luer plug and flush moments later.

'Any word from Sally?'

'Sorry.' Beth shook her head. This was the kind of thing she hated about starting a new job. 'I don't know who Sally is.'

'She's one of our paramedics,' Maureen supplied. 'The ambulance got called not long after Jackal's mates took off from here.' Her brief smile was intended to be reassuring for Beth. 'Police back-up got activated at the same time.'

Beth nodded, pleased to find her hands steady as she completed the fiddly task of screwing the luer plug into place on the cannula hub. She was injecting a bolus of saline to check that the IV line was patent when the radio on the main desk crackled.

'Ambulance to ED. Do you copy?'

'Shall I get that?' Chelsea queried.

'I'll do it.' Mike stripped off his gloves and then glanced at Beth. 'Can you get some more fluids up?'

'Sure.'

Beth taped the cannula securely in place, having flushed the line. Then she reached for a giving set and a new bag of saline. The task was automatic enough not to distract her from listening to Mike as he reached for the microphone next to the radio set.

'Mike here, Sally. Receiving you loud and clear. What have you got?'

'Status one patient. Car vs pedestrian.'

'Roger.' Mike shook his head slowly as he pulled a pen from his shirt pocket. They all knew how unlikely this was to have been any accident. 'Vital signs?'

'Heart rate of 130. Respiration rate 36. Oxygen saturation down and blood pressure unrecordable at present. GCS of 8. Head and chest injuries. Multiple fractures.'

Sid and Dennis looked at each other again. They didn't need medical training to know that this patient was seriously unwell. Neither did they need the ambulance officer's confirmation that this was another code yellow patient.

The ETA of the ambulance was ten to fifteen minutes and any calm in the small emergency department vanished.

Extra staff began arriving as Beth and Chelsea were assigned the task of setting up Resus 2 in preparation for the new arrival.

'Have an intubation trolley ready,' Mike instructed. 'And a chest decompression kit.'

'What happens with serious chest injuries here?' Beth queried, pulling the crumpled sheet from the bed. 'We don't have a cardiothoracic surgeon, do we?'

Chelsea shook her head. 'We stabilise them and then chopper them to Wellington.' She flapped the clean sheet to spread it over the mattress. 'Same with head injuries. We don't run to a neurosurgeon either.'

Chelsea told Beth who the staff members were as the level of activity in the department steadily increased.

'That's Kelly—she's a radiographer. Seth is the house surgeon on call. Looks like Rowena's coming in to help as well. She's a midwife.'

The names flowed right over Beth's head. These people were all still strangers and this was no time to start even trying to remember names.

'And there's Luke.'

Beth flicked the laryngoscope she was checking shut to turn off its light. Despite herself, her head turned sharply at that familiar name but any view of the latest newcomer was blocked by the large figure of Dennis, the police officer.

'The ambulance is here,' he told them. 'I'm going to see if they need any help.'

Two other members of the local police force had accompanied the ambulance but the paramedics had been in no danger from the hit-and-run victim they were transporting.

'Breath sounds absent on the left side now.' A blonde woman had her stethoscope on the exposed chest, between ECG electrodes. 'GCS has been dropping steadily. I've already done a decompression on the right side.'

'Bring him straight in here.' Mike pointed to the available resuscitation area and Beth stepped back as the stretcher moved swiftly towards her. Then she reached to help transfer the patient to the bed.

'On the count of three,' Mike directed, holding the patient's head and neck still by supporting the cervical collar. 'One…two…three!'

'We think he was hit at a speed of at least sixty kilometres an hour,' the paramedic informed Mike. 'Apparently he was airborne for twenty to thirty metres.'

Maureen handed Beth a pair of shears. 'See what you can do to get rid of the clothing.'

Beth was aware of more people pressing into the resus area to assist.

'Tension pneumothorax on the left,' Mike confirmed tersely. 'Someone get me a decompression kit, please?'

'I can do that.'

The calm voice should have eased some of the tension but the shears in Beth's hands closed with an uncontrolled snap. Her gaze shifted just as emphatically to the speaker and for a split second she actually forgot what she was supposed to be doing.

Luke.

It couldn't be.

But it was.

Luke Savage.

At Ocean View hospital?

If Beth had tried to think of the last possible place on earth she would expect to see this man again, a small-town hospital would have been way up on the list. A prison cell might have beaten it to top spot, of course, but not by much.

He hadn't noticed her. The surgeon was completely focussed on the task of inserting a needle between the victim's ribs to release air trapped in his chest, which was preventing his lungs from functioning.

'Pelvis is unstable.' Mike was doing a survey for other major injuries while Luke was attempting to establish adequate breathing.

The consultant's statement was enough to start Beth's hands moving again, her momentary lapse unnoticed. She peeled leather trousers clear of the deformity on the right thigh.

'Open fracture of the femur,' she advised.

'Cover it,' Mike responded. 'We can't deal with that just yet.'

Beth reached for a large gauze dressing and tried to concentrate on squeezing a sachet of saline onto the pad to dampen it, but she simply couldn't help glancing back towards Luke.

Had Luke recognised her voice as easily as she had recognised his?

Apparently not.

'Oxygen sats aren't climbing.' Luke was staring at the monitor above the bed. 'We'll have to intubate.'

'I'll get another IV line going,' Mike said. 'We need to speed up this fluid resus.'

A new face peered in through the curtain. 'Luke? They just called to say they're ready for you in Theatre.'

His glance seemed to bypass Beth effortlessly as she used the damp dressing to cover the gaping wound on their patient's leg. 'Thanks. I'll be up as soon as I can.'

Mike took the cannula Beth was holding out for him. 'Could you help Sid take Jackal upstairs, please?'

'Sure.' The prospect of making an exit was appealing.

Was Luke simply being professional, ignoring her—quite properly—due to the emergency treatment of a patient? It was possible that he had not yet recognised or even noticed her.

It was also quite possible that he just didn't give a damn.

And why, in God's name, should that bother her so much anyway?

Beth turned her back on Luke but she wasn't going to escape quite so easily. The sound of breaking glass made everybody pause.

'What the hell was that?'

'We locked the doors when we came in.' The male ambulance officer had abandoned his paperwork to step closer. 'Sounds like someone really wants to get in.'

A police officer appeared behind him. 'ETA for the chopper is only two minutes. We've got a bit of a skirmish going on in the car park right now, though.'

The sound of a shotgun being fired was unmistakable.

So was the alarm that sounded on the new patient's monitor in the tiny silence that followed.

'He's in VF,' Luke warned.

Mike was already reaching for the defibrillator paddles. 'Everyone stand clear.'

'I don't want anyone moving from here until we get some back-up,' the police officer ordered.

'Stand clear,' Mike ordered.

Beth stood clear. In fact, she was quickly penned into the corner of the area, along with the paramedic and Chelsea, and couldn't escape the awareness of how appalling the situation was.

They watched as Maureen squeezed air into the patient's lungs and Luke readied himself to do compressions when the initial series of shocks was completed. Mike pressed the paddles into position and pressed the buttons to deliver the second shock and then the third.

Beth closed her eyes for a moment. This was all so bizarre it was almost a joke. Some huge, cosmic joke. And whoever decided which way the winds of fate were going to blow was laughing at her right now.

She had come here to get away from the stress of dealing with violence and was now up to her neck in the most major incident she had ever encountered.

And she had also come to get away from the lingering effect Luke Savage had branded on her life. She had just ended her extremely brief engagement to Brent, for heaven's sake, because she had recognised that the only qualities he had that were attractive had been the ones that reminded her of Luke.

The prospect of actually crossing paths with Luke Savage had haunted Beth for far longer than the fear of finding herself living Neroli's nightmare, and coming to a small town like Hereford had seemed like the perfect way to escape that particular ghost.

And here she was, only a few feet away from the man. And it felt like the first time she had seen him all over again. He was just as physically attractive, but it hadn't been simply his looks that had drawn her so convincingly at that first meeting. It had been his presence. The feeling she'd got that this man would be able to handle any situation he found himself in, no matter what it was. And she could feel that again right now. Luke was just…exactly the same.

It was so bizarre. It went way beyond being a disappointing start to a new beginning. This was gutting. Maybe she *should* have taken up Neroli's invitation to go to Australia with her. Melbourne would be a nice place to live and Neroli's sister was always short of waitresses in that coffee-shop.

The static cleared from the monitor screen after the third shock to show a pattern that settled over several seconds into normal sinus rhythm. The quiet was broken by the steadying beeps of the monitor, loud but muffled shouting from somewhere outside and then the crescendo of an approaching helicopter's rotors.

Relieved glances were exchanged between staff

members and it was only then that Beth's gaze met that of Luke. The, oh, so familiar dark grey eyes beneath that shaggy mop of black hair widened and Beth realised that he hadn't been ignoring her.

He couldn't look this shocked if he had known she was so close.

Her presence was a surprise. And it wasn't a pleasant one.

It shouldn't have hurt but it did. Any fantasies she'd ever had of looking into those eyes again and seeing the love that had once been there were crushed in an instant, and Beth could hear echoes of that cosmic laughter.

She wanted nothing more than to get away, and Mike's repeated instruction to help shift Jackal up to Theatre seemed timely.

It wasn't until Beth pulled the curtain back and stepped outside the resuscitation area that they realised the move had been premature.

Black-clad, helmeted and armed offender squad members were filing rapidly into the emergency department of Ocean View hospital, but the skirmish that had been taking place outside had also moved in. Somehow one of Jackal's mates had gained access and was now standing outside Resus 1 with a knife in his hand as a member of an obviously rival gang advanced rapidly towards him.

And Beth had inadvertently stepped right between them.

Was this the punchline of the joke?

There was nobody close enough to help but the fear that should have swamped and immobilised Beth simply wasn't there.

'Don't even *think* about it!' she snapped.

Beth drew herself up to her full height of a not very impressive five feet four inches. Her lack of height was irrelevant because the misery over the personal disaster she had engineered for herself in coming here had just morphed into pure fury.

'You!' She jabbed her finger at the leather-clad chest of the man whose progress towards Resus 1 she had just blocked. He was at least six feet tall and his bearded, tattooed face was bleeding heavily from a jagged laceration. 'Go and *sit* down and behave yourself.'

Whirling to confront Jackal's mate, Beth was dimly aware that the police officers rushing to her assistance had slowed involuntarily, their jaws drooping.

'Drop the knife,' she commanded.

'*No!*' she yelled as both men made a move to close her further into the middle of the potentially very dangerous human sandwich. Her voice remained at a furious shout. 'Do as you're bloody well *told*! I am just *so* not in the mood for this.'

Amazingly, the gang members froze. The hand holding the lethal-looking knife began to drop and suddenly the police were right there. As fast as the incident had occurred, it was defused and the space cleared.

Beth was aware of a curious shaking sensation in her knees. She turned her head slowly to see the occupants of Resus 2 staring at her.

'Woo-hoo!' Chelsea called softly. 'You go, girl!'

Mike had an astonished grin on his face but it was Luke who drew Beth's gaze. He was staring at her as well, of course. Who wouldn't be? He wasn't looking shocked any more. He was looking as though Beth were a complete stranger.

A rather impressive stranger, in fact.

Straightening her back made that weak-kneed sensation subside almost completely. The calm, confident smile Beth was aiming for probably came out more like an embarrassed grin, but it didn't seem to dull the respect she could detect from her small audience.

An audience that included Luke Savage.

How cool was that?

CHAPTER TWO

GOOD grief!

Luke was still shaking his head in disbelief as he scrubbed up for Jackal's emergency laparotomy ten minutes later.

Seeing Beth again after all these years was unbelievable enough. Seeing her doing that warrior princess act with the gang members had been…

The sexiest damn thing Luke had ever seen in his life.

He scrubbed beneath his nails hard enough to cause real pain.

Beth was the only woman who had ever made him seriously consider marriage.

And she was the only woman who had ever dumped him.

The hurt and the ensuing anger that had caused should have been rendered inconsequential by the blows life had meted out since then, so it was incredibly disturbing to find how easily the years could be peeled back.

One good look into those bright blue eyes and there he was again. Not measuring up. Just not being good enough, no matter how much love he had to offer.

What the hell was Beth doing in Hereford of all places?

Luke took his foot off the water control and reached for a sterile towel. She'd probably come here to give her kids a nice, healthy rural upbringing or something. Snapping on gloves, Luke turned abruptly to let the scrub nurse tie up his gown. That flash of something astonishingly like jealousy at the thought of the father of those children was ridiculous.

So she was still an attractive woman. So what?

So she had grown up a bit and become brave about confronting things she didn't like. Again, so what?

Luke had more than enough to deal with in his life right now, without complicating things by renewing any kind of relationship with Beth. The last thing he needed was to try poking an old scarred area when the potential to find a tender spot was so clearly possible.

A deep breath was called for here. And rational thinking. This disturbance was probably just part of the surprise factor of seeing Beth again. All he needed to do was ride it through and there would be no shortage of distractions if that proved in any way difficult. It was a relief to use the one immediately available.

'Let's get this show on the road, shall we?'

With his hands held carefully crossed in front of his chest, Luke used his shoulder to push open the swing doors into Theatre.

At just after 3 a.m. on a Tuesday morning, Ocean View's emergency department was stretched to slightly over its full capacity.

One of the high-tech resuscitation areas was still occupied by a seriously injured patient, the other one having just been vacated by the hit-and-run victim, who had gone up to Theatre 2 for the attention of an orthopaedic surgeon. All the beds in the cubicled area were also full and half of those patients were still waiting to have bones X-rayed or lacerations sutured. The treatment rooms were full and there were no spare seats in the waiting area either.

A few people with minor injuries were in Reception but most of them were simply there to offer solidarity to their mates, and they included some of the loudest and most unpleasant women Beth had ever encountered.

They were all unkempt, tattooed, pierced in multiple places and inebriated, and only too happy to demonstrate their contempt of any authority figures or lack of appreciation for any medical assistance. But the police presence was strong enough to ensure the safety of staff and the background noise of obscene language and shouting was so constant Beth could tune it out now.

It had already become automatic to seek the company of a police officer before approaching or treating a patient, and all the nurses remembered to wait until a member of one gang had left the X-ray department before escorting a member from the rival gang down the corridor.

Hopefully, the stab victim who was currently in Resus 1 would also be sent up to Theatre soon. When the doctors could be freed from attending the critically injured patients they should be able to deal with the minor injuries rapidly. They would be able to clear the department and then they could all have a well-deserved break.

Oddly enough, the chaos and unpleasantness of her current environment had been quite enjoyable over the last hour or so. Not the patients, of course, but their uniform lack of co-operation or appreciation had provided a bond of camaraderie amongst the staff members that had only increased under pressure.

And Beth was very firmly one of them. Thanks to that inadvertent episode of venting her tension, having stepped into the path of the converging gang members, Beth had not only been welcomed into the ranks of Ocean View's emergency department staff, she was currently being used as a lynchpin.

Even though it had only taken a few seconds and could quite easily have been a huge mistake, the fact that Beth had taken control had become a kind of emotional bank in which snippets of humour or stamina were being deposited and could be withdrawn whenever someone needed the lift of a shared smile or a pat on the back.

'I'm just *so* not in the mood for this' had become the catch-phrase of the night and never failed to produce a smile.

Dennis, the local cop, had claimed Beth as one of their own with a hint of pride.

'Keep your eyes open,' he had told one of the Nelson police officers about to accompany Beth when she needed an escort to Radiology. 'You might learn something from our Beth they never thought to teach you at police college.'

How ironic that Beth could feel so at home in a new place so quickly when she was still having serious doubts about the wisdom of having come here at all. She even knew her way around the storeroom now, having gone in there so often to fetch new supplies, and she was there again now, checking the fridge, as requested, to see how much O-negative blood they had on hand. Then she moved towards the shelves supporting boxes of dressings.

A number of extra-large gauze pads had been needed to staunch the arterial flow from the blood vessel severed by a knife wound in the car-park skirmish. And a fresh intubation pack was needed to restock Resus 2. Searching for the location of cuffed endotracheal tubes, Beth's eye was caught by the sterilised, draped rolls of surgical gear.

The obstetric pack was probably useful, but how often would they have the need for a thoracotomy kit here? Beth had only ever seen someone's chest opened in an emergency department once, and that had only been done because it had been in a big hospital and they'd had a cardiothoracic surgeon available for back-up.

Luke had had ambitions in cardiothoracic surgery so why on earth was he working here? And how could Beth hope to start a new life when there would be such constant reminders of the past?

If she didn't stay at Ocean View, though, would she end up being back in some emergency department large enough for the triage staff to wear headsets and microphones? Beth's sigh was heartfelt. She had really been looking forward to the change of working in a much smaller and potentially friendlier environment. And what on earth was she going to say to the nurse manager?

Sorry. This is a great place to work but I can't possibly stay because the man I was passionately in love with years ago happens to be working here as well, and I'm not sure if I could handle seeing him every day.

How pathetic was that?

Especially when it had been her that had broken up the relationship.

Beth added some other sizes of gauze dressings to the load she was carrying and wondered how the supplies of lignocaine were holding up. A lot of local anaesthetic was being used in the repair of lacerations.

The thought was only fleeting, however, and Beth did not reach for any ampoules. She was too busy thinking about something else.

It hadn't *been* her that had broken things up, though, had it? Not really. Ending it had been the last thing Beth had wanted. And having her nose rubbed in the puddle of her lost dreams by living in the same small town as Luke Savage was just unthinkable.

And finding him beside the bed of the stabbing victim in Resus 1 was unexpected enough to add considerably to those doubts about her new job. She had thought Luke would be tied up in Theatre for the rest of the night and that maybe encounters with the surgeon would be the exception rather than the rule. Beth averted her gaze hurriedly to avoid renewed eye contact but the surgeon was listening too intently to Mike to notice the arrival of a nurse carrying supplies.

'...femoral artery,' Mike was saying. 'Class III haemorrhage. Estimated blood loss of around two litres, but we've finally got it under control with the pressure bandage.'

'Blood pressure?'

'Coming up finally. Ninety-five on fifty now. We've run in two litres of saline and I'm just waiting for blood results.'

Beth was behind Luke now. It was quite safe to risk a glance. Not that she needed to confirm the impressions gained earlier, but it was tempting to add to them.

The shaggy black hair was a little longer than it used to be and there was just a hint of silver at his temples. Thirty-six seemed a bit young to be going grey, but Beth had found the odd white hair amongst her own recently and she was two years younger than Luke.

His face was browner and leaner, which made him look more serious somehow. Judging by the arms and the smooth V of chest visible around the baggy scrub suit, the rest of Luke's body was browner and leaner than it used to be as well.

Beth had to take a rather deep breath all of a sudden. No. Luke Savage had not lost his looks in the last ten years. Quite the reverse, really…damn it!

'Beth?'

'Sorry, were you talking to me?'

'I just wondered how the supplies of O-neg were looking.'

'There's two units. Plus some packed cells.' Beth continued putting the dressings into the drawer of the trolley but it would have been rude not to look up again. Mike was nodding. Luke was looking at the patient.

'How are you feeling?' he queried.

The gang member gave a noncommittal grunt.

'We're going to have to take you up to Theatre and repair that gash in your leg,' Luke explained. 'Have you had anything to eat or drink in the last four hours?'

'Yeah. I had a feed.'

'How long ago was that?'

'Dunno.'

'And you've been drinking?' The question was superfluous, given the smell of alcohol that hung over most of their patients that night, but Luke managed to sound nonjudgmental.

'Yeah. Had a few beers, man.'

The gang member actually smiled at Luke. 'You going to fix up my leg, then?'

Beth was slipping out of the cubicle as Luke turned towards Mike. 'Looks stable enough to go upstairs. We should be ready in twenty minutes or so, I guess. What about…?'

Beth was now far enough away for Luke's voice to be covered by the general noise in the department. Or maybe it was because the noise level had suddenly increased out here. A wave of weariness hit as Beth wondered if she needed to call for more police assistance.

But it was a police officer who was doing the calling.

'Help! We need some help here.'

Beth moved fast towards the reception area. She could see a woman lying on the floor near the seats in the waiting room. Another woman was struggling to get away from the grip the police officer had on her arm.

'I *told* you Stella was sick,' the woman shouted. 'And you wouldn't listen, you bastard!' She kicked at the officer, who winced but held on.

Beth dropped to a crouch, reaching to shake the apparently unconscious woman's shoulder.

'Stella? Can you hear me?' With no response to the shaking, Beth pinched the woman's ear lobe. 'Open your eyes.'

The woman groaned and rolled her head from side to side. Beth could see her chest rising and the groans were loud enough to suggest that her airway was clear. She was feeling for a pulse on the woman's wrist as she heard a deep voice behind her.

'What's happened?'

'She fainted or something,' the police officer said. 'One minute she was sitting on that chair and the next she was on the floor.'

'She's been bloody *hurt*, that's why!' The second woman was clearly furious. 'She's been feeling like

crap but nobody would *listen*!' With the stream of obscenities that followed this statement, it didn't surprise
Beth that nobody had wanted to listen. Still, there was
no excuse for missing a potentially serious injury.

Luke was frowning as though he'd had the same
thought. He crouched down close to Beth and put his
fingers on the woman's neck, feeling for a carotid pulse.

'There's no radial pulse,' Beth told him quietly.

Luke nodded, acknowledging the information that
the woman's blood pressure had to be very low. He
glanced up at the people standing nearby. 'Can some-
body tell us what happened to her?'

'She got hit in the chest,' the second woman spat.
'With a bloody softball bat, that's what *happened*.'

'How long ago?'

But Luke's query was ignored.

'And it was that bitch over there that did it. And I'm
going to *do* something about it.'

Fortunately, two more police officers arrived to deal
with the woman who was making a new and more
frenzied attempt to get free.

'It must have happened in the car park,' the first
officer told Luke. 'Probably well over an hour ago.'

'Thanks.' Luke slid an arm beneath the woman's
back, the other under her legs, standing up with
apparent ease despite the weight of his burden. 'Let's
go,' he said to Beth. 'What's free?'

'Resus 2.' Beth led the way, relieved to move away
from the tension in the waiting area, which was now es-
calating thanks to the screams of their new patient's
friend.

'Let me *go*! Where are you taking her? She's bloody
dead, isn't she?'

Stella wasn't dead but she wasn't looking at all well. Mike came into Resus 2 as Luke gently deposited the woman on the bed.

'What's happened?'

'Collapse,' Luke told him succinctly. 'Possible blunt chest trauma from a softball bat more than an hour ago.'

Beth slipped an oxygen mask over the woman's face and turned the flow up to 10 litres a minute, before swiftly turning her attention to pulling open Stella's shirt. Then she grabbed a pair of shears to cut through the singlet top beneath the shirt.

'She's tachycardic,' Luke told his colleague. 'And she's got JVD.'

Beth hadn't noticed the distension of the jugular veins on the woman's neck but she recognised the significance of the sign, reaching for the ECG leads as she dropped the shears.

'Chest-wall contusion,' she reported.

Stella groaned loudly, swore incoherently and tried to move as Mike put his hands on the obviously bruised area on the left side of her chest.

'It's all right,' he reassured their patient. 'We're just checking you out.' He looked up. 'Do we know her name?'

'Stella,' Beth supplied.

'I know it hurts, Stella. Hang in there.' He looked up again. 'Fractured ribs,' he said. 'But she seems to be moving air all right.'

Luke had wrapped a BP cuff just below the tattoo encircling Stella's upper arm. 'Hypotensive,' he noted. 'Systolic's barely 80. Let's get an IV started.'

'Make it two,' Mike said. 'Beth, can you get a line in on your side, please?'

'Sure.' Beth stuck the last ECG electrode in place and

turned to grab a tourniquet. Mike was watching the screen of the cardiac monitor.

'Sinus tachycardia,' he said. 'And…yes, we've got electrical alternans.'

Luke's grunt sounded almost satisfied as he pulled the cap off a cannula. 'Thought so. Pericardial tamponade.'

Beth glanced up at the screen, noting the way the spikes of the QRS changed direction every few beats, indicating a change in the cardiac axis. She knew the first line of treatment for an acute pericardial tamponade was a rapid infusion of saline. Bleeding around the heart, trapped by the membrane encasing the organ, was interfering with its ability to pump blood. By increasing the fluid volume of the patient, the output of the heart could be improved.

Pleased to have known to choose a wide-bore cannula without being told, Beth had also gone for easy venous access inside the left elbow. The cannula slid into place and she occluded the vein at the end of the tubing as she withdrew the needle and reached for a luer plug.

Luke was reaching for a luer plug as well. For a split second they caught each other's gaze and there was a hint of a smile lurking on the surgeon's face.

'Snap,' he murmured. 'Guess we'll have to call that one a draw.'

Mike watched them both as they finished attaching giving sets and started the fluids running. 'Definitely a draw.' He smiled. 'Nice work.' Then his face settled into a frown of concentration as he placed his stethoscope on Stella's chest.

'Heart sounds are pretty muffled.'

'Jugular veins are more distended now.'

'Stella!' Mike raised his voice. 'Open your eyes for me.'

There was no response. Mike pinched her ear lobe but her level of consciousness had dropped enough for the pain to be ignored. 'GCS is dropping,' he warned.

'Beck's triad.'

Beth wasn't aware she spoken aloud until she caught Mike's glance. 'You know your stuff, don't you?' The older consultant sounded impressed. 'What do we do next, then?'

'Pericardiocentesis?' Beth *was* aware that Luke was watching her. She'd been little more than a student nurse when they had worked together all those years ago. Would he also be impressed at the level of knowledge and the skills she had acquired since then? 'Removal of as little as 20 mils of blood can improve cardiac output and patient condition considerably, can't it?'

'Spot on.' Mike nodded. 'You'll find the kit on the shelf above the IV cannulas.'

Luke drew up the local anaesthetic while Beth swabbed the skin on Stella's chest. Mike inserted the six-inch, plastic-sheathed needle, aiming towards the base of the heart, and they all watched the monitor screen carefully for ECG changes.

'QRS complex is widening,' Luke warned at one point. 'Draw back a little, Mike.'

Beth held her breath. If it wasn't blood around Stella's heart that was causing the problem then their patient was in serious trouble. She relaxed slightly as she saw the needle fill with blood.

'Here we go.' Mike drew back on the syringe. 'Five mils,' he noted. 'Ten…fifteen…'

Then the flow stopped. It seemed that enough blood should have been removed to help, but there was no improvement in Stella's condition. In fact, it got worse. The ECG began to change, with the heart speeding up and missing beats. Stella wasn't moving or even groaning any longer.

And then Chelsea called out from the adjoining resuscitation area.

'Mike? He's bleeding again. I can't seem to find the right spot to apply manual pressure. Shall I take the bandage off?'

'Coming.' Mike glanced up at Luke. 'Can you manage?'

Luke glanced at Beth. 'Sure.'

The management of the femoral artery bleed next door was obviously difficult and the rest of the department was still humming. Nobody could be spared to assist in Resus 2 even when Stella's heart gave up the struggle of trying to pump against constriction.

The electrical stimulus was still there but their patient was pulseless and Luke's attempt to draw more blood from the pericardium with the needle proved fruitless.

'Start CPR,' he instructed Beth.

She worked hard to make her chest compressions as effective as possible, but Luke shook his head as he felt for a carotid pulse moments later.

'We're still not getting a pulse.' He raised his voice. 'Mike? I'm going to have to go for a thoracotomy here.'

Beth's jaw dropped but Mike sounded perfectly calm. 'That's fine,' he called back. 'I'll come and intubate for you in a second.'

Luke had caught Beth's astonished expression and

his tone suggested he had taken her reaction as a personal criticism. 'You'll find a thoracotomy kit in the storeroom, Beth.'

She was pleased to be able to turn away. 'I know where it is.'

He *was* a surgeon after all, and maybe Luke had had experience with opening people's chests. He certainly seemed confident enough, and it was probably the only procedure that was going to save a life here, but it was still horrific to watch him divide Stella's sternum with a saw in what seemed like only a few minutes later.

It was just as well she'd had theatre experience in the past, Beth decided, handing instruments and wound towels to Luke. It was how they'd met in the first place. Luke had been a surgical registrar and Beth had just been starting work as a theatre nurse. She'd transferred, of course, when their relationship had hit the rocks and the fascination and pressure of working in the emergency department had gone from being a welcome distraction to a real passion.

And here they were again. The bizarre impression of being in a time warp was heightened after Luke took a scalpel and carefully incised the membrane of the pericardium. The rush of blood wasn't enough to suggest a fatal cardiac injury and there was a collective sigh of relief as the vigorous pumping of Stella's heart could be actually seen.

Mike had his fingers on the side of Stella's neck. 'Great output,' he said delightedly. 'Fantastic!'

His voice startled Beth. The feeling that she and Luke had been a single—and isolated—unit had been so strong she had actually forgotten Mike was there in the last few minutes. She had been standing so close to

Luke. Their hands had touched more than once when she had handed him instruments, and that closeness—that touch—had wrapped them into a space that had been theirs alone.

Luke merely nodded in response to Mike's delight. 'We're not out of the woods quite yet,' he warned. 'Let's cover everything with dressings and sterile drapes and get her up to Theatre to finish.'

But he paused fractionally when he caught Beth's gaze and for the third time that night she was trapped by the expression in those dark grey eyes.

There was no hint of displeasure in them this time. Or the suggestion that she had changed beyond recognition. And, very oddly, the flicker of warmth that she saw was far more of a shock than Luke's earlier reactions to seeing her had been.

His voice touched exactly the same tender place as that fleeting glance had.

'Thanks, Beth,' Luke said softly. 'You were *brilliant*.'

CHAPTER THREE

IT WOULDN'T go away.

That flash of warmth in Luke's gaze had been contagious, and Beth could still feel it, hours later, when she was finally able to follow Chelsea to the staffroom where Maureen was making a pot of tea.

She could still abandon her new job and leave Hereford, she reminded herself as she sank gratefully onto a chair. Her head was telling her that in no uncertain terms again and again. Her heart, on the other hand, was insufferably smug in the knowledge of how difficult it would be her to talk herself into walking away. From this place. From the new job.

From Luke Savage.

And all it had taken had been that one little spark from the warmth in those grey eyes and the tone of his voice when he'd said she'd been brilliant.

Brilliant!

Beth's toes actually curled inside her shoes as a new wash of the glow spread through her.

'You're looking happy.' Maureen placed a steaming mug on the table in front of Beth. 'Sugar?'

'No, thanks.'

'I reckon she's just relieved it's all over.' Chelsea reached for the sugar bowl. 'What a night!'

Beth smiled wryly. 'It'll certainly go down in history as the most memorable first shift I've ever had at work, that's for sure.'

And the major incident with the gang members had only been the half of it.

'You did an amazing job out there.' Maureen pushed a plate of chocolate biscuits closer to Beth. 'Well done.'

'Yeah…' Chelsea was eyeing Beth curiously. 'You were brilliant.'

Beth hadn't blushed like that since she'd been a teenager. She reached for a biscuit to cover an embarrassment that had little to do with any modesty concerning her professional skills.

It hadn't been the first time she had been a key player in a dramatic life-and-death scenario in an emergency department. Not that she'd assisted with a thoracotomy, of course—in a big department there was always a queue of more senior staff eager to participate in something that big, but there had been that emergency Caesarean that time. And the puncture wound in a carotid artery and…

And none of that history mattered a damn because any praise that had come her way had been strictly professional.

As the comment that Chelsea appeared to have overheard from Luke had been, she reminded herself firmly.

But it hadn't *felt* like that, had it? The approbation from Luke had touched a place that hadn't been touched since…since…

Since she had been Luke's lover.

Beth crushed the thought relentlessly because

Chelsea was still giving her an odd look. As though she was determined to read her mind.

So was Maureen, come to that. Beth's eyebrows rose sharply.

'What?' she asked. 'Have I got chocolate all over my nose or something?'

'We're just curious,' Maureen explained.

'About the thoracotomy?'

Chelsea laughed. 'No. About whether you're going to ask or not.'

Beth was mystified. 'Ask what?'

'What every new female staff member always asks.'

So the interest had to concern a male staff member, and Beth suddenly knew exactly whom Chelsea had in mind. She could stop this conversation right now. Change the subject. Pretend that an urgent trip to the bathroom was called for. But her mouth had other ideas. It smiled.

'Which is?'

Chelsea exchanged another significant glance with Maureen. 'Whether Luke Savage is married or not, of course.'

The fact that the answer was expected did not stop Beth's heart stumbling over the next beat or two, but she actually laughed and shook her head in a valiant attempt to feign indifference. She picked up her mug of tea with a remarkably steady hand and took a sip.

Her lack of any verbal response did not faze Chelsea but she did seem puzzled.

'Well, that's a first, then.'

'What? A woman not throwing herself at Luke Savage?'

'Yep.'

Beth couldn't pretend to be all that surprised. She'd had a vivid reminder tonight of what it had been like the first time *she* had clapped eyes on Luke. There must be countless women out there who would feel that same level of attraction. What was surprising was the distinct impression she was getting that Luke was, in fact, still single.

'Not that any of them succeed,' Chelsea added wistfully enough for Beth to wonder if she had been one of those women herself. 'Maureen and I have a kind of running bet to guess how long it will take for them to realise he's not interested.'

That explained the significant glances but it left rather a lot still not explained.

Like *why* was Luke not interested in the women who clearly made themselves easily available?

Why was he *here*? In a medical backwater that lacked so much of the resources a larger hospital would have in the way of specialty expertise and facilities?

And *why* was she experiencing such an overwhelming level of curiosity?

The need to escape took on greater urgency and Beth glanced up at the wall clock.

'Nearly time to go home,' she said in relief. 'Is there anything I should be doing before the day shift arrives?'

'No.' Maureen smiled at Beth. 'You go and get some sleep. You've done more than enough on your first shift. We'll take care of the paperwork and handover.' She waved aside the protest Beth was clearly about to make. 'Go on,' she ordered. 'And if you see Mike out there, tell him his cup of tea's getting cold. I don't know why he hasn't come in yet.'

* * *

Beth soon found out. Mike was leaning against the central desk, in a now deserted department, talking to Luke. Both men looked exhausted but Beth could sense their satisfaction.

'How's Stella?' she queried.

'Stable,' Luke answered. 'We'll be transferring her to Wellington pretty soon.'

'Thanks to you two,' Mike added. 'You're a pretty good team, aren't you?'

Beth gritted her teeth. The old wound must have opened more than she had realised for Mike's words to have the effect of rubbing salt into it. This wasn't good.

'Runs in the blood for Beth, mind you,' Luke told Mike lightly. 'Did you know that her father is Nigel Dawson?'

Beth could barely suppress her groan. Of course Mike didn't know. It was the last thing *she'd* be pointing out to any new colleagues.

'Not the Nigel Dawson of heart-transplant fame?'

'That's the one.'

Mike's glance towards Beth was openly interested but it was Luke he directed his comment to. 'How on earth did you know that?'

'Beth and I worked together for a while, years ago.' Luke made it sound completely impersonal. 'She did a stint as a theatre nurse.'

'Lucky for Stella that you did.' Mike was smiling warmly at Beth but it was almost impossible to return the gesture.

Not only had Luke dismissed their past relationship as not rating a mention, he had revealed a large chunk of Beth's personal history that had been the other major part of her past she had been hoping to leave behind in coming to Hereford. It was the last straw and the balance finally tipped. No. Thanks to Luke, there was no way she could envisage the future she'd hoped to find here.

'I'd better go,' she said aloud.

Of course, her new colleagues couldn't detect any undertones to her statement. They both smiled understandingly.

'I'll walk you out to your car,' Luke offered.

'No need, thanks. I'm walking.'

'I'll come anyway,' Luke said infuriatingly. 'I need to grab my shaving gear from my car. Besides, we haven't even said hello properly, Beth.'

Beth ignored the quirk of Mike's eyebrow but she could feel her shoulders slump as she turned away. On top of discussing her famous father, she could just imagine how interested Chelsea and Maureen would be to hear that Luke was insisting on escorting her out of the building.

Her first shift at Ocean View hospital was ending with just as much of a disaster as it had begun with. Beth was in no mood to give a polite response to Luke's query about how she was.

'I would have been a lot better if you hadn't told Mike who my father was.'

Luke looked justifiably taken aback by her sharp tone. 'What's the problem? He *is* your father.'

Beth couldn't deny it, however much she would have preferred to. 'I came to Hereford to make a new start,' she said curtly. 'My family was one of the things I was more than happy to leave behind. Now I'm going to have everybody I meet asking questions.'

The calm, early morning sunshine that they emerged into made the drama of the last six hours seem totally unreal. This conversation with Luke seemed just as unreal. How crazy that they could slip back into an argument the first time they got to talk to each other.

'Well, I'm sorry.' Luke didn't sound sorry at all. 'But what's so wrong with your family? If he was my father I'd be proud of what he's achieved in his career.'

'Yeah…*you* would.'

'What's that supposed to mean?'

The tone was enough to force Beth to slow her pace and turn to face Luke. He looked so tired, she thought. And annoyed. And genuinely puzzled.

'Your opinion of my father was always higher than mine.'

'I only met the man once. If you remember, you kept me away from your family for so long I thought you were an orphan.' Luke shook his head. 'For heaven's sake, Beth. When did you start hating your father?'

'I don't hate him. I don't hate any of my family. They're strangers.' Beth's anger was more than ready to spill out. Gone were the days when she had responded to a conflict by bottling things up. 'We were just an item to add to our parents' CVs. Our son, the cardiologist. Our daughter, the paediatrician. Oh, there's Beth, of course, but the only thing she ever did that we really approved of was to produce Luke Savage as a potential son-in-law.'

Luke had stopped walking completely now. He was staring at Beth with that look she had seen earlier. The one that implied she was a total stranger.

He opened his mouth but Beth didn't give him a chance to say anything.

'I wanted to escape from that "not living up to the family tradition" rubbish. Now, thanks to you, that's going to be impossible.'

Luke merely blinked. 'Was that all you came to Hereford to escape from?'

'What?'

'Is there anything else I should know about so I don't put my foot in my mouth and make your new start any more difficult for you?' Luke didn't actually sound as though he was trying to be helpful. His polite tone had a distinct edge of sarcasm. 'Have you left a boyfriend behind as well perhaps? Or a husband maybe?'

The tone pushed a button Beth had almost forgotten about. As if he cared about any answer she might supply!

'A fiancé, actually.'

The effect on Luke was quite satisfying. His jaw dropped. 'You're *engaged*?'

'Not any more.'

Luke's expression became carefully blank, as though a switch had been thrown. 'Who finished it?' he asked quietly. 'You…or him?'

'Me.' Beth glared at Luke. Just how much of her past was going to be dragged up before she could even find some time alone to come to terms with it all? It had gone beyond any kind of joke, however unfunny. Right now, it felt like her entire life was unravelling.

Luke met Beth's glare without moving a muscle. 'Not good enough for you, huh?' he suggested casually.

Beth could feel the heat leaving her gaze but she couldn't drag her eyes away from Luke. What would he say if he knew that her fiancé hadn't measured up because it was Luke who had set the standard? Staying in a relationship with Brent would have been settling for second best. No, not even that close. It would have been stepping onto another emotional planet.

The thought was gone as quickly as it had come and Beth could feel her anger draining, but it was Luke who looked away first.

'Maybe I should start a club,' he muttered. He turned towards a black Jeep parked nearby. He took a step away from Beth then stopped again. Luke looked more than tired now. He looked…sad.

'You've changed, Beth. I would never have thought you could stand up to trouble with gang members like that. Or start hating your family. Or go around dumping fiancés. I don't feel like I even know you any more.'

The sadness in Luke's expression was enough to bring the sting of tears to Beth's eyes and she turned away quickly to hide them.

'You never did, Luke,' she said softly. 'That was the problem, wasn't it?'

The walk to the motel unit the hospital was providing until she found somewhere to live was not long enough to calm the spin-cycle effect Beth's brain was having on her thoughts, and despite her exhaustion she knew she had no hope of sleeping yet. A walk on the deserted beach over the road from the motel seemed the perfect way to wait out the cycle.

Somewhere beneath the emotional roller-coaster the night had provided was a quiet pride in the fact that she had actually coped with it all. And the knowledge that she could cope again, if she had to. She wasn't going to follow Neroli's path and give up the work she loved because of intimidating patients.

Seeing Luke again had been just as much of a shock. But she had coped with that, too. Or had she? Somehow, it was crushingly disappointing that their conversation in the car park had ended up feeling just like one of the arguments that had marked the disintegration of their relationship. Nothing had changed.

But everything had changed. There was something different about Luke. A mystery that was never going to be solved if Beth didn't stay in Hereford long enough to find out why Luke had chosen this quiet place to live and work.

And the tension created in the car park was never going to be resolved the way the old arguments had been. Until that last, horrible conflict, they had always made up their differences…in bed.

Any lingering tension would have been channelled into love-making that had made anything else totally insignificant. The world could have stopped turning as far as Beth was concerned when she had been in Luke's arms like that. She wouldn't have cared. She probably wouldn't have even noticed.

An echo of Luke's touch reached through the years and surfaced strongly enough for a spiral of desire to clutch something deep within Beth. A sound like a strangled groan escaped her lips and she sank onto a sun-warmed boulder.

How could she cope with this?

It was the ultimate reason to leave, wasn't it? A very clear alarm sounding. If her body and heart were going to rebel against her head and decide they still wanted Luke, then she was going to be vulnerable. She could get hurt.

Again.

The thought was terrifying.

And exhilarating.

The spark was still there. Even if the result was a negative tension, it was better than indifference would have been, wasn't it? When Beth had thought Luke had been ignoring her because he didn't give a damn, she had felt astonishingly let down.

But it hadn't been entirely negative.

He'd told her she'd been brilliant. He had looked at her—for just a fraction of a second—with an expression that had spoken of appreciation. Pride even.

And for the briefest pinpoint of time Beth had felt the sensation of pure joy that had always come from Luke being proud of her. Turning her face up to the sun, Beth closed her eyes and sighed softly. That sensation, however brief, was unforgettable. It was precisely what had been missing from her life for far too long. It was that elusive 'x' factor she had been searching for in all her attempts at other relationships. She had thought she might have found it more than once, only to gather enough doubts to ruin things.

And she'd been so right. Because now that she'd experienced the genuine article again, Beth knew she'd never found anything comparable. The craving to feel it again was undeniably powerful. The fear that she couldn't protect herself if she did was equally strong.

The chance of experiencing it again if she stayed was minimal in any case. Luke hated her now. She was a stranger to him. An angry stranger who confronted people and hated her family. He was clearly bitter about their past. Did he really think that Beth had ended things because she'd thought he Luke 'wasn't good enough'? And how many fiancés did he think she might have had in the intervening years?

It was almost too hard to open her eyes again. It was definitely too confusing to try and make any long-term decisions. Beth needed sleep if she was going to be ready for her next shift tonight.

At Ocean View hospital.

The short-term decision she needed to make was suddenly easy. She wasn't going to leave Hereford just yet. If revisiting her past was too much to handle, how on earth did she imagine she could build herself a future?

Besides, even if she only stayed for a little while, she might find answers to the questions that seemed astonishingly important. If they went unanswered they might haunt her for ever, and the further she moved away from Luke the less likely she would be to ever find those answers.

The minor celebrity status Beth had gained on her inaugural night in Emergency had worn off by the end of her first four night shifts but then, after three days off, she began on days and found it starting all over again.

'I'm Roz,' the red-headed nurse in the locker-room introduced herself. 'And you must be Beth, right? I've heard about you.'

'Oh, no!' Beth grimaced. 'It was a one-off, honestly. I don't go around looking for trouble from gang members. Quite the opposite.'

'Actually, I was talking about the thoracotomy.' Roz closed her locker, smoothed the tunic top of her uniform and gave Beth a curious glance. 'Have you done anything like that before?'

'Hardly. Cracking a chest in an emergency department is not exactly a common procedure, even in big hospitals.'

'First time it's happened here, that's for sure,' Roz said. 'And it wouldn't have happened at all if it wasn't for Luke. He's amazing, isn't he?'

'He's a good surgeon,' Beth agreed cautiously. She pulled her sweatshirt off and reached into her locker for the dark blue tunic, hoping this wasn't going to be another fishing expedition to gauge whether or not she was attracted to Luke. 'I hear the girl's been discharged from Wellington hospital already.'

Roz nodded again. 'Apparently, she's giving up her gang associations and going home. Being in hospital gave her mother a chance to see her for the first time in years.'

'That's a nice, happy ending. She's been very lucky, having the chance to start again.'

'Thanks to Luke.' Roz was waiting for Beth to lace up the comfortable trainers she wore for work. 'He could have been a cardiothoracic specialist by now— you know, working somewhere like the Mayo Clinic. We're so lucky to have him here.'

The look Beth received implied that she had been lucky to have the opportunity to assist him so closely and it was too good an opening to pass up.

'Really?' Beth's eyebrows rose. 'What made him come and work in a place like Hereford, then?'

'Something to do with his family, I think. I heard he had a sister who died a few years back.'

'Oh?' Beth's response was genuinely surprised.

'And he grew up here.'

Beth had not known that. For a horrible moment she wondered if he *had* told her and the information had been buried in her subconscious, ready to sabotage her after she'd chosen a new place to live. No. He'd talked of Nelson as his childhood stamping ground—a much larger town than Hereford but still not exciting enough for Luke. He hadn't been able to wait to get away…and stay away. Working somewhere like the Mayo Clinic had been right up there on the career ambition list.

Beth shut her locker and then waited as Roz paused in front of the mirror to redo her ponytail and catch errant strands of her long hair.

Losing his only sibling—and a twin at that—would have been dreadful but did it explain the change for someone as determinedly ambitious as Luke had been? Especially when he had never talked about his family in more than general terms. Had he been that close to his sister?

Had it been her own influence that had prevented him sharing that aspect of his life? She had certainly avoided families as a topic of conversation because she'd had no desire to let her own family diminish the joy of being with Luke.

She had made the accusation that it had been Luke's lack of knowledge about her that had caused the failure of their relationship, but how well had *she* actually known Luke?

Surely well enough to guess that the death of a family member wouldn't have been enough to sway the whole direction of his life. There had to be more to it than that but Beth wasn't about to appear too interested by asking questions. If Maureen and Chelsea had a running bet going, how many other staff members would have their antennae up?

Imagine if it got back to Luke that the newest staff member in Emergency appeared to fancy him? The thought was enough to make Beth cringe and she willingly accepted a new topic of conversation as she followed Roz into the department for the 6:45 a.m. staff changeover.

'So, how are you finding work here?'

'It's great.'

'Know your way around now?'

'I'm getting a good handle on the emergency department but I'd still get lost pretty fast if I had to go much further afield.'

'I'm supposed to keep an eye out for you today.' Roz was smiling, apparently happy with the assignment. 'If we get a quiet spell I'll see if can take you on a tour.'

There was to be no quiet spell in the early part of the day. Beth was kept busy monitoring an 84-year-old woman from a local rest home who had a history of cardiac problems and was now developing pneumonia. She required blood tests and X-rays, fluids and antibiotics, and her family needed reassurance that she was getting the best possible care. It was nearly 9 a.m. by the time the elderly woman was transferred to the medical ward and Roz signalled Beth as she returned from accompanying her.

'Would you mind taking the baby in cubicle 3? He's been vomiting all night and I won't be popular if I take a bug home to my boys.'

'Sure.' Beth collected the referral note from the GP. 'How many boys have you got?'

'Five. Six, if you count my husband, Gerry.'

'You're kidding!'

'I wish I was sometimes.'

'How on earth do you manage to find time to work here?'

'I only did one night a week until my youngest, Toby, started school last year. Gerry's very supportive.'

'Five kids!' Beth shook her head, as she moved away. 'That's a big family these days.'

'The first one wasn't exactly planned.' Roz grinned.

'But we figured that since we'd started we might as well carry on. We kept hoping to get a girl eventually.'

'You're not...' Beth stopped speaking as she realised that the question was rather personal, but Roz laughed.

'No. We're not still trying. Have you got any idea what it's like, living with six men? I may as well just nail the toilet seat to the wall.' She pointed towards the IV trolley. 'You'll need to take that. They've sent the baby in because the GP's concerned at her level of de-hydration. I'll get one of the docs to come and put it in.'

Beth was still smiling inwardly at the thought of Roz and her toilet seat as she helped the houseman get an IV line into ten-month-old Barry. He was the first child for the anxious mother and Beth did her best to reassure both of them after the young doctor had left to arrange admission.

'Barry's going to be fine, honestly. The worst part's over now that the line is in. He's just going to need watching and some fluid replacement.'

'I just can't bear him being so sick.' Barry's mother was holding him tightly enough to make him protest. Her eyes filled with tears. 'It's awful!'

'He's going to be fine,' Beth repeated. 'Whoops! It might take a while longer for that vomiting to stop. I'll go and a get towel so you can clean up a bit.'

Roz pushed a wheelchair past the linen trolley as Beth collected supplies and she wondered just how many minor or even major crises Roz would have fielded with her tribe of children by now. The feeling of envy was fortunately muted by familiarity but it still stung. Beth was running out of time to hope for much more than one or two children, let alone the big family she had always dreamed of.

Acceptance might have to be the next step. She wouldn't have any children if she wasn't with a partner she truly loved. She had come here to avoid just such a compromise, hadn't she? The notion of a childless future was still not acceptable, however. Beth smiled at Roz. She wasn't going to give up yet. She was only thirty-four, for heaven's sake, and she was in a new place, starting a new life.

She was a whole week into that new life now but Beth had yet to catch another glimpse of Luke. No night time emergencies had occurred that required a surgeon to be called into the department. Disappointingly, it looked as though her first day shift might go the same way.

Having made the decision to stay, Beth had been preparing herself for the next time her path crossed Luke's, quietly confident that she would be able to cope without the confusion and angst that first meeting had sparked. With every passing day she was feeling happier with her decision so why did that knot appear in her stomach when the call for a surgical consult on her next patient was answered…by Luke?

The young girl had come in by ambulance from her school, looking pale and complaining of severe abdominal pain, and Beth hadn't been surprised when the houseman made a provisional diagnosis of appendicitis and referred her to the surgeons.

Luke's smile at Beth, after being introduced to the patient and her mother, was friendly. Professional.

'What's been happening?'

'Katy's had dull, generalised abdominal pain for the last twelve hours.' Beth repeated what the houseman must have already told the surgeon. 'No nausea but she's been anorexic. The pain's settled into the right lower quadrant and she felt too unwell to stay in class this morning. Vital signs are all within normal limits but she's running a mild temperature of 37.4.'

'Got a white-cell count yet?'

'On its way.'

'So, Katy.' Luke's smile for his patient was much warmer than the one Beth had received. 'Got a bit of a sore tummy, huh?'

'It feels better now.'

'Mind if I take a look anyway?'

Luke pressed on the left side of Katy's abdomen first.

'Ow!'

'Where does that hurt?'

'Here.' Close to tears again, Katy pointed to the right side of her abdomen, well away from the pressure.

Luke glanced up. 'Know what that is, Beth?'

'Rovsing's sign.' Beth nodded. 'Associated with rebound tenderness.'

His eyebrow twitched. 'You do know your stuff, don't you? No wonder Mike's been so impressed with you.'

Had the emergency department consultant been talking about her to Luke in the last few days? Was *Luke* impressed? He didn't appear to be.

Neither did Katy's mother. She looked worried.

'What are you talking about? The sign? *Is* it Katy's appendix?'

'It's a definite possibility. Rovsing's sign is one of the things we look for. There are a few other possibilities, though, so we'll need to run a few more tests. Like an ultrasound or CT scan. Beth, could you see if CT is free at the moment?'

'Sure.'

Katy looked frightened. 'Does that hurt?'

'Not a bit, sweetie,' Luke said reassuringly. He rested a hip comfortably on the side of the bed and smiled as Beth slipped out of the cubicle. 'You getting your periods yet, Katy?'

Beth headed for the phone. When had Luke become so comfortable talking to children? Or laid back enough to practically sit on their bed for a comfortable chat? The Luke she had known had always been moving way too fast to pause that long. In far too much of a hurry to get to the top.

This new Luke was even more attractive than the old one. Beth's confidence that she could cope with working in the same place dropped a notch. Possibly two.

Beth's first day shift at Ocean View hospital was almost finished by the time Roz took her on a quick tour.

They bypassed the area adjacent to Emergency that Beth was now familiar with. The minor theatre, Radiology and CT and the plaster room. Roz paused near the pharmacy and small gift shop, manned by volunteers.

'Outpatients is down that corridor. There's also Physiotherapy, Occupational Therapy, Mental Health Services and so on. A few people wander into ED by mistake so it's worth knowing where to direct them.'

Beth peered past Roz. 'It looks busy.'

'It always is. Hereford's only small but the hospital has a huge catchment area.'

'That explains why the staff is so much bigger than I'd expected. I must say I was surprised. I'd expected this quiet little small town hospital.' The number of staff hadn't been the real surprise, though, had it? More the calibre. 'I'm still amazed at how many consultants there are.'

'Yes, we have a lot. The private work fills in any slack time but there seems to be less and less of that these days.'

'There are private patients?' Beth couldn't hide her astonishment.

'Just one ward. It's shared by all the consultants doing private work. They use the hospital facilities and I guess the insurance companies pay the government. The consultants and anaesthetists get a separate fee, of course.'

'Of course. I suppose Luke Savage does most of the private work?'

'What makes you say that?'

'I…um…' Beth bit her lip. What *had* made her say that? Because fame and fortune had been so important to the man she'd known? Because his desire to become a kind of clone of her father had started the rapid downhill slide of their relationship? The fact that private work was available had seemed like another small piece to fit into the puzzle of why Luke was here, but the expression on her colleague's face was making her wonder now. 'I have no idea,' she concluded lamely. 'It just seemed to fit.'

'Weird.' Roz shook her head. 'He's the only surgeon who *doesn't* do private work. Len does any general stuff and the orthopaedic guys share out the hip replacements and so on.'

'Is that the maternity ward?' Beth was eager to change the subject.

'Yes. And that's Paediatrics beside it.'

Beth latched onto a good way to distract Roz. 'My sister's a paediatrician. In Sydney.'

'Really?'

'And I've got a brother who's a cardiologist in London.'

'Wow. That's a very medical family.'

'Mmm.' Beth suddenly regretted the change of subject because the look Roz was giving her was rather too familiar. Maybe Luke hadn't spread the interesting information about her background any further.

'Dawson…you're not related to *Nigel* Dawson, are you? That heart surgeon guy?'

Beth suppressed a groan. 'He's my father.'

'Wow!'

Beth shrugged her eyebrows. Despite the feeling that she and Roz could end up being good friends, she wasn't about to start spilling the beans about how her father's personality and career had had such an adverse effect on her family and childhood.

'I read about him not so long ago,' Roz continued. 'Isn't your mother medical as well?'

'An anaesthetist,' Beth confirmed. 'They met in a theatre and have worked together ever since.'

'How romantic!'

'Mmm.' Was it romantic to allow nothing, including three children, to interfere in any way with accruing fame and fortune?

'And you went into *nursing*?'

'I'm the black sheep,' Beth confessed lightly.

Roz laughed. 'Every family should have one, I guess. Do you know where the surgical ward is?'

Beth nodded. 'I went up with Katy when she got admitted for surgery.'

Luke hadn't been there. And Beth had been irritated with herself at finding that disappointing.

'OK. I'll show you the really important stuff now,

like the staff swimming pool. You'll be diving in like the rest of us at the end of every shift in summer, believe me.'

'I love swimming,' Beth said, 'but I prefer the beach.'

'You'd better talk to Luke, then.'

Beth's spine prickled as her pulse quickened. 'Why?'

'He lives on the most perfect beach around these parts. Boulder Bay. You'll have to wangle an invitation and try swimming there. It's gorgeous.'

'But New Zealand has public access to any beach. They can't be private.'

'It's not, but you need four-wheel drive to get up and down the access road safely. Have you got a four-wheel-drive vehicle?'

'No.'

'So that's why you'll need to talk to Luke. He won't mind giving you a lift if you leave your car at the top of the hill. That's what we all do. Look, that's him just over there. I could ask him for you, if you're shy.'

Beth laughed. 'No, thanks. I can do my own asking. He looks a bit busy right now.'

He was talking to a woman who had just emerged from the pharmacy and was looking into the contents of a paper bag. She was an attractive blonde, probably in her late twenties, and the diamond rings on her left hand caught the light as she moved. Whoever she was, and despite her obvious marital status, she had Luke's full attention.

'I'm just going to grab a chocolate bar from the gift shop,' Roz said. 'Want something?'

Beth shook her head. 'No, thanks. I'll just wait here.'

Where she could appear to be admiring the display of flowers and teddy bears for sale while Roz waited in a small queue. Where she could still see Luke talking to the pretty blonde.

The woman seemed to be scrubbing tears from her face when Beth flicked a glance in her direction. Was she the relative of a patient perhaps? She saw the blonde nodding as though whatever Luke was saying was what she needed to hear. Then she saw Luke's arm going around the woman's shoulders and the impression of closeness touched a very deep chord in Beth. This was no professional relationship. She would never believe that Luke would be having an affair with a married woman, but whoever the blonde was, she had a bond with Luke that clearly meant a lot to them both.

And it hurt, dammit! There was no way Beth could reason her way out of this reaction. Had she really thought she could cope? This was jealousy, pure and simple. A nasty feeling that Beth wanted to eliminate as quickly as possible. Roz was finally paying for her chocolate. Beth moved to meet her at the door of the shop. A rapid escape seemed entirely possible.

Until Luke called out. And waved. And came towards her.

'We got to Katy's appendix just in time,' he told Beth. 'It looked like it wasn't that far off perforating.'

'That's good.' Beth edged closer to the door. She didn't want to talk to Luke. Not while she was struggling with the knowledge that she still cared enough to be jealous of any other potential women in Luke's life.

Luke's smile hadn't lost any of its charm. 'Look, I'm sorry about the other night. I shouldn't have said anything to Mike about your father. I really don't want to make a new start any more difficult for you.'

'It doesn't matter,' Beth muttered ungraciously. It

was on the tip of her tongue to say something about how hard it was to escape the past no matter how much you might want to but fortunately, perhaps, Luke spoke again first.

'We should have a coffee one of these days, Beth, and catch up on the last few years.'

He was being so *friendly*. Casual. As though she was simply an old acquaintance and it really didn't matter if they 'caught up' or not. The evil claws of jealousy were still digging into Beth and they sharpened her tone far more than she liked.

'I came here for a change of lifestyle, Luke. I don't see much point in raking up the past.'

'Fair enough.' The upward inflection on the last word was subtle but nevertheless conveyed that Luke had received the message. He wouldn't be making another attempt to engage Beth socially in a hurry. 'See you around, then.'

Roz emerged from the gift shop and received a smile from Luke warm enough to highlight just how chilly his words to Beth had been.

'Hiya, Roz. Sorry, I can't stop and chat just now. We'll have to catch up soon with a coffee or something. Everything all right with that tribe of boys you live with?'

'Great, thanks. You'll have to come to dinner soon.'

'Love to.' And Luke was gone with a friendly wave to Roz and not even a glance back at Beth.

Beth straightened her spine. She didn't care. Luke would probably be avoiding her from now on and that should make things a lot easier.

She should be happy.

'Are you all right?' Roz was giving her a curious look.

Beth pasted a smile to her face. 'I'm fine, really. Just a bit tired.'

'Me, too. It's been a busy day.' Roz nodded her understanding and smiled back, clearly convinced that Beth was being honest.

It was just a shame she couldn't convince herself so easily.

CHAPTER FOUR

THE cigarette was ground out in the gravel of Ocean View hospital's car park with an angry gesture and the pretty blonde woman sighed heavily as she climbed into the black Jeep.

'I've just wasted my money, haven't I? On those nicotine patches?'

'Consider it an investment.' Luke smiled. 'They'll keep.'

Maree Winsome sighed again. 'I'm hopeless, aren't I? My brother is dying of lung cancer and I can't give up smoking.'

'Kev's cancer has nothing to do with cigarettes. You know he's never smoked in his life. The pancreas was the site of the primary tumour. It's just spread to his lungs.'

'I know. It's so bloody unfair. It should be *me*.'

'Don't be daft. Life is often very unfair. We both know that.'

Maree broke the silence after Luke started the vehicle and moved off. 'This is really hard on you, too, isn't it? You and Kev have always been so close.'

'We've been best mates since we met at play centre

when we were about three. The terrible duo, they used to call us.'

Maree smiled. 'I used to get so jealous of Jodie because she got to hang out with you guys. Did you know I had a huge crush on you when I was, like, twelve or thirteen?'

'No kidding? No, I never knew that.' Luke grinned. 'Does John know about this?'

'Of course. I was well over it by the time I met him.'

'How is John?'

'He's fine. A bit worried about me. He's coming over for the weekend and he said he's looking forward to catching up with you.'

'I haven't seen John since…' Luke had to clear his throat. 'Hell, I haven't seen him since Jodie's funeral— just before you guys moved to Sydney.'

'And I met him at Jodie and Kev's wedding.' Maree's smile was poignant. 'Small world, isn't it?'

'It's smaller when you come from a place like this.' Luke headed uphill and turned into a tree-lined avenue.

'I miss it sometimes,' Maree said. 'Part of it, anyway. Not that I'd want to live here again. I like the pace of city life too much.'

'I used to think like that. I'd never have come back for more than a few days' visit if Jodie hadn't got sick. And then I kept coming back because I couldn't stay away.'

'And now you wouldn't live anywhere else, huh?'

'It's home,' Luke agreed simply.

Maree nodded. 'I'd forgotten how much like an extended family a small community can be when you need support. Two of the neighbours turned up with casseroles last night and old Mr Donaghue from the end of the road came and mowed the lawns today without even being asked. And Mum would have no hope of coping with any of this if it wasn't for your mum, Luke. She's practically living at our house.'

Luke pulled up in front of the old villa that badly needed a coat of paint as she spoke. 'That's what best friends are for.'

'She's amazing. And it must be *so* hard. I know it's been four years but it must be bringing back so many memories of Jodie. For all of you.'

'The memories have always been there. Kev was never able to let go.'

Maree made no move to get out of the car. Her face was serious. 'Do you think that's made a difference, Luke? I mean, he hasn't put up any kind of a fight, has he?' She didn't wait for a response. 'It's makes me so angry sometimes. What right has he got to just give up the will to live? Do his family and friends not count for anything?'

'We count,' Luke said gently. 'But it isn't our battle, love. All we can do is be here for him and help in any way he wants us to.'

'Well, I don't want to help him die.' Fresh tears rolled down Maree's cheeks and she wrenched the car door open and then slammed it shut behind her. She turned away from the house, however, reaching into her handbag for her packet of cigarettes. 'You go on,' she instructed Luke. 'I need a few minutes to pull myself together.'

'Want some company?'

'You want to make me feel even guiltier by subjecting you to secondhand smoke?' Maree managed a watery smile. 'No. Go away, Luke. Kev's been asking for you. You go and do the visiting thing.'

It was no surprise for Luke to find his own mother

completely at home and busy in Joan Winsome's kitchen but, then, this house had always been a second home for him. The two families had been linked long before Kevin and Luke had become inseparable friends. Luke's father, Don, had been more than an honorary uncle to the Winsome children after Joan's husband had died when Maree had been a baby.

The tragically brief marriage between Kevin and Luke's twin sister, Jodie, had only deepened an already unbreakable bond, and Luke's mother, Barbara, and Joan Winsome were closer than sisters. The twist of fate that was putting them through the unbearable pain of losing another young life was appallingly unfair but Luke knew they would get through this by leaning on each other.

They all would. There was simply no other choice.

The hug Luke gave his mother conveyed that message well enough for her to nod as she pulled away. And to smile.

'Did Maree find you? She walked into the hospital to collect the morphine prescription.'

'I gave her a ride home. She's outside at the moment beating herself up over her smoking.'

Barbara sighed. 'I'll go and talk to her. She's quite stressed enough right now, without putting herself through any more. She's been feeling too sick to eat properly for days now.'

'I know. It's tough all round, isn't it?'

'I persuaded Joannie to lie down for a while. She got really upset when Kev decided to plan the music for his funeral.'

Luke groaned softly. 'Oh, no!'

'He's been asking when you were coming. He's got

a list of CDs he wants to borrow. Said he can't guarantee he'll give them back, though.'

Luke was still shaking his head, smiling, as he went through to the sunroom at the closed-in end of the villa's long verandah. That was so like his mate, to be making jokes to try and lighten such a bleak atmosphere. Jodie had died in her husband's arms when she'd succumbed to the vicious form of leukaemia she had contracted, and Kevin swore she had been still smiling at the last joke he'd told her.

'Hey, Kev.' Luke sat down on one of the chairs beside the bed that the palliative care department of Ocean View had provided. The electronic adjustments could be varied enough to provide comfort and the soft cushioning of the inflatable mattress cover and the sheepskins was a bonus. 'What's all this I hear about the concert you're planning?'

Eyes too large for a wasted face were fixed on Luke. 'Is Mum still upset, then?'

'I haven't seen her. She's asleep, I think. Anything I can get for you, buddy?'

'Yeah. Your retro CD…that's got Procul Harem… "Whiter Shade of Pale"?' Kevin Winsome's lung capacity was reduced enough now for him to need to catch his breath after every few words. 'Nice and ghostly…huh?'

'It's no wonder your mum's upset, mate. You just can't stop stirring, can you?'

'I'll stop soon enough.' Kevin smiled slowly. 'And then you'll…be sorry.'

'Yeah.' Luke couldn't keep up the banter. Maybe Maree was right. Kevin was too accepting of all this. 'What I meant was, did you need a drink or some more jungle juice or something? How's the pain?'

Kevin's hand movement was weak but still dismissive. 'We've got better…things to talk…about. Can you…make a list…for me? Of songs?'

What had Luke just said to Maree? That all they could do was to help in any way Kevin wanted them to? 'Sure thing,' he said softly. He pulled out the notepad and pencil that he always kept in his shirt pocket. 'Fire away,' he instructed Kevin. 'What's first?'

'That soppy one that…Jodie chose for our…wedding song.'

Luke's gaze went to the most prominent photograph in the clutter of pictures lining the window-sill beside Kevin. His sister had been the happiest bride in the world, no question. Thank God none of them had known she would be diagnosed with a fatal illness within a year.

Kevin had followed Luke's line of vision. 'Gorgeous, isn't she?'

Luke nodded, the lump in his throat precluding speech.

'I could never…have found anyone…to take her place…you know.'

'You two were soul mates, that's for sure.'

'Not many people…are that lucky.' Kevin was tiring and had to catch his breath several times before he could speak again. Then he caught Luke's gaze. 'I'm not afraid…to die, mate… I'm kind of hoping…to see Jodie…again.'

Luke's mouth twisted. 'You'll have to say hi from me, then. I miss her.'

'You have to find…your soul mate…otherwise I'll come back…and haunt you.'

'I'm being haunted already, thanks. You remember that theatre nurse I was planning to marry? Beth Dawson?'

Kevin's nod was painfully slow. 'She's the only

one…who ever made you…think about getting… married.'

'Well, she's turned up here. Taken a job in the emergency department at Ocean View.'

'Why?'

'That's what I'd like to know.'

'Is she…married now?'

'I don't know. She's not wearing any rings but she might just take them off for work.'

'Ask her.'

'I can't do that. Can't ask anyone else either. You know what hospital gossip is like. She might think I was interested in her again.'

'You are.'

'No way. She dumped me, remember?'

'You didn't try very hard…to fix things, mate.'

'I wasn't going to beg her to take me back, if that's what you mean. There were plenty of others who wanted to play. Anyway, it's all water under the bridge and I don't want to go swimming in that particular river again. Neither does she.'

'How do you…know that?'

'I met her in the corridor this afternoon and she gave me a look that would have curdled milk. The woman still loathes me.'

'Flip the coin.'

'What?'

'Hate's just…the other side of…love, isn't it?'

'You're getting a bit philosophical in your old age, aren't you?'

'May as well.' Kevin was giving Luke a very intense look. 'She still cares… You could find…a way to flip… the coin if…you wanted.'

'Doubt it.' Luke grinned. 'Beth has her foot on that coin very firmly. I don't think she has any intention of even speaking to me again.'

'I have no intention of *ever* speaking to him again.'

'You'll have to at some point. You work in the same hospital.'

'Maybe I won't stay after all. I could learn to make cappuccinos, Neroli. Surely your sister could take on another waitress or something?'

'You don't want to do that.'

'Why not? You're having fun, aren't you?'

'I think the novelty's starting to wear off.' A sigh echoed over the phone line. 'I really miss nursing. I think I might have overreacted by chucking it in. I could have just made a change from the emergency department. I'd quite like to be a theatre nurse, actually.'

'Good thinking. The patients are knocked out so they can't give you any grief. And you never know your luck. You might even meet a hot surgeon!'

They both laughed but then it was Beth's turn to sigh. She was staring at her feet. 'I'm wearing those rabbit slipper socks you gave me for Christmas last year.' If she wiggled her toes the whiskers on the bright pink rabbit faces twitched and the ears that were attached near her ankles bent forward as though listening to something interesting. Beth smiled. 'I really miss having you around, Neroli. I could use a best friend.'

'Luke could be your best friend if you gave him a chance.'

'Have you not heard a word I've said?' Beth clicked her tongue sadly. 'I shudder to think how much I've spent on this phone call already and now I have to tell you all over again. I'm curious about the man, not *interested* in him.'

'Doesn't sound like it from this side of the ditch, chick. I think you're jea—'

'Good grief!' Beth interrupted. 'What the hell was *that*?'

'What *is* that?' Neroli's voice was very faint as Beth held the phone at arm's length so she could see out the window. 'Sounds like someone's screaming. Beth? Beth? Are you all right?'

'Got to go. Looks like someone's come off their motorbike just outside.' She didn't wait to hear her friend's farewell. She didn't even stop long enough to change the fluffy slipper socks, but nobody seemed to notice as she arrived at the scene of the accident seconds later.

'Beth!' The woman from the dairy opposite the motel had learned her name within a week of her arrival. Beth had liked the friendly interest from the shopkeeper. 'Thank goodness. You're a nurse, aren't you?'

'Did you see what happened?'

'He shot round that corner and just went straight into the lamppost. Is he dead?'

'No.' Beth could feel a good carotid pulse. The black helmet the youth was wearing seemed undamaged but his left leg was bleeding and one arm was bent at an unnatural angle. Right now, though, Beth was more concerned about his breathing. And his neck. 'Has someone called for an ambulance?'

'I did.' The man was still holding the carton of milk he had obviously purchased in the dairy. 'It's on its way.'

'And isn't that Dr Savage?'

'What?' Beth lost count of both the respiratory and pulse rate she had been trying to take simultaneously.

'What kind of name is that for a doctor?' The man with the milk sounded incredulous.

Beth almost smiled. Luke had said exactly the same thing once. 'And I'm not savage,' he'd added with a winning smile. 'Am I?'

And Beth had assured him he was anything but. Determined, yes. Confident, certainly, but she hadn't thought it tipped over into arrogance. Not then, anyway. Ruthless? Unlikely. But very definitely not savage. He was capable, in fact, of being the most gentle man Beth had ever known. She opened her mouth to say something in defence of Luke and his name but there was no need.

'He's a wonderful doctor,' the woman from the dairy informed her customer stoutly. 'He looked after my dad last year and you wouldn't want anyone else after you've had Dr Savage, let me tell you. You'd know all about that, wouldn't you, Beth?'

The groan was fortunately contained in her head. Luke had slammed the door of the sleek black Jeep behind him and had clearly heard the final piece of that interchange. His startled glance at Beth set a confused whirl of thoughts into that spin-drier action again.

You wouldn't want anyone else after you've had Dr Savage.

The comment stabbed at something astonishingly raw. Neroli had been about to tell her she was jealous of that blonde woman she had seen in Luke's company. And it was true. She *was* jealous. And she had never found anyone she truly wanted after Luke. Imagine if she'd agreed with the woman from the dairy? Both she and Luke would know she wasn't referring to any professional skills the man possessed, however wonderful they were.

Again, thankfully, there was no need or opportunity for her to say anything. Luke's glance had been even briefer than the painful flash of insight. He was now crouched beside the young man on the road.

'Airway's clear,' Beth told him. 'But I haven't been able to assess his breathing properly with the way he's lying.' The crumpled figure was almost in a recovery position and while she could feel the movement of his chest and abdomen, it was hardly adequate for a proper assessment.

'We've got enough people to do a log roll.' Luke moved to hold the helmeted head. 'I'll look after his neck.' He looked up at the bystanders. 'You're Mrs Coulter, aren't you?'

'Doris.' The woman from the dairy beamed at the recognition.

'I need you to help us, Doris. We're going to turn this man over so he's lying on his back but we need to be very careful with his neck. We'll need you as well,' he told the man with the milk. 'Beth will show you where to put your hands.'

It took only moments to achieve spinal alignment and the movement made the injured man groan.

'It's OK,' Luke told him. 'Try not to move, mate. You've had an accident. Can you open your eyes?'

The groan was louder this time but there was no response to the command. Luke frowned, adjusting his hold on the man's head. 'Stay as still as you can,' he instructed. 'Beth, can you undo that jacket? OK, chest wall movement looks equal from here.'

Beth nodded. 'I can't feel any rib fractures. Sternum feels stable and trachea looks midline.'

'What's happening with that leg? Looks like there's some blood loss that needs controlling.'

The wail of a siren was getting steadily closer as Beth removed the now bloodsoaked blanket Doris had helpfully fetched and then used to cover the lower half of the injured man.

'Looks like a degloving injury.' Beth eyed the mangled skin and flesh dubiously. 'I can't see any obvious fracture.'

'Use that towel that Doris has to cover it.' The ambulance was pulling to a halt and Luke was watching for the paramedic to emerge. 'Sally—good to see you. We need some large dressings, stat. I didn't have my first-aid kit on me.'

Sally's partner put an oxygen cylinder on its side near Luke and attached a high-concentration mask to the outlet.

'Can you grab a collar, please?' Luke asked him. 'And, Beth, could you help me get his helmet off so we can put a collar on? Sally can deal with that leg. She's got gloves on.'

They should all have gloves on, Beth realised. She slipped hands that already had smears of blood on them inside the bike helmet to hold the youth's head as Luke gently eased the bulky item clear. His movements were very careful and he was making very sure he didn't move the man's neck as he removed the helmet.

It was inevitable that their hands would touch. And not just briefly. At one point Luke's hands overlaid Beth's as he inched the helmet clear with tiny increments of zigzagging pressure from his thumbs. Every second of that physical contact seemed to Beth to stretch into infinity. The effect of the most fleeting touch that night of the thoracotomy had been noticeable and they had both been wearing gloves that night.

This was bare flesh against bare flesh and the nerves

in Beth's hands had caught fire. The burning sensation was travelling up her arms and then spiralling down to somewhere deep in her abdomen.

'Right. Keep holding that position, Beth, until we get the collar into place.'

Things seemed to happen fast after that. Too fast. The injured man was given oxygen. An IV line was inserted. His level of consciousness was improving rapidly as his leg was covered with sterile dressings and then a pressure bandage put on to control the bleeding. His neck was encased in a semi-rigid collar and then he was strapped to a backboard, with cushions and straps ensuring that no untoward movement could worsen a neck injury.

Within fifteen minutes they were ready to load and Luke was heading for his vehicle.

'I'll go in with him,' he told Beth. 'He's going to need that leg cleaned out under anaesthetic. Do you want a lift home?'

'No. I'm living just across the road.'

'Really? You're lucky. Places this close to the beach don't come up very often.'

'I'm in the motel.' Beth felt inexplicably embarrassed and dropped her gaze. It felt like she was admitting some kind of failure. She was a displaced person with no home. 'Just temporarily.'

'Oh-h.' The drawn-out monosyllable had an odd tone to it. Beth glanced up but could then see why Luke sounded odd. He was staring at her feet and Beth blushed.

'They were a present,' she muttered. 'From a good friend.'

'Very cute.' Luke looked up and caught her gaze.

And then he smiled. Beth smiled back and for just a moment there was a connection of shared amusement. And then, suddenly, there was a much deeper connection and their smiles dimmed as quickly as if a switch had been flicked.

And they both turned away at precisely the same moment. The ambulance edged past and Sally was looking out of the driver's window.

'Shall I tell them you're on your way, Luke?'

'I'll be right behind you.' Luke got into his vehicle and drove away. Beth had no idea whether he looked back or said goodbye because she was walking back to her motel unit and she did not turn back.

At least, not until his car was just a black speck at the far end of the road.

Daytime shifts at Ocean View were busy enough to leave Beth little time to think about personal issues, which was just as well because she seemed to see rather a lot of Luke over the next four shifts.

Did he never have days off? Why didn't he send a registrar or houseman down when surgical opinions were sought in the emergency department?

And how did a population base as small as that which Ocean View serviced manage to produce so many patients requiring the skills of a general surgeon? There had been two cases of obstructed bowels and a perforated duodenal ulcer. A baby had come in with a Meckel's diverticulum and there had been an elderly man whose colostomy had broken down. Then there had been a case of rectal cancer, a femoral hernia and a nasty abscess or two.

Beth counted them off on her fingers. OK, so Luke

hadn't appeared to assess them all but he *had* appeared in the department at least once every day. There had also been the times she had spotted him in the staff cafeteria and he had driven past her when she had been walking home yesterday. There was simply no way to avoid the accumulation of reactions that required considerable thought when she had her quiet moments away from the hospital.

None of those occasions had provoked more turmoil than the encounter on Tuesday evening, however. It had been a long and very hot day and Roz had persuaded Beth to have a quick swim in the hospital pool before heading home.

'But I don't have any swimming togs.'

'Chelsea keeps some in her locker. She won't mind if you borrow them.'

And Chelsea had arrived for her night shift and agreed wholeheartedly. 'Go for it,' she'd urged Beth. 'My togs should fit you.'

They had, though rather too snugly for Beth's comfort. She had never been a stick figure but the cut of the costume had given her a cleavage that had made her wish she'd had a T-shirt available to wear on top. At least it had been black, which had helped the hip line, but Beth had regretted her decision to swim the instant she had surfaced from her first dive into the deliciously cool water.

Luke was dropping a towel onto one of the deck chairs surrounding the pool. His swimming shorts were boxer style and hardly revealing, but Beth's memory banks happily filled in the area covered by the modest costume and suddenly the water lost any of its power to cool and soothe.

Like his face, the whole of Luke's body was browner and leaner than it had been six years ago. There wasn't an ounce of fat to blur the outline of muscle on those long, long legs and broad shoulders. The evening sun gave his bronzed skin a warm glow and Beth had to duck below the surface of the water to stop herself staring.

Luke was still, by far, the most gorgeous man she had ever met.

Going underwater was her second mistake of the evening. She had to come up for air eventually and it was unfortunate that her timing and position coincided with Luke completing his initial dive. He surfaced close enough for Beth to be liberally splashed by the water he shook from his head and she could almost feel those long fingers as they raked hair back from his forehead and out of his eyes.

'I sure need a haircut.' Luke blinked droplets from the thick, dark eyelashes Beth had once coveted, and then his gaze focussed. 'Oh…hi, Beth.'

'Hi.' Being below the surface for so long had left her breathless. Beth trod water but the sight of Luke's near-naked body scrambled her brain and she was totally unable to think of anything else to say.

'Hey, Luke!' Roz was waving a large Frisbee. 'Catch!'

He did and then he flung the Frisbee back to Roz, who immediately flicked it on to Beth. She missed, thanks to her reluctance to launch herself any closer to Luke, but then she caught the mood of the group of people intent on having as good a time as possible as they cooled off and her own agenda could be shoved aside.

It was fun. Seeing Luke's glistening body as he leapt and dived as enthusiastically as anyone else was simply a part of that enjoyment. Beth even decided that the wayward reaction her own body was producing was simply another memory that hadn't been adequately filed.

The mental filing proved difficult, however. It was easy enough to locate the pocket it should go in once Beth was alone later that evening, but the temptation to ruffle through other memories of Luke's body proved too powerful.

The way he had kissed her. No, the way he had looked at her *before* he had kissed her. As though she had been the only thing in the universe that Luke had been aware of. The only thing that had mattered. His hands would cradle her head so gently and Beth would watch his eyes and then his lips as he started to slowly close the distance between them. And Beth would be in freefall, the anticipation and excitement and sheer driving lust making her as completely focussed on Luke as he was on her.

The memory had been enough all by itself to stir a physical reaction that could only leave pure frustration in its wake. Beth had shoved the memory back, thrown in the one of Luke in the swimming pool and tried to slam the drawer shut on the mental filing cabinet. She had tried *very* hard.

And yesterday, Wednesday, she had avoided even looking at Luke when he'd been in the department, in case that drawer broke a lock she knew was weak and started sliding open. She had kept her head down and repeated very firmly to herself that nothing had changed.

Just because he was still such an attractive man

didn't change a thing. The fact that her relationship with Luke had been enough to sour any later attempts to connect to other men also changed nothing. Luke Savage was *not* the man she needed in her life right now. She was not going to go down that road again no matter what Neroli thought because she knew there was an accident scene at the other end of the road and that the victim would be herself.

She didn't need Luke in her life. She didn't need any man in her life. At least, not until she had sorted herself out a little more. No wonder her relationships in the last few years had never worked out. How could she hope to be happy with someone else if she wasn't happy with herself?

What she needed, Beth decided, was a focus that was purely selfish. Something that would keep her busy outside working hours. Busy enough to get past the mental block Luke had presented. Heavens, if she kept up thinking about the man this much, she would have to admit it was becoming an obsession and that would be totally unacceptable. Pathetic, even.

Beth used her days off to search for that new focus. One of the benefits of living in a motel was the wealth of pamphlets available that extolled all the attractions of the area she was now living in. On her first days off after the night shifts, Beth travelled the short distance to the Marlborough Sounds and she fell in love with the seemingly infinite number of sheltered bays and islands. The wildlife cruise she took let her see tiny blue penguins for the first time and almost touch a dolphin that cruised on her side of the shallow boat.

There were plenty more attractions. Hereford was a town in an area now famous for its vineyards and crafts.

There were fabulous restaurants to try, gardens to visit, riverboat cruises and the most wonderful shopping at numerous craft galleries and markets. Beth set out to explore and found herself tasting treats like early cherries, asparagus and crayfish caught just down the coast at Kaikoura. She made plans to attend the upcoming wine and food festival that was now a major attraction for Marlborough, and she stopped her car on several occasions just to admire the views.

She loved it all. The sea and forests, the hills and mountains. She loved the fabulous climate and the casual way people dressed. The way Doris from the dairy always greeted her by name and the wonderful sunsets she was in the habit of watching from a now favourite boulder on the beach near the motel.

What she didn't love was the motel unit and the way the walls closed in on her when she had to return to sleep, but on her second day off Beth found the answer. She had started making an effort to stop at every tiny craft gallery she passed in her explorations the previous day but she almost missed this one. The hand-painted sign advertising pottery was only just visible beneath the ivy creeping up its pole. The shop was just as low key—part of a shed that housed the artist's kiln.

But there it was. The Answer. Staring at Beth in the form of a casserole dish. The pottery was gorgeous. With a base colour of a rich, earthy brown, a golden-hued glaze had been applied so that it looked as if something had boiled over and oozed down the sides to finally trickle into droplets that ringed the base like jewels. What really captured Beth, however, was not the piece of pottery so much as what it represented.

Home. An oven from which the aroma of a hot,

meaty dinner wafted on a cold winter's night. A family big enough to warrant cooking the size of casserole this dish would hold. A table big enough for them all to gather around. Beth could almost hear the laughter and feel the love around that table, and the yearning was strong enough to be painful.

That was what she wanted in her life. What she had always wanted even when she had been too young to understand what had been missing. Waiting for the right partner to provide a home was never going to work. And it didn't matter because Beth could do it for herself. Well, maybe not the family bit but she could certainly do the rest.

'I'll take this dish, please,' she told the owner of the kiln. 'I just love it. And you wouldn't happen to know any local real estate agents, would you?'

The first step was taken late the same afternoon and it was with a sense of growing excitement that Beth found herself being chauffeured around Hereford by Ronald from L. J. Homes Ltd, viewing any available properties within easy commuting distance of Ocean View hospital.

'I'd like something old,' she told Ronald. 'I'd be happy to renovate.' Restoring an old house would be a wonderful project to keep her occupied outside work, wouldn't it? And it would be a home. A real home. She would spend all the money she had saved so carefully ever since she had started working. She would buy at least part of the dream symbolised by the casserole dish that was now looking oddly out of place on the tiny kitchenette bench of her motel unit.

'I'd really like to be near the beach,' she added.

'Might be a bit pricey for you, love.' Ronald consulted

a printout of listed properties he had in his briefcase. 'We could get you up on the hills maybe, with a *view* of the sea. Or what about south of town, near the river?'

Beth was looking at the printout as well. 'That cottage looks cute. Can I see that first?'

So they drove a little north of Hereford. Ronald's car slowed to negotiate the bend at the top of a hill and Beth turned her head sharply to peer at the yellow wooden arrow on her side of the road.

'So that's where Boulder Bay is!' she exclaimed.

'Do you know it?'

'I've heard of it.' Beth wished she hadn't sounded so interested. To have any thoughts of Luke encroaching on this new adventure took some of the excitement away.

'Nothing for sale down there,' Ronald told her. 'And even if there was, you couldn't afford it, I'm afraid. Besides, the road's awful and the residents aren't going to pay for it to get upgraded. They like their privacy.'

'How many houses are down there?'

'Only one.' Ronald was increasing speed as the road led down the other side of the hill. 'Belongs to one of the docs at the hospital. You said you were a nurse, right?'

'Yes.'

'You probably know the bloke, then. Luke Savage?'

'I've met him.' Beth's tone prompted a glance from Ronald who instantly dropped the subject and left them in silence until he pulled up outside the cottage Beth wanted to view.

Not that she took that much notice of the tour. Ronald had said 'they'. If there was more than one resident to the exclusive Boulder Bay, it had to mean that Luke was sharing his house.

Who with? The woman wearing the wedding ring? No. Beth actually shook her head. It simply didn't fit.

Ronald had noticed the unconscious gesture. 'Not what you're looking for?'

'Not really.'

'Right. Let's try something else, then. There's a house not too far from here. We might as well have a look while we're on this side of town.'

Beth took more notice of this property but it was an isolated cottage and so rundown it would be a daunting prospect to renovate. She loved the acre of land that came with it, however, and spent some time exploring the sheds. It was Ronald who called it a day.

'It's getting late,' he reminded Beth. 'I'd like to drive you past another place while there's still enough daylight to see. And then I'd better get you home.'

But Beth wasn't quite ready to go back to the sterile motel unit.

'I might walk,' she told Ronald. 'Can you drop me at the top of the hill?'

'It'll take you hours.'

'It's only a few kilometres. I often walk for an hour or more on my days off. I could do with the exercise.'

'If you're sure.' Ronald stopped the car but looked dubious. 'It's going to get dark before you get home.'

'I'm sure. Thanks very much for your time, Ronald. I'll have a think about those houses and call you tomorrow.'

The walk would be a good time to think and Beth really did want some vigorous exercise. It wasn't until the taillights of Ronald's car blinked as he slowed further down the hill that she realised just where she had requested the stop. Her breath left her lungs in an incredulous huff as she saw the yellow arrow sign.

Boulder Bay.

How far would she have to walk down the road in order to see the house Luke lived in? Beth's steps slowed but didn't stop. No. It would be just too embarrassing if he caught her acting like some sort of stalker.

But was the beach as beautiful as Roz had told her? And what sort of house did Luke live in? Ten days ago Beth would have been quite confident that any real estate Luke purchased would have to be an architectural statement that advertised status. If it was, maybe the mystery of why Luke had compromised his career to such a degree would be solved. Had he been so successful already that he was in a kind of early retirement?

The thought was intriguing enough to make Beth stop. Just a quick look to satisfy her curiosity, she decided. With a rapid scan for traffic, Beth almost scuttled across the road and set off towards Boulder Bay at a brisk pace. Twenty minutes later she could see the outlines of a house set into the cliffside at the far end of a picture-perfect bay, despite the light fading more rapidly than she had expected. There were no lights on. Maybe Luke had been held up at work. He could be sitting on a deck, enjoying the sunset, or maybe he used this part of his day to wander on what had to be almost a private beach.

And no wonder it had been named for its boulders. The white sand of the beach gleamed in the soft light but only small pathways towards the water were visible. Enormous boulders ringed the beach and were strewn across the sand. Beth had never seen such huge, smooth black rocks. And how come they glistened as though they were wet when the conditions were far too calm to have thrown any spray that far?

Puzzled, Beth walked a little further. Then she stopped abruptly, put her hand up to shield her eyes from the last rays of sun for the day and she stared intently at the beach.

It had to have been her imagination.

But then it happened again.

One of the boulders *moved*.

And then a jet of spray of water coming from another of the enormous rocks caught enough light to resemble a tiny fountain and an odd, mournful sound carried clearly up the hill to where Beth finally realised what she was seeing.

Whales.

She had heard of mass strandings, of course. Had seen pictures of people fighting to save the huge mammals on more than one occasion but Beth had no idea what to do right now.

She had to call help and find someone who *did* know. How long would it take her to run back uphill and then find a telephone? Who would she call? The police maybe?

Beth was in the process of turning to retrace her steps when her peripheral vision caught something and she turned back and then breathed a sigh of relief.

A light had come on at Luke's house. He was home and he would know what to do.

Keeping to the side of the gravel road where the grass verge gave more secure footing, Beth began to run downhill.

Towards Boulder Bay beach.

Towards Luke's home.

CHAPTER FIVE

'WHAT the—?'

Luke braked sharply enough to cause a slight skid in the loose shingle of the road leading to his home as his headlights picked out the solitary figure running down the verge.

Being the back view of a person in an unnaturally bright spotlight was no hindrance to recognition, and Luke knew exactly who it was almost instantly.

At least this time the curvy figure was fully clothed. The last time Luke had seen Beth out of uniform had been at the staff swimming pool on Tuesday, and the image of her body in a swimsuit that had to be a size too small had been plaguing him ever since.

Not that that had stopped him frequenting the emergency department of Ocean View far more often than was customary. If anything, he was even less able to resist that magnetic 'scab-picking' effect than he had been the night she had appeared back in his life. That moment after dealing with the motorbike accident victim when he'd noticed the slippers had replayed itself in his mind countless times since.

Knowing that Beth was living in the motel unit allocated to new and single staff members had piqued his curiosity, but *he* had been largely in control of any encounters they'd had so far. And he wanted to keep it that way. He wasn't going to risk another put-down like the one he'd received when he'd suggested they get together for coffee.

Right now Beth was apparently hell-bent on reaching his home. His sanctuary.

It was too much!

He braked again, this time coming to a halt. He pressed the button to unroll the window on the passenger side of the vehicle. Beth had seen him coming, of course, and she actually looked eager to speak to him, but Luke got in first.

'Where the hell do you think you're going?'

'Luke!' Beth's jaw dropped. 'I thought you were at home.' She peered in at him, clearly disconcerted. 'There's a light on at your house.'

'It's automatic,' Luke snapped. 'To deter intruders.'

The rebuke went right over her head. 'I need a phone. There's—'

'Hang on just a minute,' Luke ordered. 'How did you know it was *my* house?'

'Ronald told me. No, Roz told me. Ronald just showed me where it was, but that's not important, Luke. There's a—'

'It might be important to me. Who the hell is Ronald when he's at home?'

'For God's sake, Luke!' Beth raised her voice. 'There's a whole bunch of whales on your beach.'

'What?'

'I thought they were big rocks but then one of them moved and I saw—'

'Get in.' Luke had started rolling downhill again even before Beth could shut her door properly. 'Have you reported it?'

'I didn't have my mobile with me. That's why I was going to the house. I mean, *your* house.'

Luke reached for the phone plugged into the Jeep's dashboard and punched in three numbers.

'Emergency services,' the voice responded promptly. 'What service do you require? Police, fire or ambulance?'

'Police.'

A new voice was on the line within seconds. 'What is your location?'

'Boulder Bay. Just north of Cloudy Bay, Marlborough.' Luke knew that the call was probably being answered in a major centre such as Wellington or Christchurch.

'And what is your emergency?'

'A mass whale stranding.' Luke could hear the surprised silence at the other end of the line as he concentrated on getting round a sharp bend in the road. 'Sorry, but this was the fastest way I could think of to activate a rescue operation. I don't have any numbers easily accessible for the Department of Conservation. They handle these sort of emergencies and we'll need some assistance pretty quickly.'

'Can you keep your mobile phone with you, sir?' The officer from the police communications centre had recovered from the surprise. 'We're onto it. Someone should contact you very soon.'

'Good. I should have some more information by then.' Having stopped the vehicle and killed the engine, Luke unhooked the phone and clipped it to his belt. 'Come on,' he said to Beth. 'We'd better go and have a closer look.'

Beth looked quite nervous about approaching the whales, but Luke had no hesitation in walking right up the nearest mammal. They were big, but not monstrous. Its blowhole was about level with Luke's waist and the whale was eight to ten feet long. Mostly black, there were large patches of white and the size of the fins was another good clue to their species.

'These are pilot whales,' he told Beth. 'That's good.'

'Is it?'

'If they were sperm whales there would be no rescue operation. They'd all have to be killed and buried.'

Beth was horrified. 'Why?'

'Because sperm whales have virtually no chance of survival once they're grounded like this.' Luke's head was turning rapidly, scanning the length of the small beach. 'It must have happened within the last hour or so. The tide's turned so we're going to have a long wait for enough water to try refloating them.' He shook his head. 'I'm amazed no one saw the pod coming in. There must be twenty or thirty animals here.'

Beth had come closer to the whale Luke was standing beside. She reached out a tentative hand and touched the rough cluster of barnacles that had seaweed trailing from it like an odd clump of hair. Then her hand stroked the black skin.

'It feels warm,' she said in surprise. 'But it's dry. Is it dead?'

'Hard to tell just by looking,' Luke said. 'They can hold their breath for an extraordinarily long time. They can go into a diving reflex when they're stranded like this.' He walked to the head of the whale and gently touched the edge of its eyeball. The eye and then the whole whale twitched.

'Watch out for the fluke.'

'The what?'

'The tail. It can swish pretty fast and it packs a punch.'

'Oh.' Beth hurriedly stepped away from the tail end of the large mammal.

'Don't step on the flippers!'

'OK.' Beth sounded out of her depth now and a second later she was clearly distressed. '*Oh!* Is that a baby?'

The whale she moved towards was only about the size of a large dolphin. It was lying on its side, a flipper moving weakly, and it made a mewling noise that had Beth dropping to a crouch beside it and reaching out to touch it.

'You poor wee thing. Luke?' Beth's face was upturned to him and her tone was beseeching. 'Can't we *do* something? Can we save it?'

'We'll certainly do our best.' How could he not respond to that heartfelt plea? The involvement of a baby in any kind of disaster exerted a greater tug on the heartstrings, but getting too emotionally involved with this kind of situation was a mistake that could easily affect the outcome. Luke turned away. 'Come up to the house. We need a whole heap of stuff.'

'Like what?'

'Blankets and sheets. Shovels. Buckets. We're going to have to keep them all cool and damp. We'll need to dig trenches to get any of them lying on their sides upright again. We also need to dig moats around their flippers and tails. This way.' Luke led Beth up the path that wound between boulders and into the native shrubbery that comprised his garden.

This was a bad idea, inviting Beth inside his home,

but what choice did he have? He couldn't carry everything himself and it could be some time before any further assistance arrived. The thought made Luke reach for his phone.

'Who are you calling? The police again?'

'No. My parents.' It was sad, the way a puzzled frown appeared on Beth's face. *Her* parents would probably be the last people she would think of contacting in any emergency. She had always had such a clear vision of the kind of family she wanted and it had come because she felt it had not been provided in her upbringing. The opposite had happened in Luke's case, but it had taken extreme circumstances to show him the value of what he had always had.

'They're involved with Project Jonah,' Luke explained. 'And they've had a lot of experience with whale rescues over the years. Hi, Mum— Hang on just a sec?'

Luke opened his front door and turned to Beth. 'There's a linen closet next to the bathroom. Get as many blankets and sheets as you can find. Take the ones off the bed as well.' He knew he sounded terse but he couldn't help it.

Beth was going inside his house. It was never going to feel quite the same again, was it? He would think of her being there. Wondering what she thought about the things she saw. Whether she was drawn by the simplicity and homely feel of the place as much as he was. He would just be thinking of *her*, dammit, and he was already doing more than he should be of that.

'Mum? Are you still there? Listen, there's a pod of whales that's beached itself practically on my front doorstep…'

* * *

Luke's conversation with his mother faded as he went, presumably in the direction of a tool shed, and Beth went inside the house.

By the time she had taken a few steps she was feeling very puzzled. This must have been a holiday house in the past. Small and simply built, it had the feel of a quintessential New Zealand 'bach'. Modifications had been made in recent times, like the new kitchen and bathroom, but Luke choosing this as his home seemed inexplicable. It was so far removed from the kind of mansion he had aspired to as his career had been taking off. The kind of home her parents had owned.

Beth loved it. She could imagine how perfect a spot the small living area would be to watch the sun rise or set, but there was no time to stop and admire the sea view right now. The main bathroom was on the opposite side of the house, looking into a small garden, and the linen cupboard was easy to find.

Beth stacked all the sheets and blankets from the shelves near the front door and hesitated before fulfilling the other part of her instructions. She really didn't want to find Luke's bedroom and take the linen from his bed.

It was as difficult as she had anticipated. The bed *smelt* of Luke. Beth couldn't believe how she could have remembered that faint, musky scent that she associated so strongly with lazy early morning lovemaking or just lying in someone's arms, feeling loved and protected and so…*safe*.

She couldn't help glancing swiftly around to see if there was any evidence of a female resident. A comb or lipstick maybe, or a feminine robe hanging behind the door. The only evidence she found anywhere suggested that Luke's interest in housekeeping hadn't grown much since his days of sharing a house with other young doctors.

The aroma from the pile of dirty socks and underwear in the corner of the new-looking *en suite* bathroom did not evoke any poignant memories. Beth's nose crinkled and she hurried outside with the first armload of linen. Going back for the rest, she noted the dirty dishes on the kitchen bench and the CDs scattered on the floor of the living area.

The cover of the uppermost disc caught her eye. *Seventies Retro* it was called and it brought back a sudden and unwanted memory of the fancy-dress party of that era that she had attended with Luke to celebrate the thirtieth birthday of one of the surgical registrars he lived with. Beth had gone dressed in an orange Paisley caftan she had found in a vintage clothing store and she had covered her black curls with a long blonde wig.

She'd had the *best* time. The only really good time she had ever had attending the kind of parties Luke had preferred. Maybe that had been because the elite of the local medical community had all been in disguise that night, letting their hair down and having too much fun to be concerned with flaunting position or wealth or superiority.

And she had gone home with Luke well before the others had left the party venue and Luke had slowly removed her wig and that caftan and had looked at her with *that* look and said softly, 'I just *love* unwrapping presents!'

But it had been Beth who had received the gift that night. Love-making so intense but so gentle. Until Beth had demanded more and had been given a lot more than she had bargained for. A lesson, in fact, on just how wild sex could be with a partner you trusted completely.

She had never trusted anyone else that completely, but that was only to be expected, wasn't it? Luke had been her first real love and she had given him her heart. Maybe he still had a piece or two of it. Or perhaps she had lost them when she'd tried to put her life back together. It would explain why she'd never been able to offer anyone else the kind of love and commitment she had felt for Luke.

Could anything else ever be that good again?

It was a relief to leave the house and the memory behind. Luke was on the path with a laden wheelbarrow and her first armload of linen was balanced precariously on top of buckets and tools.

'Help's on its way,' Luke informed her briskly. 'A Department of Conservation team is flying in from Wellington and Mum and Dad are rounding up local volunteers. The police are going to cordon off the road so we don't get inundated with sightseers, and I've offered the house as a base for the operations manager. They'll need kitchen facilities and so on.'

'You sound like you know all about this kind of thing.'

'Not really. I helped at a stranding years ago on Farewell Spit, which is a much more common place for this to happen. I would have thought Boulder Bay beach was too steep and rocky, but there you go. It's happened.'

'They do it when one of them gets sick or injured, don't they?' Beth stumbled a little as she followed Luke. At 9 p.m. it still wasn't completely dark but it was hard to see her feet around the pile of blankets she held.

'Sometimes it's because the leader is sick or disorientated and sometimes they just don't know why it happens. There'll be people coming to study the scene. They make a site map and examine and take samples from any dead whales.' Luke looked up as a set of car headlights appeared on the road winding down the hillside.

'I hope that's my parents,' he said. 'I've asked Dad to ferry other volunteers down from the top of the hill. We don't want too many vehicles down here or there won't be room for the heavy stuff.'

'Heavy stuff?'

'Tractors. Boats. Generators for the lights, that sort of thing.'

'Good grief! I had no idea how much was involved in rescuing whales.'

'Are you working tonight?'

'No. And I've got the day off tomorrow.'

'Good.' Luke smiled. 'How about coming to help me with a spot of triage, then, Nurse?'

'Certainly, Doctor.' Beth smiled back. 'Do you have some colour-coded triage cards in that wheelbarrow first-aid kit of yours?'

'No, but I've got a can of spray paint. We'll put a big "X" on any obviously dead whales and that will save time later.'

The feeling of excited anticipation that the prospect of working with Luke was engendering evaporated. Beth didn't want any of these whales to be dead. This was an extraordinary experience to be thrown into and Beth's connection suddenly went way past being the person to have discovered the emergency.

She wasn't about to stop and try to analyse why it was so important to her. Maybe it was because the whales had chosen Luke's beach to strand themselves on. Or maybe she had accorded the situation the status of an omen regarding her new life in this place.

It didn't matter. Her determination to succeed was

powerful enough to feel like desperation and there was no time to lose.

At least fifty volunteers had gathered within an hour, and until the Department of Conservation officials arrived it was Luke's parents, Don and Barbara, who took charge of the rescue operation. One whale was already dead—possibly the sick or injured member of the pod that had prompted the rest to strand themselves.

Pairs and trios of people were assigned a now numbered whale each to care for. Beth waited until finally Barbara shone her torch on the piece of paper she was writing on and then looked up.

'Beth Dawson?'

'I'm here.'

'We'll get you to look after the baby. Jack—you can help. You've got some experience.'

Jack showed Beth how to gouge a shallow trench in the sand parallel to the tiny whale's body. Luke came past just as they were completing this first task.

'That looks deep enough. Let's try getting him upright. Dad?' Luke's father was talking to a man as he shone a torch on one of the larger whales. 'Could you give us a hand?'

Don was also satisfied with the trench digging. 'Make sure you keep his flippers flat against the body when we roll him,' he advised. 'They're easy to injure.'

The four of them managed to roll the baby whale from its side quite easily, and the trench looked as though it would keep him upright securely.

'Do you know about making a moat around the flippers and tail?' Don asked Beth.

She nodded. 'And Jack said we can't make it too deep because that might make it difficult to shift him later.'

'Sorry, Dad.' Luke was draping a folded sheet over the whale's body behind the blowhole. 'You know Jack, don't you? This is Beth Dawson.'

'Hello, there.' Don Savage had a smile identical to his son's, and Beth found herself smiling back just as enthusiastically at the wiry man who looked to be in his seventies. 'That name sounds familiar.' He peered at her more closely. 'You're not *the* Beth, by any chance, are you?'

'Um…' Beth had no idea what she could say to that. What did he mean? Had Luke been bitter enough to describe her in lurid detail to his parents perhaps?

'Your mate, Pete, is just over here.' Luke took his father's elbow and steered him away without acknowledging the interchange. 'He and Doris are looking after number fifteen. You might like to come and check out their moats.'

Doris was the woman from the dairy and Beth had been astonished at how good it was to see a familiar face amongst the volunteers. A not-so-pleasant surprise came when she saw the arrival of the pretty blonde woman she had seen Luke talking to that day. At least she was directed well away from Beth's position to join the group caring for the large bull whale who was assumed to be the pod leader.

Jack, Beth's only partner in caring for the baby whale, was a man in his fifties and he was rapidly becoming a friend.

'You're going to be OK, Willy,' he told their whale.

Beth grinned. 'Willy? As in *Free Willy*?'

'Yup. It's the only whale name I know. Unless you can think up a better one?'

'Willy's fine by me.'

Naming the baby made it all seem even more personal. Beth joined people queuing to share buckets and make trips into the surf and back, carrying water to fill the moats and tip carefully over the whales' backs. Beth knew without being told not to tip water into Willy's blowhole but she hadn't known it still needed to stay moist. Using a corner of the wet sheet to dampen the skin on the whale's head, Beth leapt back and nearly fell over when it released a breath with a noise like the vent being opened on a pressure cooker.

She laughed, but the spray was cold. Her legs were now soaked from the knees down from filling the bucket in the surf, and it all got colder over the next hour or two. The first of a supply of hot drinks was provided at the same time as the generators were set up to flood the area with artificial light, and the atmosphere changed as the rescue operation went into another gear under the expert supervision of Department of Conservation experts.

No one was more determined or focussed than Beth, however.

'I think number fifteen must be Willy's mother,' she told Jack excitedly. 'Have you noticed how she answers every time he makes a sound?'

Number fifteen didn't just respond vocally to the baby. It had a tendency to thrash its tail, which had Doris and Pete scrambling out of the way at regular intervals. The operations manager became concerned.

'We might have to try moving the baby. You're kind of hemmed in here and it could be dangerous if this one gets any more distressed.'

'But we think that's Willy's mother,' Beth exclaimed. 'If we separate them, she'll only get more upset, won't she?'

'Willy?' The Department of Conservation official shook his head, clearly unimpressed with Beth's bond with the baby whale. 'We'll see how it goes,' he said noncommittally. 'I'll be back.'

Jack took a turn hauling buckets of water just after 1 a.m. 'The tide's turned,' he told Beth. 'It's on its way back in.'

'How deep does it need to get before we start refloating the whales?'

'We'll be about knee deep by the time the adults can be shifted. We'll have to hang onto this little chap for a while, though, or even shift him further up the beach. Once we get them all back into the water we have to keep them together in a group for an least an hour to try and reorientate them.'

'Is that so they won't just beach themselves again?'

'That's right. And after we've let them go, we'll all have to stand in a line in the waves and bang metal things together to try and persuade them to head out to sea. We're in for the long haul, I'm afraid. You're not too tired or cold yet, are you?'

'No.' Beth's tone was valiant but she *was* tired. And very cold. And her stomach was hurting. When the next cup of soup came her way she found she couldn't swallow more than half of it. The warmth was welcome but it made her feel sick.

Cramp, she decided, from crouching over Willy too long without stretching her muscles.

'I'll get some more water,' she told Jack. 'Be back in a minute.'

Luke saw Beth struggling to carry a full bucket of sea water.

She looked exhausted. And very pale. Luke couldn't

suppress the memory of how much he'd always loved the smooth, milky quality of Beth's skin, but seeing her right now did not make him want her the way it had in the swimming pool the other day.

What it did make him want to do was to take her in his arms and hold her until she warmed up. Until the lines of strain on her face eased. He wanted to tell her what a great job she was doing and how impressed he was at the way she threw herself so wholeheartedly into helping others—people or animals. He wanted to tell her that everything was going to be all right. She didn't have to be so worried.

The only comfort he could offer, however, was a smile and an outstretched hand to relieve her of the burden of the heavy bucket.

'Here, let me help you with that. You look done in.'

Beth hesitated, as though she was about to refuse his assistance. She gave in and let him take the bucket but she didn't return his smile. She grimaced, in fact, and dug the fingers of her right hand into her abdomen just beside her hip.

'I'm OK,' she said. 'I've just got a stitch from carrying that bucket.'

'Have a rest for a minute.'

'Mmm.' Beth looked away abruptly. Had she read a level of concern she didn't appreciate? Luke carefully made his expression and tone as neutral as possible.

'I'll bet you're wishing you hadn't come to live in Hereford after all.'

A startled glance let him know he'd said the wrong thing…again.

'I meant this,' he added quickly. 'There's not many

places you could go to and end up having to knock yourself out saving whales.'

'No.' Beth sounded incredibly weary. Was she thinking of other reasons why she might wish she hadn't come to live in Hereford? Like seeing him again?

The mournful cry of a nearby whale seemed to echo Luke's melancholy thought. He stared at the back of Beth's head for a second as she started walking slowly back towards her own whale. Then he followed.

'Why *did* you come here, Beth?'

'I told you. I wanted a new start.'

'But why *here*? In Hereford.'

Beth shrugged. 'The job just happened to be in the nursing gazette. I'd been out to the airport to say goodbye to a friend and I guess the time was right to make a decision. I didn't want to do anything as drastic as Neroli had done, though, like leaving nursing. Or New Zealand.'

'Neroli? Your friend with the red hair and freckles? The one that always laughed a lot?'

'That's her.' Beth turned and smiled, as though pleased that Luke had remembered so clearly. 'She hadn't been laughing much in the last few months she was here, though.'

'Why not?'

'She got held at knife point in ED by a gang member who was as high as a kite on drugs. It was terrifying enough to make her throw in the towel and give up nursing. I can't say I blame her either. It *was* pretty scary.'

Luke caught his breath. 'Were you *there* when it happened?'

'Yes.'

And she'd been caught in the middle of a gang war on her first night at Ocean View. She must have been as terrified as Neroli had been and yet she'd defended herself without hesitation. More than that—she'd set the tone for the whole department to cope with a nasty few hours.

A peculiar sensation sneaked up on Luke. It wasn't that Beth had changed into some stroppy individual who went around sorting out anybody who displeased her. She had always been amazing. Brave and clever. She wouldn't attack anyone without justification.

He'd never understood why she'd wanted so little to do with her family until her bitter remarks in the car park that morning.

He'd never understood quite why she'd dumped him either, but the thought that she might have been justified was not one he wanted to explore. He'd been put down enough by Beth, and this wasn't the time to go looking for any more emotional injuries. Besides, she'd made it quite clear that she didn't want to start raking up the past.

'What?' Beth had turned again and was looking at him oddly.

Luke blinked. 'What?' he echoed.

'You just muttered something about raking up the past.'

'Did I?' Luke tried to dismiss the embarrassment of having spoken that last thought aloud. 'Maybe that's what *I* was doing when I came back here.'

Beth gave him a sharp look. 'I had no idea *you* were living here.'

Her tone implied that it was the last place she would have come if she *had* known. Luke gritted his teeth. And he'd been trying to avoid a put-down, too.

'This is the last place I would have expected you to be,' Beth continued. 'You told me you grew up in Nelson.'

'I went to school in Nelson,' Luke corrected.

'And you called that Hicksville. I seem to remember you saying you wouldn't be caught dead, trying to practise any kind of medicine in some provincial backwater.'

Luke's shrug dismissed the comment as irrelevant now. 'Things change. People change.'

Not that much they didn't. Beth took the last few steps towards Willy in silence.

Things didn't change to that kind of degree unless something absolutely catastrophic happened. The new chill that suddenly ran through Beth was enough to make her shudder.

Was Luke sick? Had all the stress of his ambition and workload and then his sister dying given him a heart attack at an early age, maybe, and forced him to slow down?

The fear the thought provoked was powerful enough to make Beth realise just how much she had been kidding herself.

She had never stopped loving Luke Savage.

She never would.

Turning back, Beth searched his face but she could find no answers.

'What changed, Luke?' she asked quietly. 'Why *are* you living here?'

'It's home.'

The simple words explained nothing and yet they explained it all.

It was precisely what Beth was searching for, wasn't it? But home could be a person as much as a place. And the home that Beth's soul craved had nothing to do with any real estate or stupid casserole dishes.

Her home could only be with the man she loved.

A man who no longer loved her.

She was still staring at Luke when she heard someone call his name with some urgency from near the car park.

And Luke, with a smile that seemed almost apologetic, handed the bucket back to Beth.

Then he turned and walked away.

CHAPTER SIX

WHY had he been embarrassed to admit that Hereford was home?

The only place Luke wanted to be. Would Beth see him as a failure, having traded his dreams of fame and fortune to be a simple country doctor? Living in a place small enough to ensure he was recognised wherever he went? Being on call every second night and quite likely to have some member of the community stop him in the supermarket to ask advice about some minor ailment?

And did it really matter what Beth thought of him?

Yes and no.

Luke smiled at the man waiting beside his Jeep, whose injury someone had alerted him to.

'What's happened, mate?'

'I fell over my bloody shovel,' the man growled.

'Let's have a look.' Luke shone his torch onto the man's shin. 'You're going to need a couple of stitches in that, I'm afraid,' he said seconds later. 'You might need a tetanus booster as well if that shovel was rusty. I'll put a dressing on it and someone will be able to run you down to the hospital.'

'Can it wait? The tide's turning. I wouldn't want to miss refloating these guys. Not when we've worked this hard already.'

Yeah. Some things were worth putting up with a bit of discomfort for, weren't they? Luke did his best to make sure the owner of the leg wound wouldn't suffer from waiting for a while. He cleaned the wound and covered it with a sterile dressing and then bandaged it carefully. He even scored a plastic bag from the team manning the barbecues and taped it securely over the bandage to keep it dry.

'Make sure you get into the emergency department as soon as you can,' he warned. 'This isn't going to hold it together for that long and I'd hate you to end up with an infection.'

He watched the determination with which his patient headed back towards the whales. They were reaching the low point of this rescue operation. It was an ordeal to hang in there and keep going. Some people had given in and gone home for a rest.

Beth wasn't one of them. Luke found his gaze wandering as he searched for the small shape of the baby whale and its carers.

Of course it mattered what Beth thought of him. He'd lost so much in his life already. He was about to lose even more, with his best mate only having such a short time left. The sadness that clouded Luke's life could easily shift to encompass what he'd lost with Beth and override any lasting bitterness.

The bitterness had only lasted this long because he'd never understood quite why it had gone so wrong. Sure, they'd started having arguments. Silly arguments over things like which restaurant he'd chosen to take Beth out to or the wine he'd chosen to accompany the dinner.

Nothing he'd done had seemed to be right and, yes, it had got his back up. When the disagreements had started on important things like his friends and his career, of course he'd had to take a stand. And, of course, he had started spending longer and longer hours at work. Why go home when time with your partner made you feel you just weren't good enough?

It hadn't been anything like that to start with, though, had it? Time together had been so precious. He had loved everything about Beth. Just being with her. Talking to her. Listening to her. *Touching* her.

Oh…*God*!

Luke shoved the last of his supplies back into his first-aid kit and zipped the pack shut.

Why *had* it gone so terribly wrong?

He hadn't deserved to be dumped but sadness still outweighed anger. Maybe if he could understand what had happened he might be able to move on and be confident that he didn't make the same mistakes in a future relationship.

What if Beth decided to stay in Hereford and they spent years avoiding really talking to each other because he was too proud to ask what he'd done that had been so wrong?

If they spent years missing out on a potential friendship because of his pride?

Luke was all too aware of just how precious friends were.

He pushed the first-aid kit into the back of the Jeep. The next opportunity he got, he was going to talk to Beth, dammit.

Really talk.

* * *

It was all becoming an ordeal.

A second adult whale died and a whisper of gloom spread along Boulder Bay beach. The waves crept a little further up the sand each time they rolled in and as they got closer, the chill increased. Jack seemed as miserable as Beth was now feeling and for some time now he had said almost nothing. They crouched on either side of the baby whale, scooping water from the moats around his flippers and tail to splash over the sodden sheet covering his back.

Beth was on autopilot, trying to ignore her wet jeans, the cold gritty sand in her shoes and the irritating pain in her side that wouldn't go away. She just needed to distract herself enough to hang on and see this through. Another half-hour or so and the waves would be covering her feet, and by then they should have started to refloat the first of the mammals.

The best method to distract herself was to watch what was happening in the circles of light away from her own, but the way her gaze invariably found Luke in the crowd of people only added to her despondency.

He was moving between the groups. Administering first aid when needed, but more often he was just talking to people. Encouraging them. Helping. Beth saw him touch someone's arm, pat someone else on the back and once he was enfolded in an enthusiastic hug from a very large and very short woman.

What became even more noticeable than the physical connection he constantly made with these people was the effect his presence clearly had. Women and men smiled when they saw him approaching and the only laughter to be heard on the beach now was always close to where Luke was.

This *was* his home, wasn't it? These were *his* people. Beth wanted to be a part of the community that Luke cared about so much.

No. If she was honest, she wanted to be singled out as special. She wanted to be the one person Luke cared for more than anyone else.

The way she cared about him.

And it could never happen. Beth had made sure of that, hadn't she, by ending their relationship in the first place? At the time it had seemed like she'd had absolutely no choice. But now, with the changes she saw in Luke—even if she didn't understand how they had happened—it felt like she had made a huge mistake.

Beth's spirits slipped another notch and when she heard Jack groan it seemed as though he was reading her mind. But that was ridiculous.

'Are you all right, Jack?'

'I've got a bit of a pain.'

'Whereabouts?'

'In my chest. It's OK, I've got my spray somewhere.'

Beth's knees protested as she straightened and the cramp in her abdomen tightened, but she was well distracted from her own discomfort.

'Is it angina? Do you have a heart condition, Jack?'

'Yeah…kind of. Nothing too serious.'

'You've never had a heart attack?'

'No.'

'How bad is this pain now? Is it the same as your usual angina?'

'It's just kind of gripping me.'

'Whereabouts exactly?' Beth had come around

Willy's head and didn't even notice the spray from his blowhole wetting her hair as she saw Jack's clenched fist against the centre of his chest. 'Is it just in your chest?'

'Goes down my arm a bit, too.'

'Where's your spray?'

'In my pocket, I think.' Jack fumbled with the zip on his jacket. 'Damn it, my hands are so cold they won't work properly.'

'Here, let me.' Beth unzipped the jacket. The small cylinder of GTN spray was easy to find in Jack's back pocket. 'Lift your tongue up,' she directed Jack. Then she sprayed two squirts of the medication. 'You sit down for a minute and rest.'

Beth felt his pulse, which seemed quite steady and strong, but she was alarmed, nonetheless. Even if the pain went away with rest and medication, Jack needed a check-up to determine whether this was angina or a heart attack. And he certainly shouldn't be standing around in the cold, let alone planning to battle the surf to help refloat the whales.

Beth wasn't surprised that Luke noticed what was going on. He was beside them less than a minute after Jack had sat down on the sand.

'What's going on?'

'Jack's got some angina. He's just used his spray.'

'Has that helped, Jack?'

'Not yet. Maybe I should have some more.'

'How are you feeling otherwise?'

'Cold. A bit sick, I guess.'

'Right. We're going to send you into Ocean View to get checked. I'll get a stretcher and we'll get you up to the ambulance at the top of the hill.'

'Don't be daft. I can walk.' Jack glared at Luke. 'There's no way I'm getting carried off this beach in front of all these people.'

'Hmm. How bad is this pain at the moment, Jack? On a scale of one to ten with ten, being the worst.'

'Two.'

Luke chuckled. 'You wouldn't be lying, would you, Jack?'

'I'm not getting carried.'

'Fine. We'll walk as far as the car park. But you'll let me support you and we'll walk very slowly.'

Beth scrambled to her feet again. 'I can help.'

Luke shook his head. 'Look after your whale. I'll find someone to come and take Jack's place for you.'

But it was Luke who came back to her a little while later.

'He looks OK,' he told Beth. 'Another dose of GTN and some oxygen fixed the pain, but I've sent him in for an ECG anyway.' He stooped to collect a half-bucket of water from the moat Beth had just refilled and dribbled it over Willy's back. 'There's no one free to help you just now so I'll stay unless I'm needed somewhere else.'

'Thanks.' Beth could think of nothing else to say and there wasn't much point in dreaming up a conversation, was there? It probably wouldn't be long before someone else wanted Luke's attention.

The silence was awkward and it was Luke who broke it.

'I'm glad you came to Hereford, Beth.'

'Really?' Beth couldn't help sounding surprised. 'That wasn't the impression *I* got. You looked horrified when you saw me in ED.'

'I *was* surprised,' Luke conceded. 'For a second I thought I was seeing a ghost.'

He smiled at Beth as he put the bucket down. Surely it was a trick of the artificial light that made the smile seem to wobble so precariously? But then Luke dipped his head, adding to the impression that something had saddened him immeasurably. He cleared his throat and the new cheeriness in his tone was definitely forced.

'So…what do you think of Hereford so far, anyway?'

'I love it.'

'Yeah? It *is* a great place.'

'I even went out yesterday to look at a couple of houses for sale.'

'No kidding?' Luke almost sounded pleased at the idea that Beth was planning to stay. She smiled and nodded as she stretched out her hand.

'Can I have that bucket? I'll go and get some more water.'

It wasn't far to go to fill the bucket now. A wave broke over Beth's feet and the icy foam reached to her knees. She was shivering by the time she arrived back beside Willy.

'What's he doing?'

'What, that sort of hiccupping? Wasn't he doing that before?'

'No. He's never made a noise like that.' Beth put the bucket down and crouched to peer at the whale's face. 'Are you all right, Willy?'

'Willy?'

'Jack named him.' Beth sighed. 'I hope he's going to be all right.'

'Who? Jack or Willy?'

'Both of them.'

The new silence was quite long enough for Beth to fret about Willy's condition. He probably still needed his mother to feed him. How long would he last without milk? He'd hardly moved for the last hour or more, come to think of it. Maybe one of the Department of Conservation officials would know enough about whales to be able to reassure her. Beth looked up to see if she could spot someone in one of the bright reflecting vests, but all she managed to do was catch sight of the blonde walking away from her group towards the car-parking area. Looking for Luke perhaps?

Beth's gaze automatically shifted. 'Friend of yours, isn't she?'

Luke turned his head swiftly. 'That's Maree.' He nodded. 'Yes, she's a good friend. She's also the sister of my ex-brother-in-law.'

Beth's heart sank like a stone. 'So you *did* get married, then?'

'No, of course I didn't. What on earth makes you say that?'

Beth's mouth opened and then closed again. Why had he said 'of course'? Surely he couldn't mean that if he hadn't married *her* he wouldn't want to marry anyone else. That was ridiculous.

But it *had* sounded like that, hadn't it?

Luke saw her expression and completely misread it. 'Oh…right. In-laws can get complicated, I guess. Maree's brother was married to my sister.' He looked away from Beth. 'I never got married.'

'Why not?' The personal question popped out before Beth even thought of preventing it.

'Never met the right person, I guess.'

'Not for lack of trying, though.' Beth's smile was wry. 'What?'

'You had a different woman on your arm every time I saw you after we broke up, Luke. Right up until you moved to Wellington.'

Even in the shadows Beth could see the way Luke's face tightened angrily. He started pulling back the covering over Willy, which was starting to slip, with jerky movements.

'What did you expect me to do when you cut me out of your life, Beth? Sit and mope? Turn into a monk?'

He seemed to collect himself. 'I was angry,' he said more quietly. 'Angry enough to try and prove that there were women out there who actually thought I *was* good enough for them.'

A wave reached as far as Beth was crouching and the icy water soaked the seat of her jeans. She stood up hurriedly.

'I never thought you weren't good enough, Luke.'

'That was the impression I certainly got.'

Beth had to stoop suddenly to catch the bucket the retreating wave was stealing. The pain in her side grabbed at her but she shook her head, denying the pain as well as Luke's impression.

'We were just too different, that's all. Our values were too different.'

'But we never disagreed about important things like values. We argued about silly things. Like that car I wanted to buy.'

'The BMW?'

'Yeah. What *was* so wrong with that?'

'I told you at the time. I didn't like that it was such a status symbol.'

'It was a good, safe car. That was the reason I wanted it. To keep us safe. To keep *you* safe.'

'So you said.' Beth hated the way she was sounding. She didn't want to argue with Luke. She didn't want to go over such old ground like this. She was cold, tired and miserable, and there still didn't seem to be an end in sight to this ordeal.

'You hated my friends, too.'

Make that both ordeals. The whale rescue *and* Luke's dissection of their break-up.

'Some of them were snobs,' Beth said wearily. 'If you weren't climbing the same social ladder they were, you weren't worth talking to. You fitted *right* in. I had no desire to be part of that set.'

'Then why the hell did you go out with a doctor in the first place?'

'I…I fell in love with you, that's why.' The words almost choked Beth. 'I thought you might be different. A country boy who had worked very hard to get qualified. Someone who came from a background very different from mine. From a *real* family. I thought you might feel the same about the things that really matter.'

'Such as?'

Beth reached out to stroke Willy. 'What I was just talking about,' she said quietly. 'Family.'

Luke groaned. 'Oh, come on! I value my family a hell of lot more than you value yours. I had to practically force you to introduce me. It was months before you would and they only lived across town, and when you did…'

Someone said hello to Luke as they passed and someone else was shouting something about getting ropes to get the first whales ready for shifting, but Luke seemed to hear nothing but his own thoughts. When he spoke again after that pause, he sounded almost bewildered.

'When you did finally take me to meet your parents—that was when things started to go so wrong between us, wasn't it?'

Beth couldn't deny it. Not that she got the chance.

'I'd set out to try and impress your parents for your sake but it backfired on me, didn't it? That was when you decided I wasn't up to scratch. Everything I did was somehow wrong after that. Even my career. You actually tried to talk me out of applying for the job I'd dreamed of getting.'

'And you applied for it anyway.'

They were at the crux of it all now. The final showdown. Beth was surprised to find so much of her anger still there.

That anger had been why she had refused to consider going to Wellington with Luke. That job had represented every doubt she had been having about their future together. When he'd gone ahead and applied for it without even telling her, all those doubts had seemed justified and his determination to accept the position if it had been offered had been what had finally split them irrevocably.

Beth had had the torment of hearing about his successful interviews from others and then watching him work out his notice in Auckland with the air of being about to move onto something much better.

'Of course I did.' Luke was still sounding bewildered. 'I couldn't understand why you were so against it. It was an astonishing position for anyone at my stage to even be considered for.'

'And you wouldn't have got that far if my father hadn't been so impressed by you.'

Luke shook his head. 'I got the job on my own merits. Sure, the director of cardiac surgery in Wellington was an old friend of your father's—'

'His *closest* friend,' Beth cut in.

Luke ignored the interruption. 'And maybe it helped my application get a second glance, but I competed on an even field with a lot of other applicants after that—applicants from all over the world, no less. I deserved that job, Beth. I *earned* it.'

'Of course you did.'

'And what the hell was so wrong with wanting to succeed? I would have had to have changed my entire career and lifestyle to make you happy then. Of course I wasn't going to do that. For anyone. You were right. I was a country boy and I *had* worked bloody hard to get where I was.'

He'd done it now, though, hadn't he? Made a complete U-turn in his career and his lifestyle. Beth wanted so badly to ask why but Luke wanted an answer to his own question. And he deserved one because he seemed genuinely puzzled.

Did Luke really have cause to look back and see her as being critical and destructive without adequate reason? If he did, it wasn't entirely her fault. She'd tried to explain but she herself hadn't really understood how crucial what had been missing from her own life had been. Her objections could have come across as being an inverted snobbery, but Luke hadn't been willing to listen hard enough, had he? He'd overridden her objections with increasing impatience until that last, dreadful fight about the job he had intended to compete for. She had been right to take her own stand then, hadn't she? Or had fear warped her perspective?

Beth could see the operations manager walking towards them but Luke was still clearly waiting for an answer.

'Nothing,' she said finally. 'There's nothing wrong with wanting to succeed.'

'So what was it, then, Beth?' Luke's tone was despairing. 'What did I actually *do* that was so wrong?'

Luke's face seemed to have captured and condensed that whisper of gloom that had been doing the rounds of Boulder Bay beach and the sadness Beth could see brought tears to her eyes.

She bit her lip and dropped her gaze. 'I was scared,' she admitted.

'Scared of what?'

Beth was unwilling to raise her face and look at Luke, but his gentle touch under her chin made hiding impossible.

'What were you so scared of, Beth?'

'That…that I'd chosen someone who was going to end up being just like my father.'

The operations manager was beside Willy now. He looked from Beth to Luke and frowned.

'Not interrupting something, am I?'

'No.' Luke's shoulders slumped a little as he turned away from Beth. 'What's up, Jim? Nobody's injured, are they?'

'No. We've got enough water to start refloating. We're probably more likely to get injuries now than at any other time, so I just wanted to make sure you knew what was happening.'

'I'll come with you.'

Beth watched the two men walk away. Dawn was breaking finally and she could see beyond the pools of artificial light. She could see the rescuers with the whales closer to the water, waves breaking above their knees and the foam up past their waists. They were hanging onto their charges and seemed to be rocking them in the water. It was only now that Beth realised how the noise level had grown as instructions were shouted. Her conversation with Luke had been so intense she had been unaware of the shift into the next phase of the rescue effort.

She wasn't sure she was ready for this. Already physically challenged, that time with Luke had exhausted her emotionally. Had she ever really tried to look at things from Luke's perspective? No wonder he was bitter.

'It's hopeless,' she said aloud. 'Isn't it, Willy?'

The sound from Willy was loud. Louder than any he'd made for hours. The answering cry from whale number fifteen was even louder. Willy wriggled and the ankle deep water was enough to let him move.

'Oh!' Beth grabbed the baby whale behind his fin. 'Don't move yet, Willy. It's all right. Everything's going to be all right.'

Someone Beth didn't know came to help her hold onto Willy, and things seemed to start moving a lot faster on the beach from that point.

A tractor and ropes were being used to move whales into deeper water and the sand and surf boiled with the movement of their huge tails. Beth did as she was told and struggled to keep her footing in the icy water and keep Willy upright and prevent his blowhole being swamped as each new wave surged in. Everywhere people were shouting and moving. Some even swam beside their whales.

And everywhere Beth found herself watching for Luke, but she couldn't find him and somehow that seemed perfectly appropriate.

Luke was gone and there was really no point in dwelling on how much either of them had been to blame for what had happened in the past.

The next wave actually lifted Beth from her feet and Willy moved away from her to tuck himself alongside whale number fifteen.

'Come away,' Beth's new partner told her. 'Don't try and get between them. Look—they're moving.'

All the whales were moving now. They slipped into deeper water and gathered into a single group. Beth joined in the loud cheer that ran through the crowd. Surf splashed her face and mingled with tears that were flowing freely.

Maybe it was finally over.

CHAPTER SEVEN

THE noise was deafening.

Clanging of metal against metal. People shouting. Outboard motors on inflatable boats revving as they patrolled the sea between the human wall and the pod of pilot whales now milling about in deep water. A helicopter overhead with cameras taking footage for a television news broadcast because it was finally light enough to see what was happening clearly.

It would have taken many more decibels, however, to silence the words Luke could hear in his head.

No wonder Beth had run from their relationship.

Luke had never denied being ambitious. He'd even recognised it as being a stumbling block in his relationship with Beth when they'd started arguing about that job in Wellington. Right now he could also see it as arrogance.

His refusal to contemplate compromise had seemed perfectly justifiable at the time. He would have been doing it for them both. His wife—and, eventually, his children—could only have benefited from his success and the more money and power and prestige he could have garnered, the better off they would all have been.

Those ambitions were long gone, of course. Jodie's illness and death had pulled an emotional rug from beneath Luke with enough of a jerk to send them flying. There was no way Beth could be afraid of him evolving into a clone of her father now, surely?

Or was there?

She'd been scared.

Why hadn't he seen that? Of course she'd been scared. But, then, Beth had always been a little nervous of anything new in those days. She'd always tried so hard to get things right and her self-esteem had never been as high as it should have been. And no wonder. How much of her life had she spent trying to win a little attention from her parents?

What had she said? That the only thing she'd ever done that they'd really approved of had been to produce him as a potential son-in-law?

Luke couldn't imagine what it would be like, growing up in an atmosphere where acceptance and love were scarce commodities.

If he'd been thinking about her, rather than the impression he'd been trying to make that night she'd taken him home to meet her parents, he might have recognised her reticence as fear then, too.

She'd been so quiet. Self-effacing. Listening to praise of her siblings with apparent interest. Simply smiling at what Luke had seen as fond teasing about her own choices.

'Beth could have managed medical school, you know, Luke,' Nigel Dawson had said. 'She's bright enough.'

'Just stubborn,' Celia Dawson had added. 'Do you know, Luke, when she was a toddler, she would wear her shoes on the wrong feet all day, rather than admit she'd got it wrong?'

And Nigel had laughed. 'Must have hurt her feet. Maybe she's not so bright after all!'

Luke had winked at Beth to let her know he'd known it hadn't been serious. That he had been laughing with her father, not at *her*. And even then, Luke realised with shame, he would have been flattered at the idea that he would become a man like Nigel Dawson.

Who hadn't heard of the famous surgeon? The man was an arrogant bastard, sure, but everybody knew he was the best. He had a terrible temper and was renowned for throwing things in the OR. He treated his wife, who was invariably his anaesthetist with contempt in the professional arena but he was a brilliant surgeon. The best.

And Luke had been hungry to be the best.

He wouldn't have been anything like Beth's father in any other respect, though. The very thought was shocking.

As shocking as suddenly being underwater when he stepped forward into a hole and found himself out of his depth. He surfaced a second or two later, swimming back to waist-deep water, but he'd lost one of the iron rods he had been striking against each other so there seemed little point in staying where he was.

They would all soon go back to the beach in any case, leaving the boats to patrol the bay and hopefully keep the whales from stranding themselves again. A huge driftwood bonfire had been built so that the volunteers could dry off and warm themselves, and he could smell the sausages and bacon being cooked up for a celebratory breakfast on the gas barbecues. After the long, hard night, a celebration was called for.

But Luke had never felt less like celebrating.

Any anger he'd directed towards Beth for the last few years had suddenly done a neat U-turn and was now directed at himself.

He hadn't had any inkling of Beth's real fear, had he? And he hadn't given an inch. He'd taken all her initially gentle objections as personal criticism and had fought back. He'd even dismissed having it pointed out that their dreams might be taking them in different directions and that could ultimately destroy what they had together. If Beth wanted to be with him, her dreams could just be modified, couldn't they? They would do it his way or they wouldn't do it at all. He'd shouted at her that night. He'd walked away.

He hadn't been so very different from her father at all, really. And if he'd kept going in the same direction, he *would* have ended up being a clone of a man Beth had done her best to avoid claiming any connection with.

Luke had brought his loneliness on himself and in some ways he should thank Beth for kicking him out of her life. If he'd had Beth with him during those grim times with Jodie he would have used that calm strength she had when on familiar territory. Depending on that could have blocked him from learning what he had needed to learn.

What Beth had always known.

Luke paused as he walked clear of the surf. He'd fallen in love with this place because being here had given him peace at a time he'd needed it badly. Now that he was thinking so clearly, he could recognise that peace as an echo of what he'd found with Beth all those years ago.

What he'd lost.

What he would give anything to get back.

He'd lost Beth because of who he had been becoming, but that person bore no relation to the person Luke really was. The person he was now being true to. If Beth knew how much he'd changed—*really* changed—would that make things any different?

Luke badly wanted things to be different.

If nothing else, he had to apologise. Properly. Maybe Beth would be able to forgive him and a friendship might be possible.

Something more than friendship was too big an ask to even contemplate right now, and it would certainly remain an impossibility if the past couldn't be put to rest. Luke had to find Beth. He had to see if she might be at least willing to talk to him.

Volunteers were returning to the beach now but Luke actually waded back into the water as he searched for Beth. The general mood of the crowd was jubilant and Luke could hear laughter and good-natured ribbing as people compared their injuries or discomforts.

'I'm frozen! My hands are blue!'

'I'm *so* tired, I can hardly stand up!'

'I'm sure I've broken this finger. Hurts like hell!'

'I'm *starving*!'

'It was all worth it, though, wasn't it?'

'Sure was, mate. It sure was.'

And there was Beth, struggling back to shore, knocked off her feet by a larger wave and being swept directly towards Luke.

He caught her, helped her to her feet with his arm around her waist, and although they were both standing in only ankle-deep water, he didn't let her go.

He couldn't.

'We've done it, Beth! The whales are safe.'

'I know.' She was smiling. The deep, dark blue eyes that Luke remembered so well were shining with joy. Even tears, perhaps.

'Willy's back out there with his mum, probably having breakfast. Are you happy?'

'It's fantastic. Of course I'm happy.'

But her smile was fading and those *were* tears in her eyes. And Luke just couldn't bear it. He pulled her closer, wrapping his arms around her and holding her shivering body against his own. Pressing his lips into the wet, salty tresses clinging to the top of her head.

Would Beth have turned her face up towards his like that if she hadn't wanted him to kiss her?

Would he have *wanted* to kiss her if he'd known what it would be like?

If he'd known that the lock would disintegrate on that part of his heart that had been so well protected for so long? That all the old feelings would still be there so completely?

Except they hadn't been complete, had they? Because now he could add the painfully gained wisdom of many years. And forgiveness for the way Beth had ended their relationship and—most importantly—he could add the understanding of why it had happened.

They were both in danger of hypothermia as they stood there in the shallows, but Luke couldn't stop kissing Beth. His hands held her close, his lips moved over hers very gently. This wasn't about passion, although that was potentially only a heartbeat away. It was about finding a connection again and asking whether that connection could ever mean enough to make it worth exploring further.

Luke would have been more than happy to stand there holding Beth for as long as it took. However, the rude shock of having someone else losing their balance in the surf and barrelling into them made it totally impossible to keep his hold on her.

And maybe it was just as well because a familiar voice was shouting from the dry sand. Maureen had some extra clothes. Some nice warm track pants and a woollen jersey.

'I've got a towel here, too, Beth. Come and get dried off, for heaven's sake, before you catch your death.'

The towel felt like sandpaper on skin so cold it felt scorched. Beth's fingers had no chance of undoing the zip on her jeans or even pulling a sodden anorak and sweatshirt off over her head.

Luke had gone off towards the fire on hearing his name being shouted, but Maureen was still there, thank goodness, clucking over Beth like a mother hen and helping her into a soft jersey and some track pants long since discarded by one of her grown children.

'There you go, love. Goodness me, you're cold, aren't you? You sound like you're going to break your teeth, shivering that hard.' The older nurse looked more closely at Beth. 'You're awfully pale. Are you all right?'

Beth simply nodded. And smiled. Because she'd never felt more all right in her life. The exhaustion didn't matter. The bruises and scrapes and strains were insignificant. Even that pain in her side was perfectly tolerable.

Luke had *kissed* her.

Really kissed her. And his lips had told her something she could never have guessed. That he still cared.

Maybe there was a way to get past the hurt they had

caused each other. Her fears might have been ground-less, given the fact that the man Luke was today bore so little resemblance to the high-flyer she had known. He might have a new perspective on more than just his career these days. He might understand why she had been afraid and be able to see that it hadn't been because she'd thought he hadn't been 'good enough'.

The kiss had told her something else as well. Beth had realised the physical attraction was still there for her. In spades, given the reaction she'd suffered seeing him in the staff pool.

She knew she still loved him, given the fear that it might have been illness that had made him change his lifestyle so drastically. What she hadn't guessed was that the depth of the love she had once felt for Luke had gained an extra dimension even while she had been so busy trying to deny it.

Ever since she had come to Hereford, Beth had been seeing a version of Luke that had all the good qualities she remembered and none of the bad ones. If he'd set out, in fact, to make himself the perfect man for Beth, he couldn't have done a better job.

Maureen was stuffing Beth's wet clothing into a plastic bag.

'Come near the fire and warm up,' she instructed Beth. 'We'll get you something hot to eat and drink and then I'll take you home. Or have you got your car up the hill as well?'

Beth shook her head. She was still shivering hard enough to make speech difficult.

Maureen sounded puzzled. 'So how did you get here?'

Shaking her head had made trickles of sea water run

down into Beth's eyes and they stung. Beth screwed her eyes shut and used an almost dry corner of the towel to try and blot the moisture from her dripping scalp.

'I walked.'

'Oh?'

Beth looked up at the tone and Maureen smiled at her.

'Don't worry, I won't tell anybody what I saw.'

The blush had the welcome effect of heating Beth up from the inside and the violent shivering abated. 'There's nothing to tell,' she said. 'Not really. We were all happy, that's all.'

Looking over her shoulder out to sea, Beth could just see the dark shapes of whale fins in the distance beneath a hovering helicopter. Looking ahead of her, she could see people crowding the edges of the bonfire and somewhere in that laughing, talking group would be Luke.

Beth was still happy. She felt oddly dizzy as she started the short trek across the sand and she was more than happy to take a seat on one of the boulders. Someone offered her a piping hot bacon sandwich but Beth shook her head.

'I'm really not hungry, thanks. I'll eat later.'

'Coffee? Or tea? How about some hot chocolate?'

'No, thanks. I'm fine, honestly.'

She wasn't shivering any more. The bonfire was extraordinarily hot, in fact. Beth could feel herself starting to perspire and the odd dizzy feeling increased. Maybe she should have something to eat after all, even if she didn't feel like it.

'I think I will go and find a sandwich,' she told Maureen.

Her legs felt like jelly and Beth regretted her decision

to stand up, but Maureen was watching so she made an effort to shake off her physical weakness. She hadn't done any more than anyone else here during the night. It would seem rather pathetic if she collapsed into a heap and fell asleep on the sand now, and Beth did not want to appear pathetic. Not when there was every possibility that Luke could be watching her.

Walking was even more of an effort and Beth's vision blurred slightly. Not enough for her not to recognise Luke, however. Or the blonde woman hanging round his neck like a human pendant as they stood on the edge of the parking area.

Maree appeared to be crying. And Luke looked absolutely terrible. He disentangled himself from the woman's arms and helped her into the passenger seat of his black Jeep. Then he turned back towards the beach.

He saw Beth, she was sure he did, but he stared at her as though he'd never seen her before in his life. For a second he bowed his head, his forehead resting in one hand, as though whatever he was thinking about was unbearable. And then he shook his head, very slowly, and turned to get behind the wheel of the Jeep.

Beth watched the vehicle climb the shingle road up the hill. Away from Boulder Bay beach.

Away from her.

Any joy from the successful rescue mission of the whales and the kiss she had shared with Luke vanished. Its place was filled instantly by sheer misery—both physical and emotional. Fighting back a flood of tears, Beth retraced the few steps she had taken.

'Maureen? I really need to get home and get some sleep before I fall over. Can I take you up on that offer of a lift, please?'

* * *

Sleep hadn't helped one little bit.

The exhausted slumber had lasted until well into the afternoon but Beth woke to find herself feeling extremely unwell.

Her head ached so badly it took a huge effort to get it off the pillow. She was bathed in sweat. Her heart pounded and it felt like there simply wasn't enough air in the room. When she tried to sit and then stand up, Beth became so faint that black spots danced before her eyes and a roaring sound came from nowhere and rushed in to engulf her.

Lying down again, Beth closed her eyes and tried to slow her breathing. This couldn't be the aftermath of exhaustion or even hypothermia. Something was very wrong with her. A bad dose of flu, maybe. She hurt all over. Her joints ached, her whole abdomen was painful and even her skin felt raw.

What time of day was it? Beth rolled onto her side and found her watch on the bedside table. Five o'clock. But it was too light to be 5 a.m. Why was she asleep at 5 p.m.? She was supposed to be at work at 6 p.m., wasn't she?

Panic elbowed space in the confusion and Beth gave up trying to figure it out. She needed some help. Sitting up more carefully this time, she took a few sips of water from the glass beside her watch. Then she picked up her mobile phone, but the screen was blank and the connection for the charger lay on the floor.

Beth tried to insert the little pin into the socket on the back of the phone but it just didn't seem to fit any more and she was horrified to find tears of frustration welling.

This was ridiculous. OK, she wasn't feeling well but

she wasn't a small child and she could look after herself. She didn't need her mother, or anyone else, to come running to care for her. So why did she have this overwhelming urge to be cradled in someone's arms right now? To close her eyes and have someone tell her that everything was going to be all right?

Not just someone.

Luke.

Now Beth did begin to cry. She wanted Luke. She needed him. And he wasn't there. He never would be there because he was with someone else. Maree. The good friend.

Snatches of the jumbled dreams she had just been having returned. There was a beach with impossibly bright diamonds of light dancing in the surf. She and Luke were swimming effortlessly in the clear, green water. They were naked. Twisting and turning like dolphins. Touching. With their lips, their hands…their entire bodies.

But she had clothes on now. Weird clothes. Baggy old track pants and a well-worn jersey. Where had they come from? And why had she been in bed with clothes on, anyway? No wonder she had been sweaty and feeling dreadful.

She was feeling better now. She could stand up. Walk even. It was almost like floating. She could see the door of the motel's office. Why was she here?

Oh, yes. She needed to use the phone. To call Luke and tell him she needed him.

No. Beth stopped and shook her head. That wasn't right. She mustn't do that even if she couldn't quite remember why.

She turned but had no idea what she was supposed

to do next. Easier to just keep floating. Her feet seemed to know where they wanted to go.

A loud noise hurt her ears. Blaring and unpleasant. Beth put her hands over her ears but she could still hear the shouting.

'What the *hell* do you think you're doing, woman? You're in the middle of the *road*.'

The voice was familiar. Beth tried hard and found she could open her eyes. She tried to focus on the owner of the furious voice.

'You *idiot*! I could have *killed* you!'

Luke.

The word was in her head. Her lips moved but no sound came from Beth's mouth.

'Beth?' Luke's face was swimming into view now. 'My God, Beth! What on earth's the matter?'

He looked pale. Tired. And very, very sad. Beth reached out her hand to touch him. To let him know that everything was going to be all right.

But her hand reached into nothingness and that floating sensation had gone. She was being sucked down now. Taken away from Luke and swallowed by the waiting blackness.

Very faintly, she could hear a horrified echo of her name.

'*Beth!*'

CHAPTER EIGHT

NOTHING much could faze Senior Nurse Maureen Skinner.

She'd seen so many and varied emergencies coming through those automatic doors into Ocean View's A and E department she could cope with anything.

Mind you, the car that had come through those very doors recently had been one out of the box, but it hadn't been nearly as alarming as what she was now seeing.

'Luke!' Maureen dropped the file she was holding and ran towards the surgeon. It wasn't until she met him halfway across the tiled reception area that she recognised the face on the limp figure he held in his arms. 'It's *Beth*,' she cried in horror. 'What's happened?'

Luke kept moving towards the resuscitation rooms. 'I found her standing in the middle of the road just outside the car park. She looked totally out of it and then collapsed. Completely unresponsive, and I can't find a radial pulse.'

He laid his burden down on the bed with extraordinary care. It was good clinical practice to tilt Beth's head back and maintain an open airway, but Maureen had never seen a doctor brush loose strands of hair from a patient's face quite like that. Not that this was the time to process such information.

'She's tachypnoeic.' Maureen estimated the rate of Beth's shallow breathing to be well above normal. Close to forty breaths a minute probably. 'I'll get some oxygen on.'

Luke had pushed up the loose sleeve of the old pullover to wrap a blood-pressure cuff around Beth's upper arm. 'Where's Mike?'

'In the small theatre, cleaning out a dog-bite wound.' Maureen slipped an oxygen mask over Beth's face, turned the flow up to ten litres and clipped an oxygen saturation probed over a finger. She could feel the clamminess of Beth's skin and her anxiety level increased sharply as she noticed what looked like a touch of cyanosis darkening the younger nurse's lips. 'I'll get him,' she said tersely.

Luke simply nodded, his gaze fixed on the mercury slipping down inside the sphygmomanometer. 'Unrecordable,' she heard him mutter as she left the area swiftly. 'My God, Beth...what's going on here?'

Maureen returned with Mike seconds later, a house surgeon right behind them, having left Chelsea to complete the dressing and bandaging of the dog-bite wound.

'She's in shock,' Luke informed the emergency department consultant. 'Tachycardic at 130, BP is unrecordable and her oxygen saturation is down to ninety-four per cent.'

'What happened?'

'We don't know.'

'She was out with that whale rescue last night, wasn't she?'

It was Maureen who answered. 'I took her home about seven o'clock this morning. She said she was just very tired but she didn't *look* well.' She picked up a pair of shears. "She was very pale and she had refused anything to eat or drink before we left.' Maureen was cutting away the pullover. 'She hasn't even changed her clothes. These are the dry ones I gave her at the beach.'

'Was she injured in any way?' Mike had his stethoscope on Beth's chest.

'She didn't appear to be when I spoke to her last.' Luke caught Maureen's glance and looked away hurriedly. Did he know she had seen him kissing Beth? That the way they had been clinging to each other had suggested the embrace had been far more significant than the celebratory gesture Beth had made it out to be? 'She was very cold,' Luke said quickly, 'but we all were by then.'

'Equal air entry and no sign of trauma, but she sounds congested.' Mike slung the stethoscope around his neck and reached for a tourniquet. 'Let's get Kelly through for a chest X-ray. This could be a pulmonary embolism.'

It took several seconds for Mike to successfully locate a vein on Beth's arm and he shook his head. 'She's completely shut down. Start another IV on the other side,' he instructed the house surgeon, Seth, 'and get some fluids running. Maureen, I need some blood tubes. A full biochemistry screen to start with and…' Mike frowned. 'Let's do a coagulation profile and cultures as well. She could well be septic. What's her temperature?'

Maureen put the kidney dish full of blood-test tubes on the bed beside Mike. 'I'll find a thermometer.'

'Is she wearing a medical alert bracelet?'

'No.'

The radiographer arrived to take the chest X-ray and the other staff members moved briefly behind the lead-lined screen.

'Does anyone know anything of her medical history?' Mike asked. 'Luke?'

Maureen was holding the tympanic thermometer she hadn't had a chance to use yet. 'She's never said anything but, then, she's only been here for a short time, hasn't she?'

'I knew her years ago, Maureen,' Luke said. 'We worked together in south Auckland. But, no, she didn't appear to have any major health issues then.'

Was he avoiding any eye contact with her, Maureen wondered, or was there another reason why Luke's gaze was fixed so firmly on Beth's still figure on the other side of the heavy glass?

Definitely another reason, she decided on hearing him sigh almost inaudibly and watching the way he raked his hair back from his forehead with stiff fingers. She had never seen Luke look this perturbed before.

His colleague's distress hadn't escaped Mike. 'You shouldn't be here, mate,' he said quietly. 'Go home.'

Luke's head shake was terse. 'Not yet. Not until we know what's going on here.'

'It could take a while.'

'I know that.'

Mike cleared his throat. 'I was sorry to hear about your brother-in-law, Luke. Early this morning, wasn't it?'

'Yeah.' Luke's face settled into even grimmer lines. 'Apparently he was watching for the whales from his window. His mum said that as soon as he saw them heading out to sea, he closed his eyes and just stopped breathing.'

Maureen's heart squeezed. No wonder Luke was looking so perturbed. Even if his connection with Beth was not as significant as she suspected, it would still be too much of a blow to lose another young life right now. She touched Luke's arm with a comforting gesture.

'I saw Maree leaving before the refloating started. Was she there with Kevin at the end?' She could see how hard it was for Luke to swallow.

He nodded grimly. 'I should have been there, too.'

'Maybe you were needed just as much where you were.' Maureen's suggestion was soft and this time Luke's eyes acknowledged what she had seen on the beach, but was the pain she was seeing because of his feelings for Beth? Maybe involving himself to this degree here was simply a distraction from the agony of losing his best friend and feeling that he had let Kevin down by not being there at the end.

Mike must have sensed something of what Maureen was wondering. 'How well did you know Beth, Luke?'

His words gave nothing away. 'Well enough, I guess.'

Mike was moving in response to a signal from the X-ray technician. 'Then do stay,' he urged. 'A familiar face could be just what she needs.'

Luke was still there an hour later when the anaesthetist was called down to intubate Beth and put her onto a ventilator after the oxygen levels in her blood dropped to dangerously low levels.

Luke's counterpart, Ocean View's other general surgeon, Len Armstrong, was there as well. 'She's not in the best shape for surgery yet, Mike.'

'We can't afford to wait,' Mike decided grimly. 'The dopamine infusion has at least brought her blood pressure up a bit and we're getting some urine output, thanks to the diuretics.' He glanced towards the ultra-sound machine he had been using a short time ago to examine Beth's now rigid abdomen. 'We've started aggressive antibiotic cover but the longer that perforated appendix is in there, the harder this is going to get.'

'Right.' Len turned away. 'I'll head upstairs and get scrubbed, then.'

'Has someone got in touch with her family yet?'

'I can do that,' Maureen offered.

'No. I will.' Luke looked grey with fatigue now. 'And then I'll come upstairs.'

'Only as a spectator, mate.' Len's smile was clearly intended to cover a concern for Luke's state of mind. 'I'm the one who's on call here, remember.'

'I just need to be there.' Luke pushed himself away from his position and paused for a second beside Beth. Reaching out, he laid the back of his fingers, very gently and very briefly, on Beth's cheek.

Maureen saw the glance that passed between Mike and Len. Puzzled and questioning initially and then accepting. They had even less of an idea of what might be happening here than she did but they knew that some connection existed between Luke and this very unexpected and now critically ill patient. And that connection had just markedly increased the urgency and tension of this case.

Seven p.m. on a Friday night.

The address was still the same but what was the chance of finding Beth's parents at home? Luke punched new numbers into the phone, having just hung up from talking to Directory Service.

Nigel and Celia Dawson were highly likely to be out at a social gathering of some description—if they were even in the country. They were just as likely to be somewhere else, attending one of the numerous international conferences that needed a star line-up of speakers.

Then again, the Dawsons had to be well into their sixties by now. Maybe they had retired and were embracing a quieter lifestyle. Sure enough, the phone call was answered on its third ring by a gruff but familiar voice.

'Yes?'

'Mr Dawson?'

'Who wants to know?'

'This is Luke Savage, Mr Dawson. I'm calling from Ocean View hospital in Hereford.'

'Savage? That name rings a bell. Do I know you?'

'I'm a surgeon, sir.' Old habits died hard, Luke thought wryly. Like respect for an eminent specialist. 'I met you several years ago when I was going out with your daughter.'

'Ah…' Nigel sounded thoughtful. Or possibly disinterested.

'It's Beth I'm calling about.'

'Who?'

'Beth.' Being so tired made it easier to keep his tone even. 'Your daughter,' he added wryly. 'I thought you should know that she's—'

'Savage,' the older man interrupted. 'Weren't you the young chap thinking of a career in cardiothoracic?'

'Yes. I wanted to tell you that—'

'And *where* did you say you were calling from again?'

'Hereford.'

'Where the hell is Hereford? England?'

'No. Marlborough. South Island, New Zealand.'

'Never heard of a cardiothoracic unit down that way.'

'There isn't one. I'm a general surgeon.'

'Oh?' The monosyllable carried a distinct edge of contempt. 'I seem to remember you as a lad who was going somewhere, Savage. You reminded me of myself, in fact.'

'I've got to exactly where I wanted to go, sir.' So Beth hadn't been the only one to pick the unsettling similarity. Luke tried to push away the weariness threatening to allow any further distraction. He didn't care what Nigel Dawson thought of him any more and he certainly wasn't about to start defending his career choices. 'Right now I'm heading up to Theatre where your daughter is about to undergo surgery.'

'What the hell is she doing in…Hereford, did you say?'

'She's been working in the emergency department here for a couple of weeks now.'

'First I've heard of it. What's she having surgery for?'

'A perforated appendix. Beth is critically ill right now, Mr Dawson. She's in septic shock and is on life support.'

'Well, she shouldn't be in a tin-pot hospital in the middle of nowhere, then, should she? Get a damned helicopter and ship her out, son. What's the closest tertiary centre? Dunedin? Wellington?'

'Beth couldn't possibly be moved right now. She's far too ill.'

'It should have been done earlier, then, shouldn't it? Who's in charge down there?'

Luke ignored the bluster. 'We're doing everything that can be done,' he said firmly. 'And we have excellent intensive care facilities available.'

He could hear another voice in the background. A
female voice, calling for Nigel. Maybe Beth's mother
would be more appropriately concerned with her child's
state of health rather than her whereabouts or finding
someone to blame for her condition.

'You should be able to get a commercial flight to
Nelson,' Luke said into the silent line. 'It'll take about
ninety minutes by road from there. Otherwise there are
small airlines operating out of Hereford airport.'

'I can't go to Hereford.' Nigel sounded astonished at
the suggestion. 'I'm about to take a flight to Rome. I'm
the keynote speaker at a conference that's due to kick
off in less than twenty-four hours. The taxi's here now,
as a matter of fact.' The voice became fainter, as though
the phone was being held at arm's length. 'I'll be there
in a second, darling.'

'Perhaps I could speak to Beth's mother?'

'There's no time for that. We're going to miss our
flight at this rate.'

A wash of something like desperation hit Luke and
he closed his eyes for a moment. Her parents were
strangers, Beth had said. She had never known the kind
of love Luke had been blessed with from family and
friends. Could Luke ever hope to make up for that?
Would she trust him enough to let him try?

'Look. I'll pass the message on.' Nigel's tone was
dismissive. 'I suppose I'd better try and let that young
man know what's going on as well. Or is he down
there already?'

Luke's eyes opened smartly. 'Who?'

'Her fiancé, of course. Brent what's-his-name.
Ranger or Granger, maybe.'

The heaviness engulfing Luke became unbearable.

It was an effort to draw in a deep breath. 'I was under the impression that Beth's engagement had ended before she came to Hereford.'

'News to me. Mind you, I haven't actually spoken to the girl since she stormed out of here that day. When was it, two years ago? I hear any news secondhand, through her brother or that Brent chap. She's the worst of the lot as far as keeping in touch.'

'I wonder why?' Luke muttered.

'Pardon?'

Luke cleared his throat, suddenly more than ready to end this conversation. 'Please, do pass the message on to anyone who may be concerned about Beth's welfare.' He wasn't worried that his criticism might not be veiled well enough to avoid causing Nigel offence. He might find out whether the man actually cared a fig for his daughter. 'Rest assured that we will be taking the best possible care of her in the meantime.'

'Good lad.' Beth's father sounded relieved at the opportunity to abdicate any responsibility. 'You do that.'

Not that there was much that Luke could do except to be there for Beth. The effort that took, however, made it possibly the hardest thing he'd ever done in his life.

Never before had he felt like this in any operating room. Every unusual blip on the cardiac monitor—and there were plenty as the anaesthetist struggled to keep Beth's blood pressure at a level that could sustain life—made his own heart skip a beat and then start racing in alarm. He had to look away from the initial incision because it made him feel physically sick. This was Beth's flesh being cut.

Luke's professional side noted how well Len was

dealing with the surgery. The caecum was identified. The appendicular artery was secured, clamped, divided and ligated. The appendix mesentery was divided. The nasty, swollen and infected appendix was clamped with artery forceps and removed with care to avoid it spilling any more of its poison into the surrounding tissues and blood vessels.

But that damage had already occurred and it was no less nerve-racking for Luke to be beside Beth's bed after she was transferred to the intensive care unit. Her blood pressure was still marginal and the function of vital organs like her kidneys and lungs was severely compromised. Central venous pressures were being monitored by a Swan-Ganz catheter, which had been threaded right through her heart to rest in a section of her pulmonary artery and Beth was kept intubated and ventilated.

The consultant now in charge of her care was more than a little concerned about her renal function, but Luke was only half listening to the professional interchanges as he sat there holding Beth's hand and talking quietly to her whenever her medical attendants were occupied with the machinery rather than with Beth's body.

'I'm here, Beth,' he whispered, time after time. 'You're going to be all right.'

Barbara came up to the unit just after midnight, and Luke left Beth's side to meet his mother on the other side of the double swing doors.

'What are doing here, Mum? Is everything all right?'

'I was worried about you, love,' Barbara told her son. 'Nobody would tell my anything except that you were keeping a sick friend company.'

'I'm sorry,' Luke said sincerely. 'I should have called. I should be with you at the Winsomes' but I lost track of time.'

'It's all right.'

'I can't leave Beth just yet. It's still touch and go.'

'Of course you can't, darling.' Barbara squeezed his hand.

How could she know? Luke wondered. How he *really* felt about Beth when he hadn't known himself until faced with the prospect of losing her like this? He'd lost track of time all right, because minute by minute his feelings for this woman were growing stronger. He *wasn't* going to lose her.

He *couldn't*.

'How is she?'

'Not good. She waited too long to get help. The infection has really taken hold. We'll just have to hope the antibiotics kick in soon.'

'But she *is* going to make it, isn't she?'

'I hope so, Mum.' For just a split second Luke lost control and fear tangled its icy fingers around his heart just a shade more tightly. Had he found Beth again and been given the possibility of making things right just in time to lose her for ever?

Was it somehow *his* fault that he lost the people he loved the most?

'This is *not* your fault, Luke,' Barbara said softly. 'None of it. Not Jodie or Kevin. Or Beth. And Beth's going to be fine, I'm sure of it.'

Luke couldn't go there. Not right now. 'How's Maree?' he asked. 'And Joan?'

'Coping. John brought his flight from Sydney forward and he arrived early this evening. Kevin's come back from the funeral parlour. We're going to keep him at home until the funeral on Monday. The vicar's been to visit. All the arrangements are made now.' Barbara's smile wobbled. 'Kevin and Jodie are finally going to be together again.'

'Did you remember the tape I made? The music Kev wanted?'

'It's all done. Joan said to say thank you.'

'I'll get in to see everybody just as soon as I can.'

'They understand why you're here, Luke. It's OK.'

'Do they?' Luke ran a hand over his eyes. 'I'm not sure I understand myself. I haven't seen Beth for six years. How can I feel like this when she's only been back in my life for a matter of days?'

'I think you always felt like this.' Barbara smiled. 'You just did a very good job of hiding it. From everyone, yourself included.'

'So how come you guessed?'

'I'm your mother. It's my job to know about stuff like that.' Barbara had to reach up a long way to stroke her son's hair. 'You need some sleep. And you need to stay with Beth. She needs you more than Kevin does right now. And who knows? Maybe he's here somewhere, practising a bit of guardian angel stuff.'

Luke hoped so. He managed to return his mother's smile but the moment she turned and stepped into the lift his face crumpled and he had to scrub the burning pain of tears from his eyes with both palms.

But maybe his mother was right. His thoughts turned often enough to his friend in the quiet moments of the rest of that night, and the feeling of Kevin's presence was strong enough to make him smile at times. He wished he could have told his mate that he understood now why Kevin had had no fear of dying. Why life without his soul mate had been so grey.

Luke thought he'd found peace in his own life in the last few years. Happiness, even. But it was so clear now what was still missing, and the only person who would be able to fill that gap was lying on the hospital bed beside him with tubes and wires snaking from her body, attaching her to machines that were, hopefully, improving her chances for survival.

And those chances needed to improve, dammit. Right now they were probably about fifty-fifty and the odds were terrifying. Luke covered one of the small, cool hands on the bed with both of his own.

'I'm here, Beth,' he whispered yet again. 'You're going to be all right.'

It seemed so wrong that it was Luke receiving the visitors at the intensive care unit and not Beth.

Barbara returned early on Saturday morning with a change of clothes and some shaving gear for Luke, and later on Maree came.

'How's Beth doing? Has there been any change?'

'Not for the better. They're trying some different drugs to see if they can improve her kidney function and she's...well, we're waiting for the results on another set of bloods to see if she needs a transfusion.'

'Why would she need that?'

'There's a thing you can get from septic shock called DIC—disseminated intravascular coagulation. Basically means that the mechanisms that control clotting pack up so the patient can bleed to death.'

'But you don't know that she's got that?'

'No.' Luke ran his hands through his hair. 'But some

of the puncture sites seem to be bleeding more than they should be.'

Maree sat on one of the chairs in the relatives' room and patted the one beside her. Luke obediently sat down.

'Does Beth know how much you care about her, Luke?'

He thought of the kiss they'd shared in the surf and started to nod cautiously, but then he remembered the conversation when they had been looking after Willy.

He could hear the angry echo of the list of criticisms he had harboured for so long and the nod turned into a miserable sideways movement. Maybe Beth had responded to that kiss simply because it had represented closure of some sort.

'I don't know, Maree,' he sighed. 'Probably not.'

'Then you'll have to tell her,' Maree said calmly. 'It's possible she can hear you, isn't it? Even if she's unconscious?'

'It's possible,' Luke agreed. It was possible that Beth was aware of the touch of his hand on hers as well. Maybe not in any real sense, more like the way he could feel Kevin's presence. His mate might only be there in his memory but the presence was real enough to matter. Enough to make a difference.

Luke squeezed his eyes tightly shut but couldn't prevent an errant tear from escaping. 'I'm going to miss your big brother,' he told Maree. 'So much.'

Maree just nodded, silent for a minute as she struggled with her own tears. Then her lips twisted into a crooked smile.

'Kev approved, you know.'

'Of what?'

'You and Beth. I told him that you were looking pretty cosy as you looked after that baby whale together. He gave me a thumbs-up sign and I couldn't stop him talking for ages after that.'

'What did he say?'

'Oh, that she was the one for you. I'm supposed to tell you to do the job properly this time or you'll be the first person he's going to haunt.'

Luke groaned. 'What are we going to do without him?'

'I know what you're going to do.' Maree hugged Luke fiercely as she took her leave. 'You're going to go in there and tell Beth how you feel. Tell her just how much she's got to live for.'

It took an hour to get a private enough moment. Luke had to wait until Beth's consultant had been and gone yet again, having reviewed all available results, adjusted some of the settings on the life-support machinery and ordered another raft of tests. Then the blood-sample technician came and went and finally Beth's nurse, Claire, frowned at the chart.

'Why haven't they been in for that chest X-ray yet? I'd better go and ring. Can you watch Beth for a minute, Luke?'

'Sure.'

He could do more than watch. He took her hand, carefully avoiding the IV port and line taped to the top but managing to twine her fingers with his own. He leaned very close so that his lips brushed her ear.

'I love you, Beth Dawson,' he whispered. 'I didn't realise till now but I never *stopped* loving you.'

He had to pause long enough to swallow the lump in his throat and take a deep breath.

'I always will love you,' he continued softly. 'I hope you

can hear me but it doesn't really matter if you can't because you're going to get better and I'm not letting you leave here until you understand just how much I do love you.'

Was it his imagination or did Luke feel a tiny flutter from the fingers laced with his own?

It was probably just that he had to let go of Beth's hand hurriedly as her nurse returned. He was providing enough food for gossip by being here as an old friend for Beth. How much worse would it be if everyone knew how much he was really suffering?

And it was hardly a professional look for those who didn't know him. Like the man wearing a gown and mask to accompany the nurse to Beth's bedside.

'Beth's got a visitor, Luke.' She turned to the newcomer. 'Brent, this is Luke Savage. He's one of our surgeons and a friend of Beth's.'

Luke stood up slowly. Claire hadn't finished her introductions yet. She hesitated just a fraction, as though wondering how Luke was going to react. She was, no doubt, curious about his relationship with Beth as everybody else probably was.

'This is Brent Granger, Luke,' she said finally. She bit her lip but her tone was calm. Admirably professional. 'Beth's fiancé.'

CHAPTER NINE

STAYING positive was going to be a big ask.

Not on Beth's account, thank goodness. The improved results on all the most recent tests filtered back as Ocean View's ICU consultant arrived to speak to Beth's visitor in the privacy of his office. There was no real reason for Luke to be present other than his delivery of the chest X-ray, which he clipped onto the viewing box and then perused intently.

The consultant shook hands with Brent. 'You're a cardiologist, I hear?'

'That's correct. I'm in private practice at The Sisters of Mercy in Auckland.'

'And you're Beth Dawson's fiancé?'

'Also correct.'

The short silence echoed with the unspoken question of why Beth had come to Hereford if that was the case, but the consultant let go of any curiosity quickly.

'Beth's been a very sick young lady,' he told Brent, 'and I wouldn't say we're entirely out of the woods yet, but we can at least be confident that she's going to pull through this.' He smiled as he scanned the biochemistry report he was holding. 'As you've seen, renal function is almost back to normal and we're definitely onto the right antibiotics.'

'Which are?' Dr Brent Granger's tone was clipped. He could have been speaking to a junior houseman rather than an experienced specialist.

'We're using clindamycin with gentamycin and clox-acillin. We wanted to make sure we were covering any anaerobic organisms as well, of course.'

He glanced up at the X-ray illuminated on the wall. 'Looking good, isn't it, Luke?'

'Hell of a lot better than last night's. Lung fields are almost completely clear.'

'The fluid balance was tricky,' the consultant confessed. 'We had a bit of a juggling act to improve perfusion without aggravating her pulmonary oedema.'

'You've been combining an albumin infusion with diuretic therapy, I suppose?' Brent's gaze left the X-ray and settled on Luke for a split second. Then he, too, was seemingly dismissed as irrelevant.

'Yes. I'm happy enough with her pressures to take out the Swan-Ganz catheter now and we should be able to get her off the ventilator later today. Then it should just be a matter of keeping a close eye on her for a few days.'

'There's no reason she couldn't be transferred within the next day or two, then, is there?' Brent reached to pick up Beth's notes from the desk and began to flick through them.

'I'd prefer to keep her in Intensive Care for another twenty-four hours or so.' The consultant smiled at Brent. 'Then we'll certainly transfer her into our medical ward.'

'No.' Brent shook his head. 'I'm talking about taking

her *home*. To Auckland.' The cardiologist certainly had a charming smile but its effect was lost on Luke.

'Beth may prefer to stay in Hereford,' he suggested mildly. 'She might not have been here very long but she's made a lot of friends.'

The flick of a dark eyebrow was subtle but the message was clear. *Like you?* Luke held the eye contact steadily, refusing to be intimidated. *Yes*, he said silently. *Like me.*

'I think discussion about discharge could wait a while yet,' the consultant said.

'Of course.' Brent seemed happy to co-operate. 'The plane I chartered will be here until I have to head back on Monday. That should give us plenty of time.'

'And you have somewhere to stay in Hereford? The hospital has a good relationship with one of the closest motels if—'

Brent waved his hand. 'No need. My secretary made arrangements for me to stay at the Millhouse. I'm hoping that will be quite satisfactory.'

'It should be, at the kind of prices they charge.' Beth's consultant looked amused. 'In any case, perhaps Luke could show you the facilities we have at Ocean View. Beth's going to be asleep for a while yet. You'll need to know where to find our cafeteria and so on. Luke? Have you got the time?'

'Sure.'

The need to get away from the hospital and spend time with his own family and friends would be satisfied very soon. Luke could hardly continue his vigil at Beth's bedside playing musical chairs with her fiancé, could he? He might even try and fit in a walk on a beach because some breathing space was definitely called for here.

It was impossible not to feel alarmed at the turn of

events. Luke was quite sure that Beth had been sincere when she had told him her engagement was over, but Brent Granger was clearly a man who was used to getting what he wanted and why would he be here now if he had no interest in reclaiming Beth's affections?

As if he guessed the direction of Luke's thoughts, Brent caught his gaze as soon as they had left the consultant's office.

'I expect you're a bit curious.'

Luke tilted his head fractionally. 'Beth did mention a fiancé. An *ex*-fiancé.'

Brent's confident gaze didn't flicker at all. 'Beth needed a little time to think about things. I'm sure she'll be delighted that I've made the effort to rush to her sickbed.'

It was certainly a lot more than her family had done. The thought that Beth might well be delighted at such an obvious expression of concern was not a pleasant one. If Brent had been looking for a way back into Beth's life, he'd just been handed a golden opportunity here.

Maybe Luke's challenge, given the short time since Beth's arrival in Hereford, was not going to be to convince Beth that he had changed. Or that his love for her was strong enough to give them a future together.

He hadn't expected to be faced with competition from someone who had already come a step closer to marrying Beth than Luke had. Her relationship with Brent was so much more recent as well. Could six-year-old memories measure up in comparison? Could *he* measure up? Luke flicked another glance towards the man walking alongside him as he led Brent towards the lift at the end of the corridor.

Physically, Brent wasn't dissimilar to himself, being just as tall and just as dark. He was older than Luke by a good ten years but if anything that probably gave him an advantage in terms of confidence and sophistication. Not being on duty, Luke was currently wearing the comfortable old jeans and shirt that Barbara had brought in for him. Brent was wearing a pinstripe suit and carrying a briefcase, which made him look far more the part of a consultant than Luke did.

More worrying, however, was the sense of power the man exuded, which could only come from being very successful and probably very wealthy. Combined with that charming smile and an attractive British accent that hinted at a northern upbringing rather than public school, Brent could have stepped from the pages of some romantic novel. It wasn't hard to believe that Beth had accepted a proposal from the cardiologist. What Luke would dearly like to know at that moment was why she'd felt such an urge to escape.

He pushed the button to summon the lift. 'So, how did you meet Beth?'

'I worked in the same London hospital as her older brother, David. When I decided on a sabbatical on this side of the world, I wanted to meet his family.'

'So you're on sabbatical?' A temporary stay, then. This was good.

'It was supposed to only be for a year but Beth wasn't all that happy about the idea of living in London.' Brent's smile at Luke would have been engaging if it wasn't for the underlying hint of triumph. 'I've got a little surprise for her now, though. I've purchased a property and signed a contract for permanent employment at Mercy.'

The lift doors slid shut, trapping the two men in a rather too confined space for Luke's liking. He could smell the aftershave Brent was wearing. It was as inoffensive and subtle as many aspects of this man's personality, so why did they all add up to a force that felt like a human bulldozer?

Because there was steel beneath the silk, that's why. That glance Luke had received when the 'little surprise' had been revealed had carried a disturbing undertone. Brent Granger expected things to go his way. And they would, because he was very charming and generous about setting the process into place. And because he wasn't going to tolerate anything else.

Had Beth simply been railroaded into an engagement? Flattened by charm and confidence and sheer power? If so, what chance would she have of harbouring whatever doubts had caused her to break off the engagement in the first place? Right now, she would be weak enough to be incredibly vulnerable.

Luke didn't like the knot forming in his gut. Beth needed protection but what right did he have to offer it? Brent had stepped into the space he had willingly taken from the moment Beth had collapsed. Maybe neither of them had a right to assume that role, but Luke couldn't compete on the same playing field as Brent. He wouldn't even want to try exerting that kind of control.

Brent cleared his throat into the silence. 'Is there a florist of some kind based in the hospital?'

'The gift shop has some flowers available. We'll go past it on the way to the cafeteria.'

'Good. Beth's parents have asked me to organise something on their behalf.'

Luke kept his tone carefully bland. 'It's a shame they couldn't be here themselves.'

'Mmm.' Brent shook his head sadly. 'Beth's been estranged from her family for some time. In fact, that was how I met her. I was visiting a patient in the hospital she worked in and Nigel and Celia asked me to deliver a birthday gift that was too fragile to post.' He stepped out of the lift ahead of Luke.

'Beth refused to accept it. She actually got rather upset and I ended up taking her out to dinner.'

Luke could feel the tension building in his jaw. This man had started using Beth's vulnerability to his advantage right from the beginning, hadn't he? What woman wouldn't respond to someone taking charge at a time like this?

'She was such a lonely little thing,' Brent added fondly. 'Despite all her friends. What Beth really needs in her life is a family and I'm hoping things between her and her parents will improve. I expect once they've got grandchildren nearby, they'll appreciate what they've been missing.'

Grandchildren?

Brent's children?

An image of Beth holding a baby in her arms sprang into Luke's mind. And then one of her watching over toddlers playing. Brent was right, of course. Beth deserved the security and love a family of her own could provide.

It was what Luke needed in his own life.

He wanted to be a part of that picture he could see so vividly. He wanted to share the joy that a child of their own could bring.

They were passing the gift shop now and Brent paused to look at the display of merchandise.

'The bunches of flowers are a bit on the small side, aren't they? I'll have to buy the lot, I think.'

'Flowers aren't allowed in ICU.'

'They'll be ready for her transfer into the ward, then, won't they?' Brent's smile was satisfied. 'I'll get one of those teddy bears, too. Beth will love that.'

Obviously there was not going to be any shortage of gifts showered on Beth in the foreseeable future. And how long would that be? Brent had a very clear vision of permanence, it seemed, and Beth was a key player. Would his generosity make her any more receptive to his plans?

And was there anything Luke could do about it if it did?

He couldn't stay in the hospital all day. He was needed elsewhere. But leaving Beth to wake up and find Brent beside her was more than unsettling.

The cardiologist seemed to sense how torn Luke felt. He held out his hand and Luke was forced to shake it.

'Thanks for your help, old chap,' Brent said politely, 'but don't let me hold you up any longer. I'll be just fine now.'

Luke's feet felt like lead as he headed towards the car park.

It would be Brent sitting beside Beth when she finally opened her eyes later today. Even if she had been aware of a loving presence beside her for the last twenty-four hours, she couldn't possibly be certain of his identity. He himself may have been giving her messages of love that Brent would now be credited with, and there was nothing Luke could do about it without potentially making a fool of himself.

He had never felt so powerless in his life but he was just too damned tired to try and think of a way of redressing the situation.

The needs of others were calling him away from a selfish focus in any case. Kevin's family…his own family…needed comfort.

Still being tired wasn't enough to stop Luke rising early to go into the hospital on Sunday morning. The Millhouse was well away from Ocean View and surely Brent wouldn't have time to have breakfast and go visiting by 7 a.m. Finding Beth alone with her nurse was a good start.

'How is she, Claire?'

'Doing great. She's been off the ventilator since 4 p.m. yesterday and everything's looking good. They'll be shifting her into the ward today, I would think.'

'Has she been awake much?'

'She stirred a little at odd times overnight, but hasn't said anything yet.'

The knot in Luke's gut unravelled just a little. She hadn't spoken to Brent yet, then. He still had a chance to say something. To at least tell her that he loved her.

Claire smiled and Luke was sure she had guessed his thoughts. 'I'll leave you two alone for a minute,' she said. 'I'll just be in the office if you need me.'

Luke sat down on the chair and took Beth's hand. The IV line was still there but he could see the fluids were drug-free. It was just normal saline, keeping the line open and her fluid levels up. Her skin felt warm but not febrile, and while Beth's face was still very pale she looked a whole lot better.

Luke squeezed her hand. 'I told you everything would be all right, didn't I?' he asked softly. 'I'm still here, Beth.' He swallowed hard. 'And I still love you, sweetheart.'

His thumb traced slow circles on Beth's palm and it

was no imagined flicker he felt in her fingers this time. They curled around his softly. A weak grip but definitely a grip. Luke watched her face intently as her eyelashes fluttered and the corners of her lips twitched into a tiny smile. She was surfacing from a deep sleep. Any moment now she would open her eyes and when they managed to focus, it would be Luke she saw sitting so close.

The return of Claire was unexpected and she sounded as apologetic as she looked.

'I'm so sorry, Luke, but ED is wondering if you could go down?'

'I'm not on call, Claire.'

'They know that. There's someone there who's asking for you.'

'Who?' Beth's eyelashes were still again, black against her pale cheeks. Her fingers lay still also. Had the buzz of conversation been enough to send her back into exhausted slumber?

'Joan Winsome? Is she a relative?'

'What's Joan doing in Emergency?'

'Her daughter's been brought in by ambulance. Apparently she collapsed at home this morning.'

'Oh…*God*!' There was no help for it. Luke felt like he was tearing off part of his own flesh as he extracted his hand from Beth's and stood up. He walked towards the exit of the intensive care unit without looking back. He couldn't afford to look back or it would be far too hard to keep moving.

The dream was fading.

Beth tried to hang onto it but instead of being cradled in Luke's arms she was running now. Her bare feet sank into the warmth of dry sand and the soothing rhythm of breaking surf became fainter. Where was Luke? All she could see were the smooth, dark shapes of boulders. She tried to call because she could hear her name, but her lips refused to co-operate and her feet were slowing. She was just too tired to keep running.

'Beth! Wake up, darling.'

Luke! Beth made a huge effort to surface from the dream. Luke was calling her. He was calling her *darling*. Her eyelids felt too heavy to open and there was pain. Her head thumped and there was a sharper pain in her belly. But the effort was worthwhile because Luke was there. She could see the outline of his dark head. She just needed to blink so that her vision would be clear enough to see those beloved dark eyes.

Except…they were the wrong colour. Green instead of grey. Weird. And the voice wasn't quite right either. Beth blinked again.

'Brent…what are *you* doing here?'

'I came to look after you, darling.'

'But…where…?' Where's Luke? Beth wanted to cry, but her head swam with sudden confusion and she had to close her eyes again to try and sort it out. 'Where am I?'

'You're in the intensive care unit, Beth. You had a perforated appendix and a nasty dose of septicaemia. But don't worry, you're on the mend now. Everything's going to be all right.'

Of course everything was going to be all right. Luke had been saying that all along.

Or had he? Had Beth simply been dreaming all along? Creating some sort of fantasy fuelled by fever and drugs?

'You're well enough to go to the ward now,' Brent told her. 'And I've arranged to take you back to Auckland tomorrow so I can take care of you while you recuperate.'

'No…' Beth pulled her eyes open again. 'You can't…do that.'

'I already have.' Brent patted her hand. 'There'll be a few people annoyed at not getting their slot for elective angioplasty and another couple that'll have to wait for their permanent pacemakers, but I didn't want to rush you, darling. We've scheduled take off for 2 p.m. tomorrow.'

Beth tried to shake her head but it was easier to lie still. She didn't want to go home. She *was* home. Surely she could stay where she was until she felt better?

'It's kind of you, Brent, but I don't want to go back to Auckland. And I don't need looking after. I can take care of myself.'

'Not just yet you can't. I want to look after you, Beth. You know that.'

'Brent…' Beth summoned the last of her strength. 'I've already told you I can't marry you. I don't love you. I don't understand why you're here.'

'I'm not doing this to blackmail you in some way, Beth. I just want you to get better. We'll talk about other things later.'

'No.' But Beth knew she had no hope of winning this so she gave up for the moment and left her eyes shut. She wanted Brent to go away, but if he wasn't going to then she would just escape and go back to that dream. She welcomed the reprieve of unconsciousness enfolding her. This time she would find Luke.

'I don't believe it. It *can't* be true.'

'Why not?' Luke was smiling. 'It makes sense, doesn't it? You've been feeling off colour ever since you got here and Mum's been very worried about you not eating.'

'But why now? We're not on the list for more IVF for another three months. It's *been* three months since the last attempt. I've been trying to get pregnant for *years*, Luke. Why would happen all by itself and why now?'

'Maybe it's the best time it could have happened, Maree. It's going to give us all something special to celebrate.'

'I can't tell anybody. Not till after the funeral. It wouldn't be fair.'

'On whom?' Luke's smile was poignant now. 'Kevin? He'd be as happy as you should be about this, love. On your mum? She's just lost her son. Don't you think the biggest comfort she could have would be that her first grandchild is on the way?'

'A grandson.' Maree's husband, John, was holding his wife's hand tightly and still had a rather bemused smile on his face. 'I can't believe we could see him so clearly on that scan.'

'Joan's still in the waiting room,' Luke reminded them. 'Can I tell her she can come in now?'

'You tell her, John.'

'Shall I tell her the news?'

Maree nodded. 'Luke's right. And Kev was the world's worst at keeping secrets, wasn't he?'

'And then we'll get you home,' Luke said firmly. 'You need rest and some fluids to deal with your dehydration. It's no wonder you fainted, with your blood pressure dropping like that when you stand up.'

Maree was reaching for the leather handbag John had left on her bed when he'd gone to find his mother-in-law. She fished inside.

'Can you get rid of these for me, please, Luke?'

Luke accepted the packet of cigarettes. 'Have you got those patches with you?'

'Don't need them,' Maree said decisively. 'This is the best incentive I could ever get for stopping smoking, and I'm not going to use anything that might be harmful to the baby.'

Luke smiled as he squashed the half-full packet and dropped it into the rubbish bin. 'Good for you, love. You'll do it, too, I know you will.'

He excused himself before Joan came to see Maree in her cubicle. The small family needed time by themselves to absorb the startling discovery that a new member was expected. And he needed time to go back and see if Beth was awake yet.

Luke.

Beth blinked at the man beside her bed. How could she have been wrong…again? She had been so sure Luke was there. That wonderful feeling of comfort had come back. Of safety.

Of knowing she was exactly where she wanted to be.

But it was still Brent sitting beside her bed.

'You're awake again, darling. How are you feeling?'

'Better. Thirsty.'

'There's iced water. Here, let me help you sit up a bit.' Brent slid his arm behind Beth. 'And look—you've got a visitor.'

Beth looked. Luke was standing at the foot of her bed, her chart in his hand, and suddenly it felt terribly wrong to have Brent's arm supporting her as she sat up enough to be able to swallow safely.

'Luke…'

'Hi.' His smile was so much better in real life than it

had been in her dreams. So was the look in those dark, grey eyes. It was just the kind of look Beth most wanted to see. The one that made her feel as though she was the most important thing in the world. The most loved even.

'You're looking a lot better,' Luke said. 'That's great.'

Beth couldn't look away from him. But why was he reading her chart? Had he come to visit as a doctor rather than anything personal? 'Was it you that took my appendix out, Luke?'

'No.' Luke smiled. 'They wouldn't have let me do that.'

'Why not?'

'I…wasn't on call. And we were all a bit tired after that rescue effort.'

'What rescue effort?' Brent was looking from Beth to Luke and back again, and he didn't look happy.

'The whales,' Beth told him. Her gaze flew back to Luke. 'Were they all right? They didn't try and strand themselves again, did they?'

'They hung around for a while but they haven't been seen since Friday afternoon.'

'Here, darling. Drink this.'

Beth obediently took a sip from the glass of water Brent was holding to her lips, but she shook her head when he tried again. She didn't want another drink. She didn't want Brent to be here at all, in fact. She didn't want anybody to be here except Luke, but that was just wishful thinking. The numbers around her bed increased further as Claire and another nurse arrived.

'We're all set for you in the ward,' she told Beth. 'We were just waiting for you to wake up. I'm sorry, but we don't have any private rooms available. You'll be sharing with Mrs Daniels, who's just had her gall bladder out.'

'Oh.' The sound was pure disappointment. No chance of any private time with Luke in the ward either, then. Beth still felt weak enough for the frustration to bring tears to her eyes.

'It's only for tonight,' Brent said soothingly. 'It's just as well I'm going to whisk you back tomorrow to that luxury suite at the Mercy to finish recuperating.'

Beth blinked back the tears. To her dismay her voice was slower to get into line and her words came out sounding far less sure than she had intended. 'I said I didn't want to go to Auckland, Brent.'

'I don't think she should go either,' Luke said.

Beth caught her breath. Maybe they didn't need any private time. If Luke felt anything like she did then he could just say something right now. If she had been sure about how *he* felt, *she* would have said something already.

But Luke's words were disappointingly professional. 'Beth's not nearly well enough to travel yet.'

'That's why I've organised a medivac flight,' Brent said coolly. 'And hired a medical escort.' He smiled at Beth. 'I've even organised some tickets so that your friend can pop over from Melbourne for a visit. You'd like to see Neroli, wouldn't you?'

'Of course, but—'

'No "buts",' Brent said firmly. 'It's all organised. Your job is to just rest and get better.'

Say something, Luke, Beth pleaded silently. Claire was releasing the brakes on her bed. Things were happening too fast and she didn't have the strength to resist by herself.

'You should see all the flowers in your room,' Claire said. 'Mrs Daniels says it's like being in the middle of a florist's shop. All the nurses are dead jealous.'

Had Luke sent flowers? Beth tried to thank him with her eyes but to her dismay he dropped his gaze and stood back to make room for the bed.

Brent was smiling broadly. 'It's no more than you deserve, darling. And it's only the beginning.'

Beth lost sight of Luke as her bed was wheeled away.

It felt far more like an end than any beginning.

CHAPTER TEN

THE music made people smile through their tears.

'Trust Kev,' someone murmured. 'Who else would try and make us laugh at his own funeral?'

'It was a beautiful service. Are you staying for the lunch?'

'Of course.' The speaker waved at the person walking towards them. 'Yoo-hoo, Luke! You're coming back to the house, aren't you?'

Luke paused near the elderly relatives. 'I'll be there within an hour or so. I've got someone I really need to pop in and see at the hospital on my way.'

'Ah!' Kevin's aunt nodded gravely. 'I hope your patients know how lucky they are to have you, Luke.'

The corner of Luke's mouth curled into a brief, lopsided smile. 'That's what I intend to find out, actually.'

Aunty Pru looked puzzled but Luke moved on. Joan waved to him from a distance, knowing his mission, and Maree used the hand that wasn't holding tightly to John's to give him an encouraging thumbs-up signal.

The Jeep rumbled into life but Luke gripped the steering-wheel and stayed motionless for several seconds while he took a very deep breath.

The service *had* been beautiful. A celebration of life…and love. Luke's twin sister, Jodie, had been spoken of almost as much as Kevin, and the presence of the young lovers had felt real enough to add a sharp poignancy to the powerful mix of emotions.

It had been real enough for Luke to actually hear things Kevin had said so recently.

That not many people were lucky enough to find their soul mate.

That Beth had been the only one who had ever made Luke consider marriage.

That Beth still cared.

That Luke could find a way to flip that coin if he wanted to.

That Beth was *the* one for him.

And that he'd better do the job properly this time.

A lot better than he had managed yesterday. That visit to Beth had turned to custard the moment he'd neared her bed to find himself the subject of an intense stare from Brent Granger.

You're not welcome here, the message had shouted. *Don't even think about it, because you've already lost.*

The man's confidence had been palpable, and Luke had had the horrible conviction that he'd already had a significant conversation with Beth and arrangements had been made which were entirely to Brent's satisfaction.

Luke had covered that awkward stretch of time as Beth stirred into consciousness by focussing on her patient chart and quietly rejoicing at how quickly she was recovering.

He'd wanted to say he wouldn't have been allowed to be the one to remove her appendix because no surgeon should operate on someone they were so emotionally involved with—but how could he have? Brent had had his arm possessively around Beth, and he'd been holding that glass to her lips as though she was a sick child incapable of helping herself.

What would Brent Granger have said if he'd seen Beth sorting out violent gang members in a chaotic emergency department only a matter of days ago?

Not that she was really capable of standing up for herself at the moment. Beth hadn't sounded at all sure when she'd said she didn't want Brent to take her back to Auckland. And she had certainly sounded disappointed at the news she would be sharing a room with Mrs Daniels. That luxury private suite at Brent's hospital might be very welcome.

Luke's objection to her travelling, when he'd been trying to buy just a little extra time, had been so easily overridden. Brent had had all the answers. All the incentives. Of course Beth would want to see her best friend. Luke could be quite sure that Brent's generosity wouldn't stretch to flying Neroli to Hereford for a visit instead of Auckland.

And Beth had thought Luke had sent the flowers. Even if he *had* arranged a bouquet, it could hardly have competed with Brent cleaning out the supplies of the whole gift shop. He hadn't followed Beth's bed as she was taken to see the floral display in the ward. Brent's triumphant expression had placed the final brick in the wall Luke had been confronting.

He'd left the hospital feeling as if Brent *had* won, but with the prospect of his best friend's funeral only hours away the only way Luke had been able to cope with the thought of losing Beth was to put it aside in the hope of finding the head space to deal with it later.

Putting it off, however, was the worst thing he could have done. What did it matter if he made a fool of himself? Put his heart on the line and had it rejected… again. Sure, it would hurt, but he couldn't feel any worse than he did at the moment.

At least he would *know*, one way or the other. And knowledge had the power to circumvent endless agonising. Maybe it was high time Luke took a leaf out of Brent Granger's book and made an attempt to turn the tide in the direction *he* so badly wanted it to go.

By the time the final hymn in Kevin's service had been sung, Luke had known with absolute conviction that he couldn't just hand Brent victory. It would be wrong for Beth. Brent Granger was the epitome of what Luke had once aspired to be himself. Successful. Powerful. In control of his own life and the lives of those who shared it. Beth deserved better than that.

Having just been reminded so vividly how precious relationships were, Luke was not going to lose the woman he loved so much. Not if there was any chance at all that she might feel the same way, and there *had* to be a chance.

She wouldn't have been so snaky about raking up the past that time he'd suggested coffee if he didn't still have an effect on her.

He'd definitely felt something touch his soul that time their eyes had met after he'd commented on those awful rabbit slippers.

And why had she been coming to his house when she'd discovered the stranded whales if she hadn't had the intention of spending time alone with him?

She had *kissed* him, for God's sake. And that connection had taken Luke back in time. Right back to when he'd first realised he had fallen in love with Beth. Before he'd met her parents. Before he'd rushed blindly into imposing his own vision of a future that had so missed the real point of being together.

He knew where he had gone so wrong. He knew that he was on the right track now. Somehow he had to let Beth know.

It was nearly one p.m. by the time Luke arrived at Ocean View hospital. He drove straight past the car park and headed for the main entrance. What time had Brent planned to leave today?

Please… The word became a mantra.

Please let Beth still be here. Please let her want to listen.

Luke wouldn't be surprised if she wasn't keen to listen. He might deserve to be shut out. He should have been more sure of himself. And of Beth. Kevin had been so right. She was the *one*. Luke could feel the connection so strongly that Beth would surely believe him, even if she wasn't so sure herself, and any belief would give them the chance to try again. And this time Luke knew they couldn't possibly go wrong because he simply wouldn't allow them to.

Luke braked sharply. The fire escape stairs! The fastest way to Beth's ward would not be through the main entrance and along the corridors. He would go in through the emergency department and take the little-used concrete staircase that emerged near the ward kitchen.

There was an ambulance parked in the bay, but the paramedic, Sally, didn't seem to mind when Luke eased the Jeep in beside it.

'Have you come to say goodbye to Beth? You're cutting it a bit fine, aren't you, Luke?'

'I…ah…' Just how far did the grapevine extend at Ocean View?

Sally grinned. 'I'm on a bit of overtime for transport duties. I've got Beth in the back, ready to take her to the airport. Dr Granger has just gone back to the ward for the paperwork we forgot.'

Luke leapt onto the loading platform. Then he stepped around the open back door of the ambulance.

'*Beth!*' His breath rushed out in a huge sigh of relief. 'Thank goodness! For a horrible moment back there I thought you might have gone already.'

She was propped up on one of the stretchers, with pillows behind her and a blanket covering her legs. About to leave. There was too much to try and say, and not nearly enough time. Beth's eyes looked too big and dark for her pale face, but she was smiling.

'Hi, Luke.'

Luke swallowed hard. How long did he have before Brent returned with the paperwork? Minutes? Seconds? He stepped into the back of the ambulance.

'Beth, I really need to talk to you.'

Luke's sense of desperation increased as he felt the movement of someone else approaching the ambulance.

Beth's face was so much thinner, and there were dark shadows under her eyes. She looked so tired. It would hardly be fair for him and Brent to stand in front of her, competing for the right to take care of her.

But it was a female voice he could hear.

'Excuse me. I need to get in here.'

'That's Susie,' Beth told Luke. 'She's the medivac nurse who's coming with me.'

There was still too much to say, and the clock was ticking mercilessly.

'Do you *want* to go away to Auckland with Brent?'

The question came out more abruptly than Luke had intended. Was that why Beth hesitated? Why the head shake was slow enough to give the impression of uncertainty? Luke deliberately softened his tone.

'Would *you* like to talk, Beth?'

Beth nodded, but her gaze slid sideways as the medivac nurse made another effort to climb into the ambulance.

'Sorry, Susie.' Luke turned, but instead of stepping aside to make room he put his hands on the nurse's shoulders and gently but firmly turned her around. 'I need a few minutes to talk to Beth,' he explained kindly. Then he pulled the back doors closed. 'In private,' he added.

Behind Susie's astonished face was the backdrop of the automatic doors into the emergency department. Beyond them, Luke could see past the main desk to another set of doors though which a man was walking. A confident figure that Luke could recognise far too easily even from this distance.

Suddenly, and for the first time in far too long, Luke felt in total control.

Strong. Invincible, even.

Three steps took him to the front of the ambulance and he opened the driver's door.

'Sally?'

'What's up, Luke?'

'Could you do me a small favour?'

'What is it?'

'Hop in and drive us round the block, or something. I really need to talk to Beth.'

Sally caught Luke's urgency with commendable swiftness. She had a wide grin on her face as she swung herself into the driver's seat and turned the key to fire the throaty rumble of a powerful engine.

'Where to, sir?'

'Anywhere.' Luke could see out of the small square windows in the back doors. He could see Brent Granger's pace slow and a look of bemusement changing very rapidly to one of annoyance. 'Just don't spare the horses.'

'Gotcha.'

The ambulance moved away from the loading platform with a jerk that had Luke sitting down rather hurriedly on the spare stretcher. Beth was staring at him wide-eyed.

'What *are* you doing, Luke?'

'Taking you somewhere we can talk,' Luke said with a smile. 'By ourselves.'

The bumps in the road were enough to jar Beth's healing abdominal incision, but the pain in no way burst the bubble of joy inside her.

She had come so close to giving up on Luke. After she had been moved to the ward yesterday, and events had seemed so out of her control, Beth had decided she had no choice but to go with the flow.

Her last hope had been that Luke would come back and say something before she left. Anything—as long as it gave her a reason to plan her return when she was well again. She had waited all last night and all of this morning to no avail.

But he *had* come. And it hadn't been just to say goodbye. Beth had seen the expression on his face when he saw her in the back of the ambulance, and had heard that heartfelt sigh of relief.

She still felt unbelievably weak, and her own relief, on top of the misery that Luke's continuing absence had fed, was overwhelming.

So overwhelming it was too much to try and take in. A new hope was dawning rapidly for Beth. The hope that maybe what Luke wanted to talk about was what she most wanted to hear. That he would say something to convince her that this time it *would* work. That she could offer all the love she still had for Luke—and more—and it wouldn't end in heartbreak.

Of course she didn't want to go away with Brent, and of course she wanted to talk. But Beth wanted to listen even more just at the moment, so she stayed silent, simply watching Luke as the ambulance rolled through the streets of Hereford.

Luke was peering at Beth a little anxiously. 'Are you feeling all right?'

'A bit tired,' Beth admitted. She smiled. 'Must be all the excitement of being abducted.'

The ambulance was slowing. Sally turned her head.

'I'll park up here for a while,' she told her passengers. 'I'm going to go and sit in the sun and give the hospital a call to tell them what's happening. They might be getting a bit anxious at the airport.'

'Thanks, Sally.' Luke looked out of the window and grinned. 'Good choice.'

'Where are we?' Beth asked.

'Lookout Point,' Luke responded. 'If I open the back doors you'll be able to see down over the main beach.'

Sally jumped out of the vehicle. 'Take your time,' she called in through the window. 'I'm going for a walk. Cellphone reception is much better up at Lover's Leap.'

'And how would you know that, Sally?'

'Lover's Leap?' Beth could hear an echo of Luke's teasing tone in her own words.

Luke smiled. 'It's the local park-up spot where teenagers bring their dates.'

'Ohhh…'

He was giving her *that* look. The one that said she was the only thing of any importance in the universe as far as he was concerned. The one that meant he wanted to kiss her, and would do so if she gave him the slightest indication that his touch would be welcome.

Beth's mouth felt suddenly dry and her heart skipped a beat. She wasn't ready. Not quite yet.

'You…said you wanted to talk to me?'

Luke nodded. He leaned across the gap between the stretchers and took hold of Beth's hand. Then he caught her gaze and held onto that as well. His mouth opened, then closed, and then he cleared his throat. His smile was embarrassed.

'I've got so much to say I don't know where to start.'

'Try the beginning,' Beth suggested helpfully.

'Do you want the long version or the short version?'

'How short is the short version?'

'Very short.' Any hint of amusement died from Luke's face and his features settled into lines serious enough to alarm Beth.

'Three words, Beth,' Luke said softly. 'I love you.'

She could feel the words just as clearly as she could hear them. They enfolded her in warmth and the bubble of joy inside her was over-full. Little bits of that joy were leaking into Beth's bloodstream and sending the most delicious tingles into every cell in her body.

'I love you, too, Luke,' she whispered.

His face moved closer, his lips on their way to claim

hers, but Beth raised her hand and pressed her fingertips against the softness of those lips.

'Now I want to hear the long version.'

Luke groaned softly.

'Please?'

Beth could see Luke collect himself and had to hide a smile of secret joy that it was clearly so difficult to rein in the desire to kiss her. She wanted that kiss just as much, but she knew that it would be worth waiting for. That it would be even better when she knew the answers to those questions that had provided such a puzzle. Luke nodded slowly, as though he understood and agreed. Trapping Beth's hand more firmly between both of his own, he sighed softly.

'I've been at a funeral this morning, Beth.'

'Oh…that's awful!' How selfish had *she* been, then—deciding that if Luke cared about her he would have been there at the hospital with her? Beth searched Luke's face anxiously. 'Was it someone close?'

Luke nodded solemnly. 'As close as it's possible to get.'

Beth could feel her eyes widening. A *woman*? But Luke's smile was reassuring.

'Without sex, of course.' He squeezed her hand. 'Kev was my best mate. We grew up together. He and my twin sister, Jodie, fell in love at high school and they got married a year after I left Auckland. When I was living in Wellington after…after…'

After his relationship with Beth had been well over. Beth returned the hand-squeeze and nodded, to encourage Luke to continue and not get sidetracked by ground they didn't need to revisit.

'They were so in love,' Luke said wistfully. 'And they

had so much to look forward to. They spent three months backpacking in Europe for a honeymoon, and then Jodie got a job at Ocean View as a physiotherapist and Kev's electronics business started taking off. They were talking about trying for a baby just before their first anniversary, and then...Jodie got sick.'

Luke closed his eyes for a second, and when he spoke again it seemed that his professional tone was a deliberate attempt to keep still raw emotions in check.

'It was leukaemia. Acute myeloid. For a long time we thought we could beat it. I was a near perfect match as a donor—thanks to being a twin, I guess—so I had bone marrow harvested twice. I would have done it again. Hell, I would have donated any part of my body that might have done the trick, but we didn't get the chance to try again. She died four years ago, when she was only thirty-two years old.'

'Oh...*Luke*!' Beth ignored the tears she could feel trickling down her cheeks. 'I'm *so* sorry.'

'Yeah.' Luke's attempt at a smile was heart-wrenching. 'I know. Anyway, I spent as much time as I could with her over that year she was sick. My job suffered with all the time I took off, but it didn't seem to matter. I just didn't really care any more. About anything. It felt like the bottom had dropped out of my world. My parents and Kev were just as devastated, of course, so I kept coming back to spend time with them. We helped each other get through it, and about six months later I realised I didn't want to be anywhere else. I took only as much time as I needed to complete my training as a general surgeon and then I moved to Hereford and bought that property on the beach.'

'I wish I could have been here to help.'

'It's just as well you weren't.'

'Why do you say that?'

'Because if I'd had you to lean on I would have found it so much easier to cope. I would have built a bridge of some kind and just kept going the same way I had been. You *were* right, you know. About why you doubted our future together.'

Beth started to protest, but Luke shook his head gently.

'I *would* have ended up like your father,' he admitted sadly. 'I was on the same track back then, wasn't I? And I never saw it. When Jodie died I learned something. Something I suspect you knew all along.' His smile was gentle enough to bring fresh tears to Beth's eyes.

'What was that?'

'It doesn't matter how much money or prestige or power you get in life,' Luke said quietly. 'None of it matters a damn when you're dying. The only thing that counts then is being with the people you love. The people that love you.'

Luke's gaze told Beth that *she* was the person he loved. His smile was another caress.

'They say life is for living, don't they? But I reckon they're wrong. Life is for *loving*. And the more you give, the more you get back.'

Beth could only nod. No words could have made it past that lump in her throat.

'Sometimes,' Luke continued, 'if you're lucky, you find a love that's so powerful it outshines any other. Kev found that kind of love with Jodie.' Luke's voice caught and thickened. 'He told me he wasn't afraid to die, Beth. And I can understand that now.'

'You can? But he was so young! It's tragic.'

Luke nodded slowly. He let go of Beth and moved to kneel on the narrow floor space between the stretchers. Then he reached up to cradle her face in his hands.

'A love like that is so strong that even dying isn't something to be afraid of. It's living without that person that causes the fear.' A tiny tremor was transmitted from the hands holding Beth's face. 'And that, Elizabeth Dawson, is the kind of love I have for you.' Luke's thumbs moved to brush the last traces of tears from Beth's cheeks and then to follow the outline of her lips. 'I'm afraid to live without you.'

'I'm not going anywhere, Luke,' Beth whispered. 'I feel exactly the same way about you.'

'You don't have to say that.' Luke drew Beth into his arms and held her so close she could feel every beat of his heart. He kissed her softly. 'You're still nowhere near well. You're vulnerable right now. I just had to make sure you knew how *I* felt before you went away anywhere.'

'I'm not going anywhere,' Beth repeated. 'And I might be a bit wobbly, but that doesn't change how I feel, Luke. I knew the first day I saw you again that I could never leave. That…that I still loved you.'

Luke kissed her again. 'How did you know that?'

'You told me I was brilliant.' The memory of that spark and her attempts to talk herself out of giving it any significance made Beth smile. 'I realised that what you thought was more important than anything anyone else could ever think.'

'What about…?' Luke's hesitation was palpable. 'Brent?'

'I don't love Brent. He knows that. Yes, I dated him for a while. I was very lonely after Neroli had gone to Australia. I was down enough to start thinking I would never find what I really wanted in life and that I might miss out completely if I couldn't compromise in some way. It wasn't until Brent talked me into accepting his proposal that I realised that what had attracted me to him were only the things that reminded me of you. It would have been dishonest to let it go any further and I told him that.' Beth shook her head. 'We never got as far as getting a ring or anything. I explained why we could never be married. I haven't even spoken to him since, so it was a real shock when he turned up here.'

'He's not going to be happy.'

'I wasn't going back to Auckland because he wanted me to,' Beth assured Luke. 'I knew I wasn't going to be much use for anything around here for a while, and I didn't feel I knew anyone well enough to ask for help.'

'You know my mum,' Luke said. 'She's very good at looking after things. Gardens, people…whales. You name it. And she's the best cook I know.'

'I couldn't land myself on your mum. Especially right now, after a family funeral. Maybe I could just stay in hospital for a bit longer.'

'And then go back to that motel? I don't think so.' Luke kissed Beth again, rather more firmly this time. 'When you're well enough to leave hospital, you're coming home with me. Forget my mother. *I'm* going to be the one looking after you from now on.' The anxious look that followed such a firm declaration was almost comical. 'That is, if that's what *you* want, hon.'

Beth snuggled back into Luke's embrace. 'It's what I want,' she confirmed happily. 'Can you cook?'

'Of course I can cook.'

'You don't sound very sure about that.'

'Doesn't matter, anyway. My mum makes the best casseroles you've ever tasted. She can give me some lessons.'

Beth pulled back far enough to beam at Luke. 'That's great!'

'Why? Can't you cook, either?'

'Of course I can cook. It's just that I've got this really nice casserole dish that needs christening.'

Luke shook his head in fond bewilderment. Then he kissed Beth yet again, before levering himself to his feet. He slid open the narrow side window above Beth's stretcher.

'Sally? We should probably head back now. We've got a few things we need to get organised.'

'For cooking?' Beth was feeling weary enough to simply let the joy of being with Luke be the only thought she needed to hold.

'No,' Luke said sternly. 'For spending the rest of our lives together.'

'Oh…' Beth smiled up at the man she loved. 'What are we waiting for, then?'

'Just this.'

Luke bent his head and kissed her…again.

THE EMERGENCY DOCTOR'S DAUGHTER

BY
LUCY CLARK

Lucy Clark began writing romance in her early teens and immediately knew she'd found her 'calling' in life. After working as a secretary in a busy teaching hospital, she turned her hand to writing medical romance. She currently lives in South Australia, with her husband and two children. Lucy largely credits her writing success to the support of her husband, family and friends.

To Karen—thanks for always being there for
a lovely long phone chat.
They're much appreciated.

CHAPTER ONE

'OK. THAT's finished.' Amelia stood and closed the case notes she'd just finished writing up. 'I'm going to have my lunch-break now,' she told Rosie Jefferson, the accident and emergency triage sister.

'Go.' Rosie nodded. 'Tina's still around, isn't she?'

'Cubicle three, I think.'

'All right. See you back here in half an hour, if not before,' Rosie teased, and Amelia groaned.

'I order no emergencies for at least the next hour or two.'

'Is that when your shift ends?'

'About then.' Amelia smiled and headed out of the A and E department towards the cafeteria, pleased she'd managed to remember the way rather than getting lost as she'd done the other day. The cafeteria was busy, crowded with the usual mix of hospital staff, patients and their families. Glenelg General Hospital wasn't as big as some of the ones she'd worked in over the years and was definitely smaller than her hospital back home in England where she'd undertaken most of her medical training. Still, it was a nice place to work, close to the beach and the apartment she'd found for her three-month stint here.

Amelia browsed the food on offer, picking up a yoghurt and trying to decide what else she wanted to eat. An elderly woman brushed passed her, jostling her shoulder, and the tub of yoghurt slipped out of her hand.

'Sorry,' the woman called, and Amelia saw the frantic look on her face before she bent to pick up the—thankfully—unopened tub. She rubbed her shoulder and continued looking, deciding on a not-too-heavy salad roll.

Making her way back towards the A and E tearoom, Amelia heard a strange noise and stopped, listening carefully. It sounded as though someone was crying. She turned and headed down a small side corridor, which had a flickering fluorescent light casting a start-stop eerie glow.

The crying came again and she homed in on the sound, stunned to find a little girl pressed up against the wall, hugging her knees as she watched Amelia's approach with wide, scared eyes. The poor darling looked to be no more than about three years old. She had a mass of blonde ringlets which framed her heart-shaped face.

'Hello, sweetheart,' Amelia said softly. 'Are you all right?' She crossed to the girl's side and crouched down. 'Are you all right, darling? Are you hurt?'

The little girl's bottom lip began to wobble again and Amelia's heart wrenched at the sight. 'Oh, don't cry, sweetheart. It's all right. I'm a doctor.' She pointed to the stethoscope around her neck as proof. 'I can help you.'

'You doctor?' the girl hiccuped.

'That's right. Are you hurt?'

'No.'

'Are you lost?'

She nodded.

'You poor darling. You must be so scared. Would you like me to help you find your mummy?'

'Daddy,' the girl said.

'You've lost your daddy?'

The bottom lip wobbled again and a few more tears were squeezed out as she nodded.

'It's all right, it's all right.' Amelia reassured her as best she could. 'Why don't we find your daddy?' She shifted her food into one hand and held out the other to the scared girl. 'We can find him together, all right?'

The girl nodded again and put her hand into Amelia's. 'My name is Amelia. Can you say that? It's a bit of a tricky name.'

'Meel-ya,' the girl repeated.

'Well. It's obviously not tricky for you, is it? You must be very clever.'

'Yes.' The tears had dried but the way she was gripping Amelia's hand showed she was still a little scared.

'What's your name?' Amelia asked.

'*Lan*-da.'

'My, that's a pretty name and perfect for a pretty girl. Come on. Let's go see if we can find your daddy. Is Daddy sick?'

'No.'

'Daddy's not sick in a bed?'

'No.'

'Is he hurt?'

'Yes. He hurt his hand.'

'Oh. Poor Daddy.'

'I pix.'

Amelia smiled, not sure she understood what the child was saying. If her father had a sore hand, chances were he was in A and E, being treated. They walked back the way Amelia had come but a moment later a man burst from the stairwell, his gaze frantic as he searched around him.

He was wearing a pair of tatty denim jeans, a grey T-shirt with a casual checked shirt over the top, hanging open. He had work boots on, boots which were splattered with paint, as, she realised, were his clothes. He also had an old bandage around his hand, most of which was hanging off.

He turned to look at them and as Amelia watched the instant relief wash over his face, she knew they'd found Landa's father. The child broke free from Amelia and ran towards him.

'Daddy!' she squealed, and he scooped her up into his arms, hugging her so tight Amelia wondered whether the child could breathe.

'Where did you go? Daddy was so worried,' he said, and although his words were chastising, it didn't outweigh the total happiness Amelia could see. She waited a moment then the painter came towards her, shifting his daughter to his hip, holding her with his bandaged hand. It obviously didn't hurt that much.

'Thank you. Thank you so much,' he said, and smiled. The action changed his face, softening his features which had looked so drawn and anxious before. His brown eyes, so rich and deep, were filled with relief and thanks. He raked his free hand through his thick dark hair, his lips slowly starting to relax from the smile.

He had a perfectly straight nose and a slightly chiselled jaw. His shoulders were broad, giving him an air of confidence that fitted him perfectly. In fact, he seemed to radiate that rebel-without-a-cause attitude that said he didn't care what anyone thought of him.

The world seemed to have slowed down as Amelia took in the rest of his features at a glance and she began to feel a strange stirring in the pit of her stomach such as she'd never experienced before. The stirring of anticipation and excitement, that something amazing was about to happen, which was ridiculous because this man was not only a patient here in the hospital but also probably had a wife and, no doubt, a gaggle of other little blonde-haired girls at home.

He definitely had a quality about him, one that had brought out a reaction in her—something totally foreign to her. She'd never been instantly attracted to anyone in her life.

He held out his hand and she accepted it, working hard at ignoring the way the simplest touch of his skin against hers was enough to ignite her entire body. She withdrew her hand instantly.

'Thank you,' he said again. 'She got away from my housekeeper.' He looked at his daughter. 'Mrs D.'s been very worried, pumpkin. She's been looking every where for you.' Landa merely buried her face into his neck and his grip on her tightened.

'I think she's had quite a fright herself,' Amelia said. 'But everyone's reunited now. I don't think she'll go wandering off any time soon.' She smiled and sucked in a breath, knowing she should move, that she should leave, but for some reason her legs simply weren't obeying the commands her brain was sending.

'Let's hope not,' the painter said, and tickled his daughter's tummy. The child lifted her head, a little giggle escaping her lips. Both adults smiled and Amelia felt envy fill her heart at the way both man and child seemed to be so well connected. It was a pretty picture.

'Well…I'd better get back.'

The painter nodded, then pointed to the food in her hand. 'Sorry for taking up your break time.'

She waved his words away. 'I'm used to it.' She looked to Landa. 'You take care now, and keep Daddy safe.'

'Yes.' The girl nodded enthusiastically, ringlets bobbing every which way. 'Bye, Meel-ya.'

'Goodbye, sweetheart.' Amelia held out her hand and Landa took it, giving it a shake before letting go. As Amelia walked away she swallowed over the lump that had risen in her throat, wondering how she was ever going to get her salad roll past it. How she'd love to have a child like Landa. That man and his wife were lucky indeed.

She sighed and shook her head as she entered the tearoom, switching on the television in need of something to distract her thoughts.

'Terrific. A medical drama,' she groaned, but nevertheless sat to watch it. Twenty minutes later, she'd had enough of the absolute tripe on the screen, as a perfectly made-up patient in high heels and a very low-cut hospital gown fluttered her eyelids at a very handsome young doctor, who was apparently the only one who could save her life.

'Oh, for crying out loud!' Amelia looked around for something to throw at the television but, apart from throwing her spoon, which she was still using to eat her yoghurt, she couldn't find anything. The door to the A and E tearoom opened and her fellow registrar, Tina, walked in.

'Are you watching that hospital soap garbage again?' She laughed at Amelia as she headed to the urn, helping herself to coffee.

'Obviously. I need something to give a lift to my day.'

'And this is it? Honey, you're getting in a rut.'

'I know.' Amelia's pager sounded and then Tina's did as well. They checked the details and found they were both the same.

'There's something to get you out of the rut,' Tina grumbled, and flicked her blonde hair over her shoulder, looking longingly at her drink. 'Why do they insist on paging both of us?' They'd been at work since early yesterday evening thanks to a big emergency and now, being close to three o'clock on a Friday afternoon, they were more than ready to leave.

'I'll take it,' Amelia said. 'You have your break. I'll page you if you're needed.' She stood and headed over to the television.

'You may as well leave it on,' Tina said, as she sat in the seat Amelia had just vacated. 'I need something to laugh at. Plus, those actors are pure eye-candy.'

Amelia shrugged. 'I guess so.' She put her yoghurt container in the bin and washed her spoon.

'Oh, come on. You can't tell me that you don't think these guys are cute?'

Amelia smiled and glanced at the TV once more. 'Maybe.' And for some reason the painter she'd met almost half an hour ago came to mind. He was pure eye-candy and she'd definitely been attracted. Of course, she would only admit it to Tina, the two having been friends for many years. Amelia had first met Tina when the blonde registrar had come to England for part of her A and E training course and it had been Tina who, in turn, had helped set up Amelia's last three-month placement here at Glenelg General Hospital in Adelaide, Australia. Amelia had spent the previous three months in Brisbane and once she'd finished her stint here, she could return to the UK, take her final exams and become a qualified A and E specialist.

That was definitely something to look forward to and she didn't need any distractions, especially not where good-looking men were concerned. The actors on the tube posed no threat to her well-ordered life and that was the way she planned to keep it. All of those characters were just figments of some writer's imagination, with the wardrobe and make-up departments making the actors look the attractive studs they were supposed to be. Until she'd met Landa's father, Amelia had wondered whether there really were men that attractive out there in the world...*real* men who weren't models or actors and who wanted to stay home and play happy families.

Mr Sexy-Painter had certainly been that type and she was glad he'd been able to change her perception. Was he still in A and E? Had Tina fixed up his hand? She decided not to say anything as it was much better for her to put him right out of her mind.

'I'll see you later, Tina. Oh, by the way, are we still on for our girls' day tomorrow?'

'Yes. If we meet at ten, we can do some shopping and then have lunch.'

'*Really* looking forward to it.' She smiled before heading to the accident and emergency nurses' station. 'Hi, Rosie, I'm here,' she said to the triage sister. 'What's up?'

'Ambulance is just about to arrive. Two teenagers were found in the back of a school room, unconscious.'

'Drugs?

'Alcohol. Vodka.'

Amelia sighed and shook her head. 'Ages?'

Rosie consulted her notes. 'Both sixteen.'

'OK. We'll set up for gastric lavage in both treatment rooms one and two.'

'Sure. Oh, and, Amelia, the other reason I paged you?'

'Yes?' Amelia sighed, wondering what else she had

to deal with. She just wanted to get these kids sorted out and go home.

Rosie leaned in closer and said in a stage whisper, 'I heard you haven't met Harrison yet.'

'The A and E director? No. He was away when I arrived last week.'

'Well, he's back.'

'What? Where?' Amelia looked around, searching for a new, unfamiliar face. There was a woman with a stethoscope around her neck, talking to a mother who was holding a toddler. Wrong gender—obviously not him.

Then her gaze fell on Mr Sexy-Painter himself. A tingle began in her toes and started to work its way up to engulf her entire body. He was still here and he still had that tatty bandage on his hand. His daughter, however, wasn't with him as he spoke to one of the nurses. The nurse in question was smiling brightly.

'That's him.' Rosie angled her head. 'The one with the bandaged hand.'

Amelia's eyebrows shot up in surprise. 'The se—um…painter?' She couldn't believe she'd almost said sexy painter! What was wrong with her today? She needed to get herself together and focus, especially if what Rosie was saying was true. Mr Sexy-Painter was really *Dr* Sexy-Painter and her *boss*.

'Yes.'

Just then, he turned and looked her way and the previous tingling that had flooded her body started exploding like fireworks. Amelia found it impossible to look away as he excused himself from the nurse and began walking towards her with firm strides, his gaze never faltering from hers.

Within an instant, he was standing in front of her. 'Dr Watson, I presume,' he said with a slight grin.

His deep voice washed over her and for a split second she couldn't breathe. Then he blinked and it was as though she'd been released from whatever had been holding her so enthralled. Amelia glanced away and sighed, saying with forced joviality, 'Haven't heard that one before.'

'Sorry. Couldn't resist.' His smile reached his eyes and she could feel herself becoming captivated once more.

'Try.'

He watched her for a moment before nodding slowly. 'So, we meet again.'

'We do.'

'I'm Harrison. Harrison Stapleton, director.'

Amelia nodded. 'A face to the name.' She jerked back, desperate to get herself under control. 'Uh…where's your daughter?' she asked. 'Somewhere safe, I hope.'

Harrison's smile was as sexy as it had been the first time she'd seen it. 'Yes. My housekeeper has taken her home. She said they both needed to lie down.' He shook his head. 'Poor Mrs D. She'd taken Yolanda to the cafeteria to get something to eat, was standing in line to pay and turned around to discover Yolanda had wandered off again.'

Amelia thought back to the woman who'd jostled her. It all added up. 'Does Yolanda often wander off?'

'Yes. Where do you think all these grey hairs have come from?' He pointed to his temples. Amelia smiled. She liked the flecks of grey. It made him look more distinguished.

'It must be a constant worry to you.'

'It is but we're working on it. It's trying to get Yolanda to be conscious of when she's actually starting to wander, that's the difficult part.'

Amelia was intrigued. From the way Harrison spoke, she got the feeling there was something wrong with Yolanda. The girl's features showed no physical abnormality but that didn't mean to say there wasn't something else going on inside the little girl's mind. Anyway, it was really none of her business. 'Well, I'm glad she's safe.'

'You and me both.' He raised a hand to his heart and patted it, leaning in a little closer, as though he was about to take her into his confidence. Amelia automatically took a step backwards, his spicy scent teasing her senses. She could feel the warmth from his body and was surprised the way her own body responded to that heat. She met his gaze as he spoke. 'I felt as though I aged about fifty years in five minutes.'

'You looked it.' She shifted, resisting the urge to place a hand to her cheek to see if she really was blushing due to his nearness. It was ridiculous.

Harrison eased back, laughing at her words. 'How very complimentary of you, Dr Watson. Anyway, sorry I wasn't here when you started work last week.'

'It's fine. I've settled in. Besides, I was told you were at a conference.'

'I was. I would rather have been here, though.'

'Didn't enjoy it? I heard it was on the Gold Coast. That's a nice enough area.'

Harrison smiled. 'It was. I'm just not one for sitting around listening to speakers when I could be out enjoying myself.'

'Then it would have been called a holiday, not a conference.'

He chuckled. 'Good point.'

Amelia found she liked the sound as it washed over her and realised it was difficult to keep her focus with him so near. She was always focused. What was wrong with her? She had her goals and a little flirtation with her boss wasn't going to deter her…not that he was really flirting with her or anything. At least, she didn't think he was. 'Um…and your hand?' She pointed to the bandage. 'You hurt yourself while you were away?'

Harrison glanced down as though he'd forgotten. 'Oh. The hand. No. I did that this morning. I was opening a tin of paint and slipped. It's not damaged.'

'Really? Looks as though you need a new bandage on it.'

Harrison frowned at the bandage and turned his hand over to survey the handiwork. 'I think it looks quite good. A real professional job. The cutest little nurse did it for me.' His smile was one of pleasure and pride and Amelia tried hard not to roll her eyes.

'I have no doubt.'

Harrison watched her face, noting that she didn't seem impressed with his words. He smiled. 'You're jumping to conclusions.'

'Well, have you given me any reason not to jump?'

His smile was almost infuriating. 'No. Probably not.' Harrison continued to watch his new registrar's expressions, seeing her impatience and annoyance wash over her. She wasn't what he'd call classically pretty but her blue eyes had a certain fire in them he appreciated. Her auburn hair was cut short in a style that wouldn't require her to do much with it when she woke up. She was dressed in a business skirt and shirt, neat and tidy, and she was about five feet six inches, her body in proportion to her height. She wore plain gold earrings and a stethoscope around her neck.

'I guess we'd better get ready,' Harrison continued after a moment.

'For?' Amelia raised her eyebrows, trying to figure out what he was talking about. He'd given her a strange look before he'd spoken, a look that had seemed to say he was satisfied with what he saw. Amazingly, it made her feel kind of pleased when in reality she thought she should have been offended by his brief perusal.

'Emergency. Ambulance arriving. Teenagers who've drunk too much alcohol? Ring any bells?'

'Yes, Dr Stapleton, it does. Thank you for the reminder. *I'll* go now and get ready. No doubt you need to go and check on your daughter or catch up on paperwork.'

'That can wait until Monday. I'll come with you.'

Amelia couldn't help herself and glanced down at his bandaged hand. 'And you're planning to help how exactly?'

'Well, with an attitude like that, perhaps I *won't* offer my help.' His voice was still smooth, still deep, still washed over her like silk, but this time there was a hint of teasing in his tone. 'Instead, I might simply watch you. See if you're as good as Tina says you are, Dr Watson.'

'Terrific.' The word was dry and she turned on her heel, heading towards treatment room one. She wanted to get some distance between them, not have him tag along for an impromptu testing session. Harrison's sexy chuckle encompassed her and she realised he was following her. Why couldn't he just leave her alone? She wasn't in the mood for a test—not when she'd been stuck in this place for goodness knew how many hours. She sighed, trying to pull some energy from somewhere.

'Long shift?'

'And getting longer.'

'Some people would say being snippy isn't the best way to make an impression on your new boss.'

'And some other people would say testing your new employees when they've been working for hours on end isn't going to endear you to them, especially the one who took care of your daughter and returned her safely to your waiting arms.' She faked a smile and he laughed once more.

'You smile so sweetly yet your words are so full of…meaning.' The twinkle in his eyes captivated her for a moment and she wondered just how many other women felt the same way when they looked at him. All she'd heard about him was that he was a widower, his wife having died a few years ago, and apart from that, all Tina had said about their boss had been that he was fair and just. 'Let's get set up,' Harrison said.

'I'm not being snippy,' she said as she started setting things up. 'I'm punchy. There's a difference.'

'Divided by a thin line, Amelia-Jane.'

'It's just Amelia. No one calls me that.'

'Why not? I think it kind of suits you, Amelia-Jane.'

'Bit of a mouthful, though.'

'Well…' Harrison leaned against the cupboards and gave her another quick perusal. 'When we're nice and relaxed like this, I'll call you Amelia-Jane, and when we're busy, I think I'll just bark *"Watson"* and then you'll come running.'

Amelia couldn't help herself this time and laughed, shaking her head and not wanting to be impressed by him. He didn't seem to mind her exhausted attitude, which meant he'd worked long hard shifts and understood how things were near the end.

Wow. Harrison was glad he was leaning against something as the power of her true smile almost made him slide to the ground. How could he not have seen that instant beauty? When she smiled at him like that, he felt it, and that was odd in itself because there was absolutely no room in his life for anything except his job and his daughter. Yet somehow Amelia-Jane Watson, the new English rose with the alluring accent, was intriguing him more with each passing second.

'I can't believe we're discussing my name like this.' She crossed to the sink and washed her hands again, the wail of the ambulance sirens getting closer by the second. 'It's just a name. Right, Harry?'

His smile was slow. 'Make it Harrison, if you value your job and your life, Dr Watson.'

'Don't like it, eh?'

'Not particularly.'

'It doesn't suit you. Harrison does.'

'Thank you and I tend to think that Amelia-Jane suits you better. It's more…English,' he said, and she found herself captivated by him once more.

'You seem very laid back for a director.' Her words were soft and she was astonished to hear them come out sounding intimate.

'That's just the way I am,' he replied. He looked into her eyes and was taken aback at the way his gut twisted with desire. He'd never been so instantly attracted to someone before and he should heed the warning signs. Yet there was something about her…the soothing sound of her voice or the subtle scent of her perfume, or perhaps just the way she didn't seem to be intimidated by her new boss. Oh, yes, she was interesting.

The sirens were loud now, the ambulance obviously pulling into the bay outside before the loud noise ceased. Amelia pulled on a protective gown over her clothes as the doors to A and E slid open a moment later, the paramedics wheeling in the patients.

When she'd finished tying the tapes of her gown, she turned to see Harrison standing at the sink, washing both his hands, his tatty bandage nowhere in sight.

'What do you think you're doing? You'll damage your—' She looked at his hands as she spoke and was surprised to find nothing wrong with either of them. Nothing at all. 'Miraculous recovery?'

'Either that or I'm a very fast healer.'

'You were never hurt, right?'

'My dear Watson, you catch on fast.'

Amelia rolled her eyes and groaned at his pun. 'Thanks, Sherlock. So why *was* your hand bandaged?' The patients were transferred to the A and E beds but she wanted to know.

'Because I hurt my hand—nothing serious—and my daughter insisted on playing doctor and bandaging it for me.'

The cutest little nurse... Realisation dawned on Amelia and she now understood what Yolanda had told her. 'She *fixed* it.' Well, at least that explained the bad bandaging job.

He smiled. 'Yolanda's a very insistent three-year-old.'

'She seems as though she has a strong will. Good luck with that.'

Harrison nodded and rolled his eyes. 'I think I'm

going to need it.' He dried his hands and pulled on a gown to protect his old painting clothes and looked at Amelia for direction.

'What have we got?' she asked the paramedics.

'Two teenagers, both sixteen years of age. Meg and Tad. Found passed out in a classroom by the school cleaner, three six-hundred-mil bottles of vodka next to them.'

'Quite a party.' Amelia pulled on gloves. 'Harrison, take the boy,' she instructed. After all, if he was testing her, surely that meant she was the one in charge. 'Meg? Meg? Can you hear me? I'm Dr Watson. Meg?' She tapped the girl lightly on the cheek and received a slurred response.

'Pupils are enlarged,' the nurse reported. 'BP's down.'

'Why do they do this?' Harrison said as he called again to Tad and received a response. A moment later Tad started to turn green. 'Bucket!' Harrison called and stepped out of the way just in time as Tad spontaneously performed his own gastric lavage.

'Meg's airway is clear,' Amelia reported. 'Let's get the lavage started.' She administered a spray of topical anaesthetic into Meg's mouth before inserting an endo-tracheal tube that would prevent Meg from breathing in the stomach fluids into her lungs.

'Tip her onto her left side,' Amelia directed, and then they lowered her head. Next, she inserted the lubricated stomach tube through Meg's mouth, which went down into the oesophagus and into the stomach. 'Start suction.' She glanced across at Harrison. 'How's Tad?'

'Doing a good job of rejecting what he's swallowed all on his own.'

'Good. Give him activated charcoal with sorbitol-hyperosmotic. That should help speed up the emptying of his intestines. Are their parents here yet?' she asked one of the nurses.

'I believe so.'

'OK. I'll talk to them once we're done.' She looked at Meg and sighed, wondering why the teenager thought binge drinking was good fun. 'Welcome to the party,' she said sadly, then looked across at Tad, who didn't look as though he was having a good time at all. She glanced at Harrison, who seemed to have the same expression on his face as she did.

'Are we having fun yet?' He grimaced as he said the words and shook his head.

When both were stable, she went to talk to the parents, who were embarrassed and concerned as well as furious with their kids. 'Both Tad and Meg will need to stay at least overnight to be monitored. We'd also like them to see one of the social workers here so they can talk about why they did it.'

'There's nothing wrong with my daughter,' Meg's father blustered, and jabbed his finger at Tad's dad. 'It's his fault. It's *his* son who's corrupted my sweet little girl.'

Amelia dealt with the parents and managed to calm them down, conscious of the fact that Harrison was there, watching and listening but not interrupting. When the patients were stable and ready for transfer to a ward, Amelia sat down to write up the case notes, Harrison pulling up a chair beside her and doing the same.

'How did I do, Dr Stapleton? Pass your test?'

Harrison nodded slowly. 'Actually, you weren't too bad.'

'Too bad.' She thought over those words. 'See, if I knew you better, I'd know whether that was praise or not.'

Harrison kept writing the notes, not looking at her. 'It's praise.'

'Oh, goody.' Even though she spoke the words with a hint of sarcasm she was kind of pleased he hadn't found fault. 'If you're finished with the notes, I'll take them around to the ward.'

'Trying to get rid of me, Amelia-Jane?'

She shrugged, conscious of the way his thigh was very close to hers beneath the desk. Once more she could feel the warmth emanating from his body and didn't like the way it was affecting her. He was her boss and nothing more, but right now she wouldn't mind a bit of space to get her mind in gear and to try and figure out just what it was about him that seemed to knock her off balance. 'I simply thought you might like to get home and spend what's left of your Friday with your daughter.'

'What if I haven't finished testing you?'

'Well, unless you're going to test me on how fast I can clock off and leave the hospital, you're going to have to wait until another day for further testing because I am going home.' With that, she gathered up the two sets of case notes. 'See you on Monday, Dr Stapleton.'

'If not before, Dr Watson.'

Amelia tried not to smile as she walked to the ward. He was nice. He was good-looking. He was even funny. At the moment she couldn't find anything not to like about him and that was bad. She didn't want to like her new boss, or at least she didn't want to feel anything other than enjoying a platonic working relationship with him. Somehow, though, during the short acquaintance they'd had, Harrison Stapleton had made a lasting impression.

She returned to the change rooms and after having a quick shower she re-dressed, slipping her feet into her shoes and brushing her hair. At least now she felt more human and could return to her seaside holiday apartment to relax in peace and quiet for the remainder of the night. Thankfully, she'd found a place within two blocks from the hospital and therefore had no need for a car. The times when she worked late, she took a taxi home. Besides, the area in which she'd chosen to live was across the road from the beach and a street away from a shopping centre. The perfect place to complete her final months of training.

Amelia picked up her bag, paged Tina to let her know she was leaving the hospital and headed for the door. As she stepped outside into the mid-March evening, glad the sun was still up, thanks to daylight saving, she was startled to find Harrison Stapleton standing there, leaning against the wall. He quickly stood upright when he saw her.

'Ah, Amelia-Jane. There you are. I thought I might have missed you.'

'Something wrong?'

'No. No.' He shifted and shoved his hands into his pockets. 'I, er…just wanted to thank you again for looking after Yolanda. She's everything to me and I went crazy with worry when Mrs D. told me she was missing. So…er, thanks.'

'It's fine. Everything worked out.' She hunted in her handbag for her sunglasses, still getting used to the fact that March meant the end of summer rather than the end of winter, as she'd been used to all her life. She found the glasses but didn't put them on, looking at Harrison. 'Was there something else?'

'Do you have a car?' he asked.

'No. I don't live far from here.'

'Neither do I. Which street?'

'The Esplanade.'

'Really? What number?'

Amelia thought for a moment. 'Uh…number 375. I'm staying in one of the holiday apartment complexes.'

Harrison shook his head. 'That's two doors down from where I live. I'll walk you home.'

Amelia was startled. 'That's OK. I'm fine.'

His grin was immediate. 'We're both walking the same way, Amelia-Jane. It would be ridiculous to walk down the street and ignore each other.' He had no idea why he was insisting she agree, apart from the fact that he wanted to get to know her a bit more. While he told himself it was all strictly business as he hadn't yet received her file from her previous hospital and she could perhaps fill him in on some details, Harrison knew it went a little deeper than that.

The two of them had some sort of strange connection. He couldn't explain it. They'd certainly got along well, both while they'd been enjoying silly banter and whilst they'd been working.

He watched her now, seeing her indecision, and for some reason he felt like giving her a testimony to let her know that he was safe, that he was a good guy, that he would never harm her. She glanced at him and he smiled, and when she slowly returned that smile he was stunned by the instant hit to his solar plexus. In that moment, Harrison realised he *liked* Amelia-Jane Watson. *Really* liked her. As a man liked a woman…a woman he could become interested in.

That had *never* happened to him before.

CHAPTER TWO

'I GUESS it does seem silly,' Amelia said, bringing Harrison back from his musings.

'Huh? Oh, right.' He indicated the main gate to the hospital. 'Shall we go, then?'

'Of course.' Amelia slipped on her sunglasses as they headed out, conscious of keeping a bit of distance between them so they didn't accidentally bump hands as they walked. Both were silent and she felt the weight of it. She searched for a suitable topic and came up with the first polite level of small-talk she could think of. 'The weather here is certainly nicer than back where I live.'

Harrison nodded. 'Tina said you're from the Lake District.'

'That's right. My parents have lived in Barrow all my life.'

'It's a nice area.'

'You've been there?'

'On my honeymoon, actually. We…ah…toured that area. I'm a widower,' he added quickly, in case she though he was married.

'I'd heard.' Amelia couldn't believe how uncomfortable she felt. She'd liked what she'd seen so far where her new boss was concerned and while she had no intention of getting involved with him, it seemed a little strange to be walking down the street, discussing his late wife.

'Did you like it?'

'I did. Inga wasn't all that taken with it. London was more her scene.'

'Oh,' Amelia said again, wishing she could think of something else to say. 'London's not really my thing.'

'Too noisy?'

'Yes.'

'Me, too.'

A group of teenagers riding bikes came up onto the footpath near them before whizzing past, causing Harrison to step aside and inadvertently bump into Amelia. His hands came up to her arms to steady her so they didn't fall, his chest pressed against hers.

'Sorry.' He quickly regained his balance, trying desperately not to concentrate on the way Amelia felt in his arms. She was his colleague, a very beautiful and desirable colleague who would be leaving his world in just three short months and it wouldn't do him any good to go forgetting that. Dragging in a sobering breath, he finally found the will, the strength to set her from him, putting distance between their bodies, but found he was still unable to completely let go. It was an unspoken personal rule to avoid relationships with hospital personnel, especially if they were members of his department, but something about Amelia seemed to be reeling him in, making him forget everything except the way he felt right now.

'Are you all right?' Harrison's tone was deep and the sound resonated through her body, not helping Amelia to control her reaction to him. His hands were still on her arms, warm and firm yet not hurting her at all. A moment ago, when she'd been cradled in his arms, arms that were strong and protective, she'd felt a sense of perfection wash over her. She couldn't help the reaction she experienced at his touch and it was as though her body was reacting completely on its own, without consulting her brain.

'Good,' he said when she nodded that she was OK. 'Kids never look where they're going.' Reluctantly, he eased his hands open, his fingers trailing softly down her arms until they dropped heavily back to his sides.

The warmth, the tingles his touch had created stayed with her even after he'd removed his hands and for a moment Amelia found it impossible to get her legs to work. Instead, she simply stood there, looking up at him, trying to control her fingers, which itched to brush his hair back from his forehead where a dark brown lock had fallen. It was then she realised she was trembling and she clasped her hands together to try and control it.

'Are you sure you're all right?' Harrison asked, looking more closely at her, and Amelia looked away.

'I'm fine. Really.' The moment had gone, passed, and now she could hopefully begin to function like a human being again. She shifted her bag further onto her shoulder and nodded again for emphasis.

'Only one more block to go. Think we can accomplish it undamaged?' Harrison asked, with a small smile.

Was he talking about the reckless kids or what had just transpired between the two of them? Amelia decided to interpret it as the former because the latter simply threatened to break the control she'd just managed to obtain over her senses. 'It could be risky,' she countered, and was pleased when he laughed, the sound washing over her like a warm, comfortable blanket. 'I think we should chance it.'

'Excellent.' They started walking once again, both of them keeping a little more distance between them. Amelia glanced in the shop windows they were walking by and saw one laden with Easter chocolates.

Harrison groaned when he saw them.

'You don't like Easter?' she asked.

'I don't like the constant badgering for chocolates,' he said.

'Yolanda?'

He nodded. 'It's astounding. Females seemed to be genetically attracted to chocolate and Yolanda is no exception. She's even gone so far as to get the latest Easter catalogue, sit down with me and point out everything she wants.'

Amelia couldn't help but smile. 'Definitely a girl who knows what she wants.'

'That's my baby.' Harrison's smile was that of a doting dad. 'How about you?'

She smiled. 'Do you mean have I sat down with my father and gone through the Easter sale catalogues with him?'

'Exactly.' He was pleased they seemed to share the same warped sense of humour. 'Actually, I meant are you a girl who knows what she wants?'

Amelia thought about it for a moment. 'Um…most of the time, I guess. I don't always get it, of course, but as far as Easter chocolate goes, well, that one's easy.'

'It is?'

'Yes. I'm not a big chocolate fan.'

'Really?' His eyebrows hit his hairline. 'You don't like chocolate?'

Amelia shrugged. 'I'd rather have something savoury than sweet.'

'Interesting.' Harrison looked very thoughtful.

'What? Never met a woman who didn't go for chocolates? I don't like fresh flowers either.'

'Now you're starting to scare me. Just when I think I have the fairer sex worked out.'

Amelia found it hard to repress her smile. Harrison was revealing himself as a very sweet man with a playful charm that was difficult not to respond to. She wished for strength as she would need to keep herself under tight control.

Given the direction in which they were walking, they came across Harrison's house first and as they stopped outside she looked up, admiring the beautiful two-storey beach house. Its double-glazed glass front would let in a lot of the sun but keep a lot of the heat out, as well as providing wonderful views of the ocean.

'Nice place,' she said.

Harrison shrugged nonchalantly. 'It's nothing special but it's home.'

Amelia laughed and he pointed to the apartment two doors down. 'Do you like where you're staying?'

'Yes, I do. The apartment is clean, comfortable, came fully furnished and was a reasonable price. Also, there are your beaches.' She sighed as she looked across the road to where the glistening golden sand and the dark blue water shone. 'Australia has the most beautiful beaches, in my opinion.'

'You'll get no argument from me. I guess the sand here is a little more...um...golden than Brighton?'

Amelia nodded. 'It's also *sand*, which is very nice to walk on.'

Harrison agreed. 'You know, we have our own Brighton beach.' He pointed south. 'Further up that way, and I guarantee the sand is just as nice as here.'

'I'll have to check it out.'

Before either of them could say another word, a high-pitched squeal pierced the air and both turned to see Yolanda running down the front path, arms open as she hurtled herself towards Harrison.

Instantly, he bent down and scooped her up when she got close enough, her arms closing about his neck with glee. 'Daddy. Daddy.'

Harrison hugged her close and glanced over at the doorway where a woman stood. 'Hi, Mrs D.,' he called, and waved one hand.

'You're back earlier than we thought,' the woman said, her strong English accent resonating through the air. 'We've just woken from our rest and have finished making some biscuits.'

'Dey are berry yummy, Daddy,' Yolanda assured him.

Amelia took in the scene and took a step away. 'I'd better get going,' she said. 'See you at work.'

'Uh…' Harrison shifted Yolanda to his hip, his arms still firm around her as the little girl planted a few kisses on his cheek. 'Would you like to come in?'

'It's fine. I don't want to intrude.'

'Oh, nonsense.' Mrs D. beckoned them inside. 'It's the least we can do for you helping us out with Yolanda earlier. I'll go put the kettle on and we can all sit down and have a nice cup of tea.'

'Half an hour,' Harrison said, and started up the garden path.

'Are you sure?' Amelia hesitated, not sure if she should accept, although tea and biscuits with Harrison and his family sounded very nice.

'Come on. Mrs D.'s right. Look upon it as our way of saying thank you for finding Yolanda.' Harrison angled his head towards his home and Amelia decided it couldn't hurt. As she walked in, she admired the décor and wondered whether he'd hired a decorator, but as she continued through the house to the rear, where the kitchen was situated, she passed a room that was bare except for drop sheets, ladder and paint tins.

'Doing a bit of renovating?'

Harrison smiled and looked down at his clothes. 'It relaxes me.'

'Harrison's almost done the whole house,' Mrs D. said as Amelia walked around the kitchen bench. 'Please, dear, have a seat,' she said, pointing to the stools. 'I'm Mrs Deveraux or Mrs D., as Harrison so eloquently calls me.'

'Forgive me my manners,' Harrison said as he deposited Yolanda on a stool. 'Mrs D., this is Amelia-Jane, a new registrar all the way from your homeland.'

'Stop teasing her, Harrison,' Mrs D. admonished. 'How do you take your tea, dear?'

'Black, thank you.'

Harrison continued. 'Mrs D. was a dear friend of my mother's and sleeps in the back bedroom where she keeps telling me she's quite comfortable and doesn't want me rearranging furniture or repainting her walls.'

'Quite right,' Mrs D. said as she pulled bone china mugs from the cupboard.

'And you remember Yolanda,' Harrison continued, dropping a kiss on his daughter's head.

'How could I forget?'

'Do you remember Amelia-Jane from the hospital?' Harrison asked his daughter.

'Meel-ya,' Yolanda said, but didn't bother making eye contact until she had a biscuit secured in each hand.

'It's good to see you again.' Amelia smiled at the gorgeous little girl, determined to ignore the emptiness inside she always felt on meeting well-loved children. It had been clear within the first few seconds of seeing Harrison with his daughter that Yolanda was very special to him and she was pleased to find he was a man who appreciated the important things in life.

She pasted a smile on her face and pushed aside the thoughts that she would never have such a beautiful child of her own. It was something she was still trying to accept and whenever she was faced with such a touching scene, it made it all the harder.

The tea was lovely and the biscuits were mouthwatering. When Amelia said as much, Yolanda took full responsibility.

'*I* did it. *I* mixed da flour. *I* mixed da…da…'

'Sugar,' Mrs D. supplied.

'Shoogar,' Yolanda repeated, and climbed down from the stool. 'Come see dolly.'

Amelia blinked at the quick change in topic but allowed herself to be tugged away by the three-year-old, glancing at Harrison who lifted an eyebrow but didn't say a word. Instead, he followed as Yolanda pulled Amelia into her bedroom, which was painted in pink and white with a border of flowers around the edge near the ceiling. A pink and white bed was against the wall opposite the wardrobe and a pink and white bookshelf was against the other wall. Soft toys were all around, and a doctor's set, complete with bandages, lay on the bed, but in pride of place in the middle of the room sat a beautiful dolls' house.

'Ta-da!' She dropped Amelia's hand and ran over to the dolls' house. 'My daddy made it.' There was pride in her voice and Amelia looked at Harrison, who was leaning against the doorjamb. He merely shrugged as though it was nothing.

'My daddy made da shelves.' Yolanda ran to the book-shelves. 'And he made da bed.' She ran to the bed. 'And da *dollies'* house.' She said the word as though it were a sweet she couldn't get enough of, her eyes wide as she lay down next to the dolls' house and opened the front panel.

'Quite the carpenter.' Amelia glanced at Harrison, who allowed himself a little smile. She sat down on the floor, being careful of her skirt, and looked inside.

'Is pink and white,' Yolanda said proudly.

'Do you like pink and white?' Amelia asked, already knowing the answer, and Yolanda nodded enthusiastically.

'However did you guess?' Harrison walked over and sat down next to Yolanda. 'I'm sure when she eventually changes her mind, I'll have to repaint everything all over again.'

'Perhaps she won't change.' Harrison looked doubtful but Amelia nodded. 'My favourite colour is red and has been ever since I can remember. I certainly haven't changed, nor am I about to.'

'Favourite colour is red, doesn't like chocolates or flowers, prefers savoury to sweet and has black tea, no milk, no sugar.' He ticked the points off on his fingers. Amelia was also the only member of his staff he'd seen Yolanda bond with. His daughter was very picky and the fact she'd gone to Amelia with no hesitation whatsoever spoke volumes about the English doctor's character.

'Making a list?' she asked, wondering whether she should be scared or flattered.

'And checking it twice.' He raised his eyebrows. 'Gotta find out who's naughty and who's nice.'

Amelia laughed. 'It's almost Easter, Harrison. Not Christmas.'

'I like to be prepared.'

'Easter!' Yolanda squealed loudly and he immediately hushed her.

'Little softer, please, pumpkin.'

'Easter. Easter. Chocolate. Chocolate.' Yolanda stood up and jumped around the room, clapping her hands.

'See what I mean? Obsessed with Easter.'

Amelia watched the little girl, noting that she still wore a nappy and also that her speech wasn't as advanced as it could be for a three-year-old. Then again, all children developed at different rates but she wondered if Harrison had picked up on anything.

'Come and play with your dolls,' Harrison said, and in the next instant Yolanda was back on the floor, lying on her stomach, picking up a doll and handing it to her father.

'Dis one for you, Daddy, toz you da boy.'

Amelia smiled as Harrison took the male doll and straightened his clothes.

'Dis one for you, toz you a gel.' Amelia found a doll with long blonde hair thrust into her hands.

'Oh. Thank you.'

Harrison's gleam was one of satisfaction. 'Didn't think you were going to get away that easily, did you?' He cleared his throat and walked his doll over to Yolanda's. 'Hello, there, my little girl. Are you ready for the party? My, my, that is a pretty dress you're wearing.'

Yolanda answered him with her doll while Amelia simply sat there and watched the two of them. It was such a precious moment, one of the ones that if she had her choice of capturing and freezing it, she would immediately accept.

'Is dere chocolate at da party?' Yolanda's doll asked.

'Most certainly. Lots and lots of chocolate,' Harrison answered, and Yolanda's doll jumped up and down just as the little girl herself had been doing a few minutes ago.

Amelia's heart welled up with need and longing and to her disgust she felt tears begin to blur her vision. Biting her lip, she tried to control them and took a few deep breaths. It simply wasn't fair that she would never have this when she longed for it with every fibre of her being.

When Harrison glanced at her, his face instantly changed. 'What's wrong?' he asked in his normal voice.

Amelia shook her head and forced a smile. 'Nothing.' She handed the doll back to Yolanda. 'She's a very pretty doll, Yolanda. I'm pleased to see you take such good care of her.'

'Berry prwetty dolly,' Yolanda agreed, and took the doll from her.

'I have to go,' Amelia said and carefully levered herself up from the floor.

'Now?' Harrison said.

'I have a few things to do, plus I've just finished a very long shift.' She looked down at Yolanda. 'Goodbye, Yolanda. I'll see you another time.'

'Bye,' the little girl called, more interested in her dolls than in anything else.

Harrison scrambled to his feet. 'Daddy will be back in a minute, pumpkin.'

'O'tay.'

They walked to the kitchen and Amelia picked up her bag and thanked Mrs D. for the tea. 'It was lovely. Thank you.'

'You're most welcome, dear. Drop by again soon.'

Amelia wasn't sure whether that was going to be possible or not, so she merely smiled before heading through to the front of the house, aware of Harrison following behind her. She had no idea what was currently happening between herself and Harrison, or whether or not it would go anywhere.

At the front door she turned to face him. 'Thanks. It was nice of you to invite me.'

'I'll walk you to your door,' he said.

'It's all right. It's not necessary,' she started, but he'd closed the front door behind him and stepped past her, heading down the path.

'It's no trouble.'

Amelia shook her head, realising it was pointless to try and argue with him.

'So…are you sure you're all right?' he asked as they walked past the house between his home and her apartment complex.

Amelia rubbed a hand against her temple and sighed. She didn't want to talk about it. Not now and not with him, but how did she say that without intriguing him further or possibly hurting his feelings?

'It's nothing. I… She's just so gorgeous. Besides, there are things I need to do.'

Harrison nodded slowly. 'Mind if I don't believe you?'

'That I have things to do? Why would I lie about that?'

'There's something you're not telling me.'

'There's a lot I'm not telling you. Harrison, we only

met a few hours ago.' She stopped at the corner of the apartment complex. 'I don't find it easy to open up to people. It's just who I am.'

'So there is something bothering you?'

'A lot of things bother me, just as I'm sure the same could be said for you or Mrs D. or anyone else for that matter. It doesn't mean I want to talk about them all.'

Harrison shrugged, realising he'd have to let it go if he didn't want to upset her. That wasn't his intention but neither could he help the concern that had gripped him at seeing her eyes mist up the way they had. He knew it was far better for him to maintain a professional distance between the two of them. 'Fair enough.' He pointed to the building. 'Home at last, eh? Go and rest, Dr Watson. I'll see you at work.'

The next week seemed to fly by and Amelia didn't see much of Harrison as they were on different shifts. But on Thursday, when she was on a regular day shift, he sought her out in the cafeteria.

'Is this seat taken?' Harrison asked, and she looked up from the book she'd been reading, trying to squash the feeling of pleasure at seeing him.

'Hi. Uh…no. Please, sit.' She closed her book.

'Is the book good?' he asked, and she shrugged.

'I've read it before. So, how are things?'

'Good. I heard you had afternoon tea with my daughter yesterday.'

Amelia nodded slowly, concerned at what his reaction would be to the news. 'I did. I met Mrs D. and Yolanda on the beach when I was taking a walk and they invited me back. I hope you don't mind.'

'No. Yolanda was happy to have someone to play

dolls with. At least, she told me your dolls had gone to a party with lots of chocolate.'

Amelia smiled. 'They did.'

'That's good.' He nodded and unwrapped his sandwich. 'So, tell me, Amelia-Jane, what have you been doing the past few days, besides working, walking along the beach and having afternoon teas?'

'Hmm. Let me think. I've been working, walking along the beach and having afternoon teas.'

'Just as I thought,' he said, and she laughed. He enjoyed the sound of her laughter and liked the way her face lit up, her blue eyes sparkling with merriment. He took a bite of his sandwich and they talked about the patients they'd seen and other general hospital matters. It was amazing how much they agreed on and Harrison was pleased with the way Amelia seemed to be settling in with the rest of the staff.

'That's good to hear,' he said. 'Staffing issues can be real nightmares, especially when employing doctors from overseas. You never know exactly what you're going to get until they arrive.'

Amelia raised her eyebrows. 'Very flattering, I'm sure.'

'Oh, not you, of course.' Harrison looked contrite, as though he'd temporarily forgotten she was from overseas, or perhaps he'd said it on purpose just to tease her.

'Why not?' she prompted.

'Because you came highly recommended.'

She smiled. 'Tina's a good friend.'

'You've known each other long?'

'Quite some time.' Her pager beeped and she sighed and slowly rose to her feet. 'Sorry I can't keep you company while you finish your lunch.'

Harrison shrugged. 'You're better off going. If you

make Rosie wait, you won't get a moment's worth of peace.'

'Who's in charge of this department?'

'Uh…me?'

'Or so you think,' she agreed. 'See you later, Harrison.' As she walked away from the cafeteria she was surprised at how happy she felt. He really was a nice man and she found she liked talking to him.

She bumped into Tina on her way to A and E. Her friend had a large smile on her face. 'I saw you talking to Harrison,' she said in a sing-song voice.

'Yeah. He just came and sat down to eat his lunch.' Amelia put her paperback into the pocket of her white coat.

'Had any more afternoon teas?' Tina raised her pinky in the air and mimicked Amelia's accent.

'Ah, yesterday, actually, but only with his daughter and housekeeper.'

'Oh. How disappointing.'

'Not really.' Amelia dropped her voice as she said, 'You know how difficult it is for me to open up to other people. It takes me a while to feel comfortable around strangers.'

'And you really get the opportunity to do that when you're moving hospitals every three months.' Tina's sarcasm was evident. 'Why on earth did you choose to do your twelve-month overseas rotation in four different hospitals?'

'I wanted to see as much of Australia as I could. You know that.'

'I also know that's not the real reason. Anyway, I have to say that you look very comfortable around Harrison.'

Amelia sighed and nodded sadly. 'And that's a problem.'

'Why? He's single, he's good-looking, he's funny.'

'He has a daughter.'

'That should be a bonus as far as you're concerned. He won't be too bothered about you not being able to have children because he's already got one.'

Amelia stopped and looked at her friend, more than used to her bluntness. 'I can't get involved. I leave at the end of June and I have plans back in England.'

'Plans such as not staying and working in one hospital for any extended length of time?'

Amelia started walking again, faster this time, her annoyance showing. 'Plans such as experiencing a variety of situations around the world,' Amelia countered. 'There's nothing wrong with travelling while I have the opportunity, Tina.'

'Travelling? No. Running away? Yes.'

They took the stairs to A and E. 'I am not running away.'

'No. It's impossible to run away from yourself.'

Amelia huffed. 'Go home and sleep,' she told Tina. 'I need to work.'

'All right. Hey, I noticed you're rostered off on Saturday. Do you want to meet for coffee? I don't start work until eleven.'

'Sure.'

'We can talk more about you know who.'

'Goodbye, Tina.' Amelia waved and headed for the nurses' station.

The two registrars met for coffee on Saturday morning and managed to squeeze in a bit of shopping before Tina started work. Amelia bought a new pair of shoes, two new skirts for work, three new tops and a new jacket.

'Planning to go out on a few dates?' Tina teased.

'No. The clothes are cheaper here than back home. That's all.'

'Oh, good excuse.'

'It's the truth.'

'Look, why don't you admit that you like Harrison Stapleton?'

'Why?'

'Because at least then you can do something about it.'

'Or not.'

'He's a great guy. Everyone at work likes and respects him and personally I think it would be wonderful if you two started dating. You're perfect for each other.'

Amelia opened her mouth to refute Tina's claims but decided it wasn't worth the effort. Tina had a bee in her bonnet and that was fine. Just so long as it didn't come buzzing around her.

'See? You can't even deny it.'

She sighed. 'Fine. I like him. All right? Are you happy now?'

'You should go for it.'

'Tina. I've already told you I don't have ti—'

'Save it, sister. I've heard it all before.' Tina checked her watch and then shrieked. 'Oops. Gotta go. I'll see you when I see you.'

Amelia rolled her eyes and waved then decided to go and have another quick cup of coffee before she went looking for a new pair of earrings. She was sitting down to enjoy it when she looked up and was surprised to see Harrison. He was coming out of the shop opposite and had Yolanda on his shoulders, her brown eyes shining with delight. His hands were on her legs, holding her steady, but she sat straight without a care in the world and obviously queen of all she surveyed. Amelia couldn't help smiling at the picture they made.

Mrs Deveraux came out of the shop behind him, carrying a shopping bag. Harrison asked her something and she looked around, then pointed to the coffee-shop where Amelia was. Harrison spotted her straight away and waved, heading in her direction.

'Amelia-Jane,' he said as they walked over. 'Fancy meeting you here.'

'Fancy,' she replied, and said hello to Mrs D. and Yolanda. Everyone seemed to stand still for a moment, no one wanting to make a move to stay or go, and in the end Amelia realised it would be up to her to make the first move. She cleared her throat and indicated the empty chairs at her table. 'Would you care to join me?'

'Excellent idea.' Harrison instantly pulled out two chairs and lifted Yolanda from his shoulders. 'Time for a drink, wouldn't you say?' he asked his daughter as he planted a kiss on her cheek and sat with her on his knee. 'Mrs D. could certainly use the break.'

'Definitely,' Mrs Deveraux replied, putting the shopping bags on the floor. 'Time for tea.'

Harrison glanced briefly at the menu then gave their order to the waitress who came to attend them. 'AJ? You right for a drink?'

She opened her mouth to say something but stopped at the abbreviation of her name. It was what her family called her and although she had no objection to the name, it surprised her that someone she didn't really know that well was using a nickname so soon in their acquaintance. It made them seem more familiar, closer, intimate somehow, and that was hardly the case.

'I'm fine, thank you.'

When the waitress had gone, Harrison leaned on the table. 'Is it all right if I call you that?'

'Uh…sure. You just surprised me. It's more a family pet name. Just sounds strange hearing it in this environment but, hey, it's just a name.'

He shrugged. 'AJ suits you.'

'What? Two letters. Short, sharp and shiny?'

Harrison chuckled at that. 'No.' For a moment she thought he was going to say more but he didn't.

'Teaset. Teaset,' Yolanda said, and climbed down from his knee to rummage around in a big bag Mrs D. had been carrying.

'Yes, here you go, dear,' the woman said, and pulled out a container, opening it for Yolanda. The girl climbed back onto her father's lap and withdrew little plastic cups and saucers and a teapot then proceeded to pour them all 'tea'. Mrs Deveraux's phone rang and she answered it with a sigh, looking at the name on the display.

'Excuse me,' she said, and stood again, leaving them alone while she took her call.

Harrison looked from Yolanda to Amelia and back again. 'Yolanda. Do you remember Amelia-Jane? She came and played dolls with you.'

Yolanda nodded her head, curls bobbing all over the place.

'Can you say hello to Amelia?'

'Hey-yo, Meel-ya,' she said, and again Amelia had the feeling something wasn't quite right with the little girl. Then Yolanda handed Amelia a cup and saucer, and she willingly sipped the imaginary tea, enjoying the child's delight. 'Tareful. Is hot,' Yolanda warned.

'Quite right,' Amelia said, and blew on it first. She glanced at Harrison, who seemed to be watching her closely, and she began to feel as though she was under a microscope. She handed the cup back to Yolanda. 'Thank you for the tea. It was delicious.'

'She just loves tea parties,' Harrison said, still watching Amelia closely.

'What little girl doesn't?'

'Did you?'

'Most certainly. I used to do exactly what she's doing and force everyone to drink their imaginary tea. That was until I graduated to sugar water.' She shook her head. 'I can't say my parents were too fond of that.'

'You're an only child?'

'Yes.' That was all she was going to say on the subject.

Harrison sipped his imaginary tea and realised Amelia wasn't going to say anything else about her family—at least, not this time. 'When I saw this teaset I couldn't resist it, and I'm glad I bought it. She only plays with this one when we're out and about and has a pink one at home for her dolls.'

Amelia smiled at the 'pink' part. 'Naturally. It wouldn't do to just have *one* teaset. How ordinary!' Harrison laughed, enjoying the way she drawled her vowels. 'So, how's the E-a-s-t-e-r shopping going?' She deliberately spelt out the word so she didn't set Yolanda off again, jumping about the shop.

Harrison returned her smile and nodded. 'Almost finished. Hard to believe it's just next weekend.'

Yolanda poured the tea again and both adults dutifully drank from their tiny cups before returning them.

'So…how's your week been?' Harrison asked.

'Busy,' she said. 'Although I'm sure you know that.'

'I've read the stats and reports.' He paused. 'And you've settled into your apartment all right? Nothing you need?'

'No. Everything's just fine.'

'Your paperwork still hasn't arrived,' he said. 'Brisbane General are slack in the admin department. If it wasn't for Tina vouching for you, I'd be calling the police to do a background check.'

'Really?'

'No.' He laughed, enjoying her gullibility.

Amelia watched as his eyes filled with merriment at her expense, not that she minded. Still, it didn't seem fair that his eyes should be so mesmerising, so deep, so rich and vibrant in colour that it would be all too easy just to sit there and look at him all day long. 'I need to go.' She started to gather up her packages at the same time Mrs D. returned to the table and the waitress brought their drinks.

'Stay.' The one word came from Harrison's lips before she'd even managed to push herself to her feet. She looked at him and wondered why it was so important to him that she be there.

Harrison couldn't believe that he wanted to spend more time with her. He was already behind in his renovation schedule due to thinking about her too much. The way she smiled, the way she laughed at his silly jokes and the way they seemed to be on the same wavelength.

'Please, stay. We'd feel terrible if we thought we'd driven you off.'

'You're not driving me off. I have more shopping to do.'

'Shopping!' Yolanda said loudly, froth all over her lips from the warmed milk she was drinking. It was enough to break the ice and they all smiled.

'She *loves* coming to the shops,' he explained.

'And you?'

'Loathe it. Especially on Saturdays when there are more people here.'

Amelia nodded, understanding exactly what he meant about the amount of people. It was one of the reasons she usually preferred to have her days off in the middle of the week. 'Really, though. I need to get going. It was nice to see you all again.'

Why did he look so disappointed? It was strange. Ridiculous, but this time he didn't protest. 'Fair enough.' He stood and for a moment, she wasn't sure why. Then she realised he was just being a gentleman and the action endeared him to her. 'See you at work,' he said with a nod.

When she'd walked out of the coffee-shop she paused and momentarily closed her eyes. Harrison Stapleton was nothing more to her than a boss and colleague. She headed towards the escalators, deciding she'd head home, suddenly feeling exhausted. She was halfway up towards the second floor of the indoor shopping mall when a loud scream pierced the air.

She turned just in time to see a pregnant woman lose her balance on the down escalator and tumble head over heels, knocking into another man who, though he was pushed quite heavily, managed not to lose his balance and somehow stopped the woman in one motion.

Amelia pushed ahead of the people in front, stepping quickly off before making her way down the descending escalator again, pushing her way through the people staring in horror and disbelief at what had just happened. 'Let me through. I'm a doctor,' she called. A little boy was crying as she rushed towards the woman who was now lying on the floor at the base of the escalators.

Amelia stepped off and put her bags down, reaching the woman at the same time another person came into view. She glanced up and almost breathed a sigh of relief.

'Harrison. Thank goodness.'

CHAPTER THREE

HARRISON quickly took in the situation and turned to the big burly man, who was kneeling next to the woman. 'Are you her husband?'

'No. No. She bumped into me.'

'He caught her,' Amelia supplied.

'Right. Press the emergency stop button, then get the rest of these people off and out of the way. Then get hold of the shopping mall security. We'll need an ambulance.'

'Are you a doctor?' the man asked as Harrison crouched down beside the woman and put his hand on her abdomen. Amelia took the woman's pulse and called to her.

'We both are,' Harrison stated, his tone brooking no argument. 'Just do it.'

'Can you hear me?' Amelia called. The woman was groggy and moaning but conscious. There was blood flowing from somewhere and she searched, finding a large gash on the woman's arm. She pressed her hand firmly to the area while feeling the woman's head with her other hand. 'What's your name?' No answer. 'Stay with me,' Amelia urged. 'What's your name?'

'Mummy? Mummy?' The little boy was sitting at the woman's feet, crying.

'What's your name, sport?' Harrison asked, as he continued to check their patient for any fractures. The little boy just continued to cry and Amelia's heart went out to him. 'My name's Harrison and this is AJ. We're both doctors and we're going to help Mummy, OK?'

Amelia lifted the woman's eyelids and was pleased when her pupils reacted to the light emanating from the shops in the centre. Her breathing was shallow and starting to come in gasps. Amelia carefully continued to feel the woman's head, checking for contusions, not surprised when she felt something wet and sticky in the woman's hair.

'She's having contractions,' Harrison said.

'Braxton-Hicks?'

'Feels like it at the moment but a fall like that—'

'Can induce labour,' she finished. 'I can feel two lacerations to the head. Both open wounds—not bad, though. Can you hear me?' she called again, and once more received a moan in response. 'Good.'

'Mummy?' The little boy had obviously had enough of sitting there, still not seeing his mother move. He stood and tried to push past Harrison in order to get closer to his mum. Amelia's heart contracted tighter and the urge to simply pick him up and hold him close was almost overwhelming. People were everywhere, milling around them, walking past and not interested. At least the escalator had been switched off so people weren't coming down in droves.

Harrison shifted so the boy could come closer. 'Here you go, champ. Can you help me by holding Mummy's hand? You talk to her because I'll bet she loves to hear you talk.'

'My mummy?'

'Yes. We're going to help your mummy,' Amelia said. 'You hold her hand. What's your name, sweetheart?'

'Ethan?' It was the woman who mumbled the word.

'Mummy?' Ethan's big blue eyes widened even more. Poor lamb. He couldn't be more than three. 'Mummy. Get up. Get up.' His tears were starting to flow now.

'Ethan's fine,' Harrison immediately assured the woman.

'What's your name?' Amelia asked.

'Liv Davis,' the woman murmured.

'I'm Amelia, this is Harrison. We're doctors.'

'The baby?'

'Is fine but starting to get impatient,' Harrison said gently. 'You have a few other injuries, too, Liv. It looks like you may have fractured your shinbone, given the amount of swelling around it. You have lacerations to your legs, arms and head, but you've been very lucky.'

'Ethan?'

'He's fine. Scared, but fine.'

Liv seemed to relax a little but Amelia saw her squeeze her son's hand in an attempt to reassure him as best she could. It was the bond between mother and child and she felt the familiar sadness touch her heart.

'AJ,' Harrison said and she looked over at him. 'You all right?'

'Fine.' She nodded, quick to assure him. Thankfully the security team from the shopping mall arrived on the scene, bringing a first-aid kit and a stretcher so their attention was taken up with getting Liv organised.

'Excellent,' Harrison said, as Amelia opened the kit and ripped open a pad, pressing it to Liv's skull where she'd previously been applying pressure. With her other hand she found a bandage, pulled the sterile dressing open. She began to wind the bandage around Liv's head, holding the pad in place. Next she applied a padded bandage to Liv's arm, which would probably end up needing sutures, but they had other things to concentrate on for the moment.

'Harrison?'

Amelia looked up and saw Mrs Deveraux standing there, holding Yolanda's hand.

'Ah, Mrs D. Good.' Harrison's voice was calm. 'This is Ethan.' He indicated the boy. 'We're going to move Ethan's mummy to a nice quiet room while we wait for the ambulance. Perhaps you and Yolanda can help look after Ethan.'

'Of course,' replied Mrs D.

'Daddy.' Harrison's daughter came to stand right beside her father, leaning on his back a little. 'Are you doh-ing to made a baby?' she said, pointing to the woman's stomach.

'Deliver,' Harrison automatically corrected his daughter's word usage. 'Possibly. Come and say hello to Ethan.'

'Hey-yo. I'm free.' She held up her fingers to indicate her age, almost shoving them in poor Ethan's face. 'I'm a *big* gel,' she said proudly.

'*I'm* free, too.' Ethan puffed his chest out as he stood and looked at Yolanda. He was still holding his mother's hand but he had something different to interest him—a bossy girl.

Amelia had finished bandaging the head. 'Pain relief? We need to give her something before we move her.'

'Liv? Are you allergic to anything?' Harrison asked. 'Not that I know of?'

'Did you have any problems with Ethan's delivery?' 'He was breech.'

Harrison put his hands on Liv's stomach again and felt the position of the baby. 'Not this one.'

Liv groaned and her muscles tensed and she started to push.

Amelia and Harrison looked at each other before they both burst into action. 'We need to get her moved now.' Harrison called to the security man. 'Have you had first-aid training?'

'Yes.'

'Right. I need something to use as a splint and I need it now. Amelia, get me some bandages out. Bring that stretcher closer. Mrs D., please, try to distract Ethan so he's out of the way while we move his mother. Little ones have a habit of getting underfoot right at the wrong time,' he said by way of explanation.

'Sounds like experience talking,' Amelia said, knowing Liv was aware of everything they were saying. 'You'll be fine, Liv. We just need to sort your leg out before we move you somewhere more private.'

'My back hurts. My stomach. The baby!' Liv's voice broke on the last word and she started to cry. 'This isn't fair. It isn't fair.'

'I know. You're doing great, though. We're here, we're looking after you. You'll be at the hospital before you know it. Unfortunately, at the moment we can't give you any pain medication, not until one of us does an internal examination. You might already be in labour,' Amelia said as she opened the packet of tissues from the first-aid box and dabbed at Liv's eyes.

'Ethan?'

'He's here,' Harrison assured her. 'I have a three-year-old daughter and the two of them are talking. Can you hear them?'

There was so much noise going on around them, the general hustle and bustle of the shopping centre, the bad music played through the speakers, announcements, footsteps, crying babies, shopping carts being rattled about, but through all that Liv strained to hear her son talking to Yolanda.

'Oh, yeah? Well, *I've* got a new truck. That's better than your doll,' Ethan was saying, and Liv almost smiled with relief. Then the look on her face changed to one of pain again and she tensed, pushing once more. Amelia met Harrison's gaze, the unspoken communication between doctors working like a charm. The contractions were quite close.

'These aren't Braxton-Hicks.'

Amelia smiled.

The security man returned and Harrison was able to splint Liv's lower left leg. While he did that, Amelia fashioned a cervical collar from a few of the bandages in order to support Liv's neck when they moved her.

'Right. AJ. You support her head and neck. You…' he pointed to the security man '…support her legs. I'll support her body. Bring the stretcher in closer and someone clear a path to the room we're heading to. We don't need to be waiting for people to get out of the way. Mrs D.?'

'I've got the children,' she called from the side. 'Oh, and I'll take your bags for you, Amelia.'

'Thanks,' she answered, having forgotten about her shopping purchases. Thankfully, they were able to move Liv to a much more private environment without further complication. It was a small room with a bed, chair and washbasin. They left Liv on the stretcher rather than putting her onto the bed, not wanting to move her more than was necessary. Just outside the door was an area with chairs and a beverage machine, and a box of toys was in the corner. Down the hall were the management offices for the shopping centre. Liv had asked that her mother be called and the security man had quickly volunteered to take care of that. When they'd enquired after the baby's father, Liv had simply said he wasn't in the picture any more.

Mrs D. stayed outside with the children while Harrison and Amelia examined their patient once more. 'Liv?' Amelia called as she pulled on a pair of gloves. 'I'm going to do an internal, just to check how far you're dilated. All right?'

'Yes.'

They helped Liv remove her clothing, Harrison finding a blanket in the cupboard beneath the washbasin and placing that over their patient, more for modesty than anything else. 'Have you done many deliveries?' Harrison asked Amelia as he washed his hands.

'A few, but I haven't done one for a while.' She stood next to him, their voices barely above a whisper so they didn't alarm or upset their patient.

He grinned. 'It's like riding a bike. You take control of the delivery angle, I'll monitor Liv.'

Amelia nodded. 'Good.' She met his gaze and it was then she realised how close they were standing together. The room was by no means large so she would have to take care not to bump into him.

'Uh…' Harrison looked into her blue eyes, amazed at how deep the colour was. Every time he'd seen her during the past week at the hospital, he'd come to realise just how beautiful she really was, both inside and out. He'd also been curious to know what had upset her the afternoon she had come to his house for tea and biscuits, and today that brief flash of sadness in her face when Liv had reassuringly squeezed little Ethan's hand had given him a clue. Had she lost a child in the past? Was that it? It had to be something and it was a puzzle he was determined to somehow put together.

Amelia turned back to their patient, clearing her throat. 'Liv, did you have any back or stomach pain before coming to the shops today?' She crouched down and began the examination.

'A bit. I didn't sleep much last night but that's to be expected.'

'Did you simply lose your footing on the escalator or were you pushed?' Harrison asked as he rechecked her bandages.

'I…er…lost my footing, I guess.'

'You remember it all?'

Liv closed her eyes. 'Yes.'

'That's a good sign, then. No memory loss.'

'Do you remember your waters breaking?'

'What? No,' Liv replied, then gasped. 'I had a funny sensation in the shower this morning but I thought it was just loss of bladder control.'

'Did you feel heavier afterwards?'

'Yes, come to think of it.'

'Well, your waters have definitely broken because you're fully dilated,' Amelia announced. 'This baby is coming now.'

Liv tensed again as another contraction took hold of her body and she pushed again. She grabbed hold of Harrison's hand and squeezed it, but he didn't seem to mind. When the contraction finally subsided, she apologised to Harrison.

'That's all right. I've been on the receiving end before.'

Amelia watched as he smiled down at their patient, his voice reassuring and relaxing. Yes, she was sure he would have been very supportive to his wife during Yolanda's birth. He was such a doting father and she admired him for tackling the world of single parenthood, rather than leaving Yolanda's care to nannies. Sure, he had Mrs D. but from what Amelia had seen, the woman filled the role of grandmother and housekeeper. She was a part of their family unit, not just the hired help. Besides, she'd seen for herself the amazing relationship between father and daughter and was envious of the bond they shared.

Harrison glanced at her and Amelia immediately looked away, hoping he hadn't seen that wistful and longing expression on her face. She couldn't help her thoughts and the knowledge she could never have children, would never know what it was like to feel a life grow within her, was a part of her and something she lived with daily. She couldn't turn her emotions on and off like a tap, no matter how hard she tried.

'Oh, yes,' Liv said as she closed her eyes. 'You have a little girl.'

'See? Memory is definitely good.'

There was a pause, then Liv choked on a sob. 'The baby's not...? It's all right, isn't it?' A tear trickled down her cheek.

'It's not breech, if that's what you mean,' Amelia answered reassuringly as she did another check. 'In fact, I can see the head, so no problems on that side. Did you have a long labour last time?'

'Yes, and then ended up with an emergency Caesarean.'

'Second babies tend to deliver faster and also this one's probably had enough of being warm and cosy inside you. It wants to come out and join the fun.'

'When are you due?' Harrison asked, taking hold of Liv's hand as she groped for it yet again.

'Two more weeks.'

'Well, this one's impatient to make an entrance.'

'It was kicking so hard.' Liv ground the last few words out as she clenched her teeth and went with the flow of the contraction.

'That's it,' Harrison encouraged. 'Breathe. Remember to breathe.'

'You're doing well, Liv,' Amelia looked up and smiled. 'The head is coming.' When the contraction had eased, Amelia glanced at Harrison. 'Do you mind seeing when the ambulance will get here, please?'

He nodded and returned a moment later. 'About another five minutes.'

'Good. OK, Liv. When the next contraction comes, I want you to really concentrate on your pushing. I know it's difficult, I know you're uncomfortable, but you need to concentrate.'

'My head hurts.'

'We know,' Harrison said gently. 'Soon you can rest. Soon.' He was checking beneath the washbasin again and pulled out another blanket, opening it up and putting it on the chair. He looked into the medical kit and pulled out a pair of scissors, as well as some string, which he cut into suitable lengths so they could tie off the umbilical cord.

'Hand! I need to squeeze your hand,' Liv demanded, and Harrison was once more by her side as the next contraction came. Amelia had to admit she was impressed. Harrison was sweet, attentive and compassionate towards their patient. He had a reassuring bedside manner, which she knew was part of the reason Liv was able to stay calm. He chatted to her, encouraged her and turned on that charm of his.

She'd heard him checking on Mrs D. and the children when he'd gone to ask about the estimated time of arrival of the ambulance. He'd shared a few words with Ethan and was now telling Liv that her son was having fun playing trucks and tea parties with Yolanda. He also told her that her mother was on the way and that, too, seemed to calm Liv so she could cope with the delivery of her second child.

When Liv started to push again, Amelia shook her head, focusing her thoughts and getting them off Harrison. 'OK. That's it. That's it. Keep pushing,' she encouraged. 'One more and the head will be out. That's it.'

'Breathe,' Harrison reminded Liv.

Amelia held her own breath as she watched the baby's head finally come out. 'You've done it. Wonderful.' She reached her fingers around to check for the cord. 'Now, don't push. I just need to check.'

'But I need to,' Liv said.

'No.' Harrison's voice was clear and firm. 'Squeeze my hand. As hard as you can.' He watched Amelia's expression go from pleased to concerned in a split second and instinctively knew the cord was around the neck.

Her next words confirmed it. 'Don't push, Liv. The cord is around the neck. I'm going to try and unhook it.'

Liv was now panting, her gaze focused on Harrison who was helping her to control the very natural urge to push. 'I can't. I can't.'

'You can,' he said, and the words were filled with such assurance that even Amelia believed him.

'It's tight.' Amelia tried again, knowing she couldn't pull on the cord or she'd risk damaging the baby further. 'It won't move.' She racked her brains, knowing Liv would soon be overpowered by the urge to push.

'Cut it,' Harrison said.

'That's what I was thinking.' She reached over to where he'd prepared the pieces of string. 'Hold on, Liv. Just keep holding on. I'm going to do this as quickly as I can.' It was very slippery but Amelia managed to slip the pieces of string around the umbilical cord and tie them off as tightly as she could.

'I can't. I can't.'

'Almost.'

The urgency, the tension filled all three of them and at that moment the paramedics burst into the room.

'Get out!' Harrison ordered, his voice so fierce, they immediately retreated. Nothing could break the concentration, the link between the two doctors, their patient and the little baby whose life was in danger.

Amelia secured the last piece of string then reached for the scissors. 'All right. I'm cutting now, Liv. Just hang on.' She could feel the perspiration peppering her brow as she slid the scissors carefully around the cord, the baby's skin all covered in vernix.

The scissors weren't the sharpest ones around as they were more than likely used to cut bandages rather than hard, thick, rubbery umbilical cords, but finally she was through and the baby was free.

'Done,' was all she said, and took a moment to breathe. 'Shoulders are now rotating. Push when you're ready.'

When the next contraction came, Liv pushed and the shoulders were out. It took just one more push until a baby boy slid into Amelia's waiting hands. He was very slippery and she juggled him for a second, but Harrison was there in an instant, the blanket he'd prepared ready and waiting. Amelia placed the baby onto the blanket before he wrapped him up to keep the infant warm.

There was a little cry and all three adults in the room smiled at the sound. Never had Amelia heard anything more beautiful in her life, tears starting to sting her eyes as she glanced down at the baby. The miracle of life had a way of affecting everyone, but especially Amelia.

'You have a little boy,' Harrison told Liv as he carried the bundle over so she could see her son for the first time. Raising a shaking hand, Liv touched the baby's face, then dropped her hand and closed her eyes.

'He's gorgeous,' Amelia crooned, and sniffed. Harrison smiled, both of them captured in the moment, and in that instant she felt a bond form between them.

'Can I sleep now?' Liv said weakly, smiling at her new son.

'I think I'll get the paramedics in.' Amelia stood, wanting to pull herself together after seeing the way Harrison's deep brown eyes had grown rich with unspoken caring. He cared about her? No. Surely she was reading that wrong. She ripped off her gloves before tossing them in the bin, glancing down at her clothes and seeing the stains. She didn't care. If stained clothes were what it took to ensure the health and well-being of Liv and her son, then so be it. She opened the door and beckoned the paramedics in, apologising for kicking them out a few minutes before.

'Understandable,' the man said as he came into the room. 'Want me to deliver the afterbirth?'

'Be my guest.' Amelia crossed to Liv's side and

brushed a few loose strands of hair out of her patient's eyes. 'You did good.' She sniffed as she crossed to where Harrison was sitting on the seat, the baby on his knee as he checked him out.

'We can probably cut the cord a little shorter now. He's breathing just fine.'

'Sure.' She looked down at the crying baby. 'Nothing wrong with his lungs.' She turned to one of the paramedics. 'Do you have a pair of locking scissors I can use?'

'Of course.'

Amelia and Harrison dealt with the baby, placing a dressing over the rest of the cord before wrapping him up again to keep him warm.

'Do you want to hold him?' Harrison asked, holding the crying baby out to her.

Amelia knew she shouldn't, but she simply couldn't resist and held out her hands for him. The little mite was adorable and she smiled down at him. 'Hello there, handsome.'

He was opening his mouth, rooting around for something to suck on, and she walked to the sink, washed her little finger and placed it into his mouth. 'Good sucking reflex,' she said a moment later, and after a second he spat her finger out again and started to cry once more. She patted his bottom and crooned to him, trying to get him to quieten for a moment.

Harrison watched her and was overcome by how natural she seemed. It only strengthened his resolve that she may have once had a child of her own. The other thing he realised was that she looked highly desirable, standing there, holding a crying baby. It was ridiculous. Most men were attracted to fashionable women, not ones covered with stains, messy hair and holding a newborn, yet to him she looked…just right.

Amelia dragged in a deep breath, loving the feel of the small baby in her arms, but it did nothing to stop her from wishing that things had been different. She felt tears burn her eyes and she knew she had to get out of there, cursing her inability to hide her feelings. When she looked up she was surprised to find Harrison watching her.

'I need to get changed.' She gently placed the baby into his arms and rubbed at her eyes, pretending she was just tired. 'Just as well I went shopping earlier.' She knew her voice was shaky but she couldn't help it.

'Just as well,' he said, shifting the baby so one of his hands was free. He grabbed hers before she walked away. 'Hey. Good job, AJ.'

Amelia glanced down at their hands, surprised to find hers holding his equally as tight. It was strange to see her fingers linked with his and in that one moment she felt a strange sense of calm wash over her as she realised it was all right. It was all right for her to like someone…to like *him*.

His eyes were as dark as warmed chocolate and just as inviting when she looked into them, and she was faced with another revelation—Harrison was experiencing the same sensations she was. It wasn't just a figment of her imagination. Perhaps it was the birth that had made them both lower their defences.

'You, too,' she finally said, her voice barely above a whisper.

Harrison's lips lifted into a smile at her words and for some reason her heart seemed to pound even faster at the way this handsome, gorgeous man was looking at her. Puzzled and needing some space, she backed away, almost knocking into the paramedic. 'I'll…um… get changed.' She turned, opened the door and stepped out, closing it behind her. Mrs D. took one look at her and instantly held up the shopping bags.

'I think you'll be needing these,' she said, and Amelia accepted them with thanks. Yolanda and Ethan were playing on the floor but both stopped when she came out. Yolanda was the first one to her feet and with her hands on her hips, demanded, 'Is dat paint? I like painting.'

Amelia smiled. 'No, sweetie. This isn't paint.' The security man instantly pointed out the way to the nearest female restroom and, nodding her thanks, Amelia headed in that direction.

She wished she could shower as well but the change of clothes certainly did the trick and when she'd bundled her soiled clothing into one of the shopping bags, she stopped in front of the mirror and looked at her reflection.

'It's nothing,' she told herself. 'There's nothing special between the two of you. Just forget him. He's your boss. Nothing more. That moment you shared was because of the miracle of birth. That's all.' She splashed some cool water on her face, dabbed herself dry with the paper hand towel and finger-combed her hair.

'Amelia?'

She was startled when Mrs D. came into the restroom but she was instantly alert. 'Is there a problem?'

'No. No. The paramedics are ready to go.'

'Oh. OK. Thanks.' Amelia gathered up her things and they walked back to the little area where the children were playing. She put her bags down against the wall and went over to where Liv had been transferred to the paramedics' stretcher. 'How are you feeling?'

Liv smiled. 'Tired.'

'I understand. Has your mother arrived yet?'

'About a minute ago,' Harrison said, as he walked out of the room where they'd delivered the baby. Liv's mother was with him, cradling her new grandson. He took one look at Amelia and found it difficult not to stare. She'd changed her clothes and she looked stunning, the blue of her top changing her eyes to a deeper colour, and his gut tightened.

'You are coming to the hospital, aren't you?' Liv said, breaking the moment, and Harrison looked at their patient who was speaking to both doctors.

'Of course,' Amelia said.

Harrison nodded. 'See you there,' he said as the paramedics wheeled Liv away, Ethan and his grandmother following behind with the new baby. Now that it was just Harrison and his family, Amelia knew she had to extract herself once more and quickly picked up her bags.

'Mrs D.,' he said softly. 'Why don't you take Yolanda home while I head to the hospital with AJ? I shouldn't be long.'

'OK.' Mrs D. told Yolanda to pack up her toys but the girl wasn't having a bar of it.

'Daddy tum home, too.'

Harrison crouched down and touched his daughter's hair. 'Daddy needs to go to the hospital. Just for a little while.'

'No!' Yolanda stamped her foot. 'No. My daddy.'

'I don't think she liked seeing you hold that other baby,' Mrs D. said softly. Amelia just watched, knowing she was intruding and should probably leave but she found it impossible to move.

'I won't be long, pumpkin.'

'No, Daddy.' Tears instantly sprang to Yolanda's eyes and she flung herself into his arms. He cradled her tightly and picked her up as she cried on his shoulder.

'She's tired,' Mrs D. said. 'Come on, Yolanda. Daddy won't be long. You've been such a good girl, you can have a treat when you get home. You can watch your favourite show on TV and sing and dance and have lots of fun.'

'I want my daddy,' she said stubbornly, and Harrison was clearly torn.

'It's all right, Harrison,' Amelia said. 'I can do the check on Liv. Go home.'

'But I told Liv…'

'Liv has a three-year-old as well. She'll understand. Spend time with your family.'

Harrison knew the grown-up thing was to leave Yolanda with Mrs D. and quickly go to work to check on his patient. Yet he had promised Yolanda they'd spend the day together and if he left her now, it might cause more issues later.

As he looked at his beautiful daughter, who so badly needed him, it hit home just how pointless it was to even think about the attraction he felt for AJ. He'd been stunned when they'd shared that moment after the baby's birth, wondering if he'd been correct in reading the signals. Signals that he knew he should ignore.

He'd stayed away from relationships since Inga's death, not only because of Yolanda and not wanting to upset the routines he worked so hard to create, but also because he himself wasn't that good at trusting women. Inga had done a number on him and had left Yolanda scarred for life. He knew people couldn't see Yolanda's disability, it wasn't evident in her features, but mentally the child needed help and he was the only one who could provide it. He was her father. She needed him.

His mind made up, he nodded to Amelia. 'Thanks. I'll head home.'

'OK.' Amelia hesitated. 'I can…um…stop by on my way back from the hospital and give you an update, if you like?'

Harrison appreciated her thoughtful gesture as well as the opportunity to see her again but he quickly squashed it. 'It's fine. I can check it out at work on Monday.'

Amelia was a little disappointed but hid it well. 'Of course. Well, have a nice afternoon.'

'You, too. Don't stay too long at the hospital. Goodbye, Amelia-Jane,' he said, and walked out of the room, leaving Amelia with the impression that he'd been saying goodbye for good.

CHAPTER FOUR

AMELIA didn't sleep well that night, wondering if she'd done something wrong where Harrison was concerned. Although she couldn't help but like the man and his gorgeous little girl she knew the attraction between them couldn't go anywhere. Still, the way he'd said good-bye…it rankled and she didn't want her thoughts to be constantly disturbed with thoughts of him.

Amelia was rostered on for day shift and reported to work bright and early on Sunday morning, ready for whatever the day was going to throw at her. She'd pushed Harrison and his daughter to the back of her mind, closed the door and locked it—tight. At the end of June she would be leaving Australia and heading back to England and she needed to remain focused.

The steady Sunday morning trickle of patients was enough to keep her busy but just before lunch Rosie took a call from an ambulance on its way in. 'Oh, my goodness.' Rosie put the phone down, her hand resting on the receiver for a moment.

'What is it?' Amelia asked, and Rosie snapped back to reality.

'Ambulance is on its way in with Harrison's housekeeper. Apparently she fell and couldn't move. Suspected fractured hip.'

'Mrs Deveraux? Oh, poor woman.'

'That's the lady.' Rosie stood. 'I'll assist on this patient. Usually when it's a staff member's family or relative, the head of unit is called in.'

'That would be Harrison.' Amelia nodded and headed towards TR1. 'What's the ambulance ETA?'

'Five minutes.'

'Right. Where's that fancy new digital X-ray machine?'

'I'll organise it,' Rosie said.

'Page the head of orthopaedics and also head of an-aesthetics. If she has fractured her hip, she may need a total hip replacement and Harrison's going to want it done as soon as possible.'

'I'll get it organised.'

'Get Mrs Deveraux's case notes ordered up. I want to know her blood type and anything she may be allergic to.'

Rosie headed off to instruct her nursing staff while Amelia checked everything in TR1, going over differ-ent scenarios in her head. Poor Mrs D. She wondered what had happened. Had Yolanda seen the fall? Was the little girl upset? Had Harrison been there or had he been out for a run along the beach?

When the ambulance siren came closer, Amelia headed out to meet it, not surprised when Harrison opened the doors from the inside and climbed out the second the vehicle stopped. 'Come here, pumpkin,' he said, turning and holding his arms out.

'No!' came the wail from Yolanda.

'It's all right.' Harrison soothed. Amelia walked over, noticing he was once more dressed in his painting garb. He looked so handsome, all scruffy like that.

'Hi,' she said, and peered into the back of the ambulance to see Yolanda clutching Mrs D., the chubby arms wrapped around the woman's hand. 'Oh, Yolanda. Did you come to see me at work?' she asked with delight, and the little girl looked up in surprise. Amelia noted the tear-stained face and realised Harrison must have already had a tough morning. Mrs D. was also trying to do her best to get Yolanda to let go. 'Why don't you come out with me and let the ambulancemen get Mrs D. out? Then you can use my stethoscope to listen to her heart because you're a good doctor.'

'I da doctor,' Yolanda said and slowly loosened her hold.

'You're an excellent doctor,' Harrison said, and held his hand out for his daughter once more, the paramedics waiting impatiently to get to their patient. There was no point in removing Yolanda by force or trying to get her out any sooner than necessary if he didn't want her to end up having a complete tantrum, which he was trying to avoid at all costs.

'Yes, remember how well you bandaged Daddy's hand the other day,' Amelia agreed, and Harrison could have hugged her. He had no idea how or why Yolanda had taken to Amelia, but the fact that she had was a godsend at this moment.

Amelia held out her stethoscope. 'Here you go, darling. You come and hold this while Mrs D. gets to ride on the wheely-bed inside.'

'I want a ride, too.'

Amelia glanced across at the porter standing by the door, looking on interestedly. 'Do you have a spare wheelchair I could borrow?' she asked.

'Sure.' He brought one over.

'I've got something better than the bed,' Amelia said with delight. 'I've got a wheely-chair.'

'Oh,' Mrs D. said with disappointment. '*I* wanted to ride in the chair not the bed. You're so lucky, Yolanda.'

Instantly, the child released the woman and headed for her father, who lifted her from the ambulance and into the waiting wheelchair. Amelia handed over her stethoscope and the child took it eagerly, hooking it into her ears and listening to her heartbeat like a pro.

'I see she's done that before.' Amelia smiled at Harrison.

'Thank you.' His words were soft but the look in his eyes was totally heartfelt.

'No problem.' She pushed the wheelchair into the hospital.

'Tumming froo,' Yolanda called loudly, and several people turned to look, smiling at the picture they saw. 'Det out of da way,' she said crossly to a nurse. Amelia set the wheelchair to the side of TR1 and held out her hand to Yolanda.

'Come on. Let's see how Mrs D. is doing.' Pleased that Yolanda accepted her hand, they went to where Mrs D. was being transferred onto the hospital barouche. 'See? She's all right.'

'I listen,' Yolanda said, with her stethoscope ready.

'Listen to my heart first,' Amelia suggested, noting they weren't quite ready. She crouched down and let Yolanda do her doctor routine, all the while listening to Harrison explaining what had happened and then giving orders as to what he wanted. Apparently, Mrs D. had slipped in the kitchen and fallen hard.

'Stick tongue out,' Dr Yolanda instructed, and Amelia

obliged. 'Say, "Ah."' Again, Amelia did as she was told. 'You O-tay. Now Mrs D.'

'OK but I'll need to pick you up.'

Yolanda immediately held out her arms and Amelia lifted her, holding her close for a moment and breathing in the sweet scent of powder, sunshine and innocence. Delicious. When the blonde ringlets brushed the side of her face, Amelia smiled and couldn't help but drop a kiss on the flaxen head.

'All right, bring her over, AJ,' Harrison said. Although he'd been dealing with his housekeeper and making sure she was all right, he'd been watching and marvelling at the way Amelia had dealt with Yolanda. Was she good with all children or was it just his daughter? The two had certainly formed a bond, which, given that Amelia wasn't going to be here for very long, he wasn't sure was a good thing.

Amelia held Yolanda as she listened to Mrs D.'s heart and then made her stick her tongue out.

'Ooh, dat tongue not good. You need op-ray-shun.'

'She's good,' Rosie said with a chuckle.

'What do you expect?' Harrison preened. 'She's a chip off the old block. I just wish I could diagnose someone just by looking at their tongue.'

'Would save us all a lot of time,' Amelia agreed. 'Dr Yolanda, do you think we need to take some X-rays?'

Yolanda thought for a moment. 'Yes. X-rays now.' With that, she wriggled out of Amelia's arms and all but tossed her stethoscope back at her, Amelia catching it just in time. 'I do da witing now.'

'I'll take her,' one of the nurses said, but Yolanda flatly refused, clinging to Amelia's hand.

'No. I stay Meel-ya.'

Amelia was filled with pride and pleasure at the acceptance from the three-year-old. Never before had she become this close to a child and it was…lovely. 'We'll go to the nurses' station and write up the notes,' she said, and again Harrison nodded.

'I'll let you know when we have an image.' Harrison smiled at her, then winked. Amelia headed off with Dr Yolanda in tow, trying to control the warm and fuzzy feeling he'd given her by winking. She wished he hadn't done it because winking was intimate, personal and it only served to enhance the connection she felt with him.

She sat Yolanda next to her at the nurses' station, giving her a piece of paper and a pen. The little girl began writing, mumbling to herself as she made important squiggles on the page. Amelia listened to her, recognising 'tongue' and 'op-ray-shun' as she continued her earnest reporting.

When Harrison came to get her, Yolanda was still very busy. Amelia smiled at him. 'Do you mumble when you write up notes?' she asked, and watched as he shrugged with slight embarrassment.

'I might,' he said slowly, then chuckled. 'We have an image.'

'What's the verdict?'

'Come and see. Yolanda? Do you want to see the X-ray?' he asked, and she stopped her 'work' and went willingly into his arms. The three of them headed back to TR1.

'The fact that you're not looking so stressed must mean it's good news,' Amelia commented.

'It's better than I'd hoped,' Harrison replied, surprised she'd been able to read him so easily.

Amelia looked at the digital image they'd captured and nodded. 'Excellent. Acetabula cup is intact, the head of the femur looks good. Mrs D., you've fractured the neck of femur in just the right place. Any higher and you would have needed a total hip replacement.'

'That's what Harrison said.'

'And me, too,' Yolanda demanded, trying to touch the digital screen, but her father kept pulling her hand back.

'You're the best little doctor,' he said, kissing her cheek.

'I a *big* doctor.'

'Yes, of course. I'm sorry.'

The orthopaedic surgeon arrived and Amelia offered to take Yolanda again while Harrison spoke to him, but this time Yolanda chose to stay with her father.

'The break is easily fixed with a few screws, possibly a plate if we need it, but for the most part surgery should take about forty-five minutes,' the orthopod reported.

'What time can you get her in?' Harrison asked, and the surgeon checked what time Mrs D. had last eaten.

'I'd say around three this afternoon.'

Harrison nodded. 'Great.' He shook hands with the orthopod and the anaesthetist, leaving Mrs D. in their hands.

'Are you heading home now?' Amelia asked as they walked back to the nurses' station.

'No. I think we'll hang around.'

'That's a long time to hang around,' she said, glancing at Yolanda, who'd scrambled out of her father's arms and resumed her medical reporting, adding another sheet of paper. 'Won't Yolanda get bored?'

'No. She's used to the hospital. Besides, I think she'd like to go to the zoo.'

Amelia frowned. 'I thought you were going to stay—'

At the word 'zoo', Yolanda had stopped what she'd

been doing, her face filled with delight. 'Zoo! Zoo!' She clambered off the chair and started jumping around, clapping her hands.

'I think I'm missing something,' Amelia said. 'The zoo's in the city, isn't it?'

Harrison took Yolanda's hand. 'Why don't we show AJ the zoo?' he asked his daughter, who immediately nodded and slipped her other hand into Amelia's, putting herself between the two adults. 'Let's go.'

They headed down the corridor to the lifts, Yolanda running ahead to press the button. 'I do it,' she said, and when the lift arrived, she pressed the button for the fourth floor.

'They have a zoo in the hospital? Isn't that against health regulations?'

Harrison smiled. 'It's what she calls the children's ward because there are animals all around the playroom and there's a gate that keeps all the live little animals…' he tickled his daughter as he said the words '…safe inside.'

'Oh. I haven't had a chance to see the children's ward yet.'

'That's why we brought you along.' When the lift arrived on the fourth floor, Yolanda was out like a shot and running down the corridor. Harrison quickened his pace but knew exactly where he'd find his daughter.

'She certainly knows her way around.'

'As I said, she's used to the hospital and she's been to the children's ward many times before.'

'Oh. Was she sick?'

Harrison considered the question for a moment. 'Not healthwise. She has regular appointments here, though.' He didn't have time to say anything else as Yolanda was standing by the gate into the 'zoo' and begging to be let in. He unlatched it and she rushed in, ignoring the other four children who were in there and headed straight for the soft animal toys.

'I'll just go speak to the sister, let her know Yolanda's here.' He disappeared and Amelia watched the little girl, noting the look of absolute delight on her face as she began pulling out one soft animal after another and lining them all up, talking to each of them in turn. When Harrison returned, he went in, holding the gate for Amelia who hesitantly followed.

'All right, pumpkin,' he said. 'You stay here until Daddy comes to get you.'

'O-tay.'

'What does she do if she needs you sooner?' Amelia asked.

Harrison turned to his daughter. 'What do you do, Yolanda, if you need Daddy?'

'I get da zoo-teeper and she get Daddy.' Yolanda nodded with satisfaction and accepted a kiss from her father before going back to bossing the animals around.

'I presume the zoo-keeper is the ward sister?' Amelia asked as they left Yolanda.

'Correct, Dr Watson.'

They headed back to A and E and Harrison went off to check on Mrs D. Rosie had another case for Amelia and she collected the notes and went to cubicle four to investigate. Two hours later, she was writing up a different set of case notes when another ambulance arrived.

The patient was wheeled in, yelling and screaming abuse at the staff. Amelia headed over, glad the paramedics had prewarned them about this one.

'June?' Amelia said, looking at the woman's large, pregnant belly. 'June, you need to calm down.'

The woman let go with a string of curses and the alcohol on her breath was both stale and putrid. 'Leave me alone. I don't have to do anything. I want to go. You can't make me stay.' As she spoke, she clutched her heart and Amelia immediately hooked her stethoscope into her ears.

'Let me listen, June.'

'Get away—'

'What is going on here?' Harrison demanded so loudly he made Amelia jump. 'You are disturbing my A and E department. Let Dr Watson examine you.'

His presence momentarily startled the woman and Amelia took the opportunity to listen to the woman's heart.

'It's rapid. Get a blood test, check her alcohol levels. There's swelling of the fingers.' She placed her fingers around June's ankles. 'Swelling there, too. I'll need a urine sample and get the obstetrics registrar here, stat. Possible pre-eclamptic patient.'

June again let her mouth run foul. 'You can't…get away—'

'She's irrational due to the alcohol,' Harrison said as one of the nurses tried to take June's blood pressure. Amelia noted a hardness to his tone she'd never heard before. 'Don't give her anything until the obstetrics registrar has seen her. Get a social worker here, stat. And while we're waiting…' he glared at June '…I think you need a little lesson on the detrimental effects of alcohol on your unborn child.'

June spat at him but missed.

'Charming. Just so you know, your current condition is serious. Both you and your baby could die due to the amount of alcohol you've poured into your body. If your baby doesn't die, it will be subjected to birth ab-

normalities. That means a high probability of facial de-
formities, growth retardation and brain abnormalities.
All this *just* so you could have a good time and drink
yourself stupid.' Although his voice had been soft, the
hardness remained and Amelia realised there was more
going on here than a thoughtless patient. Thankfully
June had settled a bit while Harrison had been talking
and the staff had been able to do the tests they needed.
When the obstetrics registrar arrived, Amelia handed
over June's care and grabbed Harrison's arm, tugging
him from the treatment room.

'I'm going on my break now,' she called to the sister.
Still holding his arm, she headed for the A and E
tearoom, thankful it was empty. 'Are you all right?' she
asked, closing the door behind them.

Harrison walked away from her, rubbing a hand over
his face before raking it through his hair. 'It just gets
me so mad.'

'I can see that.'

'She has no idea what she's done to her baby.'

Amelia took in his agitation, listened to the fury in
his voice and realised there was much more to this than
she'd initially thought. 'I brought you in here because
I thought you needed to cool off. I still do, but if you
feel like talking, getting something off your chest, then
I'm more than happy to listen.'

Harrison paced around the room a few more times,
shaking his head.

'This is personal, isn't it?' she finally said, and he
stopped moving and looked at her. 'Yolanda?'

Harrison nodded. 'Yes. Yolanda.'

'That's what's wrong with her?'

He sighed. 'Short version first—when Yolanda was

born, she was suffering from alcohol withdrawal. When she was twelve months old, she was diagnosed under the foetal alcohol syndrome disorder banner. She has ARND.'

CHAPTER FIVE

'OH.' AMELIA was shocked. She wasn't sure what she'd been expecting him to say but it hadn't been that.

'Do you know what that is?'

'Alcohol-related neurodevelopmental disorder.' She nodded. 'I know about it but I've never dealt with it before.'

'Unfortunately, FASD is becoming more common. Like June out there. Goodness knows what she's doing to her baby.'

'It's not right.'

'You've got that straight, AJ.'

Amelia's pager sounded and she sighed, wishing they hadn't been interrupted. She checked the number. 'Orthopaedics. I'd say this is about Mrs D.' She crossed to the house phone and called.

'Is Harrison with you?' the surgeon asked.

'Yes.'

'We weren't sure how to contact him but triage sister said he was with you.'

Amelia held the phone out to Harrison. 'It's for you.'

He nodded and accepted the phone, listening for a moment. 'I'll be right there.'

'Problem?' she asked as he hung the receiver up and headed for the door.

'They're taking her in earlier and I wanted to see her.'

'Of course.' Amelia's pager sounded again and she rolled her eyes. 'Let me know what happens.'

'I will.' He paused at the door and looked at her. 'Thanks for listening, AJ.'

She smiled. 'I don't think I did much.'

'You'd be surprised.' With that he headed off and it took Amelia a moment to get her thoughts in gear before returning to her job. Now this day was really starting to drag.

Mrs Deveraux's operation went well and even though Amelia's shift had finished, she waited around until the housekeeper was in Recovery.

'You still here?' Harrison asked as she came into Recovery.

'Yes. Yolanda still at the zoo?'

He nodded. 'I've just received a call from the ward sister.'

'You mean zoo-keeper,' she corrected him, and he smiled. 'How's Mrs D.?'

'Doing well. Surgery was uncomplicated and she'll only have to be in hospital for about five days.'

'I'll bet that's better than you initially thought.'

Harrison exhaled slowly. 'I heard her scream and then rushed into the kitchen to see her lying on the floor.' He shook his head. 'Her hip was at such a bad angle, I was positive she'd need a total hip replacement. Then Yolanda came in, took one look at Mrs D. and burst into tears.'

'Well, everything's settled now.'

'Yes. I'd better go get Yolanda. Are you on your way home?'

'I am, thank goodness.'

'Want to walk together?'

Amelia smiled, tingles spreading through her. 'I'd love to.'

'Good. I'll meet you out front in about ten minutes.'

'Absolutely.' She watched as he headed off and then turned to Mrs Deveraux. A moment later, the house-keeper's eyes fluttered open. 'Hi, there.' Amelia smiled.

'It's over?' Mrs D. asked.

'You're all done. All fixed up and ready for a relaxing week eating hospital food and being put through your paces by physiotherapists.'

'That doesn't sound relaxing.' Mrs D. tried to laugh but her mouth was too dry. Amelia quickly scooped some ice chips for her. 'Thank you, dear.' She swallowed them and sighed. 'A whole week, you say?'

'Around five days. Hospitals usually like to kick patients out at Easter and that starts this coming Friday.'

'Oh dear. How will Harrison cope with Yolanda?'

Amelia admitted the thought had crossed her mind but she'd told herself firmly it was none of her business. 'He'll cope. He's resourceful.'

'But she can't go into daycare. It's not good for her. The other children won't understand and…' Mrs D. was starting to get worked up and Amelia immediately calmed her down.

'Shh. Harrison will sort it out. It'll be fine. Yolanda will be fine. You concentrate on getting better.'

'Yes.' Mrs D. closed her eyes. 'Yes.'

She was dozing once more when Amelia left to go and meet Harrison and Yolanda, and as they walked home, preferring to walk along the beach rather than the footpath, Amelia wondered whether she should ask him.

For the moment they were both content to watch Yolanda running ahead, looking at the shells on the sand, stopping every now and then to pick one up and put it in her pocket. 'Where does she get the energy?' Amelia asked. 'I'm getting exhausted just watching her.'

Harrison chuckled. 'She has healthy food prepared for her, she sleeps for hours a day...not all in one go, you understand. Two hours here, five hours there,' he added. 'And she doesn't have a care in the world. She's free.'

Amelia sighed. 'Sounds lovely, doesn't it?'

'We had it once.'

'Why did we let it go?'

'Innocence.' Harrison agreed with a nod. 'And Yolanda had part of her innocence taken away the instant she was born.'

'ARND?'

'Yes. I gave you the short version before. Are you ready for the long, extended one where you get all my footnotes and if you're lucky I might even draw you some pie graphs in the sand?'

Amelia chuckled. 'You seem OK with it all.'

'I am—*now*. It's been a long and difficult two years, AJ. Why women think it's OK to drink during pregnancy is totally beyond me. It's like driving a car without your seat belt on. It's common sense not to drink, that the alcohol will damage the baby, and yet they do it.'

'Women like June.' Amelia nodded in understanding.

'Seeing her just triggered the helplessness I first experienced when Yolanda was diagnosed. Inga probably drank throughout her entire pregnancy. Even when I eventually found out, she didn't stop.'

Amelia stayed silent, waiting for him to continue, knowing how important this was to him.

'She became pregnant with Yolanda almost immediately after we married, and for that first year things were a little rocky but workable. Six months after Yolanda's birth, she'd had enough of motherhood. She said she wanted a divorce and I was happy to go along with it. She moved out, into a hotel.'

'And you became a single father.'

'Yes. Inga had a drinking problem but she couldn't see it. I think she had a romantic picture of what it was like to be a doctor's wife.'

'You mean the money, the prestige, the big house and fancy cars?'

'All that and more. Instead, she was alone a lot of the time because I was always at the hospital. She hated the phone ringing on my days off and if I offered to cover for a friend or change with someone, she became livid.'

'Sounds like a bad time.'

'The bottle became her friend, along with other *special* friends, but that wasn't really until after Yolanda was born.'

'Yolanda is gorgeous, Harrison. You should be proud.'

'Thanks, AJ. I am but, gorgeous or not, the poor baby has suffered from having two parents who didn't do enough for her when it counted.'

'Did you try to stop your wife from drinking?'

'Once I found out, yes. Nothing seemed to work. She told me she'd stopped when she hadn't but, again, I wasn't around much.'

'You're a doctor, Harrison. It's your job.'

'My daughter's life and well-being should have been more important,' he argued. 'It's been a long and difficult road for me to admit my daughter has a disability and I'm part of the cause.'

'You're not the cause, Harrison. You're her hope.'

'I'm her *father*. I should have done more.'

'You're doing more now. What happened after she was diagnosed with ARND?'

'I sought help. I've managed to find a therapist who specialises in this area and she's been wonderful. She's helped me to realise that Yolanda is Yolanda and while she might do things differently from other children, she's my child and it's my responsibility to help her. I've realised that it's the parent who needs the most training. Once we can understand and adapt to the way our children do things, it makes life a lot easier all around.'

'You said she often wanders off.'

'Yes. Sometimes I feel like putting a chain of bells around her so I know where she is at all times.'

Amelia laughed. 'I think a lot of parents probably feel that way.'

'You could be right but she stops my heart every time I can't find her.'

Amelia watched the way he was rubbing his hands together, watching the agitation he was feeling. 'It was a good thing she was diagnosed so early.'

'I was almost waiting for the signs. As you can tell, she has no physical disability, no facial anomalies, no growth retardation. She does, however, have problems with her central nervous system but, again, they're not excessive. She has impaired fine motor skills and poor eye-hand co-ordination.'

'And yet she does baking with Mrs D.'

Harrison smiled. 'Part of her therapy.'

'And she gets to have fun, too.'

'Yes. She also has cognitive abnormalities, such as lower intellectual function and behaviour and social problems.'

'Not sleeping well at night? Wandering off?'

'Exactly, although her memory appears to be improving at the moment so that's a promising sign.'

'Oh. Has she had a breakthrough?'

'Yes. With you.'

'Me?' Amelia was astonished. 'How?'

'She's remembered you. You must have made a big impact on her because she's always asking when "Meelya" is coming back to play dolls.'

'Wow. I'm…I'm flattered.'

'Good. You should be.' He paused. 'In fact, she's quite taken with you, AJ.'

Amelia glanced at him, hearing the concern in his tone, and it took a moment for his words to sink in. 'Oh. That's perhaps not so good.'

'I think it's important to be honest with her, to let her know that you won't always be around.'

'Agreed.' Amelia looked ahead to where Yolanda had bent to pick up another shell before she came hurtling back to show them what she'd found. Her heart twisted with love and she realised she was already strongly attached to the little girl, but how could she not be? Yolanda was so easy to love.

And what of her father?

The thought simply popped into her head and Amelia tried to push it away. There could never be anything but friendship between herself and Harrison, even if she secretly wanted more. Suffering from endometriosis at such a young age hadn't been her idea of fun. It also meant she needed to be very choosy in her relationships with men and although she didn't have too much experience, it was more for self-preservation than fear of wanting to commit.

'OK,' Harrison was saying to his daughter. 'Find three more shells and then it's time to go home.'

Amelia glanced around them as Yolanda ran off again and she realised they were almost level with their respective homes. 'So…what are you going to do while Mrs Deveraux is in hospital?'

'Well, I'm not a bad cook, and the cleaning shouldn't be too difficult to maintain.'

Amelia laughed, tapping his shoulder lightly. 'That's not what I meant.'

Harrison smiled but it didn't last for long. 'Yolanda?' He shook his head. 'I've been trying to figure out the best solution. There's a daycare centre at the hospital but I'm not sure if they'd be able to take her at such short notice.'

'Would she be all right in daycare?'

'With the staff or the other children?'

'Both, but more so the children. Yolanda has the disadvantage of not *looking* as though she has a disability. Other children would expect her to react to things the same way they do.'

'It's only for a few days. I can take a day or so off.'

'Use up your annual leave? But you've just returned from a conference.'

'I know, and I'm behind in my paperwork, although I guess I could try and do that from home.'

Amelia thought for a moment, wondering whether she should say what was on the tip of her tongue. She cleared her throat. 'Well…um…I could help.'

Harrison turned to look at her. 'What?'

'I live close. Yolanda likes me. You could alter my shifts, put me on afternoons. That way, I'm with her when you leave in the morning and I can bring her to work with me in the afternoon when I start my shift.'

He pondered her offer for a moment, wondering whether he was capable of completely trusting Yolanda to Amelia's care. Could *he* trust Amelia? He'd trusted once and it had ended up with Yolanda suffering for that misplaced trust. So far, though, Amelia hadn't given him any reason not to trust her and Yolanda went to her without hesitation. Surely that was good? 'You'd be starting work at around three o'clock. The earliest I could leave would be around four-thirty,' he said out loud as he tried to work things through.

'The zoo?'

'Possibly. Yolanda has therapy three times a week. Well, Friday's out because that's a public holiday for Easter, so that leaves two sessions.'

'What time does she usually have them?'

'Around ten-thirty, but if I could change it to three o'clock, when you start work, then she could have her sessions and then go to the children's ward until I'm finished.' He nodded. 'That might just work, AJ.'

'What days does she have therapy?'

'Monday and Wednesday this week.'

'Well, my rostered day off is Tuesday—'

'And I'll take Thursday off.'

'And then it's just Friday, and Mrs D. should be ready to come home.'

'I'll still need help once Mrs D.'s home, but not as much.'

Amelia shrugged. 'I can still help.'

Harrison stopped walking and looked at her. 'That's really generous of you, AJ.'

Amelia shrugged again. 'Hey, that's what neighbours are for.'

'I'm very picky about who I leave my daughter with

but the way she goes to you, the way she trusts you, it speaks volumes.'

'And once Mrs D.'s up and about, I'll start backing off and spending less time with Yolanda. Sort of wean her off so when I leave at the end of June, she'll be…' Amelia's voice trailed off and she sighed.

'Sorry to see you go,' Harrison finished. 'She won't be the only one.' He reached for her hand and gave it a little squeeze and Amelia felt the heat from his touch warm her whole body. 'Thank you for offering to help.'

'You are going to take it, aren't you? I mean, it's the best thing for Yolanda.'

Harrison nodded and dropped her hand at the same time. 'I'm going to take your offer, yes.'

'Well…good.' Now that she'd made it and he'd accepted, she was starting to have second thoughts. She took in their surroundings. 'I'd…uh…better get going.' She jerked her thumb over her shoulder towards her apartment.

'Me, too. What were you rostered on to work tomorrow?'

'Nights. Tina's on afternoons so I'll call her to swap tomorrow and then we just need to sort out a swap for Wednesday—I was on a day shift.'

Harrison nodded. 'I'll do that tomorrow.'

'Thanks.' She headed off then stopped. 'I almost forgot, what time do you want me?'

His gaze widened. 'Pardon?'

'Uh…to report for duty in the morning,' she added quickly, realising the double-entendre.

'How's seven-thirty?'

'Great.' She started up the beach again, stopping to say goodbye to Yolanda on the way. The child gave her a shell and was then happy to part, and as Amelia walked quickly to her apartment, she knew she'd treasure the gift for ever.

Once safe behind the door of her apartment, she crossed to the phone and tapped out Tina's number. After four rings the answering-machine began its recorded message and Amelia growled down the phone.

'I'm here, I'm here,' Tina said, and switched the machine off. 'Who's growling at me?'

'It's *me*,' Amelia said.

'Oh, hey, there. How's life?'

'Miserable. You'll never guess what I've gone and done.'

'Do I need to get comfortable?'

'Very.' Amelia blurted out everything to her friend. 'And then I find myself offering to look after his daughter!'

Tina chuckled.

'What's so funny?' she demanded.

'I love the way you go to extraordinary lengths to keep yourself apart from people, to not get involved in people's lives, and here you're slap-bang in the middle of a relationship before you know it.'

'Relationship?'

'Yes, Amelia, or should I call you AJ?' Tina teased. 'You and Harrison. I've seen the way you two look at each other.'

'But I hardly know the man.'

'You're going to get to know him much better after the coming week.'

Amelia groaned. 'Perhaps I should go and tell him I can't help. I mean, you're right. I go to such lengths not to involve myself because happy families aren't for me. It's not healthy for me because I so desperately want to have a family but can't. It just isn't fair,' she wailed.

'That's very true.' Tina cleared her throat. 'But think about it this way, Amelia. You can't have kids and so even if you do find a gorgeous, handsome man and get married, you'll never have the happy children fantasy.'

'Your point?'

'You've just been given an opportunity.'

'I don't follow.'

'To play happy families. For the next few days you get to spend time with Yolanda. You get to be a mother figure to her. You know it can't last. You've told me that once Mrs D. is back on her feet you'll start withdrawing into your shell once more, so why not take this opportunity, Amelia?'

'It's cruel.'

'For who?'

'For me. It'll give me a taste of what I can never have.'

'It'll also give you one or two glorious weeks of heaven, especially if you and Harrison get closer.'

'Stop.' Amelia sighed. 'I guess it's too late to back out now.'

'Especially as I've already agreed to switch shifts with you.'

'You think I should do this?'

'I do.'

So Amelia-Jane Watson reported for duty to her boss's house at seven-thirty the next morning. Harrison opened the door and ushered her in. 'Sorry. I'm running late and I can't get Yolanda to eat her breakfast.'

She nodded and followed him through to the kitchen, where Yolanda was sitting up at the bench, a bowl of cereal, a plate of toast, a boiled egg, milk, juice and water sitting in front of her.

'She keeps changing her mind but I can't seem to get her to eat more than one mouthful and she's refusing to drink.'

Amelia tried to hide her smile at the mess but Harrison caught her.

'Don't you dare,' he said, pointing his finger.

'Sorry.' She covered her mouth with her hand but noticed his own lips twitching. 'Look, you head to the hospital, I'll try and get something into her.'

'No biscuits until she's eaten at least one of those,' he said to Yolanda, pointing to the food in front of his daughter. 'Daddy's got to go to the hospital.'

'Landa tum, too.' She started climbing off the stool but he stopped her.

'No, pumpkin. Daddy gets to go to *boring* work but you get to stay here and play *dolls* with *Amelia*. You lucky duck.'

Yolanda thought about that for a moment. 'Yay. I lucky duck.'

'OK. Kiss Daddy.' She did. 'Drink your juice.' She didn't. Harrison snapped his fingers and shrugged. 'I just can't win.'

Amelia laughed as he started putting papers into his briefcase. 'How's Mrs D. this morning?'

'She's doing well. I'll stop by and see her and if there's any change I'll give you a call, but I'm expecting her to make an uncomplicated recovery.' He glanced around him. 'Where are my car keys?'

Amelia looked on the kitchen bench and saw a set of keys. She picked them up and dangled them from her finger. 'These?'

'Ah. AJ. You're brilliant.' He snagged the keys and then headed for the door. 'I'm taking the car today so call me if you need anything or if there's any trouble. Keep the doors locked while you're in the house as she's as slippery as an eel.'

'Noted. Go.' She watched him walk out, realising they'd just played out a perfect domestic scene... except for the ending. The ending was usually where the husband kissed the wife before leaving for work. At least, that was the way it worked in the stereotypical world. Even the thought of Harrison kissing her, and she'd thought about it on quite a few occasions, was enough to make her feel hot and cold all over.

When his car had disappeared down the driveway, she made sure the door was locked and returned to Yolanda's side. The child was still sitting at the bench but the food was now smothered and smeared all over the kitchen bench, the cup of juice dripping down the sides and onto the floor.

'Perfect domestic scene,' Amelia muttered to herself before she set about getting things cleaned up. The two of them had a good day and she even managed to get both food and drink into Yolanda, but the cherry on top was when the child gave way to sleep after lunch and dozed in the lounge for a good hour and a half.

Amelia picked up the phone and called Harrison at the hospital. 'Hi. It's me,' she said.

'Hey. I was just about to call you.'

'I figured as much as it's almost an hour since your last call.'

'Oh. I haven't been calling too much, have I?'

'Hourly check-ups might be considered a bit much

but it's the first day so I'm letting it slide. Try it tomorrow and you might get a different story.'

Harrison chuckled. 'Sorry. Over-protective father and all that.'

'I understand,' she said, letting the sound of his laughter wash over her. 'Anyway, I just wanted to let you know I've managed to get her to sleep and didn't want you ringing in case the phone woke her.'

'Good going.' He was impressed.

'We'll see you around three o'clock.'

'Looking forward to it,' he said, and rang off.

Amelia settled back next to Yolanda, her hand resting on the child's head. She'd known the little girl would be a lot of work but the morning had been very full. Not that she hadn't enjoyed it—she had. They'd both had a ball, playing dolls and dancing in front of the television and having tea parties, but she had to go to work soon and somehow stay awake. She was glad the next day was her rostered day off.

Just after half past two they packed a bag for Yolanda, stopped at Amelia's apartment so she could quickly change for work and then set out, walking along the beach towards the hospital. Yolanda managed to collect two pocketfuls of shells and by the time they arrived at the hospital Amelia had to stop and brush all the sand off the three-year-old before presenting her to her father.

'Here she is. All in one piece.'

Harrison gave Yolanda a big cuddle then looked at Amelia. 'Can't say the same for you. You look a little frazzled, Dr Watson.'

'I feel it. How does Mrs D. do it?'

'Ah, that's elementary, my dear Watson. She doesn't

have to come and work a shift at the hospital after spending all day running around after an active three-year-old.'

'I guess. I think I even slept for half an hour while Yolanda was sleeping, I was so worn out.'

Harrison chuckled. 'That's what wise parents do. Now, if you'll excuse me, I'll get Yolanda up to her therapy appointment.'

Amelia nodded, pleased with his reference to wise parents, and she hugged herself. She may be exhausted but she'd had an amazing time playing with Yolanda and she couldn't thank Harrison enough for giving her the opportunity to play happy families for a few days. Tina was right. This might be good for her.

Tuesday panned out much the same only this time Amelia not only knew what to expect but had better control over things. She was even able to cook dinner for Harrison so by the time he returned home from the hospital, a little later than usual, she was just taking a pasta bake out of the oven.

'Something smells good,' he said, as he scooped up Yolanda and came into the kitchen. Again, it was a domestic scene and Amelia could once more imagine him coming over and giving her a kiss.

'I'm…uh…no chef but I can get by.'

Harrison chuckled and let a squirming Yolanda go. 'Had a better day?' he asked, picking up a fork and digging it into the steaming dish.

'Hey. Just wait and I'll dish it up onto a plate for you.'

'Thanks. I'm ravenous.'

'There's a salad in the fridge so why don't you get that out? I've also made Yolanda's favourite.' She opened the microwave door and retrieved a bowl of porridge.

'Porridge? That's her favourite?'

'It is today. She's eaten three bowls of it and also demanded it for dinner.'

'A bit repetitive but, hey, she's eating and it's healthy.' Harrison nodded. 'Good work, Watson.'

'Thanks, Stapleton.' She took out one plate and started dishing up.

'Wait. Aren't you having any?'

'Uh…I…er…no.'

'Why not? There's plenty here and it seems ridiculous for you to go back to your apartment and cook. No. Stay and we can have dinner.'

She shrugged, knowing it was pointless to argue, and pulled out another plate. Harrison sat Yolanda down and watched with delight as she dug into the porridge.

'I've never seen her eat so well. Amelia-Jane, you're a miracle-worker.'

She blushed with pleasure at his compliments. The three of them sat at the kitchen bench and ate dinner together, Harrison keeping the conversation flowing on a light level. After he'd seen Amelia to the door and said goodnight, he concentrated on getting his daughter settled. Thankfully, it didn't take long and while he sat by her bed, stroking her blonde curls, he thought about Amelia and how tempting it had been to simply walk into the house, cross to Amelia's side and kiss her.

It felt natural and right and that alone should be scaring him…but it wasn't. He'd had one bad marriage, yes, but it didn't take a fool to notice that Amelia-Jane Watson was completely different from his ex-wife. For starters, Yolanda adored her 'Meel-ya' and he'd often relied on Yolanda's inbuilt radar, believing that kids could sense the goodness in a person.

He walked into the kitchen and began clearing away

the dishes, rinsing them before stacking them in the dishwasher, and once he was done he settled down to do some paperwork. Five minutes later he crossed to the TV and turned it on. Two minutes later he turned it off and started to pace around, wondering what was wrong with him. Amelia-Jane was on his mind and along with thoughts of her came thoughts of kissing her, and he realised the urge to press his mouth to hers was intensifying faster than he'd anticipated.

Also, for some inexplicable reason, his house felt all wrong. Perhaps it was because Mrs D. wasn't around but after a moment he dismissed that thought. It was Amelia. For the past two days she'd been there, caring for his daughter, and somehow she'd put her stamp on the place. She hadn't rearranged anything, nothing had outwardly changed, but when he walked into the kitchen he could smell her perfume. When he looked at Yolanda's room, he pictured Amelia and his daughter, side by side, playing dolls. Thoughts of her, visions of her were all around his house and it felt…right.

It also made him feel lonely, and until that moment it was a feeling he hadn't thought he'd ever experience.

CHAPTER SIX

WEDNESDAY was a repeat of Monday, the only thing different being the overwhelming urge to kiss Harrison hello and goodbye whenever she saw him. Amelia was glad when Thursday came and it was Harrison's turn to stay at home and look after his daughter. Amelia caught up with Mrs Deveraux at the hospital, pleased to see the housekeeper up and about.

'I can go home tomorrow,' she told Amelia the instant she saw her.

'That's fantastic news.'

'Yes, and thank you, dear, so much for helping Harrison and Yolanda.'

Amelia smiled. 'It's been my pleasure.' And it had. She'd lived a few days of utter happiness and it had provided her with memories that would definitely be keeping her warm on the cold English winter nights.

When she finished work, pleased it was a day shift, she headed home, eager to relax and put her feet up. At least, she told herself she was eager. She wasn't scheduled to see Harrison or Yolanda that day, Harrison not needing her babysitting services, and that thought was highly depressing. She liked seeing them, *both* of them, but not that night. Besides, it was almost Yolanda's bedtime.

After she'd had a quick shower and changed into a hot pink tracksuit, all nice and snuggly, there was a knock at her door. When she opened it, she was astonished to see Harrison and Yolanda there.

'We got dinner,' Yolanda announced, as she marched into Amelia's apartment, quite at home.

'We thought it was the least we could do to say thank you,' Harrison said after she'd invited them in. He'd had an overwhelming urge to see her and now that he looked at her, in that bright tracksuit, he was extremely glad he'd given in.

'Ooh. Is pi-i-in-n-nk.' Yolanda ran her hands up and down Amelia's arms and Harrison couldn't believe how jealous he felt of his daughter, being able to touch Amelia when she wanted to.

'I thought you'd like it.' Amelia smiled. 'So, do we need to eat this while it's hot? I'll get some plates. Yolanda, can you help me to set the table, please?'

Yolanda followed Amelia around and Harrison simply watched the two of them. With Yolanda wearing pink and white pyjamas, they were almost like two peas in a pod...just different sizes, of course.

Once more he kept the conversation light, prompting a tired Yolanda to tell Amelia what they'd made.

'A big pickshure for Mrs D.' She stretched her arms out wide.

'A welcome-home poster,' Harrison added. 'And it kept us busy for a good portion of the day.'

'I can well believe it.'

They exchanged hospital news and when Yolanda had yawned twice, Amelia told Harrison to take her home. Reluctantly, he picked his daughter up, the child resting her head on his shoulder. He didn't want to go. He wanted to stay, to prolong the time he had to spend with Amelia. Yes, Mrs D. was coming back tomorrow and he was looking forward to that, but it also meant that Amelia's help would be scaled back and he wouldn't see her nearly as much.

'Listen,' he said when she was about to open the door. 'What are you doing on Saturday morning?'

'Easter Saturday?'

'Yes.'

'Uh…no plans, really. Why?'

'Feel like coming out for breakfast?'

'Breakfast?'

'Sure. Mrs D. and Yolanda will be there.' He smiled down at her. 'I assure you, you'll be quite safe.'

'Are you going out somewhere?'

'We're having breakfast on the beach. It's sort of a tradition. So all you'll need to do is walk outside your door, down the footpath and cross the street and there we'll be, waiting with breakfast on the sand.' He pointed in the direction of the beach. 'A bowl of cereal for me and one for you.'

'Really? Cereal. Be still, my beating heart.'

Harrison chuckled. 'Actually, I think we can do better than just cereal, although if that's all you want, you're more than welcome to eat it.'

'Why on the beach?' She'd never thought of it before but why not? The beach was right there, right outside their windows, so why not make use of it?

'I don't know. We did it for Yolanda's first Easter and we've just sort of continued. We'll have healthy start-the-day-right foods, so hopefully Yolanda will eat more than a bowl of porridge.'

'Oh, well, so long as it's with start-the-day-right foods, you can't possibly go wrong.'

'Funny, AJ.' He shifted Yolanda, who appeared to have fallen asleep. 'You'll come?'

'Will there be any Easter eggs?'

'I thought you didn't like chocolate.'

'I never said I didn't like it. I simply said I prefer savoury to sweet.'

'Well, to answer your question, no. No eggs tomorrow. They're for Sunday. The eggs signify new life, remember. No. No eggs tomorrow.'

'You don't need to convince me,' Amelia said, laughing.

'Good. I'll see you at eight-thirty on Saturday, then.'

'Do I need to bring anything?'

'Just yourself…oh, and your swimmers. We might take a dip before we eat.'

'OK.'

'Sleep sweet, Amelia-Jane.' With that, he opened the door and left, carrying his sleeping daughter home. He carefully put her into her pink and white bed, knowing she'd only stay there for a few hours before joining him in his big king-sized bed because she couldn't sleep. He made himself a drink then sat at the kitchen bench and thought about Amelia. She didn't like fresh flowers and he couldn't give her chocolates but he desperately wanted to give her something. He told himself it would be a thank-you gift for everything she'd done for him and Yolanda that week but he shook his head, knowing he needed to be honest, at least with himself. He wanted to get her something personal, something she could take back to England and remember him by.

So what did a man give a...*friend* for Easter?

On Good Friday, the A and E staff were usually run off their feet and this year was no exception. Amelia had dealt with three drunks, two teenagers who had gone overboard with the happy pills and needed to have their stomachs pumped, one woman with a broken arm after she'd 'fallen' down a flight of stairs and a young man who'd been having heart palpitations. A basic, average late shift.

She'd had conversations with her colleagues, spoken to social workers, contacted parents, checked X-rays and filled in mounds of paperwork, yet the entire time thoughts of Harrison remained at the back of her mind.

Saturday morning dawned bright and early and Amelia worked at containing her excitement at seeing him, having missed him terribly yesterday. She knew she shouldn't. She knew if one day went by when she didn't see her boss that it shouldn't be a big deal, but after spending so much time with them over the past few days, she couldn't help it. How was she ever going to withdraw herself from his life? From Yolanda's?

She shook her head, preferring not to think about it. She closed her apartment door and walked outside, surprised to find so many cars parked and people on the beach at that hour of the morning.

As she walked down the street, she saw Mrs Deveraux come out the house, carrying a large bowl and trying to juggle her walking cane. Amelia called out and Mrs D. turned and smiled as she walked up.

'Let me take that for you,' Amelia said, relieving Mrs D. of her burden.

'Thank you, dear. It's good to see you again.'

'Likewise. How are you feeling? Not overdoing it, I hope.'

'Harrison won't let me.' She pointed across the road. 'He's already over there with Yolanda.' Amelia turned and from where she stood she could see Harrison running down the beach, chasing after his daughter. 'He thought she should get some exercise first. Hopefully, that will help her build up an appetite,' Mrs D. continued.

Amelia nodded and they slowly headed across the road and over the sand dunes to where the beach became flatter. To her surprise, a small table had been set up, with chairs around it and a beach umbrella to provide shade—although it wouldn't provide much at that hour of the morning but, still, it was very picturesque. She put the large bowl of fruit salad down and turned to watch Harrison.

He was wearing knee-length swimming shorts and nothing more. His torso was firm and brown, his legs long and lithe as he pretended to miss capturing his little girl. His hair was ruffled in the breeze and the smile on his face completed the picture of one hundred per cent eye-candy. Amelia found it difficult not to sigh with longing.

Harrison spotted her, waved and then scooped up Yolanda who squealed with delight and giggled with glee, before heading in her direction. 'Hey, AJ. Glad you could come.' He lifted his daughter and blew a raspberry on her tummy before putting her down. She ran off the instant her little feet touched the sand.

Now that he was so close to her…and so much of him was on offer for her to ogle, Amelia found it difficult to know where to look. So she met his gaze and held it, feeling slightly overdressed in her flowing summer skirt and top. She also felt highly self-conscious knowing Mrs D. was taking in every glance, every word and every unspoken word between them.

Harrison reached down and took her hand in his, giving it a little squeeze. 'I really am glad you decided to come.'

Amelia smiled, looked down at their hands, then back to his eyes. 'Me, too.'

'Daddy!' Yolanda called laughingly. 'You tarn't tatch me.'

Harrison reluctantly let go of her hand and shrugged. 'Duty calls,' he said as he took a few steps away. 'Sit down. Be comfortable.' With that, he turned and went to chase his daughter once more. Amelia sat and watched him, laughing at the two of them together. He'd intrigued her right from the first instant she'd met him and now her intrigue had turned to admiration at the way he loved his daughter. It was enough to melt any woman's heart and hers was no exception.

Finally, they were ready to eat and they all enjoyed a feast of cereal, toast, yoghurt, fruit salad, croissants and breakfast muffins. Yolanda did indeed eat quite a bit and her father was very satisfied. It was a picture-perfect morning and Amelia couldn't remember spending a better time at the beach—ever.

Afterwards, Yolanda picked up her bucket and spade and sat down to make sandcastles. 'Daddy,' she called. 'Tum and help me.'

'What's up?' Harrison asked, crossing to his daughter's side.

Yolanda stood there and looked down at the sandcastle she'd made. Her hands were on her hips and she was studying it carefully. 'It need be bigger, Daddy. Much, much bigger.' Now she waved her arms around above her head, showing him how big it needed to be.

'We might need some more help.' Harrison pointed to Amelia.

'Yes.' Yolanda decided her father was right and crossed to Amelia's side, taking her hand. 'Use dis one,' she instructed, putting a sandy bucket onto Amelia's lap. Then she stopped, took a moment to rub her wet and sandy hand over the fabric. 'Dis prwetty.'

'Thank you.' Amelia allowed herself to be pulled up, catching the bucket with her free hand. Next, she found herself sitting on the sand, filling buckets and tipping them over to create the great palace Yolanda was demanding.

'How about getting some shells to decorate it?' she suggested, and Yolanda instantly agreed, tugging Amelia to her feet.

Harrison simply sat there and watched the two of them walk away, hand in hand, their eyes glued to the sand as they looked for pretty shells. Contentment washed over him and tension seeped out as he realised he trusted Amelia. He completely, utterly and totally trusted her with his precious daughter! After Inga he'd thought he'd never trust again yet somehow, during his short acquaintance with Amelia-Jane, his ability to trust had been restored.

By the time Amelia and Yolanda returned from collecting their shells, Harrison had packed everything away. The sandcastle took on an amazing form, with Amelia sculpting the most beautiful structure from sand and water.

'More water, Daddy,' Yolanda said again, holding out a bucket to him.

'Manners,' Harrison reminded her.

'Peeze, Daddy.'

'That's better.' Harrison met Amelia's gaze as he took the bucket from his daughter and headed off. She watched him, admiring the magnificence of his body. Thankfully, before they'd settled down to eat, he'd donned an old T-shirt which had the words 'Professional Beach Bum' written on it. Amelia totally believed it because he certainly looked the part.

Hats, sunglasses and the constant slathering on of sunscreen were all part of the Aussie beach code of practice but when she'd watched Harrison rub cream into his arms, legs and face earlier, she'd been mesmerised…much as she was now.

She continued to watch him as he scooped up some water, navigating his way through the throng of people and little kids enjoying the shallows, the lifeguards on duty making sure people swam in the safety zone between the flags.

When he returned, he sat down next to his daughter, who was all but lying on Amelia's legs as they patted and shaped the sand. Because Yolanda was close, it now meant Harrison was equally as close, his leg brushing one of hers causing a powerful jolt of desire to explode within her. Their eyes met and held, both of them too stunned at their mutual need to hide their reactions.

'Need more shells,' Yolanda said, and scrambled to her feet. 'Tum on, Meel-ya.' She reached for Amelia's hand but Harrison protested on her behalf.

'Why don't you let Amelia have a rest this time? Besides, the shells you find are always the prettiest because *you* are the prettiest.'

Yolanda nodded as though his words made complete sense. She started off but Harrison told her to just look in the area they were sitting in. The number of beach-goers had almost doubled since they'd first started their breakfast and it would be all too easy to lose sight of her.

'So…' he drawled as he patted the sand. 'This is quite a castle. In fact, it's a brilliant sculpture.'

'Yolanda's very clever. She knows exactly what she wants.'

'And you're able to shape and mould and give it to her. This isn't just a sandcastle, AJ, it's a work of art.'

Amelia smiled and shrugged. 'I used to sculpt when I was younger and, besides, the sand here is so fine and easy to use.'

'You don't sculpt any more?'

'No time.'

'Come on. Tell the truth. I know how busy your job is, remember. I've been there, I've done it and, despite what people think, doctors do get a few hours off here and there.'

Amelia dipped her hands in the bucket of water and smoothed a section of the turrets with her fingers. 'I stopped and until today I haven't had the urge to start again.'

'Why did you stop?'

'I uh…got sick. Kind of.'

Harrison sat up straight. 'Are you OK now?' His tone was filled with concern. 'Is everything all right?'

Amelia was touched. 'It was quite a number of years ago and yes, I'm…fine.'

'Do you think you can tell me what happened?' Harrison glanced at her and then back to where Yolanda was starting to wander a bit further away. 'Hold that thought,' he said, and ran off to collect his daughter. When they returned, both adults allowed themselves to be distracted by Yolanda until she declared the masterpiece was finished. Mrs D., who had been watching them from the shade of her umbrella, pulled out a camera and took some photographs of the prettiest princess palace ever.

'That's simply amazing,' she said as she took a snap from a different angle. 'You're extremely talented, Amelia.'

Amelia merely smiled and stood, brushing the sand from her clothes. Harrison watched her, mesmerised by the way she fluffed her fingers through her short hair, her skirt blowing gently around her legs with the slight sea breeze.

'Why don't you two go for a walk?' Mrs D. suggested quietly. 'It's time for Yolanda to be inside, enjoying the air-conditioning, and I could certainly do with resting my leg.'

'OK.' Harrison wasn't about to look a gift horse in the mouth. Time alone with Amelia-Jane…just what he wanted. Harrison told his daughter he was going to go for a walk with Amelia, and Yolanda was more than happy to let him go, especially when Mrs D. was offering icy-poles and a video of Yolanda's favourite kids' entertainment group.

'What parent can compete with four grown men, wearing colourful skivvies, singing and dancing their way into our children's hearts?' he said as they waved to Yolanda before starting off down the beach. As they navigated their way around a few people sunbathing, Amelia wondered if he was going to hold her hand. She hoped so.

Her question was answered a moment later when

she stumbled over the undulating sand and he instantly reached out to steady her. When she was steady, he didn't let go, linking their fingers, the warmth from his arm running up hers. She wasn't sure whether to say something about it or simply to let it happen.

'It's all right if I hold your hand, isn't it?' he asked, then a smile touched his lips.

Amelia nodded. 'It's just been a long time since anyone's held my hand in this way.'

'That's kinda sad, Amelia-Jane.'

'Probably,' she sighed.

They walked in silence, going further down the beach where it was slightly less crowded so they didn't need to dodge as many people. 'I meant to tell you, your file finally arrived from Brisbane.'

'Oh, good.'

'I find it interesting that you've broken your year in Australia into four three-month rotations. That's not normal.'

Amelia shrugged. 'I wanted to see as much of Australia as I could.'

'So you've seen Perth, Melbourne, Brisbane and now Adelaide. Right?'

'Yes.'

'Three months hardly gives you time to make a lot of friends, AJ.' He felt her tense at his words and realised he'd struck a nerve. She loosened her grip on his fingers but he didn't release her hand.

'I'm not looking for friends, Harrison. I'm looking to finish my training.'

'Your file doesn't say anything about you being sick.'

'It won't affect my job performance, if that's what

you're worried about.' She hadn't meant to snap but her words came out brisk.

'That's not what I'm worried about and you know it,' he countered. 'Why did you stop sculpting? Why were you sick? Are you better now?' He shook his head. 'I don't mean to bombard you but there's so much I don't know and I want to, AJ. I want to know about you very much.'

'What's the point, Harrison? I'll be gone soon.'

'The point? The point is, I like you.'

'Oh.' She didn't know how to respond to that and the annoyance she'd felt at him quizzing her disappeared. In its place came a feeling so warm and encompassing she wanted it to last for ever. No man had ever affected her the way Harrison did.

'Please, AJ. Talk to me. It's all right.' He stopped walking and turned her to face him. Gently, he lifted her sunglasses and placed them on top of her head, before lifting his own. 'I understand it's difficult but if there's going to be anything between us, AJ, I need to know.'

'Anything but friendship?'

'I think we know friendship is only a part of what we feel for each other. I'm not denying its importance—in fact, after one failed relationship, I've come to realise a bonding of the minds is more important than a bonding of bodies.' He took both her hands in his. 'But a friendship, one where we can grow, needs to be forged with open and honest communication.'

The way Harrison was talking made Amelia want to run a mile. She couldn't get involved with him, they both knew that but she also knew what he said was true. They *did* feel more than friendship for each other but was it wise to take it any further?

She found it difficult to look at him, wanting to

believe in what had been building between them during the past few weeks but also knowing she'd be setting herself up for an even bigger hurt later on. 'I agree,' she finally said. 'But…'

'But?' he prompted.

'I'm leaving at the end of June. I don't think it's wise to get any closer than we are already.'

'What if it's too late for that?'

Again, his words stunned her and she started to tremble. 'Is it?'

'I like you, AJ. Is it so wrong that I want to know more about you? Can't you bring yourself to trust me enough to at least tell me why you were sick?'

Amelia sighed and closed her eyes for a moment, wondering if she was making a mountain out of a molehill. She wasn't sure but while she didn't like blurting out her past to all and sundry, she also recognised Harrison meant more to her than just a passing acquaintance. She opened her eyes and met his gaze.

'I have endometriosis.'

Harrison paused, almost waiting for more. When it didn't come, he nodded slowly. 'That's why you were sick? Why you stopped sculpting?' He knew there were varying degrees of endometriosis but if she'd been sick, it probably meant her case had been extreme.

'Yes.' Amelia dropped his hands and sat down on the sand, staring out to sea.

'Is it hereditary?'

She nodded. 'I'm an only child, my parents were in their forties when they had me. My mother suffered badly from endometriosis and back in those days all the doctors thought women exaggerated their pain whenever menstruating. Mum was bad, though, and finally was able to find a doctor who would listen. After twenty childless years of marriage and many operations she somehow became pregnant with me. She was bedridden for the entire pregnancy and even then I was premature.' She pulled her knees to her chest and hugged them.

Harrison continued to wait.

'I've been on medication for it since I was a teenager and while it's under control I still get days when I get depressed and upset. Lethargy and headaches sometimes strike but eating right and ensuring I don't exhaust myself are key elements in controlling them as well. When I was eighteen, I had a conservative laparotomy.' Amelia couldn't look at him while she spoke.

'They were initially just going to burn the cysts off, remove the adhesions and endometrial implants, but when they opened me up it was far worse than they'd originally thought. I woke up to discover my body was minus one ovary and Fallopian tube. Of course, I knew the risks involved and had discussed this possibility with my surgeon, but to have it actually happen…'

'AJ.' The emotion in his voice was what brought her tears to the surface and when he gathered her close, she went without hesitation. Neither of them spoke for five minutes, Amelia listening to the beat of his heart and comforted at the feeling of having someone hold her.

Eventually, she eased back but took hold of his hand, entwining their fingers tightly as though she never wanted to let go.

'So the chances of you having children?' he asked, and Amelia closed her eyes. She'd told him enough for one day. Dredging up the emotions was never easy and she'd had enough. She was drained. He was waiting for an answer, though, and she opened her eyes, looking out at the surfers, so wild and carefree—at least, that's how they appeared. Her answer was to shrug and Harrison nodded, accepting that.

'This is why you find it difficult being around small children? Babies?'

'They're always so gorgeous, Yolanda especially. She may have her problems and you may have some humdingers just waiting to happen but, Harrison, at least you appreciate her. You love her so much and it's evident every time you're together.'

'She's my world,' he said easily.

'Exactly. Children are so precious, so valuable. People who become parents should know how lucky they are—there are so many out there who might never get that chance.'

Harrison nodded, in total agreement with her, and they were both quiet for a while, both looking out to sea and both lost in their thoughts. Now that she'd told him, he'd probably leave her alone and that thought made her sad. There was only one other man she'd told, one very important man she'd confided in because they'd been heading to a serious place in their relationship. It had happened a few years after her operation and where she'd thought he'd loved her enough to take her as she was, she'd found out she'd been wrong. The news hadn't been what he'd wanted to hear and although he assured her he was fine, he'd high-tailed it out of her life as fast as possible. That had been over ten years ago now and Amelia had grown wiser.

'Thank you for talking to me,' he finally said.

'I'll confess, it wasn't easy.'

'You're not used to opening up to people, are you Amelia-Jane?' he said gently.

'No. Not about that.'

'This is a step in the right direction,' he said firmly.

'It is?'

'Yes. We've both opened up and that's a good thing.'

'I guess.'

He smiled at her. 'You guess? It's good because it means we're ready for the next step.'

'Step? What step?' she asked.

'The steps of getting to know each other.' His lips were curved into a small smile which slowly disappeared as he carefully lifted her hat and sunglasses off her head and then tenderly brushed his fingers through her hair, loving the colour. 'You're beautiful, Amelia-Jane.' His voice was soft, intimate and she couldn't believe how incredible he made her feel with his lovely words. He brought his fingers across her cheek then tilted her chin up so their lips could meet.

It was tentative at first, both of them wanting it, still not sure of the other, and his touch was feather-light. Once, twice his lips brushed across hers and she found herself trembling with repressed desire. The next time he touched her, she leaned in closer, adding more pressure to let him know she wanted this as much as he did. Need and desire ripped through him like nothing he'd ever felt before. Who was this woman who could make his blood boil with such ease? He felt like an out-of-control adolescent, unable to contain the way she made him feel. He tried to remember if he'd ever felt this way before but his mind came up blank. She surrounded him, not only by her scent but by her total capitulation, and he enjoyed every single part of it. The giving, the receiving.

He drew her closer, needing to feel her body pressed close to his but not wanting to rush her. Impatience and patience warred within him but it seemed she was also fighting a losing battle as she once more increased the pressure of the kiss. She leaned in, opened her mouth more, drew his lower lip between hers and nibbled at it with her teeth. There was no way he could resist what she was offering, her sweetness encompassing him as he took what she was so willing to give, pleased that when a ripple of excitement coursed through her, he affected her just as much as she affected him.

When he finally touched his tongue to hers, she thought she might burst with wanting. He was driving her wild, taking her places she'd never been before. Usually when it came to experiencing something new, she would shy away until she'd had a chance to figure out all the angles. Yet this time she didn't care. He made her feel so wonderful, so cherished and feminine, simply by the way he was holding her, by the way he was kissing her, by the way he seemed more than happy to lose himself completely in her.

She raised her hands and touched his chest and when she made that initial contact he strained a little before leaning into the touch. When her palms were pressed against his chest, her fingers exploring the contours of the firm torso she'd been itching to touch since she'd first arrived that morning, he groaned with crazed delight.

It was maddening. Totally maddening what was happening between them. The pheromones whirled around them, enticing them to take it to the next level, and when he nibbled on her lip then ran his tongue along first the lower then upper lip, Amelia moaned with shivering delight and wrapped her arms about him, her fingers impatiently urging his head down, holding it in place while they gave way to their mounting hunger.

Nothing mattered. Nothing at all. It was just the two of them. The need. The desire. The passion that continued to flare. The past, the future were forgotten. There was only the present, only this moment in which they both seemed content to live for ever, even though both acknowledged it was impossible.

Eventually the need for oxygen broke them apart but Harrison merely used it as an excuse to press butterfly kisses across her cheek and round to her ear where he nuzzled, his breath coming out in gasps as they slowly floated back to earth.

'Wow.' Amelia panted the word into his shoulder, her eyes closed as she revelled in the way she was allowed to touch him, her fingers running lightly up and down his back in a sweet caress.

'You can say that again.'

'Wow.'

He chuckled and reluctantly eased back to rest his forehead against hers. 'Amelia-Jane. You are a special woman. Did you know that?'

'Uh…'

His smile increased. 'You find it difficult to accept compliments.' She merely shrugged. 'Believe me when I say I find you irresistible.'

'I want to believe it but…'

'But?'

'But if I do, it means I'm opening myself up.'

'That's definitely the hard part and I'm sorry if you feel things got out of control just now.' He lifted his

head and looked around them, realising they were
getting a few strange looks from people. 'Although,
thankfully, not *too* out of control.' He gathered her to
him, pressing a kiss to the top of her head. 'You make
me forget where I am, AJ.'

'That's how I feel.'

A loud cry pierced the air, snapping them out of their
bubble. A young swimmer was hurtling out of the
waves, running as fast as he could towards the lifeguard.
'Shark!' The teenager screamed. 'Shark! There's a shark
out there. It's got someone!'

CHAPTER SEVEN

HARRISON felt Amelia stiffen in his arms and when he looked at her, she'd gone deathly pale. 'AJ?'

No response. He gave her a little shake. 'Amelia?'

She snapped her head around and looked at him, her eyes wide with fear, her body beginning to tremble. Panic gripped her and breathing became erratic.

'What's wrong?'

'I hate sharks.' She swallowed. 'I'm English. Shark attacks aren't exactly common at home.'

'You'll be fine,' he said pulling her to her feet and peering out to sea. 'Same as any triage. One step at a time.'

Amelia glanced around. She could hear the screams of the people, could smell the fear in the air, and she swallowed the distasteful realisation she was about to become a part of this situation. It was their job and they were on hand. Both of them, trained A and E doctors at the right place at the right time, could go along way to saving the surfer's life.

'AJ, there'll be blood and lacerations. Amputations are common with shark attack as well.' Harrison grabbed her hand and started walking as he spoke, Amelia following alongside him. 'You've dealt with those types of injuries before. You'll be fine.'

The lifeguard was peering through his binoculars to where the teenager who'd raised the alarm was pointing. A team of lifesavers was coming from the clubhouse with their emergency boat. People were everywhere, streaming out of the water, gathering up toddlers and babies. One woman was calling her daughter's name as she searched frantically for the child. Harrison silently thanked Mrs D. for taking Yolanda back to the house. At least he knew she was safe.

The lifeguard on duty was being bombarded with people and questions and was trying to keep a state of calm on the beach. Many people started packing up and heading for their cars. Others lined the water's edge and looked out to where there were several surfers, all heading over to help whoever was in trouble. They stuck together and adhered to the rule—never surf alone.

'Let's go offer our services,' he said, and she nodded, her gaze still scanning the waves out to sea, trying to make out what was happening. Harrison looked as well. The surfers were starting to head to shore, the lifeguard rescue boat only just hitting the water. 'Those first few minutes are going to be critical.'

'What do you want me to do?' she asked, her voice calm, her breathing even.

'Go to my house and ask Mrs D. for my medical kit. She knows where it is.'

'Do I need to call the ambulance?'

'I'm sure that's already been done.' Harrison turned and headed over to the lifeguards, who were setting up an area to accept the surfer. His mates almost had him out of the water, the patient being balanced on the boards of others.

Harrison went up to the lifeguard in charge and introduced himself. 'I'm a doctor,' he said, and the relief that came over the young man's face would have been almost comical if the situation hadn't been so dire.

'Great. Great. I'm Jonah, by the way. Uh…we're gonna put him here.' He indicated the area to his left, which had a medical kit and a pile of blankets.

'Good. Get these people back. I'm going to need some room.'

Jonah turned to one of his colleagues and yelled instructions.

'I'm presuming the ambulance has been called?' Harrison asked.

'Yes.'

'My colleague is just over the road at my house, getting my medical bag.' Harrison bent down and opened the first-aid kit to check what it held. 'When she arrives, she'll need to be let through without question. She'll be carrying a black medical bag so I think you'll recognise her.'

'So…uh…you know what to expect, then?' Jonah asked.

'If you're interested in my credentials, I'm the director of Accident and Emergency at Glenelg General. Can't get more qualified than that.' Harrison glanced up the beach and saw AJ making her way across the sand. When he looked the other way at the water, the surfers, with the assistance of the lifeguards, were carrying the injured man towards them.

'Get back. Make room,' Jonah was ordering.

People were such sticky-beaks at times, Harrison thought, wishing they'd all go, but he focused his thoughts on what was going to happen next.

Amelia arrived about ten seconds before the surfer

was carried over and she instantly opened Harrison's medical bag and began checking the contents. 'You have saline—good.'

'Is Yolanda OK?' he asked.

'She's watching TV,' Amelia answered.

'Good.'

When the surfer was placed before them, Amelia frowned for a moment. The man was alive and conscious. For some strange reason she'd thought he'd be either half-mangled or almost dead. Instead, he was chatting away as though being attacked by a shark happened to him every day. These Aussies! She doubted she'd ever understand them.

'What's your name?' Harrison asked as he reached for the scissors and began slicing open the surfer's wetsuit.

'Troy.'

'How old are you, Troy?'

'Twenty.'

'Been surfing long?'

'Ten years.'

'Allergic to anything?'

'Nope.'

'Good.' While he'd been talking, Harrison had done a quick appraisal of the injuries, as had Amelia. There was a lot of blood around the foot of the right leg and she ripped a sterile pad from its wrapper and applied pressure over the area with the most blood. As she held it firmly, she could feel something was missing and when she lifted the pad a moment later she realised Troy was missing his forth and fifth toes.

'Can you take a deep breath for me?' Harrison asked, and was pleased with Troy's effort. 'Lacerations to right arm and right leg,' he said quietly yet firmly, and Amelia knew he was talking directly to her. Harrison felt Troy's head. 'Got any bumps up here?'

'No.'

He held up his finger. 'Look at this.' He moved his finger from side to side and up and down before asking for his medical torch. Amelia pulled it from the bag and handed it to him.

'Amputation of forth and fifth metatarsals. Increased blood loss.'

Harrison nodded and called one of the lifeguards over. 'Get a blanket on him. We need to keep his body warm. Find something to elevate his leg with.' As he spoke, he pulled a few padded bandages from the medical kit and pressed them on the injured area. 'Jonah,' he called. 'Hold this.'

'Is he gonna be all right?' Troy's mate asked.

'He's going to do just fine,' Harrison answered, not looking up at him but performing neurovascular observations again. He checked Troy's pupils. 'Equal and reacting,' he announced. 'Pulse is starting to weaken. Troy. Take another deep breath in for me.' He kept his fingers pressed to Troy's wrist. 'And again. That's it.' He nodded. 'Better. Keep that breathing up. Not too fast. We don't need you getting dizzy.' Harrison now looked at Troy's friend. 'Make sure he keeps those deep breaths up.' The other young man was pale as well, but hopefully because Harrison had given him something to do, he would calm down. They didn't need him or anyone else going into shock.

'AJ?'

'Bleeding controlled,' she said as she bandaged up Troy's foot. 'I'll get a drip set up next.'

'Good.' Harrison took a closer look at the lacerations to the arm and thigh. 'He tried to take a good chunk out of your leg, mate.'

'Yeah.'

'In fact, it looks as though he just missed your femoral artery.'

'That good?'

'That's brilliant, mate.' Harrison checked Troy's pulse. 'Keep that deep breathing up. We like our patients breathing, don't we, AJ?'

'Absolutely.' She clipped the tubes together and attached them to the bag of saline. 'Here.' She handed the bag to the lifeguard who'd helped her elevate Troy's leg on an Esky. 'Hold this.' She withdrew the needle and shifted over to Troy's left side, rubbing an alcohol wipe on his arm. 'Not squeamish with needles, Troy?' She knew that he probably wouldn't even be aware of it going in because of everything else his body was trying to cope with, but if he looked at it, she didn't want him passing out.

'Nah. I'm fine.'

'Good.' She inserted the needle into his arm but a second later there was a thud next to them as Troy's friend keeled over.

'Check him,' Harrison ordered Jonah.

'Just fainted,' came the report, and a moment later Troy's friend came round, more embarrassed then anything else.

'Hey,' Troy said to Jonah. 'Do you have to report this?'

'Of course we do. A shark attack is very serious.'

'But the shark. They'll kill it.'

'That's what happens when one attacks. Its destruction is ordered and that's all there is to it,' Jonah said with authority in his voice. 'We can't risk them attacking someone else.'

'But I'm fine and Great Whites are a protected species.'

'It could have killed you,' Jonah pointed out.

Amelia was surprised at Troy's attitude. She'd never thought she'd hear a person who'd just been attacked by a shark advocating for them. She was stunned.

'But surely you don't need to report it,' Troy said.

'It's my job to—'

'Enough!' Harrison said, glancing at both men and then AJ. 'Now is not the time for bickering or this type of discussion. When is the ambulance due? Someone find out.' He looked at Amelia again. 'You OK?'

'Fine.'

'Good.' He returned his attention to Troy's lacerations. 'These will need suturing,' he said, finishing off the pressure bandage. 'AJ, obs, please.'

Amelia reached for the medical torch and checked Troy's eyes, then his pulse, which was still a little weak. 'Deep breaths, Troy.' His face had a little more colour in it and his lips and fingernails were turning from their earlier bluish tinge to more of a healthy pink. 'Any dizziness? Nausea?' she asked, her fingers still pressed to his pulse.

'No.'

'Ambulance has just arrived,' someone called, and the crowd around them parted as the paramedics carried their stretcher and equipment down the beach.

'Amelia?' Gina Douglas, the first paramedic, said, and then looked at Harrison. 'Hey, Harrison.'

'Hi, Gina, Ben,' said Harrison, nodding at the second paramedic. 'Good to see you.' Gina and Ben knelt down and started hooking the oxy-viva up, placing the non-rebreather mask over Troy's mouth and nose.

'Twenty-year-old male.' Harrison started the report.

'Multiple lacerations to the right arm and right leg. Spontaneous amputation of the fourth and fifth metatarsals. No head trauma, pupils equal and reacting to light. Pulse slightly weak and rapid at times. Saline given and no analgesics as yet.'

'What do you want to give him?' Gina asked as she adjusted the oxygen levels.

'Troy, are you allergic to morphine?' Harrison said.

'No. I've had it before and I was fine with it.'

'What did you have it for?' Harrison asked.

'Uh…after having my appendix out when I was seventeen.'

'Are you currently on any medication?' Amelia asked as she adjusted the blanket around Troy and saw the appendicectomy scar.

'No. Uh…I was drinking last night.'

'You should be fine,' Harrison said, and when Gina had drawn up the injection Harrison administered it. They managed to lift Troy onto the stretcher using the pat-slide and soon he was being carried up to the waiting ambulance. Jonah, the lifeguard, who'd taken over holding the saline drip bag, walked beside him.

Amelia glanced at Harrison as they gathered up his medical supplies and followed the patient up to the ambulance.

'Are you all right?' Harrison asked, taking her hand in his as they walked across the sand.

'Sure. It was just like you said. Take it one step at a time and follow the rules of triage.'

Harrison smiled and tugged her closer, putting his arm around her shoulders and dropping a kiss to the top of her head. They were almost at the kerb now and Gina climbed out of the back doors of the ambulance. As she shut them, she glanced at the two doctors and smiled. Amelia shifted slightly, feeling a little uncomfortable, but Harrison didn't drop his arm.

'Thanks, Gina,' Amelia said. 'I can do any paperwork on this when I come in this afternoon.'

'Sure. I'll leave it in your pigeonhole.' With that, the dark-haired paramedic went around to the driver's side and with a flash of lights and the whirring of the siren, the ambulance drove off.

Harrison turned and slipped his arms about Amelia's waist and she didn't hesitate to go into them. It felt nice, to be held close by Harrison, nice and re-assuring. She couldn't remember ever feeling as comfortable with a man as she did with him. She closed her eyes and breathed in deeply, the salt and sand mixed with his own personal scent a memory she would keep for ever.

The wind blew around them, the temperature dropping momentarily as the sun was hidden behind a cloud, and Amelia shivered, the action causing Harrison to tighten his hold on her. Was that where she was deep down inside? Was she behind a cloud, trying to figure out how to get out, to find the sun again? She listened to his heartbeat, so loud, so strong and so powerful.

'You feel so right, AJ,' he murmured, and she leaned back, looking deeply into his brown eyes. 'I can't explain it but it's just the way it feels.'

Amelia nodded and sighed.

'Come on, you need to rest if you're working this afternoon.' He shifted so they could walk, one arm still about her shoulders, holding her close. Now that he'd touched her, kissed her, he felt an overwhelming need to protect her and he didn't take his duties lightly.

She pointed to his house. 'I might just go and say goodbye to Yolanda, if that's all right.'

'Sure. Of course.'

Yolanda was up and dancing to her favourite DVD, but when she saw Amelia she broke off and came running over, holding her chubby arms out.

'Meel-ya. Tum and dance.'

'Can I watch you dance?' Amelia asked, and found a willing participant in the three-year-old. 'You are such a beautiful dancer,' she praised as the girl wove and wiggled around the room in time to the music, copying the actions of the actors on television. She ended up staying for three songs but finally was able to say goodbye, Yolanda dismissing her with an uninterested wave of her hand.

'I'm just going to walk Amelia home,' Harrison called to Mrs D., who was sitting at the bench, resting her leg, while she read a book.

'All right, dear.'

They walked down the footpath, Harrison linking their hands. Amelia was simply amazing. This woman who had been through so much. This woman who had opened up to him. This woman who fitted perfectly in his arms, against his body, their lips pressed together.

It was as though they'd travelled so far through their lives, experiencing disappointment, turmoil, pain and grief to arrive here and now. Harrison had always thought that one day he might meet someone new, someone he could learn to trust. They'd become friends, their relationship would grow and he'd eventually marry once more, giving Yolanda a mother who loved her as well as siblings to play with.

'Have you ever told any other man about your operation? About what you live with every day?' As a doctor, he'd treated women and young girls who'd been afflicted with the condition and from what he'd read and studied, endometriosis was a very painful disease to have.

'Once. A long time ago.'

'Let me guess. You told him about your operation and he bolted?'

'Exactly.'

'Which makes trusting difficult.'

'It does.'

'I understand that. Really I do, and I'm honoured you trusted me because it's not an easy thing to give, especially once it's been abused.'

'Your wife?'

'Ex-wife. Well, technically she wasn't but if Inga had lived, we would have divorced. It was the right thing to do, it was what I *needed* to do for both Yolanda and myself.' He looked at their entwined fingers and rubbed his thumb over her knuckle. 'Two weeks after Inga moved out, I received a call from the police, asking me to meet them at the hospital. I had to identify her body.'

'Oh, Harrison.' Amelia gasped, her heart going out to him.

'Her blood-alcohol reading was well over the limit and she had been driving.'

Amelia gaped at him unable to fathom how horrible that would have been.

'It was a difficult time and Yolanda wasn't doing well either.'

'But you got through it. That shows how strong you are deep down inside.' He shrugged and Amelia continued as though she needed to convince him. 'I know how important Yolanda is to you. It's clear to anyone when they see the two of you together. You're a wonderful father and I have no doubt you will raise a daughter who is self-sufficient and self-assured. No parent could ask for more than that.'

He sighed. 'Some days, though, AJ, I wonder what on earth I'm doing. Her therapeutic management, the exercises, the constant need for supervision, it's all so intense. There are days when she simply sits and stares at a wall because she can't cope with the world around her. It all becomes too much. What if she doesn't grow out of that? What if I can't fix her?'

'You don't need to *fix* her, Harrison, and from what I've seen, you're doing an amazing job. You haven't left her in a daycare centre, you have specialised one-on-one care in her own environment provided by a person you both love. You have a demanding job but working in a nine-to-five position is the best place for you to be and you've realised that.' Amelia's tone was imploring, desperate for him to believe every word she was saying.

'Yolanda is wonderful. The fact that she was diagnosed so early is a credit to you. You knew what the situation was, you knew what signs and symptoms to look for and because of that, she has benefited.'

'But you still picked up that there was something wrong with her.'

'Yes, but I'm a doctor so that's different. Besides, it's not as though you're trying to hide Yolanda's disability. You're simply trying to give her what she needs, the tools, if you like, to make the most of her life and to grow into an independent woman.'

'You think so?'

Amelia couldn't believe his self-doubt. He had

always seemed so strong, so in charge. 'Yes, I do. You're a wonderful father, Harrison. Try not to doubt that.'

He was silent for a moment, letting her words sink in. 'You're good for me, Amelia-Jane. Do you realise that? I've really enjoyed spending time with you today and I can't thank you enough for everything you did for Yolanda during the week.'

Amelia was filled with warmth. 'It was my pleasure. She's such a joy to be around.'

'I don't want to impose on you but Mrs D.'s recovery is going to take at least another fortnight before she is back on her feet, so to speak. Would it still be possible for you to call in, to check on how things are going? When you have your days off, of course.'

'Sure. I said I'd be happy to help and I still am.' She just didn't seem to able to say no to this man.

'That really means a lot to me, AJ. I'll see you tonight, then.'

'What?' They were outside her apartment door now and she turned to look at him in total confusion. 'I'm working.'

'I know. You finish around midnight, right?'

'Some time around then, yes.'

'Well, I'll come and walk you home from the hospital. Make sure you're safe.'

'I was going to take a taxi.'

'It's forecast to be a lovely evening.'

'Harrison, I don't understand.'

'You said you'd be willing to help when you weren't working.'

'And I am.'

'Well, you won't be working then.'

'And you'll need help?'

'I'll need help walking you home. How can I do that if you're not there?'

Amelia closed her eyes for a second and shook her head. 'You're confusing me.'

Harrison raised his eyebrows, his lips twitching into a grin. 'Good.' He leaned down and gave her a peck on the lips before turning and walking away.

Amelia pulled her keys from her skirt pocket and unlocked her door, her body still getting over the feel of the brief kiss he'd given her. The man was crazy. Why did he want to walk her home at midnight? She wasn't even sure she should have agreed to help him over the next few weeks. Yes, the last few days had been amazing but she could feel herself getting in way over her head and she had to pull back…but she didn't want to.

She groaned as she walked into her apartment. 'I'm so confused.'

CHAPTER EIGHT

WHEN Amelia arrived at work that afternoon, she'd pushed her confusion to the back of her mind and was ready to focus on her job. As she walked through the hospital, she realised she was getting little smiles from people…different smiles from the usual.

When the door to the change rooms opened, she turned and found herself face to face with Tina. 'So? Tell me. The hospital is abuzz with the news that you and Harrison are a couple. As I hardly saw you last week, due to the fact that you were off playing happy families with him, I can't say I'm all that surprised, but anyway…tell me the latest.'

'Well…' Amelia began. 'We've kind of…connected.' She turned and closed her locker door.

'That's a good thing, right?'

'How? How can it be a good thing? I have ten weeks left in this country.'

'But you've just said you connected with him.' Tina paused. 'Ooh. Connected lips?'

Amelia sighed and turned away from Tina.

'You did, didn't you? He kissed you. I can see it. It's written all over your face.'

'It is?' She peered in the mirror.

'I meant figuratively.' Tina laughed. 'Gee, happy families must agree with you.'

'Oh, it does. I don't want it to but I can't help it. I like spending time with him, with Yolanda.'

'Then spend time with him. You *only* have ten weeks.'

'But it's wrong to get involved and then just leave.'

'Is it? Look, how many times has this sort of thing happened to you? Like *never*, Amelia. Harrison—if he makes you feel something, then surely you owe it to yourself to find out what might happen.'

'I have to leave the country.'

'And why should that stop you from exploring this?'

'Because of Yolanda.'

'No. You're just using her as an excuse. You're scared. You're so scared that he'll reject you like that drongo did all those years ago.'

'I cannot have children, Tina. You don't think that would matter to him?'

'How do I know? Ask Harrison.'

'I can't.'

'Why not?'

'Because he'll reject me. It's so obvious he wants more children and why wouldn't he? He's a brilliant father. He deserves to find a woman who can give him what he needs.'

'What if you're that woman? What if you're reject-ing him? Ever thought of that?'

Amelia was silent for a moment as Tina's words sank in. 'No. I haven't thought of it that way.' She sighed. 'I gotta go.'

Amelia focused on her work, seeing her first patient before tracking down Troy who was settled in the orthopaedic ward, still waiting to see an orthopod about his foot.

'Hi, there,' he said when she walked over to his bed. 'Thanks for coming to see me.'

'I'm surprised you don't have more visitors,' Amelia said.

'My parents have just gone to get something to eat. Now that they've seen I'm OK, Mum can start to relax.'

'I'm glad. You were very lucky, Troy.' Her words were soft but Troy merely laughed.

'Luck doesn't have anything to do with it. The shark didn't mean any harm.'

'How can you say that? It might have killed you.'

'But it didn't and I'll tell you why.'

'I'm listening.'

'Because I wasn't surfing alone. I had mates there and they were on that shark, breaking me free before even I knew what was happening. Careful surfers know what to do, know what to expect. We had our anti-shark packs on. We're not stupid but, still, things happen.'

'How can you be so calm about it?'

'The same way you were calm when you were dealing with my injuries. You're a doctor. You're trained to deal with things when the body goes wrong. I'm a surfer—professional beach bum.' The words were said with a smile and Amelia immediately thought of Harrison and his T-shirt. Every thing in her world seemed to come back to him, wherever she was or whatever she was doing.

'Will you ever surf again?'

'Sure.'

Amelia was speechless and stared at him open-mouthed.

'It's in my blood, it's a part of who I am. I guess that seems reckless and careless to you but you wouldn't stop practising medicine if something went wrong with your body. You'd get it fixed and get back to doing what you do best.'

He had a point. That was exactly what she'd done after her own body had failed to co-operate with her plans for the future. 'You've made a valid point, Troy.' She smiled. 'Just concentrate on getting better.'

'Will do.'

She nodded and started to walk away.

'Oh, and, Doc…'

She turned back.

'Thanks…for, uh…you know…fixin' me up.' This time it was Troy who had tears in his eyes and she realised that his lucky escape had affected him far more than he was letting on. She nodded, her smile increasing before she headed back to A and E.

The next few hours ticked by, Tina not saying one more word about Harrison, which Amelia was grateful for. As they seemed unusually quiet for a Saturday evening, she had a lot of time to think…and she didn't want to think.

Amelia's head slumped forward onto the table in the tearoom where she was having her dinner-break. The whole time she'd been thinking about Harrison and trying to figure out what to do next. The man occupied her thoughts constantly and it was getting more and more difficult to shove him to the side when she needed to focus on work. She moaned, not at all sure what she was supposed to do.

'That good, eh?' a deep voice she recognised all too well said, and she sat up straight, eyes wide, and looked at Harrison. 'What…are you doing here?' Her heart leapt in her throat at the sight of him. Slowly, she drank her fill, wondering how he could look equally as handsome in jeans and T-shirt, which he was wearing now, as he did in either a suit or swimming shorts. She'd only seen him that morning yet until he'd stood in the doorway, she hadn't realised how badly she'd missed him. 'Is Yolanda all right?'

'Yes.'

'What are you doing here, then? Mrs D.?'

'Yolanda and Mrs D. are both fine, AJ. Tina called me in.'

'Why?'

'Big emergency.' Harrison came and sat down beside her. 'You don't know?'

'I've been on break for the past half-hour.' She shifted slightly, trying to put a bit of distance between them. Her nose was attuned to his scent and she could feel herself crumbling with need and longing.

He nodded and leaned closer. Amelia automatically leaned back in her chair. 'I won't bite,' he said softly. 'Not unless you want me to.'

'Harrison!' It was a cheesy line at best but it had the full effect. His eyes were so deep, so vibrant that she struggled to ignore how incredible the man was. She swallowed over the sudden dryness in her throat, her gaze flicked down to his lips and her own parted with a burning desperation to have his mouth on hers once more. She looked back at his eyes and realised he knew exactly where her thoughts were.

Harrison leaned back and took a deep breath, holding it then letting it out before he indicated the doorway. 'Shall we go see what Tina has to report?' He held out his hand to her and Amelia looked at it, knowing she should refuse but finding it impossible to pass up another opportunity to touch him. When she slid her hand into his, felt the warmth of his skin on hers, her heart rate, which had only just started to return to normal, picked up instantaneously. Once she was standing, he squeezed her fingers slightly. 'Let's go, Dr Watson.'

He continued to hold her hand as they walked through A and E towards the nurses' station. A few staff saw them together and smiled, one porter even giving Harrison a friendly pat on the back.

'Way to go, boss,' he said, grinning from ear to ear.

'Ah, Amelia,' Tina said. 'I see Harrison found you. Have a nice dinner?'

'Yes, thank you.'

'Good. I'm just waiting for two more staff members then we'll start the brief.'

'Harrison said there's been an emergency?' Amelia looked down at the hastily scribbled notes sitting beside the phone, trying to decipher them, but her mind was too full of what was happening around her. Everyone was grinning and smiling at them and Harrison was still holding her hand.

'Oh,' Rosie sighed dreamily as she entered the nurses' station. 'It's so nice to see you looking so happy, Harrison. You, too, Amelia.'

Tina edged closer and said softly, 'So I take it you're the boss's girlfriend.'

Amelia found it impossible to look at any of her colleagues, knowing that her cheeks were flaming red. She wasn't an openly demonstrative person and if she'd known holding hands with Harrison would have caused this much of a stir, she probably wouldn't have done it…probably.

'Oh, here they come,' Tina said, and the moment was broken, everyone returning to their professional personas. 'OK.' She held everyone's attention as she briefed them on the situation. 'Apparently, the rock concert being held on the foreshore got out of hand, the crowd going a little crazy with quite a few fights breaking out. At last count eight ambulances have been sent to the scene. We're going to have walk-ins, fractures, abrasions, lacerations, possible burns, not to mention people pumped up on alcohol and goodness knows what else.'

'I guess Saturday night *is* all right for fighting,' one nurse said to her friend, and they both laughed.

'Focus on your jobs, please.' Harrison's voice was quiet but firm. 'According to Tina, we're going to be inundated.' He spoke to everyone gathered. 'Work through each problem as it comes. If the patient isn't critical, patch them up and ship them off. They can come back tomorrow or see their GP on Monday. AJ, you and I'll be in treatment room one. Tina, put a team together and take treatment room two.' The wail of the ambulance siren broke the air and for a second everyone was still, as though waiting for a director to call, 'Action.' The next moment everyone was moving.

Amelia didn't have time to think about Harrison or anything else for the next three hours as they worked through one injury after another. She liked working side by side with Harrison and tonight they were definitely in tune with one another, pre-empting and assisting with little spoken communication.

Just after midnight, the patients were still coming, although a number of cases had been diverted to other hospitals. The police had also been called to the hospital to break up a fight that had started in the waiting room because there were so many people. The staff had tried to explain that it didn't matter in what order you arrived, patients were seen in priority order of their injuries.

Gina arrived, wheeling in a new patient. 'Who wants this young man?' she said.

'We're free,' Harrison called. Amelia came around him to the other side.

'Lift on three,' Harrison said. 'One, two, three.' They shifted the patient across as Gina gave a quick report.

'Nineteen-year-old male. Kevin Western. Half a pack a day smoker. Has had beer tonight, blood-alcohol reading is below point-oh-five. Sustained blunt force trauma to the right chest, with bruising and fractured T3 and T4. Patient is finding it difficult to breathe. Oxygen given. Possible pneumothorax.'

'Thanks, Gina.' Amelia pulled on a pair of gloves. 'Hi, Kevin. I'm Amelia. Can you talk?' She pressed her fingers to his wrist and found the pulse quite weak. Harrison was checking his pupils.

'No drugs tonight?' he asked, hooking his stethoscope into his ears and listened to Kevin's breathing.

'No,' Kevin said, his breathing laboured as his clothes were cut off and a blanket placed over him.

'There are no breath sounds on the right side and there's increased hyper-resonance,' Harrison stated for Amelia's sake before he had a closer look at the chest wound, touching it carefully.

'No time for X-ray?' Amelia asked.

'Exactly. Most likely scenario is that the fracture has punctured the lung, causing it to collapse.' Harrison looked at their patient while the nurses continued with the observations. 'Get it set up.'

Amelia nodded and went to the cupboard, pulling out a needle and valve tube as Harrison explained.

'When you were hit, your ribs broke and have poked a hole in your lung. That's why you're having trouble breathing. Your lung has collapsed due to a collection of air between the chest wall and the lung or the pleural cavity, as we like to call it. When you breathe out, some of that air is going into the pleural cavity. We need to insert a tube into your chest and then we can suck the air out.'

Kevin's eyes were wide with this news but Amelia wheeled a trolley over, smiled at him and administered a local anaesthetic.

'You'll be fine,' she reassured him. 'Once we've re-established the negative pressure within the cavity, the lung will expand again and you'll be able to breathe again. First, though, we need to elevate you a bit so just lie still. You're on the super-dooper bed, as we like to call it.' Amelia pressed a button and the bed started to rise, lifting Kevin up into more of a sitting position.

'Super-dooper?' Harrison asked as he ripped open the package which contained the needle. 'Is that the technical term back in England?'

Amelia's eyes twinkled with humour. 'Actually, it is.'

They were all starting to get a little light-hearted. It happened when they'd been going at it non-stop for a few hours but although they were all joking and happy, it didn't stop them from being serious about their work.

'Ready?' Harrison asked Kevin, and made a small incision into the pleural space. Amelia inserted the catheter through the second intercostal space, which would remove the air. The tube went down into an un-derwater-seal drainage bottle.

Harrison sutured the tube to the chest wall, then

stepped back so the nurse could cover it with an airtight dressing. The tubes were kept clamped while they performed the procedure and once it was done, they activated the drainage system.

Kevin was able to breathe a lot easier. 'There you go,' Amelia said to her patient, before turning to the nurse. 'See if there's any room in the men's ward. Kevin will need these drains in for at least the next twenty-four hours.' Amelia ripped off her gloves and looked across at Harrison. 'How much longer do you think this is going to go on?'

'I'm not sure but at least the patients aren't coming in as fast as they were a few hours ago.'

'Good point. Right. If we have no more ambulances coming in, I'll go grab a chart and see another patient.' It was another hour and a half later before A and E looked almost bare compared to the wall-to-wall people who had been there earlier. 'I'm going to get my bag and go home,' she said, smothering a yawn.

'Why don't you sit down for a minute?' Tina suggested.

'I can't. If I sit down, I doubt I'll get up again.' Amelia looked around her, assuming Harrison was with a patient.

'I haven't seen him,' Tina said.

'Pardon?'

'Harrison. I haven't seen him but I think he's still here.'

'Good, because he said he was going to walk me home. Or maybe after all of this he'd prefer to take a taxi.'

'Nah.' Tina shook her head. 'Tired or not, if he walks you home, he gets to spend more time with you.' She chuckled. 'The boss has it bad.'

'Bad what?'

'Bad for you, honey.'

'Don't say that,' Amelia groaned.

'Don't say what?' Harrison asked as he walked towards them.

'Um…nothing.' Amelia sat up straighter in her chair, not wanting him to know they'd been talking about him.

'I've got another patient here,' Rosie said, waving a file. 'Who wants her?'

'I'll do it.' Amelia stood, needing to get herself under control, and accepted the file. 'The sooner I start, the sooner I finish.'

'Thanks, Amelia. This poor woman has been waiting for two hours to be seen.'

Amelia went into cubicle three. 'I'm sorry you've been waiting so long, Ms Franklin.'

'It's OK,' the woman said. 'You've been busy.'

'Thank you for being so understanding.'

'I've had X-rays.'

'Oh? Let me find the packet.' Amelia went out to the nurses' station and hunted around.

'What are you looking for?' Harrison asked.

'Ms Franklin's X-rays.' Amelia yawned, tiredness swamping her. Harrison shifted pieces of paper and finally found them.

'Here you go.'

'Ah, thanks.' She hugged them to her chest.

'When you're done, will you be ready to leave?'

She smothered another yawn. 'Definitely.'

'Still OK if I walk you home?'

'Sure. I think I need some fresh air.'

'Good, then go see your patient and I'll make Tina take all the other cases.'

Amelia couldn't help smiling at his words as she returned to her patient. 'Here they are.' She flicked them up onto the viewing box and studied them. 'Your arm is definitely broken. Two hairline fractures as well. It says in your notes that you were pushed and when you fell, someone stood on your arm.'

'That's right. What a fun concert!' Her words were dripping with sarcasm and Amelia smiled.

'You've spoken to the police?'

'Yes. It won't do any good but at least I've done the right thing.'

'Good. A cast will fix that arm. You'll need to have it on for six weeks then make an appointment with either one of the orthopaedic surgeons here at the hospital or in their private practice. I'll leave a referral with the sister.'

'Thank you, Doctor.'

Amelia returned the X-rays to the nurses' station where Harrison was waiting for her, chatting with Rosie and Tina. Amelia wrote up Ms Franklin's notes as well as contacting the plaster nurse and writing the referral for the specialist.

'Ready?' Harrison asked.

'Just need to get my bag out of my locker.' Amelia hurried towards the change rooms and was back within a minute.

'Wow. That was quick. Eager to get out of here?' Tina asked.

'Most definitely.'

'All right. You two crazy kids go have a good time,' she joked, and Amelia simply rolled her eyes at her friend, ignoring the 'call-me' gesture Tina was making with her little finger and thumb.

'Goodnight, all,' Harrison said as they walked out of A and E. Once outside, he slipped his arm around her and she went willingly. Even though the early morning air was quite pleasant, it was a little cool. They'd made it out of the hospital gate and down to the street corner before he spoke. 'Aren't you going to say something?'

'Um.' Amelia cleared her throat. 'I'm not sure what to say.'

'I'm sorry if you feel uncomfortable under everyone's scrutiny.'

'They all seem very happy for you.'

Harrison shrugged. 'We've all known each other for a long time. Some of the staff I've worked with since I was a medical student, which was long before I met Inga or became a father. But let's forget the hospital. Now it's just you and me, out here, beneath the starry sky.'

Amelia was surprised at how right everything felt, although she did have a few questions. 'Well, let's just wait a minute on that.'

'On what?'

'On forgetting the hospital.'

'OK,' he drawled. 'What do you want to discuss?'

'How about the fact that everyone thinks I'm your girlfriend?'

Harrison looked down at her, a slow smile tugging at the corners of his lips. He glanced up and down the street, checking for traffic. They waited for a car to go before crossing over, the streetlights bright and illuminating the way for them.

'Aren't you?'

'Well, I don't know. I've been helping you out with Yolanda, you kissed me for the first time today—'

'Yesterday,' he corrected her, and she nodded, acquiescing.

'You kissed me yesterday and now you've held my

hand in public and the hospital thinks I'm your latest girlfriend.'

'Latest?' He seemed hurt by that. 'The last girlfriend I had ended up being my wife.'

'My point exactly.'

'It is?'

'Harrison, we can't get heavily involved. I don't mean to sound like a stuck record but I have a life back in England.'

He frowned and tightened his arm about her shoulders, not liking her words. 'I know that.'

'Then you must also realised this…thing…between us.' She shrugged. 'It can't go anywhere.'

'Why not?'

'Why not?' she asked with incredulity.

'Yes. Why not, AJ?'

'Because we live in different countries. Different continents!'

'Oh.' Was that the only reason she seemed so reticent? Was there more to it than that? She'd opened up to him, told him about her endometriosis, but was there more? His gut feeling said there was.

'Adding Yolanda to that equation provides an even stronger reason why we shouldn't.'

'Yet here you are, with your arm around me, walking down the street at two o'clock in the morning.'

'I'm not saying I don't like you—I do. Perhaps too much.'

'Well, why don't we start there and move forward?' Harrison suggested, now quite intrigued as to why she was fighting this so much.

'Because I have to finish this rotation, return to the other side of the world, study for my final exams and then, once I'm qualified, decide whether or not I'm going to take the job I've already been offered.'

'You've been offered a job?' He was stunned at this. 'In England?'

'Don't sound so surprised.'

'I didn't mean it that way. Of course you've been head-hunted. Why wouldn't you be? You're a fantastic doctor. I was just surprised because I hadn't realised that was the case.'

'There's so much we don't know about each other, Harrison.'

'Then we should at least be given the opportunity to find out.' They were walking past his darkened house but they continued on to her apartment. 'AJ, we have something very special between us and I can't seem to get you out of my mind. You've become important to me in a short space of time and when I'm with you I can't help but want to touch you, and when we're apart I wish I was with you, holding your hand, holding you in my arms, pressing my lips to yours.

'It's powerful. It's frightening and thrilling and it's growing so rapidly I think we'd be unable to stop it...if we wanted to, which I don't. I *want* to be with you, AJ. I don't know where it's going to lead or what might happen. All I know is I've never felt this way about anyone before.'

'Not even your wife?'

'No.' His answer was said without hesitation. 'She never made me feel as though I could fly, as though I could take on the world. You do. You bring out the best in me. I'd never intentionally hurt you, AJ. You're far too special.'

'I am?'

'You are.' They paused at her door and she withdrew her keys. Harrison realised he'd pushed enough for one night but that didn't mean he was going to stop seeing her. 'So, will I see you later today?'

'I want to sleep, then work. Perhaps tomorrow?'

'Meaning Monday?'

'Yes. I'm on day shift for the next two days, then off Wednesday and Thursday.'

'Right. Dinner? Tomorrow night?'

'Harrison…'

'Come on, AJ. It's just dinner. Mrs D. and Yolanda will be there. You know you want to see them.'

'OK,' she agreed reluctantly even though she knew she shouldn't. 'You'd better go.'

Harrison nodded and brushed his lips across hers. 'Sleep well.'

'Happy Easter.'

He jerked back and stared at her. 'It's Easter Sunday?'

'I know, hence the happy Easter comment.'

'I forgot to hide the eggs!'

'Have you bought them?'

'Mrs D. has.'

'Thank goodness those arrangements were left to her.'

Harrison shook his head, unable to believe he'd forgotten. 'I'd better go do that now before I try and move Yolanda out of my bed.'

'She sleeps in your bed?'

'I wasn't sure how late I'd be so I told Mrs D. to just let her sleep in there.' He shrugged. 'It relaxes her, helps her.'

'So you get to sleep in the pretty pink and white bed?' A smile touched her lips.

'Yes. Whoever said to buy your children good beds

with good mattresses because at some point you'll end up sleeping in them knew what they were talking about. I just hope she hasn't woken up.'

'Would Mrs D. have called you?'

'Yes, so as I haven't received a call, I'm presuming everything's all right.' He shook his head. 'Typical. The night I'm wide awake, she doesn't wake up.'

Amelia smiled. 'That's children for you. Go hide those eggs.'

'I will. I'll call you later,' he said and blew her a kiss. Amelia shut the door and leant against it, smiling, her heart filled with love for him.

Love!

Where had that thought come from? She stayed where she was, searching her thoughts and her heart for confirmation. Yes. It was true! She'd fallen in love with him. What was she to do?

CHAPTER NINE

WHEN she finally got to sleep that Easter Sunday morning, she had very sweet dreams, dreams of herself, Harrison and Yolanda playing happy families, although this time it was real. She was married to Harrison, Yolanda called her 'Mum' instead of 'Meel-ya' and her world was everything she'd ever dreamed of.

By the time she woke up, it was after lunch and she was glad she didn't have to go to work…or see Harrison. The realisation she was in love with him was too much for her to cope with at the moment as she hadn't expected it. To see him, to come face to face with him when her feelings felt as though they were going to overpower her… She started shaking at the thought.

She simply hadn't expected…hadn't *planned* to fall in love with him. Yolanda? Yes. She had no problem loving the child, it was impossible not to. She even had a fondness and respect for Mrs Deveraux, but falling in love with her boss? What had she been thinking?

'You weren't thinking,' Amelia whispered. Somehow Harrison had managed to break through her barriers, the ones she'd so carefully erected over the years. He'd broken through and managed to unlock her heart, the result being that she was now head over heels in love with him. She shook her head as the words repeated over and over. She loved him!

'I love Harrison,' she said out loud, looking at her reflection and knowing it was true. The emotion excited and overwhelmed her at the same time, but it also gave her clarity of mind. She knew what she had to do.

She had to make a break from the Stapleton family and the sooner she did it, the better it would be for all concerned. After she'd showered and had had something to eat, she decided to go for a walk along the beach. She needed to get out, to get some air, to find some control over her thoughts.

In an effort to avoid bumping into Harrison and his daughter, who might well be out playing on the beach, enjoying their chocolate Easter eggs, Amelia decided to walk south towards Brighton beach, away from Glenelg. Harrison had said Brighton was a nice beach so she should at least see it while she was there.

Harrison. Everything seemed to come back to Harrison.

When she opened her door to leave, she was flabbergasted to find a present propped up on the wall by her door. An envelope was attached with her name written on it— it was definitely for her. She glanced around, expecting to see someone standing there, delivering it, but there was no one about. How long had it been there?

Hesitantly, she took it inside and withdrew the card. It simply said, 'Happy Easter and a very big thank you for all your help.' It was signed by Yolanda, Mrs Deveraux and Harrison, the child having done a very good job at writing her own name but she'd obviously had some help. She'd also put three very big 'kisses' at the bottom of the card and Amelia couldn't help but smile.

How on earth was she going to extract herself from such a darling? It would be painful, more so for her than for Yolanda, because Amelia knew she didn't want to do it. She wanted to be a part of Yolanda's life, to watch her grow and change and to be there to experience those changes. She yearned for it…and that was the reason she had to stop it. It couldn't happen.

Amelia put the card down and turned her attention to the present. With trembling fingers she carefully removed the wrapping paper, folding it neatly, her heart filling with new love at the framed photograph of the pretty princess palace they'd sculpted on the beach. It was the most perfect present and she hung the picture in her room so it was the last thing she could look at before she went to sleep.

Harrison had done it again and she hated him for his thoughtfulness. It only made what she had to do even harder. She knew she'd take that picture back to England with her and it would always remind her of the flawless morning they'd had breakfast on the beach…the morning Harrison had kissed her for the first time.

Amelia closed her eyes, pain searing her heart. Why was this so difficult?

'Because you're in love with the man, you idiot,' she said out loud, and stormed to the door, deciding a run along the beach was going to be more beneficial than a walk. She needed to get these emotions under control, and fast.

She tossed and turned that night and the next morning went to work, glad it was a public holiday and Harrison had decided to stay home with his family. Still, as she went about treating patients and talking to staff, she was starting to dread seeing him for dinner that evening.

Oh, she wanted to see him. She wanted to see him

more than anything; she wanted him to hold her again, to kiss her again, to hear him call her beautiful… But it was wrong. It was a lie to let him think they could continue to spend time together because they simply couldn't. Perhaps if she hadn't fallen in love with him she could have continued to enjoy his company, as well as Yolanda's, but that wasn't the way things had worked out.

Three times she picked up a house phone and dialled his number…well, all but the last digit…before she replaced it. The least Harrison deserved was for her to tell him face to face that she couldn't continue to be involved with him. The problem was, every time she looked into his eyes she melted and her mind went blank.

On the way home from work, she picked up a bottle of wine for dinner and a drawing set for Yolanda. It contained pink and white paper and coloured pencils, all wrapped up in a box with a pink bow. It was perfect for her. She also bought a new book by one of Mrs D.'s favourite authors and then realised she didn't have anything for Harrison.

She hadn't intentionally been buying presents but now it would look strange if she gave something to Yolanda and Mrs D. and had nothing for Harrison. Well, it probably wasn't a good idea to give him a present when she was going to break up with him…even though they'd hardly begun.

Amelia dressed with care, wearing a blue knit top with matching jacket and a pair of casual black trousers. Gathering up her parcels, she took her camera with her, determined to punish herself further by taking photographs of this, their last evening together. She was trembling as she rang his doorbell and when she heard his footsteps heading in her direction, she took a few deep breaths, trying to calm her nerves.

'AJ,' he said, and ushered her inside. He closed the door then stopped to look at her. 'You look beautiful.'

'Thanks,' she muttered, trying to stay detached. Unsure what to do next, she held out the bottle of wine.

'Thank you.' Harrison accepted it, wanting to kiss her, even if it was just for a moment, but there was something about the way she stood, clutching parcels to her chest, that told him she wasn't comfortable with that idea. 'Come on through. Yolanda's very excited you're—'

He broke off as little footsteps came running in her direction and a second later Yolanda had her arms wrapped around her Meel-ya's legs. 'I done lots and lots wif Daddy today. We did da drwawing, da dancing, da *dollies.*'

'Sounds as though you've had a very busy day,' Amelia replied, as she shuffled through to the kitchen.

'Is dat mine?' Yolanda's eyes caught on the pink present in Amelia's hands.

'How did you guess?'

'Is pi-i-in-n-nk.' The little eyes grew round with delight.

'Why don't you sit up at the bench and you can open it?' Yolanda scrambled up onto the chair and then held her arms out. Amelia handed the present over. The paper was ripped and discarded and then oohs and ahhs came from Yolanda as she touched the pink and white paper.

Amelia glanced at Harrison to find him smiling at her. 'What do you say?' he prompted his daughter.

'Tank-oo, Meel-ya,' Yolanda immediately replied.

'Why don't you take that into your bedroom and you can do some drawing while Daddy finishes getting dinner ready?'

'O-tay.' Yolanda scrambled down again, collected her prize and ran to her room. Now that they were alone,

Amelia felt the atmosphere around them change. Harrison touched her arm and she turned to look at him, sucking in a breath at his caress.

He saw the same hesitation in her eyes, felt it in the way she tensed and realised something had changed since he'd kissed her goodbye early the previous morning.

'Everything all right?' He dropped his hand and went around the bench into the kitchen, lifting the lid on a saucepan and stirring its contents.

'Uh…yes.'

'Busy day?'

'It wasn't too bad.' Work. She all but sighed with relief at the topic. It was neutral. 'We had a steady stream of patients, a few stomachaches due to too much food or too much bad food. We had a child who was dressed in a superhero costume who'd cracked his head on a slide and sustained a mild concussion.'

'Did it need suturing?'

'No. I was able to just seal it with superglue.'

'Appropriate for a superhero.'

'I thought so.' Amelia sat down on a stool and watched him move around the kitchen. He was more than competent and she allowed herself a moment of pleasure at falling in love with a man who seemed good at everything. 'Smells delicious,' she said.

'Hungarian goulash, mashed potatoes, corn on the cob and green beans.'

'Mmm, sounds delicious, and here I was expecting chocolate bread, chocolate soup and chocolate cake for dessert.'

'Ugh. I think we've all definitely had enough choco-late after yesterday.'

'How did Yolanda cope?'

'We managed to restrict her to one small Easter egg per hour and she broke her big one up for dessert.'

'Sugar high?'

'Yes, although she wasn't too bad.' Harrison paused then looked at Amelia. 'We, uh…went around to your place yesterday afternoon but you weren't there.'

'No.'

She didn't provide any more details and again Harrison was left feeling there was something important she wasn't telling him. 'Yolanda wanted to show you her Easter eggs.'

'I'm sorry I missed them.'

'You…uh…weren't called in, were you?'

'No.' She could sense he was about to ask her where she'd been and so decided to quickly change the subject. 'I take it Mrs D.'s resting?'

'Yes. She'll be out soon.'

'She's doing well?'

'Better than well. The woman heals quite quickly for someone her age.'

'I heard that,' Mrs Deveraux said as she walked into the room, leaning on her cane for support. 'You rotten child,' she joked.

Harrison smiled and Amelia took a mental picture of it. He was so handsome. 'Child? I'm hardly that.'

'Harrison Stapleton, I've known you since you were younger than Yolanda and that makes you a child in my book.'

'Speaking of books,' Amelia said as Mrs D. perched herself on a stool beside her. 'This is for you.' She handed over the present. 'I thought it would give you a good excuse to sit down and put your feet up.'

'Thank you, dear. That's very thoughtful of you.' The woman carefully took the paper off.

'Just rip it,' Harrison said.

'No,' Amelia and Mrs D. said in unison, and he laughed, rolling his eyes.

'The paper's too pretty to rip,' Mrs D. said, and then gasped with delight at seeing the title of the book. 'Oh, Amelia. I doubt I'm going to get through dinner. I want to go lock myself away right now and read it.'

'Eat first,' Harrison said, hoping Mrs D. would do just as she'd suggested. He could get Yolanda into bed and then he and Amelia could have some quiet time, just talking and being with each other. 'I'm ready to dish up.'

'I'll set the table,' Mrs D. said, but Amelia made her sit down.

'No. You rest. I can do it.' Amelia went into the kitchen, mindful of keeping her distance from Harrison as she collected the cutlery. He called Yolanda and soon they were all sitting, Harrison at one end of the table and Amelia at the other. Mrs Deveraux had insisted she sit there and once more it made Amelia feel as though she was back in happy family land. The food was delicious, the atmosphere was relaxed and she couldn't help pulling out her camera to capture it all. She would need more than just her memory to get her through and even if it hurt to look at the photographs, hopefully one day, in years to come, she would be able to remember this most precious time spent with the man she loved.

Yolanda, naturally, posed for her pictures, grinning with delight, and as Amelia took a snap of the child sitting on her father's knee, a lump formed in her throat which was difficult to swallow. Breaking away from them was going to be far harder than she'd realised.

After dinner, she took the opportunity to get some

space from Harrison and volunteered to supervise Yolanda's bathtime.

She'd knelt beside the bathtub and watched with delight the way Yolanda made her bath toys talk to each other, exactly the same way she did with the dolls. 'You tate turtle,' Yolanda said, handing over an orange turtle.

'What's the turtle's name?'

'Mr Turtle,' Yolanda said, rolling her eyes as though 'Meel-ya' was silly not to know that. They continued to play in the water and once she was done, Amelia towelled her dry and then to her surprise the little girl ran, squealing, in all her nakedness through the house to her bedroom.

'She loves doing that,' Mrs D. said with a laugh as she headed towards her own bedroom. 'Goodnight, dear.' She patted the book under her arm. 'I doubt I'll be seeing you again this evening.'

Amelia smiled. 'Enjoy it.' She followed Yolanda and managed to get her dressed in her pretty pink nightie and then sat at the top of the bed, while Yolanda snuggled beneath the pink and white covers, to read her a story.

Three stories later, Amelia wondered if the child was ever going to show signs of tiredness. Then, to her surprise, Yolanda turned and put her arm over Amelia's waist, yawning as she did so.

'I wuv you, Meel-ya,' she said, and closed her eyes.

Amelia's heart constricted with pain and love as she gazed down at the child. 'I love you, too,' she whispered, and knew it was impossible to blink back the tears. Her heart swelled with such love, such protectiveness and such devotion as she stroked the little blonde curls. This child meant the world to her and Amelia knew with certainty that she never wanted to be parted from her...but she *had* to.

'Why is this so hard?' She brushed away the tears that had rolled down her cheeks.

'Why is what so hard?' Harrison asked softly from the doorway, and Amelia looked up. He stayed where he was for a moment before crossing quietly to kiss his daughter's cheek. 'She's such an angel when she sleeps,' he murmured.

'She's an angel all the time,' Amelia added.

'Then why are you crying?' He held out his hand to help her up and she hesitated for a second before accepting it. It would be the last time, she told herself. The last time she would allow herself to touch him, yet when she tried to remove her hand he held on, leading her from the room. Neither of them spoke a word until they were settled in the lounge, the table lamps on and soothing music coming through the stereo.

The whole atmosphere screamed romance and Amelia resisted sitting down until Harrison tugged her down beside him, still holding her hand. He turned it over in his, smoothing his fingers over her palm, his touch slow and intimate. Why? Oh, why was he doing this to her?

She found it difficult to look at him and remained perched on the edge of the seat, unable to relax. She knew what she needed to do, knew it was the right thing, but being with him like this, the love in her heart powering through her like a drug, it was almost impossible to resist… But resist she must.

'AJ?' She was having trouble looking at him and he sensed something was wrong. He only wished she'd open up and tell him. 'What's wrong?'

'Oh, Harrison.' Her breathing wild with panic, she wrenched her hand free of his and rose to her feet. He followed her, thinking she was about to bolt, but instead she wrung her hands together and looked about the room. 'I can't do this.'

He put his hands on her shoulders and turned her to face him. 'Can't do what? What do you mean?'

'This! You and I. I can't be your…girlfriend.'

'Why not? It's all right, Amelia-Jane.' He tried to gather her close but she resisted and he dropped his hands. 'I thought we agreed? We agreed to see where this attraction we feel for each other leads.'

'No. *You* agreed, Harrison. I put up a protest.'

'You said you were leaving at the end of June. I know that. You know that.'

'Then why are you continuing to pursue me? This has catastrophe written all over it and I can't do this to her.'

'To who? Yolanda?'

'Yes. I need to start withdrawing. It's only fair. Mrs D. is fine. You yourself said she was progressing better than you'd anticipated and although you may need a bit of help, it's not that much. I can come over and spend a few hours with Yolanda, gradually weaning that time down over the next few weeks.'

'So that's it? Just like that?'

'It's the right thing to do.'

'For who? For Yolanda? Or for yourself? Because it's certainly not the right thing to do as far as I'm concerned, but we seem to be leaving my feelings on this matter out of the equation.' He stepped closer and she breathed in his warm scent and almost sighed with longing. 'When do we discuss what's between us, Amelia? I don't care if you live here or in England or in Timbuktu, these feelings I have for you are real and honest and I won't let you just run roughshod over them, giving me some trumped-up reason why you have to end it.'

'It's not trumped up,' she said, trying to keep control over her senses, but it was proving difficult when he was so close.

'Then why can't you let go? Why can't you admit what's between us? Why can't you trust me enough to tell me what's really wrong?'

'Because I'll get hurt.' The words were wrenched from her and Harrison heard her pain. He'd realised there was more to her wanting to withdraw and he'd been trying to figure out what it was. Now, at least, she'd confirmed there was something, but what? He was positive that once he knew what he was dealing with, he'd be able to fix it.

'How will you get hurt, AJ? Certainly not by me.'

There was no way she could explain. To tell him she might not be able to have children… She couldn't even form the words, let alone get them past her lips. 'Please, Harrison. Let me go.'

'I can't.' To prove his point, he lowered his mouth to hers, capturing her in an electrifying kiss. The more he touched her, the more he craved her, and the more he craved her, the more he realised his life would never be the same again.

She clung to him and he felt her need, felt her response, and instantly knew this wasn't the reason she wanted to make a clean break from him. The power and the passion between them was incredible and right. Surely she could feel that. Surely she realised this sort of thing didn't happen every day. So why was she saying she couldn't be with him? They broke apart, both panting, Amelia limp and luscious in his arms.

'You've changed my life, Amelia-Jane. You've changed Yolanda's. I don't find it easy to trust anyone, especially not with Yolanda, but I trust you and that is so rare. Yolanda adores you, she loves you.'

'I know and I love her.'

'Then why? Why pull back? You're so natural with her. The love you have for her is everything her mother should have given but didn't. My daughter needs you, AJ, and so do I.'

With a sob Amelia shifted out of his arms and took three steps away. 'Don't make this more difficult than it already is.'

'I will. I'll fight for you. I'll show you that what we have is worth the fight. First, though, you need to tell me what's really wrong. You need to trust me.'

Amelia bit her lip, her breathing was so fast she felt as though her lungs were about to pop or that she'd pass out from lack of oxygen. She knew he was right. She at least owed him the truth and she knew once he found out, he wouldn't want her any more. And it was that pain, that searing pain, that would tear her heart apart and which she was trying to avoid.

'Is this because of your endometriosis?' he asked suddenly, and she gasped. It was what he needed. It gave him the clue that he was on the right path and his brain started working overtime, piecing everything together, everything he knew about her. 'You feel that you being sick every now and then might put a strain on our relationship?'

He watched her face closely, trying to read her expression. He'd definitely hit on the right topic. 'You've had an ovary and a Fallopian tube removed. Does that mean…?' He stopped, the light going on in his head, and he saw the fear in her eyes, the fear that he had indeed discovered the truth. 'You might not be able to have children,' he stated softly, and his heart turned over with compassion at the pain she must be feeling. He saw the truth of his statement reflected within her and couldn't believe how deeply he felt for her. 'You're so wonderful with Yolanda and yet you might be denied the opportunity to have any of your own.'

Tears started running down her cheeks at his words and Harrison moved towards her, only to have her back away instantly.

'AJ, stop. Don't run from me. Let's talk about this.' Harrison held out his hand, waiting for her to take it, to accept the help he was offering. She'd accepted it earlier when he'd helped her up from Yolanda's bed but he doubted she'd accept it this time, despite how much he was willing her to do exactly that.

She sidestepped over to the doorway. 'I can't.' She shook her head, adding emphasis to her words. 'I can't, Harrison. I won't do that to you, to Yolanda. I can't.'

With that, she turned and headed towards the front door. Harrison followed her, not willing to let her walk out of his life.

'Amelia-Jane,' he called, his voice louder than he'd anticipated, and in the next instant he heard Yolanda start to cry. He gritted his teeth, ignoring his daughter for a moment as he chased after Amelia. 'Please. Let's talk about this.'

She opened the front door and stepped through before turning to face him. 'There's nothing to talk about, Harrison.' She shook her head sadly. 'It's over.'

CHAPTER TEN

THERE was a knock at Harrison's office door and he put his pen down, glad his registrar had finally answered her pager. 'Come in,' he called, and a moment later Tina came through the door.

'You wanted to see me, boss?'

'I did. Sit down, Tina.'

Tina settled herself in the chair opposite him. 'So? What's up?'

'Amelia.'

'Oh.' Tina went to stand again but he stopped her.

'Wait. Please.' His tone was imploring with a hint of desperation. 'Come on, Tina. Talk to me. Tell me what's going on.'

'You need to ask Amelia that. I'm Switzerland.'

'Then why have you been swapping shifts with her?'

'Switzerland can help people in need and still remain neutral, you know. Remember those Von Trapp children, hiking over the mountains at the end of the movie?'

'What are you talking about?'

'Switzerland is just there, doing what it needs to do, and if people come hiking over their mountains, well…then that's OK.'

'Which means you should be able to help me as well. Can't show favouritism to one and not the other.'

Tina frowned. 'Good point.' She smiled at him. 'OK, boss, what do you need?'

'I need information. I need you to tell me why Amelia isn't returning my calls, why she never seems to be in her apartment, why she keeps switching her shifts. Every time I try to contact her, I'm thwarted.'

'You saw her yesterday. I distinctly remember the two of you working with a patient who was looking a horrible shade of green.'

Harrison couldn't believe the way he'd felt at seeing Amelia. It had been like the sun had started shining through the dark, stormy clouds that had been dogging him for the past few weeks. She'd looked fresh and gorgeous and her scent had overpowered him, but he'd had no time to talk, to do anything other than focus on the patient. He frowned as he recalled what had happened next.

'Yes, and then the patient turned a more normal-looking colour after he'd emptied the contents of his stomach all over my trousers,' he growled. 'By the time I'd changed and returned to A and E, AJ had gone.' Harrison stood and raked a hand through his hair.

Tina shrugged. 'It was the end of her shift.'

'Come on. Take pity on me, Tina. Why won't she talk to me?'

'What do you think is the reason?'

'I think it's because I've discovered her secret. I think it's because I got too close and now she's running. If she could finish her rotation tomorrow, she'd be on the next plane back to Heathrow. Too bad, Harrison. Too bad, Yolanda.'

'Yolanda? I thought she'd been spending time with Yolanda.'

'She has and she's been weaning herself slowly out of my life in the process. It isn't working. Yolanda is still asking where Amelia is, wanting to spend more and more time with her. I gave Amelia space because I thought she needed it. I thought once she'd had a chance to think things through that she'd at least *talk* to me, be polite, friendly, but she's avoiding me like the plague and it's just going too far. I don't even know what shift she's on and I'm the one who does the rosters!'

'You know I'm not the one you're supposed to be talking to.'

'I know that but she's become as slippery as an eel.'

Tina watched him for a moment and he knew he was under close scrutiny. What did she see? Did she see a man about to tip over the edge because he couldn't get two seconds alone with the woman he loved? That was certainly how he felt. Finally, Tina nodded. 'You're serious about her?'

He met her gaze, hope bubbling up through his despair. 'Dead serious.'

'What time do you finish tonight?'

'Five o'clock, or probably more around four-thirty. Yolanda has a therapy appointment.'

'Amelia's doing a late afternoon.'

He checked the roster. 'But that's what she's down to do.'

'I know. She figures you'll be gone, taking care of Yolanda. She knows your routine, Harrison, which makes it easy for her to dodge you.'

'So she'll be here just after five.'

'Can you hang around?'

'I'll make sure of it.' He nodded to Tina. 'Thanks, Switz, ol' pal.'

Tina grinned. 'Don't mention it, boss…and I *mean* don't mention it. I think the two of you are perfect for each other, which, by the way, is what I've been telling her.'

'Good. Nice to know I have an ally.'

'Just keep my name out of any reunion speeches.'

'You've got it.' He laughed as Tina left, beginning to feel as though an enormous weight had been lifted from his shoulders. So…Amelia would be in the hospital after five. He picked up the phone and rang Yolanda's therapist to see if he could delay her appointment an hour. That way, Yolanda wouldn't need to hang around as long and she'd be able to see her 'Meel-ya' when she had finished her session. Once that was organised, he called Mrs D. to let her know about the change.

Sitting back in his chair, he dragged in a deep, cleansing breath. He would convince Amelia. Before the day was done, he would convince Amelia-Jane Watson that he was the man for her. He loved her so completely that he was willing to fight every objection she threw at him in order to prove to her they were meant to be together—for ever. He would tell her everything in his heart.

He wasn't quite sure exactly when he'd fallen for his English registrar. All he knew was that it had been hard and irrefutable. She was the perfect woman for him. Yolanda loved her, Mrs D. thought the world of her, and together they would make one perfectly happy family.

Amelia walked to the change rooms and wearily opened her locker. She was exhausted and she knew it was due to her lack of sleep during the past fortnight, but work was what she was living for at the moment. She came, she worked until she was ready to drop and then could finally manage to sleep for a few hours, before waking up in a cold sweat, shaking with fear and loneliness, and sometimes calling Harrison's name.

She closed her eyes for a moment, unable to believe just how much she missed him. Her heart was breaking, she knew that, but she also knew it was better to break it now than let things get more out of control. Whoever had said that absence made the heart grow fonder hadn't been wrong. Her self-imposed exile from Harrison was only making her love him all the more.

She knew he'd tried to contact her and she'd gone to great lengths to avoid him, but deep down inside it was the last thing she wanted to do. Spending time with Yolanda had been the only bright spot in her days and now she'd cut it back to every second day and only when Harrison wasn't around.

Mrs Deveraux had tried to talk to her, tried to get her to open up, but Amelia had refused to be swayed from her purpose. She'd come to Australia to do her job, not to fall in love. So many years of hard work would be flushed down the drain if she couldn't get through these next few weeks.

'Hey, there,' Tina said, and Amelia jumped, spinning around to look at her friend. 'Whoa. You look horrible.' She placed her hand on Amelia's forehead. 'No. You're not hot. You're not coming down with this virus that's going around, are you?'

'I'm fine, Tina.'

'Yeah, right. Like I really believe you.'

Amelia closed her locker, hooked her stethoscope around her neck and pinned on her ID badge. 'Leave it, please.'

'Leave what? I'm not going to have a dig at you or lecture you. I am, however, becoming quite concerned. You look as though you're in pain.'

'I am—and I'm not talking about my heart,' she added quickly. 'I forgot to take my meds a few days ago and now I'm paying for it.'

'But it's under control, right? I don't need to get the chief gynae down here, do I?'

'No. I'm fine. I'm used to controlling it myself and I'm feeling better today than yesterday. I had horrible pains when I went home from work.'

'Hmm.' Tina nodded as though she didn't believe her.

Amelia frowned. 'What's that supposed to mean?'

'Nothing. I promised I wasn't going to start.'

'You already have.' Amelia crossed her arms. 'Go on, then. Continue.'

'Well, it's just that yesterday you saw Harrison. That's all I was going to say.'

'So you think that because I saw him I was in more pain yesterday when I left work.'

'Yes.'

'Stomach pain. Not heart pain.'

Tina shrugged. 'Whatever! Look, why can't you at least give him five minutes…or possibly ten, just so he can talk to you.'

Amelia shook her head and walked towards the door. 'This is you not starting?'

'He's in pain, too, Amelia, and he doesn't suffer from endometriosis…at least, I sincerely hope he doesn't.'

Amelia couldn't help the smile that sprang easily to her lips at her friend's words. She could never stay mad at Tina for long.

'He misses you, Amelia.' Tina was serious.

'I know.'

'Then why can't you do something about it? You're good together, you two. Don't go throwing away something that could fulfil all your dreams.'

Amelia nodded, deciding she didn't have the energy to get into a discussion with Tina about what her dreams really were. 'Noted. I need to get to work.' She headed out to the nurses' station and picked up a set of case notes, glad she had things to occupy her mind other than visions of Harrison and how incredible it felt when he held her close.

Ten minutes after she'd started, she put a blood sample she'd just taken into a packet and spoke to the triage sister on duty. 'I need a rush on this so I'm going to take it to Pathology myself. We're quiet enough here at the moment but page me if anything urgent comes in. I shouldn't be too long.'

'Righto, Amelia,' the sister replied.

Amelia was pleased to get out of the hustle and bustle of staff, walking down the long grey corridor that would eventually lead to the pathology labs. Staff were turning off lights, closing offices, eager to get home for the night. It was now the end of April and the weather had turned from warm and summery to cool and pre-wintry in a matter of weeks. She didn't mind in the slightest as the earlier sunset and colder nights fitted with her mood at the moment. Bleak and depressing.

She delivered the sample to Pathology and then headed back, amazed at how in a matter of minutes corridors that had been busy with staff were now vacant. As Sister hadn't paged her, she decided to take the long way back to A and E and had just entered the southern stairwell when a man came hurtling up the stairs.

Amelia flattened herself against the wall to let him pass, but balked when she saw who it was.

'Harrison!'

'Oh, AJ. There you are. Thank God you're still here.' He closed his eyes for a second and she saw the pain and agitation on his face.

'What's wrong?' A feeling of dread washed over her. 'Yolanda?'

He nodded and reached for her hand, tugging her up the stairs. 'She's missing.'

'Oh, no.' They came out into the corridor Amelia had just come down. 'She's not down there,' she told him quickly. 'I've just come along this way.'

'Right.' He spun her around, still holding her hand, and took her back down the stairs.

Amelia was too overcome with worry for Yolanda to even bother trying to keep her distance from him. He needed her now and, despite what was happening between them, she would support him in any way she could. Yolanda was missing! Her gorgeous little girl was missing!

When they came out of the stairwell, Amelia pulled him to a stop but he didn't let go of her hand. It was as though she were his lifeline, giving him strength, and that made her feel vitally important to him. It was a nice feeling. 'Wait. We should split up. Where was she last seen?'

'She was at her therapy appointment. That's on level three.'

'She was having therapy at this time of night?'

'I changed her appointment,' he said, guilt swamping him as he'd changed it so he could see Amelia, but now was not the time to go into that. 'I went to collect her and the therapist came out of the room as I walked up and she was looking for Yolanda then. She said she'd only turned her back for a minute.'

'That's all it would take. Yolanda's very quick.'

'And stubborn.'

'You've searched level three?'

'Yes. I thought she might have headed down to A and E but no one's seen her there.'

'What about the lifts? She might be in the lifts. You know how much she likes pressing the buttons.'

'Yes. I hadn't thought of that.'

'You check the lifts. I'll go between A and E and the third floor. Last time I found her, she was in a dark corner, crying, so we'll need to check everywhere.'

'The therapist is looking, too, so you might bump into her.'

'OK.' Amelia gave his hand a little reassuring squeeze before saying firmly, 'We'll find her.'

'We have to, AJ.'

'We will.'

They parted, going their separate ways, Amelia's heart pounding with fear in her chest as she prayed nothing would happen to the child. Yolanda was so strong-willed and stubborn that if she got it into her head to do something, she did it. The problem now was once she realised she was lost, she would then become afraid and start crying. Amelia thought back to the first time she'd seen her, crouched low with tears on her face, and her heart churned with worry.

She searched, almost willing Yolanda to jump out of a shadow as though they were playing a game…but she didn't. 'Yolanda?' she called, but her voice simply echoed down the corridor.

Amelia rounded the corner that led towards the wards

on the third floor, her gaze scanning everything. She checked every door. Most of them were locked so Yolanda couldn't have got inside.

'Yolanda?' she heard someone else call, and a moment later a small woman dressed in a suit came into view and Amelia guessed it was the therapist.

'Any sign?' Amelia asked.

'No. You looking for her, too?'

'Yes.'

'She's not around here.'

Amelia sighed heavily and shook her head. 'Can you tell me what happened just before she disappeared? Did she say anything? Do anything? Did she need to go to the toilet?'

'No, she'd just been and I'd taken her myself. I was sitting down, talking to her and playing games like we always do. The phone rang and I stood to answer it. I swear I had my back turned for all of a minute and when I turned back, she was gone. Just like that!' The woman snapped her fingers. 'At first I thought she was hiding so I checked the cupboards and under the chairs and tables but there was no sign of her.'

'That took how long?'

'What?'

'How long were you looking for her in the room?'

'About a minute.'

'A three-year-old can cover a lot of distance in a minute.'

'Who are you?' the therapist asked. 'We haven't been introduced.'

'Dr Watson. I work in A and E with Harrison. What game were you playing before she left?'

'Tea parties. Her favourite.'

Amelia nodded. She'd played tea parties with Yolanda just that morning when she'd visited. She thought hard. 'Did she say anything? Was she going to get a doll? Another toy to join in?'

'Wait a second. She mumbled something about… Meel-ya? I don't know what that means.'

At that, Amelia felt the colour drain out of her.

'Are you all right, Dr Watson? You look very pale.'

'She was looking for me.' The words were a shocked whisper. 'I'm Amelia.'

'Oh.'

'She would have headed towards A and E but I've looked everywhere between there and here.' Amelia looked behind her as though expecting to see the child but the corridor was empty. 'No. She's not here.' She sighed and thought, trying to get into the three-year-old's mindset. If she hadn't been able to find Amelia, where would she have gone?

'Has anyone checked the children's ward?'

'I think Harrison called the ward sister and asked her to call him if she saw Yolanda.'

'I'll go check,' Amelia said. 'You keep looking around here, head towards A and E.'

'OK.'

Amelia raced for the stairwell, taking the steps two at a time, her heart pounding wildly. Yolanda loved the 'zoo' and hopefully, as she hadn't been able to find Amelia, she'd simply gone there to play, to get another toy to join in her tea party.

Bursting from the stairwell, she turned right, her gaze fixed on the brightly painted children's ward. If the ward sister was on the lookout and hadn't contacted Harrison, there was no point talking to her. Amelia needed to see for herself, however, that Yolanda hadn't somehow managed to get into the 'zoo' without the 'zoo-keeper' knowing.

Amelia walked to the playroom area and stopped at the gate, which required an adult to open it. There were four children in there, a couple playing together, the others playing by themselves. Amelia scanned the area quickly, her heart plummeting when she didn't immediately see Yolanda.

Where was she? Worry gripped her so tightly she felt ill and thought she might pass out. Nothing could happen to that child. Nothing! She loved her so much, needed her as much as she needed Yolanda's father.

Now the thought of returning to England, of not being able to see Yolanda or Harrison, of constantly wondering if they were all right…the thought made her head ache and her heart break. What had she done? Had she made the biggest mistake of her life in trying to extract herself from their lives? She loved them, loved Harrison so very much.

Tears blurred her vision as she gripped the bars of the security gate. She had to find her girl… If she didn't…if something had happened to Yolanda… Amelia shook her head and sniffed, forcing her mind back from that dark place. She needed to keep her head, to help Harrison search. She hoped he'd contacted hospital security because they also needed someone to keep watch outside the hospital…just in case.

She went to go but as she moved, a little pink leg caught her eye and she looked more closely. Two little pink legs, a child lying on the floor, but there were too many things obscuring her vision for her to see clearly.

Amelia fumbled with the latch on the gate but finally had it undone and rushed over, almost tripping over another child in her haste.

'Yolanda?' She called, and the child sat up, turning a tear-stained face towards her.

'Meel-ya!' Yolanda was on her feet, rushing towards her, and in the next instant she was caught in Amelia's arms.

'Oh, baby, baby. We were so worried. We couldn't find you.' Tears of joy poured down Amelia's cheeks as Yolanda clung to her.

'I not pind you, Meel-ya. Where you go?' Fresh tears came from the child and Amelia's heart lurched with love and longing.

'I'm here, darling. I'm here and I'm never going to let you go.'

'What's all this noise?' the ward sister said, coming to the gate, but she stopped when she saw Amelia holding Yolanda. 'Oh, my goodness, you've found her. I'll call Harrison.'

'Thanks,' Amelia said as the sister rushed off. She sat down in one of the chairs, not sure her legs could hold her any longer. She gathered the child to her, settling her on her lap. 'Daddy and I were so worried. We couldn't find you, darling.'

'I no pind you, Meel-ya.' Now that the scare had passed, Yolanda was starting to return to her usual stubborn self. 'Where you go?' she demanded.

'I'm right here and you found me now.'

'And you pound me, too.'

'Yes, I did. We found each other.' Amelia kissed her cheek.

'You no go again,' she said crossly.

'No. I won't go away again.'

'Oh, my darling girl.' A deep voice came from behind them and Yolanda instantly shifted from Amelia to launch herself at her father. 'My baby. Daddy was so worried.'

'Meel-ya worwied, too.'

'Yes, I'm sure she was.' He shifted Yolanda on his hip as Amelia stood and he looked at her. 'I heard what you said, AJ. Is it true? I won't have you lie to me or my daughter. Did you mean it when you said you wouldn't go away again?'

Amelia looked at him and slowly nodded. 'I can't leave her.'

'So you're saying you'll stay? Be a part of her life?'

'I'll be a part of her life while I'm here.' She shrugged. 'We'll just have to figure out some way to explain to her that I need to return to England.'

'And after England? After you've sat your finals?'

Amelia shrugged again. 'I don't know, Harrison.'

'I play in da zoo,' Yolanda said, and squirmed out of Harrison's arms to go and finish lining up the soft toy animals she loved playing with.

'Uh…has everyone else been told to stop looking?' Amelia asked, feeling highly self-conscious under Harrison's stare.

'Yes. AJ…' He paused and opened his arms. 'I need to hold you.'

She sighed and went willingly into his arms. After the tension they'd been through it was what they both needed, to simply stop and be with each other. It was where she loved being the most, close to Harrison, listening to his heart beating firmly.

'I love you, Amelia-Jane,' he said, tightening his hold

on her. 'Yolanda ended up getting in there first, but I was the one who was supposed to ask you to stay, to be a part of my life as well as hers. I can't let you go.'

Amelia had stilled at his words, knowing without a doubt they were true. 'I need to return to England.' She forced herself to ease back but he refused to let her go, only loosening his arms a little. 'I have exams.'

'I know.' He looked deep into her eyes. 'Amelia-Jane, I want you to marry me. I wanted to tell you earlier, that's why Yolanda and I were here. It's not gone quite the way I planned it, but…'

'Oh!' She didn't know what to do, what to say, and she started to tremble. It was all too much. How could he want to marry her when she couldn't provide him with what he needed? 'But—'

'But you can't have children?' He shrugged. 'I accept that.'

'Harrison you don't und—'

'I do understand. I understand *completely*.' He paused for effect, hoping his words were sinking in. 'I. Love. You. *You*. The sooner you realise and accept that, the sooner we can get on with our lives. I understand that you've been frustrated and angry for many years about your endometriosis. You had no say in it, no control over it, and you have a right to your feelings, but it isn't the be all and end all of your existence.'

His words were heartfelt, imploring and totally sincere. 'I need to be with you, AJ. The past few weeks have shown me that to try and live without you…well, it's not living at all, it's merely existing. There was an emptiness, a loneliness in my life, one I didn't realise I had until I met you. You filled that gap, you made me whole. We have Yolanda and that's enough. We can adopt, if that's what you'd like. We can try IVF if that's your choice. Hear those words—*your* choice. You've looked at this with only one perspective for so long that hopefully I can give you another and that you are more important to me than any children we may or may not have. *You.*'

Amelia listened, her heart swelling with love for this amazing man. His words were said with total conviction and she knew he believed every single thing he'd said.

'I want to believe you,' she whispered. 'What if you say this now but later on you change your mind?'

'Change my mind about loving you? Never.'

'I meant about the children.'

'No. Not going to happen.'

'How can you be so sure?'

'That's elementary, dear Watson. You mean the world to me. You and Yolanda—you *are* my world. Without you by my side I can't breathe, I can't sleep, I can't function properly. I want you more than I want to have another child, so believe me. Believe that my love for you continues to grow so rapidly it's difficult to control. I've been married before, and what you and I have…is so different. Different from anything I've ever felt and it's right. In fact, it's perfect. You're perfect.' He held her gaze. 'There's only one thing missing.'

'What's that?'

'To hear you say that you love me, too.'

Amelia felt the weight start to lift from her heart. Could this be real? Could this be happening? To her? The man she loved and adored also loved her. He accepted her for who she was, the way she was, and he still loved her! It was a miracle—*her* miracle.

She looked into his rich brown eyes and a smile touched the corners of her lips. 'I do, Harrison. I do love you. I love you so much that my heart is overflowing with the emotion and these past few weeks have been the most miserable of my life.'

'Mine, too.' He smiled at her. 'Let's not do that again.'

'No. Oh, but what about England? We'll need to be separated when I—'

'Nope. Not going to happen.'

'What? What do you mean?'

'I mean, Dr Watson, that we have a lot of work to do in the coming weeks.'

'We do?'

'Yes, because Yolanda and I are going to accompany you back to England. We're going to stay with you, help you study and pass your exams with flying colours. Then we're going to pack up your belongings and shift everything back here to Australia—back here where you belong.'

'Oh, are we? Do I even get consulted in this?'

For the first time Harrison felt uncertain. Was he going too far, too fast? 'Well?' He swallowed and waited. 'Do you think it's a good idea?'

Amelia glanced down at Yolanda, playing happily on the floor, before looking back at the man she adored. She'd been running for so long, hiding herself away, trying not to get involved in relationships in case they ended in heartbreak. Not this one. No. Harrison had shown her, would continue to show her for the rest of her life that she was important to him. She felt it, she needed it…she needed him. He understood… somehow… He understood about her fertility problems and he was saying he didn't care. She wanted to be with him, to be a mother to Yolanda more than anything. No more running. 'I think it sounds perfect.'

Harrison breathed out with relief. 'Whew. You had me worried there for a second.'

'And when we return to Australia? What do I do then?'

'Work here in the hospital.'

'You're offering me a job?'

'Yes. You're a brilliant doctor, AJ.'

'OK. I accept—the job.'

'And the marriage proposal?'

Amelia glanced down to find Yolanda staring up at them both. 'Well, I don't think it's totally my decision.' She beckoned to Yolanda and the little girl stood, Harrison letting Amelia go for a second so he could scoop his daughter up. He shifted her to his hip and placed his other arm about Amelia, the three of them forming a family unit.

'Yolanda,' Harrison said, 'would you like Amelia to come and live with us and marry Daddy and be your mummy?'

'My *mummy*?' Yolanda's eyes almost bulged out of her head. '*Yes!* Yes, yes, yes.' Yolanda wriggled from his arms and he let her go, pulling Amelia close again, both of them watching the little girl start jumping around the room, clapping her hands. 'She tan be da mummy and you tan be da daddy and Mrs D. tan be da gwan-ma and I tan be da prwetty gel.'

Harrison's smile increased as he looked from Yolanda to Amelia. 'That sounds perfect. What do you say, my Amelia-Jane?'

'I say…yes.'

Harrison bent to kiss her, knowing he would never tire of holding this woman, of kissing her, of spending every moment he could with her by his side. When he lifted his head, he smiled. 'You be the mummy.' He kissed her luscious mouth again.

'And you be the daddy,' she said, and kissed him back with all the love in her heart.

'We be a family!' Yolanda said with glee, and both adults laughed, knowing she was one hundred per cent right.

EPILOGUE

'CAN you carry this over for me, please?' Amelia asked Yolanda.

'Of course I can.' The six-year-old rolled her eyes and took the bag her mother was holding out to her. 'I'm six now.'

'I know, darling.' Amelia took Yolanda's free hand and shut the door to their house behind her before checking for traffic and walking across the road for breakfast on the beach. Once they reached the sand, Yolanda dropped the bag, broke free and ran to where her father was sitting in the shallows, a baby boy of eight months on his knee.

Amelia picked up the bag Yolanda had dropped and carried it over to the table where Mrs D. was sitting reading a book. 'Right. I think we're almost ready to start breakfast.'

'You'll have to get them out of the water first,' Mrs D. pointed out. 'Little Scott is definitely a water baby.'

Amelia looked down the beach at her family. Scott was indeed a water baby and he'd settled into their family as though he was meant to be there. Overseas adoption hadn't been easy, but finally they'd been blessed with Scott and he was simply the most gorgeous, easygoing baby.

Yolanda had improved dramatically, being part of a two-parent family, and Mrs D. had enjoyed six months of travelling around Europe and staying with Amelia's relatives in the United Kingdom. Of course, she'd rushed home the instant she'd heard the news about Scott, and Amelia had been glad of the surrogate grandmother's help.

'You may as well join them, Amelia. The food will wait.'

'Good idea,' she said, and shed her sarong to reveal her two-piece bathing suit. The scar from her total hysterectomy was hardly noticeable and although the recovery had been long, she was now fitter and healthier than she'd been for most of her life.

Amelia couldn't help smiling as she headed down the beach, feeling happy and free, knowing she was loved for who she was and able to love those closest to her in return. Her life was like a fairy-tale and she was the princess living in the castle with her very own Prince Charming.

'Mum!' Yolanda called, and waved and ran up the beach to meet her. 'Let's sculpt another castle. We need to practise for the next competition. Everyone loved our castle last year.'

'They did, indeed.' Amelia ran her fingers through Yolanda's blonde curls, which were now halfway down her back, before she straightened her hat. Sitting down, she glanced over at Harrison who picked up Scott and brought him over, the baby holding his arms out to her the instant he spotted her.

'There's your mummy,' Harrison said, giving his son a quick kiss before handing him over. 'He's been splashing so happily. He loves the water.'

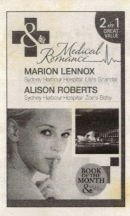

Don't miss Pink Tuesday
One day. 10 hours. 10 deals.

PINK TUESDAY
IS COMING!

10 hours...10 unmissable deals!

This Valentine's Day we will be bringing
you fantastic offers across a range of
our titles—each hour, on the hour!

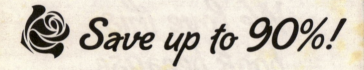

Pink Tuesday starts
9am Tuesday 14th February